Below

by Lee Gaiteri

ISBN-13: 978-1541093942
ISBN-10: 1541093941

Cover illustration by Lorena "Lhuvik" Argüelles (lhuvik.com).

For Frobozz and Rodney

Part I

Above

Nobody leaves treasure lying around. The pits, you can think of those like banks. A light guard is all you'd need on them. Maybe a few traps. A thief can't climb out on his own with his pockets stuffed with gold. That's why so much of it is still there. Who would bother with it?

Hidden chests and old strong boxes? Oh, there's surely a few. You know where to find those, lad? Mostly in the big settlements, and far from the Gates. Waste your time searching if you must, but those old empty houses aren't always so empty. A stone house makes a perfectly good nest for an animal, big or small.

And remember, I said nobody leaves treasure lying around. Mark that. If they left their gold behind, something bad happened that made them run off. Or something bad happened, and they never had the chance to run off. Maybe the descendants of whatever got them will get you too.

The Forger's Charge

They called it the Fell Current, the madness that gripped men and turned their thoughts below. Of those who felt its pull, many resisted long enough to die of more natural causes, yet on their deathbeds would grieve for a sight they had never seen, a reckless journey never undertaken. The pull was strong among those with just enough knowledge, or power, to underestimate their peril; it was stronger still among the unwary.

Gold separates the thief from the lord, the saying went. Or perhaps it was another way round; Brenish had never been sure. Gold there was, piled in pits and locked in chests deep beneath the earth, untouched by glimmer of torchlight since the Elder Kingdom vanished long ago. It was the sirens' call, the beckoning reward for great risks and great adventures under a hundred feet of stone. Brenish knew it was there, because many men had returned to the world of light laden with treasure.

Many men out of many, many more.

But those who returned brought stories of dangerous beasts and goblin hordes, of magical beings that would challenge hardened wizards. Tales spoke of cities long abandoned, vast caverns, castles left empty, bridges over deep chasms. In darkened taverns, an inebriated veteran might speak in hushed tones of a terror that left nothing of his companions but cracked bones. Some accounts were little more than boasts, carrying mere threads of truth; some were veils drawn over uncouth deeds of the teller himself, to keep from splitting a meager haul. The legends grew, condensed out of half-truths and ancient fears, and spread to the towns all about the countryside.

Brenish, raised in the little village of Ilyenis, near the river and Asaph's Gate, was weaned on those stories. As a child he snuck into the inn where returning adventurers, plied with wine, would slowly release their grip against the horror and speak. When his father had work in the city, he would listen to old travelers who told endless streams of stories to any child or fool who would listen. He learned his letters from a scholar who compounded such tales, and absorbed every book about the ruins that he could lay hands on. If a purse or a haunch of meat were found along with those books, all the better, but the books he always returned. Eventually.

He knew of a clearing in the forest west of the village, where he had once played as a boy. Tall round stonework there jutted from the earth like the tips of vast chimneys, each as wide as a hay wagon was long. He climbed to the top of one, found a sturdy stone grate covered in moss, and peered through into a hidden garden far below. A pair of bronze eyes like coins stared back at him, until he shouted down the hole and they moved away. Echoes came back out of the depths, his own voice sounding in places few men had seen over the course of an entire age. That sound had burrowed into his heart until he heard it in his dreams.

Ten years had passed since then. His twentieth year was on the wane; the full score would be under his belt come December. Men his age were tending farms, had fathered several children, or had completed studies in the city and now held positions as craftsmen and masters of lore. He was just a thief, and not a very good one. Good enough to make a living for himself, but not to support a family. He was a much better liar; but in Ilyenis he was well known, his greatest skill useless on everyone but the travelers who passed along the road, or the fortune seekers who came through on their way to the Gate, often never to be heard from again.

He bought the adventurers drinks, and never took a copper from them unless they gave it freely. At first his friends mocked him for that, because it was a foolish waste to let their coin pass beneath the earth for good. Yet some of those men were glad to speak with him, and learn something of the perils they might face from the store of knowledge he had acquired. Some came back to thank him. It had earned him a good reputation in the city; now and then, men in the grip of the Fell Current might seek him out.

Brenish had always resisted the Current. He knew his limitations. But beyond the lure of gold was the greater danger, the one that had driven thousands of better men to finally succumb: curiosity.

Pernilla Alder always insisted on giving Brenish a good meal in exchange for bringing by a stipend from the guild. They looked after their own, and her husband Willy was one of their best. In lockup they could do little but slip him extra food and a few comforts, yet he still found a way to forge documents for them behind the iron bars of the city dungeons. Willy was also a friend; he had paid Brenish handsomely on many occasions for access to his borrowed books, especially if the owner was unaware of the borrowing.

Brenish entertained the children by the hearth, showing them sleight of hand tricks and then teaching them how they worked. Willy would want no less, even if their mother didn't fully approve. She let them stay up specially on the nights he came by.

"Give us a story, Uncle Brenish," said Willy's oldest, Tamil, a girl of six years. Her younger brother John and the little girl beside him nodded enthusiastically.

He looked to Pernilla, who just smiled in quiet resignation. As long as his talk stayed away from monsters, it would be all right. The children knew something of the goblins that were said to dwell further north of the river, in parts of the ruins that hadn't been charted since the Romans gave it up. They had heard of trolls and dragons, the latter having amassed more legends above ground than below. They knew of the large insects and the rodents, and some of the less intimidating creatures like the prowling lizards. But Brenish knew to stay away from the worst dangers, the ones even he didn't like to think about.

"All right," he said, "I'll tell you one. I was told this one years ago, by a man named Kennon. He had just come from the ruins and was staying at the inn for a few days while a healer tended his friend."

"What happened to his friend?" said John.

"His friend was hurt. He said the friend's name was Harold Spellman, a lesser mage who worked as a potioner. They both came from Northhill, out west. Kennon was a swordsman, a very good one from what he said. Times had fallen hard on their families and they wanted to find their fortune in the Elder Kingdom.

"From Asaph's Gate they went west a ways, and down, following the stairs to lower levels every chance they got, until they made their way to a little village carved into the stone. No one had seen it in a hundred years."

"How'd they know that?" said Tamil.

"There was another man down there, long before, named Gressick. He was an officer of the city guard back in his day, well known, but he went into the ruins on his own one day and never returned. Kennon and Harold came back with his helmet, and the mystery was finally solved.

"But just then, they didn't know who he was. They didn't know if a monster got him, or if he just broke a leg and starved to death. His bones were scattered all over the town square. He'd found some treasure in the deep, a few bags he tucked in a corner for safe-keeping while he made his way back up. Kennon and Harold gathered up the bones and built a mound over them, and decided Gressick's gold was good enough for them."

"But how did Harold get hurt?" said John.

"They slept down there, each taking turns so one would always be on the lookout for danger, until they were rested and felt they could safely head back to the surface. When they were most of the way back, a pack of huge rats attacked them. The two friends drove them off, but one of them took Harold's leg. Kennon bound it quickly and made his friend a crutch, and they quickened their pace as best they could. The noise of their fighting, you see, might attract other beasts before long.

"But the men were lucky. They made it back to the Gate alive. Kennon used some of their gold to pay the healer and make arrangements for their transportation home. They both decided there was enough money to provide for their families, but not enough to pay a wizard for Harold to get a whole new leg. So they made their way back, and as far as I know they're still living off the treasure they found."

Brenish leaned down and lowered his voice. "But after Kennon told his story, when he was getting sleepy from wine, he got very quiet, and spoke to the visitors who were still there. He said that when he was on watch, before they came back, he saw something moving in the dark, outside the firelight. Watching them."

"That's enough for tonight, Brenish," said Pernilla.

He held up his hand for peace. "It's all right. Of course whatever it was, it would never come above ground. The deep creatures, they don't like bright light. They don't like to stray near the surface, and everything down there is afraid to come near the Gate. But I'm telling you children this so you'll understand it's dangerous to go down there. Whatever was watching Kennon and Harold, it followed them almost the whole way back. The rats didn't go near it. The men never got a good look, only glances at something that stayed just out of the light. When they finally got close to the Gate, the thing turned back."

"What was it?" said John.

"They didn't know. I have some ideas. But I won't tell you those stories just now. For now all you need to understand is that you're safe up here, and the things that live in the ruins won't ever leave there."

"But dragons go in and out," Tamil said. "Father said Visak followed one down."

"Aye, he did, as the wizard told me himself when I was little older than you. But dragons are different, and these days they leave us alone. There was a time, long ago, when some creatures like goblins dared to come out too. We taught them to fear the Gate. That's why the thing that followed Kennon turned away. All wild things fear the Gate, now. The only way you'd ever run into something like that is if you went down to the ruins yourself."

"I won't never," John said resolutely.

Brenish smiled. But he, too, had said that when he was John's age. And he had prodded, pried at the truth with clever questions, until he got the real stories about the things in the dark. The beast that had followed Kennon was likely a stalking flayer: a short, long-tailed, scaly beast that walked on two legs and was known for both its aggressiveness and skittishness. If it had caught both men sleeping, Brenish would never have heard their tale, and Gressick's fate would still be a mystery. In fact, he had long suspected that the giant rats were scared off by the flayer, and it was the flayer that took Harold's leg in the commotion, retreating back into the shadows for its meal before the men ever got a good look.

Tamil was less easily deterred than her brother. "Tell us another one!"

"No more tales tonight," said their mother. "Time for bed."

The usual grumbling ensued, but in a few minutes the children were tucked into a corner, behind a folding screen. Pernilla motioned for Brenish to follow her outside into Willy's work shed, taking out the big key she kept on a thong around her neck.

"The children love your stories, Brenish," she said. "Though I wish you'd leave out the monsters."

"If it weren't for the monsters, I'd've gone a long time ago," he said. "Fear is safer for them."

She gave the same resigned smile and put the key to the lock. It was a fiendishly heavy mechanism, requiring much of her strength to turn. The walls were thick stone outside, dry wood inside, and the door was two layers of sturdy oak reinforced with steel. It was like a miniature castle, immune to the likes of Brenish. He could pick an ordinary lock with enough time and patience, but even Tibs couldn't pick this one.

Once inside, Pernilla lit a lamp on the largest of two desks. The light came out whiter than a candle, like afternoon sun. It was a spell lamp, a piece of enchanted scrap glass drawing energy from a copper wick dipped in an amber pool of *esen* at the bottom of a collection jar. Moderately pricey, but not uncommon even in the village, and vital for Willy's work. The shed was almost as big as their cottage, but cramped: It was packed with shelves, some for books and some segmented into hundreds of little nooks for scraps and scrolls. An apothecary table, drawer ajar, held a collection of inks and brushes. Still more implements were on the desks, within reach of projects he hadn't yet had a chance to complete.

Pernilla shut the door behind them.

"You know if there's anything you need," said Brenish, "we're all here for you."

"Much appreciated," she said. "And I know you mean that beyond the guild. You're a good friend to our family, Brenish, and that's why Willy wanted to bring this to you."

"Bring what?"

She opened a drawer near the bottom of the large desk, and from it she pulled a stack of papers. At the top was one with the appearance of parchment, or spell paper, a glossy sheen hinting at durability beyond that of the documents Willy usually handled. This she picked up, and unfolded several times, until it could be spread out on the desk. It was several feet wide.

Brenish leaned over the work surface to take a better look. The paper was a map, broken into many sections and annotated with scrawls in handwriting that seemed distantly familiar. Numbers, formulas, sketches, and verses of riddles seemed to cover every scrap of available space. And suddenly his heart leaped in his chest, knowing the penmanship for what it was. He was looking at a myth, a rumor out of the depths of old stories come to life beneath his fingers. The Fell Current stirred in the deepest part of his heart.

"Pernilla," he said, almost in a whisper. "Is this *Visak's map?*"

She said nothing. But as quickly as his excitement had come on, common sense pushed it down again.

"Nay," he said to himself. "I forgot myself for a moment. This is masterful work. I saw one of Visak's books, a long time ago. This looks just like his hand. It looks like maps he drew."

"Willy's eye's like no other," she said proudly. "He's been working on this since just after John was born."

"But how did he do this?" said Brenish. "He must have had access to some of Visak's notes, and his works."

"Aye, and papers right out of the old wizard's study."

When Visak finally passed, five years ago, his legend didn't die with him. A powerful and shrewd wizard, he had bested a dragon that made its home in one of the Elder Kingdom's dead cities, and claimed the hoard for his own. Visak had never made any secret of his vast wealth nor his exploits. While he spent enough to be comfortable, no one ever believed he had tapped more than a small part of his bounty. Experts in treasure had seen the artifacts he recovered, and determined there must be much more. Visak's claims were even grander; but, trusting banks little and greedy rulers still less, he never brought more than a little of his wealth to the surface at a time. The rest was, he said, exactly where he had found it, hidden by a spell, and once or twice a year he would teleport back to the ruins to claim a little more.

Rumors had always said that Visak had a map, in case his memory ever failed him. But Brenish himself had barely ever believed it, because teleporting in and out was still the safest way for a wizard to go. A mentally infirm old wizard—that fate never befell Visak, who died sound of mind—would be little more than monster bait if he tried to follow the same long route below ground that he had taken in his prime. Still, seeing the paper in front of him, Brenish wanted more than ever to believe he beheld the real thing, that he alone held the key to such a treasure. He obviously wasn't alone, for after Visak's death his home had been stripped to the bones by scavengers.

"Where'd Willy come by the materials?" said Brenish.

"Duggle. He and a friend got hold of the wizard's work. He got some of the spellbooks, but he sold most of those. The papers he thought might be valuable. Whatever Willy makes off it, he's in for a piece."

Brenish nodded quietly, but he felt betrayed. Duggle may have been city-bred, but he was a guild-brother and a friend. More than that, he owed Brenish a steep favor; if not for Brenish's quick-talking intervention, Duggle would be in lockup himself right about now. Yet he had never mentioned this stash to Brenish, who would have had a keen interest in any artifacts left behind by the late wizard. Brenish had always wondered if Duggle was one of the men who cleaned out the estate, but he had assumed if that were really true, he would have heard something.

"Willy's in lockup six more years," Pernilla said. "He can do that time, but the children need their father. *I* need him. I know the guild has seen to it that we want for naught, and I'm grateful. But I want my husband back. With enough coin, he can buy his way out."

The thief stood silent a moment, still lost in the detail of the work. Even the wizard's speaking mannerisms were transcribed there, for Brenish remembered the way the old man loved to play with words as he spun tales by a fire. Those were the highlights of his memories from the few times he visited the city: An old man in an old rocking chair, drawing on a pipe and surrounded by the upturned faces of dozens of children whose parents conducted business at the bar. A sonorous but captivating voice, rising in laughter as often as it fell to speak of creatures man had never named.

"He wanted me to see this," said Brenish.

"He sent word. He wants you to sell it. He was worried it wasn't ready, but he thinks it's good enough. He knows you can sell it, if anyone can."

"Not in Ilyenis," Brenish said without pause.

"Nay. Besides the lack of buyers, people here know you too well. But in the city you have a better name. 'Tisn't so strange that the map might make its way to you."

"Aye," he said.

He could already imagine a few stories he might tell. If the map was taken along with the rest of Visak's things, maybe it was studied by the thief who first took it. After going to great expense to study its secrets, the thief realized the undertaking was too great, the risks too high. So it was sold, along with the secrets learned so far, to recoup the cost of the study. And so it passed, hand to hand, from one shady character to another who each decided in turn that it was too dangerous to pursue. Then finally, its last owner decided enough was enough: He could hire Brenish as an intermediary, who was known to the most informed of the adventurer type, to sell the map and its secrets in exchange for a hefty fee, an advance against a stake in the treasure.

But no. He shook his head. Not even Brenish, who had once talked a suspicious constable into letting him go while another man's purse was in his hand the entire time, could sell that story. Not to a man whose life would be on the line.

"I may have a better name in the city," he said, "but not much better. They know better."

He didn't add that he felt it would be wrong to cheat a treasure hunter, especially to knowingly send them on a wild goose chase that would almost certainly lead to their death. He had always directed them well before. He wanted them to come back safely, as many of them as possible and with more stories to tell. Always more stories.

"'Tis a tough sell," Pernilla acknowledged. "But if anyone can do it, it's you."

He sighed and kept his eyes down, on the paper. Deep regret tore through him, that it wasn't real. It looked so real; it was so much like the writings he had seen when he was younger. He remembered the wizard's face and the times he said a few kind words to him. This map meant everything to a man like himself, a man he wouldn't have the heart to deceive—not even for a friend. It meant the adventure of a lifetime, the treasure of many lifetimes, and a real future.

Time was running out for him; he knew it well. The only thing standing between Cirawyn and the altar was her father's not-unreasonable demand for a high bride price. City-folk scoffed at the idea that a villager could make a fine shopkeeper's wife or a lady of standing, but she had the smarts for it and the looks to match, as her father knew well. All the more reason he disapproved of Brenish, who could barely keep himself afloat in a disreputable profession, who had no prospects beyond the next score, and the next, until one day he'd end up in lockup like Willy—or dead—with so little value to the guild that the stipends would dry up long before any kids were grown. Eventually Cirawyn's dad would find the right suitor, and while her heart belonged to Brenish she would obey her father's wishes. The memory of the thief would fade as he grew old (if he was lucky enough to grow old) back in Ilyenis, alone.

He was obviously in for a share if he sold the map. Such things were implied. That share could be all the difference between a modest, happy life, and the destructive course he was on right now. It would probably at least cover the bride price, with enough smooth talk. But even if he could sell out a kindred spirit for gain, he wasn't sure it was possible.

He stared longingly at the map. If only it were real.

If only…

He might even be willing to chase the treasure himself, in that case. His favorite pastime was to muse on the stories he had heard, and wonder what he would have done differently: what he would have taken down, what else he would have done to respond to a threat. Second-guessing the unfortunate was an easy game to play beneath a shady tree in high summer, but he at least was a better player than most, for he had the benefit of considerable knowledge.

Stripped of financial limitations, he had in mind just what he would bring along. He wouldn't go alone; that was suicide. He wouldn't go ill-equipped. Indeed he would want all manner of potions and scrolls, enough to protect himself and his companions. And he would need an escape plan, one he was sure no one else had ever tried because it was so scandalously expensive. Yet even a modest treasure—and such treasures, while hard to find, were not uncommon in the ruins and could be found with the right magic—would yield a magnificent profit. Someone else would have to pay out for the supplies, but if he could manage to talk them into it, he could make a proper fortune.

This was the key, the thing that would convince a man of money to pay his way.

Brenish felt the Current. For the first time in his life, he felt his fingers slip a little.

"Give me a few days," he said. "I want to think about something."

"All right."

"Do you mind if I take this with me?"

"I insist. You're a good man, Brenish. Willy trusts you to look out for a friend, and I trust you too. You'll find a way to make this work, or no one will."

He nodded back to her in thanks. He would find a way to help them, and himself if he could.

That way was paved with lies. He was good at those.

A Better Plan

The inn was busy for a Monday night. A few of the faces in the crowd were outsiders, travelers, probably headed along the road to see distant relatives and get back before winter set in. Even so, they were pushing it. September was rolling out and the trees were halfway turned. The weather was turning rainier and colder, though the tail end of summer would give up the last of its warmth only reluctantly.

Brenish and Naman shared a duck at a table in the corner. Naman was almost Brenish's mentor in a way, a friend from long back who had stuck by him and sponsored his entry into the guild. The older, bigger thief was twenty-six, unmarried, supporting himself and his mother on the slim pickings around Ilyenis and occasional side jobs in the city, when he could get them. In the village, being a thief meant being a highwayman; everyone else knew your name. Money was tight in the winter and loose in the summer, and the wiser thieves saved up; Brenish had saved just enough, but that wasn't counting a few debts. Time was running out to close the gap, or it would be a lean season.

Naman's attention was on the room. He had been trying to flag down the barmaid for half an hour while she pointedly ignored the both of them, focusing instead on other patrons who sometimes tossed a coin her way. Brothers Bob and Raden were at the bar, easy to spot because they were bigger than anyone else. They spent freely when they were high on ale, but they didn't come in for revelry more than once a week. Finch sat in another corner by himself, smoking. He expected prompt service but wanted to be left alone at all other times, and paid well enough that the barmaid always kept an eye on his table. Dex sat at a far end of the bar with an open book, which Brenish always thought was like watching a snake juggle: It made no sense and was difficult to believe no matter how many times he saw it.

There were no treasure seekers in attendance. Only three parties had come through in the last six weeks, and of those only one had returned: two men out of four, empty-handed and broken. The season was as good as over.

"So you want to help Willy," said Naman, quietly enough that their conversation would still be private. "That's good, but I don't see as you can do that till spring. You're short, aren't you?"

"I am, but I have just enough time to make it up," said Brenish. "If worse comes to worst, I can borrow it. But we'll have a few more jobs before the snow."

"A few. Harry's got a line on a gold wagon tomorrow. Needs a couple more hands. You still owe Gareth, right?"

"83p. Next week it's 90." Gareth didn't share the Church's scruples about usury, and the village priest didn't bother assigning penance for it anymore. With Gareth, there were worse things.

"He'll take it off the top, then," Naman said. "Easy way to pay him back."

"Gareth's running this?"

"Course he is. Rare's the job he doesn't run, especially after Harvest. You didn't think Harry got this kind of information out of nowhere, did you?"

Brenish shook his head. Naturally Gareth had a hand in it. He'd have the connections to know when a gold wagon was coming. That didn't mean Brenish had to like it; Gareth took a sizeable cut, and so many jobs had to go through him. You could take your chances on a traveler without his help, but if he had a wagon earmarked or you robbed someone under his protection, and he got wind of it, it never ended well. Harry didn't mind dealing with him; he got on reasonably well with most of Gareth's men.

"Are you still in?" said Naman.

"Of course I'm in."

"Good."

"Back to Willy, though. Pernilla wants him out and she asked me to help. I have an idea, but I'm gonna need an investor."

Naman snorted a laugh. "Not Gareth."

"Not Gareth," Brenish agreed. "Not local. Not in the village, at any rate. I need city money."

Naman chewed on his bit of bird and grabbed another spoonful of roasted turnips, considering the proposal. "Well," he said, "I can talk to Hal. If anyone can get some investors lined up for you, it's him. What's the scheme?"

"If Willy wanted Hal involved he would've gone to him first, and Hal would've come to me," said Brenish. "It can't go through the guild."

"Why not?"

"They'll never go for it, is why."

That meant it was mad on some level, beyond what the guild was usually comfortable with. The guild couldn't con an investor, and Brenish's best work was in cons. Defrauding an outsider was acceptable, but it burned bridges; it was usually bad for business. Brenish did enough other good work for the guild that his shortcomings didn't bother them too much, but their rules really held him in check sometimes. Naman knew all this as well as anyone. He rolled back his broad shoulders and looked his companion in the eye.

"What's the scheme, Brenish?"

Brenish allowed himself a smirk. "Visak's map," he said.

Such was his power of suggestion that even Naman was taken in for a moment. "Truly? Here?" He caught himself in the same place Brenish had. "Nay, it's Willy."

"Right. But it's good, Naman. Real good. If you found it in the right place, and didn't know who made it, you'd think it was the real thing. And believe me, I know about this stuff. It would've fooled me."

Naman laughed a little at Brenish's temerity. "And he thinks you can sell it to someone because they know you like to help adventurers. That's gutsy, even for Willy."

Brenish was about to speak, but the barmaid finally came back and Naman silenced him with a look. Naman did the obligatory flirting while she refilled both mugs. She wasn't spoken for, but while she liked Naman well enough she didn't like his job nor the pittance he made at it, and told him so often enough that he kept a polite distance. The dance they did was sad enough, for Brenish was little different than Naman in his prospects, to make Brenish wonder what Cirawyn possibly saw in him.

The younger thief took a deep draft of ale when she left, giving himself time to collect his thoughts. Naman waited him out.

"I think that's what he had in mind," said Brenish, "but it will never work. If it was your life at stake, would you trust me?"

He expected Naman to shake his head, but his sturdy friend leaned back and put a hand on his clean-shaved chin as if the question were really all that difficult. "I might," he said. "I might want to believe you wouldn't purposely get me lost down there to die. 'Tis the one place you're known as honest."

"But," said Brenish.

"'Tis the one place. You're right; it will never work. No one's biting unless you take on some of the risk." He sat upright again and looked at the remains of the duck, trying to find a good piece of meat to pick off. "And you're not that stupid," he added, as if as an afterthought.

Brenish sipped his ale again, quietly, and pretended to scan the duck himself as well.

"Right?" said Naman. "You're not that stupid."

"I can't just sell it outright," said Brenish. "So I've decided to go another way."

Naman looked him in the eye and saw the twinkle there. He pounced, still in hushed tones. "You're mad. I *knew* someday you'd go Fell. I knew it."

"Calm down, will you? Hear me out first."

Naman sat back again, as if daring Brenish to wow him.

"There are other treasures down there. No one will ever find Visak's, not unless the map truly exists. But no one knows just how big his treasure is, either."

"They'll think you're skimming."

"Hear me out," Brenish repeated. "All you need down there is enough gear to survive, stout companions who will look out for each other, and the means to find a treasure and get out again safely."

"Gee, why didn't I think of that?"

"The *equipment* is the hard part," said Brenish. "That you can get, if you have an investor. I know what to bring with me and what not to. But the key things are enough goldsense potion to find a treasure pit, and a teleportation orb."

"An orb," Naman said incredulously. "Not a scroll."

"A scroll only takes one person. One person can only carry so much. An orb can do the same, or it can take your whole group and anything nearby. So a group goes in, sniffs out a treasure big enough, and teleports out to safety. You don't even need to pull the gold out of a pit, if it's in one. You claim it's the wizard's hoard, and the investor takes their cut. Everyone leaves happy, and no one is ever the wiser except for the ones who went in. And if the treasure's big enough, they won't care."

Naman was slack-jawed. He had heard out Brenish's ravings about the ruins on many nights before this one, but never had he suspected his friend was dumb enough to dive in. Brenish could see that much.

"So you see why I can't involve the guild," Brenish added. He stopped, thinking to himself. "Now the soldiers' academy, on the other hand, they might be more pliable."

"And if they're not, they'll lock you up."

Brenish gave Naman the look of disbelief now. How could he fail to talk a bunch of military men, trained for fighting and not deception, into something like this?

"Besides," said Naman, "you need companions you can trust who will also be solid enough in battle to help. No one's going to go with you on this. No one."

"This is Willy's greatest work," said Brenish. "And it's his best shot to get out of lockup early."

"I know six years is a lot. Nay, don't give me that look. I know it. I think this is foolhardy to try so soon. Give it till summer. Spring, even. Get the guild in on this after all, and do it soon. Let them plant some seeds, put out some contacts, and see what they can find. I think Willy had it right the first time. He needs you to sell it to some gullible skunk who deserves to die down there. You can't find that fellow in just a month or two. It takes time. So let the guild help you. They might balk a little, but they'll do it for Willy. You'll still get a nice cut out of it, and Willy will go free. It won't be next week, but it will be before next fall. All right?"

"Duggle gets a piece too. He gave Willy all the notes."

"They won't have a problem with that. Hal trusts Duggle; we all do."

Brenish thought a minute. Naman was his conscience; he trusted the man to keep him on the right course. It would be foolish not to listen now, after all they had been through together. And he felt the Current pulling him. Now was the time to dig in, think with a clear head, and not make any rash decisions.

"Promise me you won't do anything without giving me a chance to talk you out of it," said Naman.

"I think you mean *another* chance, but I promise."

"Are you willing to give the guild a try?"

"I'm willing to consider it awhile. Perchance you're right. I wouldn't have come to you if I didn't trust your counsel."

"I'm glad to hear it." Naman had been tense, but now he relaxed and reached across the table to slap Brenish on the shoulder. His voice came out again richer, almost a little too loud. "Give it a few days. Tonight we drink; tomorrow we work. After that, we'll both give it a lot more thought. And you come to me again before you decide *anything* for the map. I'll come to you if I have any better ideas."

"Agreed."

The sky was dark when Brenish left the inn, moonless and clouded over. He was headed for the boarding house he shared with several other bachelors in town, Naman included. Naman had gone home half an hour before, well-fed and well-liquored, satisfied his friend wouldn't make a move on the stupid plan without him.

It was, Brenish admitted to himself, a stupid plan. But he still had his doubts about Naman's.

He didn't get a lot of time to think about it, because Cirawyn was waiting outside the inn as he left. In the lantern light by the front door she seemed aglow, the bright orange shining on her pale skin as if she herself were a warm fire. Her long dark hair was braided up tight behind her, another braid bound across the top of her head. Her cheeks were rosy; there was a slight nip in the air, nothing too cold for that time of year. Her eyes glinted with happiness to see him. A longing rushed through his heart, a warmth deep in the spirit, to be with her in a cottage of their own, a simple place just like the one where Pernilla and the kids waited for Willy to return.

"Good evening," Cirawyn said cheerily, and kissed him on the cheek.

"Good evening, m'love," said Brenish.

"Naman said you needed looking after."

"He may be right. And I welcome the company."

They linked arms and walked back together. The boarding house wasn't far from her home. The whole village knew they were a couple, but it was also known that if Brenish did anything inappropriate, her father would end him. Hamish Bowman was little more than a grizzled farmer now, but he was still terrifying, and he was rumored to have once been a fighter of some distinction.

"My father's gone to the city today," she said, as if reading his mind.

"You didn't go with him," Brenish said.

"I have work to do at home. Besides, I can take care of myself."

Of that he had little doubt. Her strong personality made her father's mission to marry her off—especially to wealthy city types who had different attitudes—more difficult, but that helped assuage Brenish's fears a little. Still, someday soon her father would return, if not before this winter then certainly no later than spring, and he would have found her a husband. The old man couldn't afford any less. His son was gone, lost to disease as a boy, and there was no one left to take care of him in his old age. All the more reason he needed a good bride price, and all the less he trusted Brenish.

Could Naman's idea even work? Could it even wait till spring? Willy and his family would get along all right, one way or another. But for Brenish, the calendar was his foe.

"What's on your mind, love?" said Cirawyn.

He tried to smile, but it didn't come out right. "Time," he said. "I'll be twenty this winter, and you'll be eighteen come June. Your dad won't wait."

"I know," she replied. "I've been thinking about that too. I think you need to do something risky."

"Don't tempt me, m'love."

She laughed. "That's not what I meant, silly man."

"Not what I meant either. But what did *you* mean?"

She gestured across the fields before them. "There's naught for you in these foothills. Your talents are wasted in Ilyenis. I know you stay for the inn—"

"That's not the only reason I stay," he said.

She smiled. "And for me. But you won't make your fortune here. People know your reputation now; they know you have answers. They'll come to you in the city just as much as here. They might even pay you better. And there's more work there. Not just thief work and scams, but good honest work that you have skills enough to do. You know your letters, and you're good with figures. You could be a shop clerk."

"I'm in the thieves' guild, love."

"Not all shops will care. The guild has friends in a few. You can make a little more money over the winter. By the time spring comes, you'll have something to show for yourself. Just a little something, and I can talk my father into accepting whatever you can offer. The two of us can."

It sounded so simple. And it would fit nicely alongside Naman's suggestion that they wait for spring. If the guild was sold on the merits of the plan, they might even advance Brenish the difference so he could meet her father's price. Such things weren't unheard of, and Willy would readily sign off on the idea.

Honest work. A clerk in a shop. What would that be like?

Not half bad, Brenish thought. He might be a respectable man yet.

Whether the guild paid the difference or not, though, her father would need an awful lot of convincing. And while Brenish could talk even the stingiest innkeeper into a free meal—even Darius, time and again—talking Cirawyn's father into his blessing would be the speech of his life, even with her help. If he could do that, he felt sure he could bluff his way past the Pearly Gates.

"Love," said Brenish, "I'll do whatever it takes to be with you. There's a lot of wisdom in what you say."

"You mean you'll think about it?" she said, excitedly.

"I'll do more than that. I'll do it. Tomorrow I'll earn the coin to get square with Gareth, and I'll go to the city for the winter. Naman will talk to Hal for me. I'm sure I can find good work there."

She stopped and threw her arms around his waist. "Thank you," she said. "I know what it means to you to leave here."

"It means leaving you," he said. "Not the inn. Not the Gate. I haven't gone Fell."

"I know."

"I mean it. You're all that matters to me."

"Then work hard while you're away. I'll scrape up whatever I can. I'll do extra work around town. I'll even pick up some slack in the inn. They're always busier over winter, and Darius could use an extra hand. We'll make that money together."

"I promise I'll do everything I can."

She squeezed him again. This was all there was. If he couldn't marry her, he *would* go Fell. He would cross the Gate with whatever provisions he could beg or steal. And he wouldn't come out again, even in death.

Willy would have to wait a little while. He'd understand. Pernilla and the kids would understand. Naman would breathe a sigh of relief. Come spring, things would be different, for everybody. Things would be better.

The Wagon Job

The sky was still cloudy the next evening, threatening rain. Rain was good; muddy tracks would disappear within a few hours, making life a lot more difficult for anyone who might investigate after the fact. The sun had only just fallen, leaving the world cast in a pallid gray. Something about being out in the woods this time of night, in fall, always gave Brenish the creeps.

Besides Naman and himself, the only other man in the clearing where they met was Tibs. He was a short, moderately plump man with tiny spectacles. He could get by without them in a pinch, and usually put them away while he was on a job. Tibs was a friendly sort, the kind of fellow who would buy a round on occasion and would do almost anyone a favor. Brenish liked working with him, although as a highwayman he was most intimidating when he used his whip. Tibs wore elaborate padding under his cloak, and pads with wooden spikes on his shoulders and joints, so he would look scarier in the dark. His armor, including the helmet, was mostly decorative.

Tibs carried a crossbow as well, but without his eyeglasses it was just another accessory for effect. If it came to shooting, only Naman and Harry would be of any use, and Harry didn't even have depth perception. Brenish could barely hit the ground if he pointed straight down. Even so, he carried a crossbow too. With his skinny build, he at least looked the part of a trained archer.

"When's Harry getting here?" said Naman. He let his annoyance at their leader's dalliances show plainly. "This was his raid."

"He'll be along," said Tibs. The shorter thief seemed a bit bored, as if robbing gold wagons had become monotonous. Then again, Brenish supposed it had. Tibs was a master lockpick, and a pickpocket's pickpocket—as he had once demonstrated in the city. Banditry, the domain of thugs, was a poor fit for him. Brenish considered for a moment whether he should invite Tibs to come along with him. Might do the man some good. Tibs had a family, but surely he could make a better living for them somewhere else.

Besides, it would serve Harry right for being late all the time.

Brenish decided to play it safe and inspect his pack again: an open leather bag with thick walls, thick bottom, and thick straps, stitched with thick thongs. Their packs were meant for quickly hauling large amounts of gold, which would put those stitches to the ultimate test. He had once heard of a binder who enchanted a pack that could lessen the weight of its contents, but he had never seen any real evidence such a spell existed. Wagons were heavy as ever, and horses and men grunted under their loads. Perhaps the binding was prohibitively expensive, if it was ever anything more than a myth.

"What's the take for each of us?" said Brenish.

"300p," Tibs said. "Not bad for a night's work. How's your winter stores?"

"We don't have a place to keep any," Naman said. "We pay for meals and the boarding house. The landlord buys the stores for us. Speaking of which: Brenish, he needs your payment."

"He won't have it this year," Brenish said. "I'm taking Cirawyn's advice. Gonna move to the city for the winter. I meant to tell you earlier."

"The city?" said Naman. "What for?"

"If I don't save up enough by spring, I'm finished. Thought I'd take your advice, too, and have a talk with Hal. If you put in a good word for me, maybe he can set me up in a shop somewhere. I can wait out the winter earning some coin while my other prospects work out."

Tibs laughed that part off, knowing nothing of the business with Willy. Brenish was the sort of man who always had other prospects on the line.

"Of course," Naman said. "That's a big step, but I think you're making the right decision—about everything."

"Tibs," said Brenish, "your missus is friends with Darius' wife, right?"

"Unfortunately." The innkeeper's wife was the biggest gossip in town, with no one else running even a close second. Tibs didn't like gossip, but he always got an earful of it secondhand. Then he would complain about it to his friends, repeating everything in excruciating detail. He never saw the irony.

"Cirawyn thinks she can earn some extra coin this winter too. Maybe pick up some work at the inn. Will you help her out? Anything she can get to pick up a little more, you'd be doing me a big favor."

"Course I will, Brenish. You're actually serious about moving to the city, aren't you?"

"It's now or never. I should've done this a long time ago."

Rustling leaves announced the arrival of their fourth man, Harry Card. Like the others he had a heavy cloak with a long cowl to help disguise his face. He needed it, having only one eye. He wore a patch over the left. He liked to tell passersby that the wound was from a tavern fight, but it was really from an infection. Harry was the oldest of the bunch, in his mid-thirties, weathered and scarred and hard outside as a stale loaf of bread. His only family was an illegitimate son who thought his "real" dad was an even moodier, crustier piece of work.

"Nice of you to show up," said Naman.

"Fie, you didn't tell me you'd be bringing Brenish."

"Pleasure to see you too, Harry," Brenish said. Harry thought poorly of him for reasons that he was the first to admit were entirely appropriate. Brenish wasn't cut out for this. Then again neither was Tibs, yet here they all were. For some reason Harry was chummier with Tibs than with anyone else in the guild, maybe because of Tibs' personality.

"Aye, we're all friends here," Harry said. "Just don't bungle this for us. Try not to fire the crossbow. Last time you nearly killed a man."

"Got him to cooperate."

Tibs nudged Brenish on the arm. "If you have to do that again, just aim for him like last time. That way you're bound to miss. Just don't hit one of us."

It sounded mean, but Tibs was offering it as a joke. Brenish took the cue and laughed it off. It had the desired effect on Harry, who smirked.

"All right," Harry said. "Let's just make this a clean job and we'll each get our cut tomorrow. No unpleasant surprises."

"Got it," said Brenish.

"I still say you shoulda got Gavin. Least he can actually shoot."

Naman rolled his eyes. "Let it go, Harry. Gavin wasn't available. You'll have him next time."

"Aye, Harry," said Brenish. "After tomorrow you're good and rid of me. Whatever happens after this winter, I don't think I'll be coming back to this."

Harry spat on the ground, as if he had intended to do it all along and the timing was just coincidence. "Too good for us, lore-master?"

"Not good enough for Cirawyn's dad."

"No kidding. She's as good as taken anyway, Brenish. Might as well move on. Or just be free. Not every man *has* to get married, you know."

Brenish tsked softly. "But then what would I do? Sneak around at all hours while her husband was at the inn? Never show up for a job when I say I will? What kind of man does that?"

Harry drew back his fist, but Naman stepped between them and held him back. "Come on, Harry. You drew first blood. Just let the man do his job and tomorrow we'll part ways. No hard feelings."

"A few hard feelings," Harry said. He shook Naman off, but he put his arm down.

"Nay, I'm sorry, Harry," said Brenish. "'Twas a cheap shot. Let's just say we each have someone we'd do anything for. I'm gonna take a chance."

To his credit, Harry accepted that with a nod. It was big of him. But like the stale loaf, Harry was really only crunchy on the outside. Maybe he understood where Brenish was coming from after all. Deep down, Brenish worried that this was his fate if he failed: to live half a life in a dead-end job, promoted to chief bandit under the command of a rich landowner who treated his hired bandits worse than his lackeys. Brenish had heard whispers that the guild was keeping more and more distance from Harry, fearful he might come apart at the seams—or worse, tie them too closely to Gareth.

"Gonna rain soon," Harry said. "That's a good sign."

"Aye," said Tibs.

"Let's run through our equipment and go over our roles one more time. We'll take our places after dark."

The storm that came streaming down that night was thick and prolonged, the type of weather that sent travelers scurrying for warm inns. The cloaks protected the thieves somewhat, but in the cold and wet it was miserable work, waiting for the wagons to come. They could barely hear anything coming on the road, and from their position it was hard to see the lantern of a driver until a wagon was right on top of them.

Nevertheless they held fast, their forward barricade in place where it could be seen soon enough for a driver to stop, late enough that he couldn't avoid it entirely and back up. The bandits controlled a bottleneck in the road between dense patches of forest. This work was their bread and butter, and they had become very good at it. A wagon could be taken, moved off the road and out of sight, and the barricade removed in less than a minute, leaving no trace they were ever there. The driver and his lookout would be returned to the road with their wagon a short while later, with less of a burden.

Cooperative drivers got to keep their valuables; only the cargo mattered. Uncooperative drivers reached their destinations naked and shivering, sometimes bruised. The drivers knew this now. The quicker a driver capitulated, the more of his cargo would make the journey safely, which encouraged the senders of regular shipments to use their meekest men and load them up with a little extra just in case. The whole thing had become routine.

Except for flashes of lightning, the darkness was almost total. The four men had to perform blind, moving with precision. Brenish could handle this; it wasn't his best skill, but he had done it enough before to know his marks and his cues, like a veteran actor. It was rote. But it was rote that would not be missed.

The first hint of approaching light was easier to spot than the men had expected, thanks to a short break in the downpour. It grew steadily clearer as the wagon rounded a bend and shone through fewer trees, until suddenly it was out in the open and shining right at them. The wagon was drawn by a team of four horses and two men: one holding the reins, the other holding a lantern of the type favored by high-speed transport, curved and polished copper along the back so it would reflect into the road. Silver worked better, but those lanterns tended to get stolen.

The horses seemed to see the barricade before the light ever reached it, and came to a muddy halt right in front of it. The thieves sprang out of the woods to either side.

"Hold fast!" Naman shouted gruffly. "Drop those reins. Weapons away."

"Do as we say and you'll come to no harm," said Harry.

Brenish moved aside the curtain of vines covering their detour. While Harry and Naman forced the two men down out of the wagon, Tibs ascended and took the reins, backing up the horses and turning them aside to follow the new path. When it was safely on its way, Brenish did the rest of his job and pulled the barricade away. It was a precision operation.

The clearing was soggy but it was covered in tall grass, a pleasant change from the mud on the road. When Brenish got there, Tibs was already off the wagon and unlocking the door in the back. He was using a key, which probably galled him but kept his true talents a mystery; the less anyone knew about them, the better. Naman and Harry had the driver and lookout sit on the grass next to the wagon, the lantern shining on their faces from Harry's hand.

"All secure?" Harry shouted. He disguised his voice, as they all did.

"All clear, Alfie," said Brenish. The code names were a nice touch, one of Harry's better ideas. Alfie and his cohorts were effectively ghosts. The names changed around so there was never a consistent description to give, and Harry always kept his eye well hidden. Sometimes one of them wore makeup: a false scar that looked real enough in the dark, or a memorable fake tattoo if the weather was dry. In the city, Alfie was a man with a hundred faces.

Tibs got the back of the wagon open, finally, and climbed up inside with their reinforced packs.

"Go help," Harry said.

Brenish got into the wagon behind Tibs. Inside, he found Tibs had taken his helmet off. The shorter thief held a little wisp light, a magic lantern similar to the one in Willy's study but much smaller, meant for finding one's way home in the dark. It was sufficient to light up the compartment. Tibs squinted into the broken gloom, trying to find the sparkle of gold bars or coins. Sometimes it came in bags or closed chests.

"I can't see too well, George," said Tibs. He didn't break character. "Where's the gold?"

Brenish stepped in closer to have a better look. The front of the compartment was filled with solid boxes. He pushed his way beside and around Tibs to take a better look. There was nothing for it but to open the boxes. Brenish was already suspicious that something was wrong: The boxes weren't reinforced like a chest, and the wood grain ran horizontally. They weren't nearly strong enough to hold a significant number of gold coins, let alone bars.

He pulled down the top box and opened it up. The lid came free easily, held on only by a simple lip. Inside he found a few ink-stained papers with nothing useful written on them, and a worthless pile of straw.

He threw the box aside and opened another. More scrap paper, and more straw.

The third box had a dirty rag and a mouse. And more straw.

Brenish threw his hood back on and jumped out of the wagon. "Alfie!" he shouted. "You'd better look in there."

He took the lantern from Harry and stood guard over the prisoners. The driver didn't seem particularly smug. If anything he seemed nervous that the bandits were out of sorts. Maybe he didn't even know what he was carrying—or more to the point, what he wasn't.

"What's wrong?" said Naman.

"Everything," said Brenish. "Everything's wrong."

Harry stormed back out in a rage, Tibs hopping off the wagon right behind him. He snatched the lantern away and pushed it right up into the driver's face. "What is this?" he shouted. "What kind of trick?"

"N-no trick, sir," the driver stammered. His lookout was terrified into silence. "We're carrying gold. They *told* me it was gold." He was shaking, whether from fear or the cold no one could tell.

"They switched the wagons and didn't tell the drivers," said Naman. "We got the decoy."

A few moments later, a rushing sound and the cries of distant horses came through the trees. The light off the other lantern couldn't be seen. It didn't matter; it was long gone.

Harry was red with wrath. His fists shook uncontrollably in the rain. "I won't stand for this," he said.

"We haven't much choice, Alfie," said Tibs.

"Nay! They play games with us, they *pay* for it. We'll send them a message they won't forget. Kill one. Stick his head in one of those crates."

Naman stepped up, letting Brenish keep an eye on the riders who were now afraid for their lives. "No, Alfie," Naman said. He stayed in his character voice. "We don't do that. They cooperated. We send them on their way. Next time we'll know. They'll go back and tell their masters this trick won't work twice. Or next time we will do as you say." He turned to face the men, glaring at them as if he could see them through the cowl.

"A-aye," the driver said. "W-w-we will tell them."

Harry growled. For a minute he stood in the rain, seething, as the others wondered what he would do. Finally he waved to Tibs and to Brenish. "Get them out of here," he barked.

The horses were led back up to the road, now clear of any obstacles, with the driver and lookout marched along behind. When the wagon was ready, Naman shoved the men roughly toward the front and let them climb up, but followed that with the friendly gesture of handing the lookout his lantern.

"You remember the mercy you were shown tonight," said Naman. "Tell them it won't happen the next time they try this."

The men nodded eagerly, but refrained from spurring on the horses until Naman waved them on. The wagon took off like a startled bird, racing down the muddy road into the empty, wet autumn night.

"Well that was a disaster," Naman said.

"Gareth told me the *second* wagon was the decoy," said Harry. He was still steaming with anger. "This is *his* fault for getting the information wrong. His contacts should have been able to warn him about a switch."

"Not if it was at the last minute," said Naman. "But it's still on him."

"Aye," said Tibs, "except *we* don't get paid." He took out the wisp and put his glasses back on.

Brenish's heart sank. He still owed Gareth 83p. There was nowhere else he could get that kind of money without depleting his savings past the point of danger, making a trip to the city all but impossible. At best there was nowhere to get it in under a week. He couldn't afford much of a delay, not if he stuck to his plan. Even his more outrageous plan, revealed as childish and hollow now, was sunk. He felt trapped, like a rabbit in a snare. He would lose Cirawyn and die alone, either quickly in the ruins or, if his courage failed him as wholly as his luck, over the long march of years like Harry Card. He choked out something incomprehensible, a strangled cry of grief that didn't even have the decency to make a proper sob.

"We'll find another way," said Naman. "Do *not* go Fell on me."

"The great headman swings his axe," Brenish said, quoting an old book of verse as if in a trance, "and the stragglers perish."

Naman slapped him across the face. "Snap out of it!" he shouted.

"Men," said Tibs. His voice was so low he could barely be heard in the rain. He was kneeling in the road.

"What now?" said Harry. "What?"

"Look at the ruts." Tibs' voice quavered, on the edge of panic. "Look at the water in the ruts." He held the wisp lower for the others to see better.

"So what? What about them? We already know we missed the real wagon."

Tibs shook his head. Brenish saw Naman open his mouth, words lost before they reached his tongue. Naman saw it.

"This rut is the wagon we missed. *This* rut is the one we let go."

There was no question which was deeper.

"Nay," said Harry. "You got them mixed up. That was *definitely* the decoy."

"Aye," said Naman, but his voice wasn't primed for a joke. "That's what I want to believe too. That's what we're all gonna tell Gareth. And we'll pray he believes it even more than we do."

Brenish had nothing to say. His mind had withdrawn completely, flailing in despair. Only distantly could he understand that his friends were in trouble; for him it was too late no matter what. The city was lost to him, and with it his only real hope. One way or another, he was already doomed.

Gareth

Colin St. James was the son of a wealthy, unscrupulous financier. He traveled often from his riverside estate in Ilyenis to the cities where he grew and maintained his many political connections. His only heir was a spoiled yet clever boy, who learned his father's ways eagerly yet, by any means possible, borrowed, stole, or purchased books of deep lore. The boy stood in earshot of both Colin's dealings and the fireside tales of travelers—the wizard Visak included—who had seen the Elder Kingdom with their own eyes. As the boy grew into a man he thirsted ever more for both power and knowledge alike, and seldom was his thirst denied.

When Colin passed, Gareth St. James took the reins of his empire and sustained it ruthlessly. But unlike his father and grandfather, who viewed the estate in Ilyenis as a summer home only, Gareth expanded it. He traveled less often, but still enough to keep his lines of influence secure. Gareth was known in Northhill, Acherton, and especially nearby Eswell. He tightened his grip on Ilyenis, driving out two competing bosses with less stomach, or wit, than he. The village was the center of his power and the center of his focus. For his favorite place in the world was the high brick tower, the pinnacle of his grandfather's mansion, where in fair weather he would often look far across the nearby fields, to the grass-grown hillock in which stood Asaph's Gate.

Gareth had never gone to the ruins himself, except, it was said, to stand at the Gate as a child and listen to his voice echo back from below. He always had the good sense to keep his head above ground. But his heart, as anyone who knew him would readily say and he himself did not deny, had gone Fell long ago.

His office was decorated with weapons of every description, a naked display of power that was never lost on his visitors—especially not the four failed highwaymen who stood before him. Brenish knew, from seeing Gareth perform once in a duel, that he knew how to use every single one of those weapons. When Gareth wasn't reading about the ruins or the creatures that dwelt there, he honed his combat skills. He was at least a match for the best of his men, perhaps even the best in the city.

Four of his henchmen stood at hand, silently, as he ate his midday meal. He made the thieves wait for him, from start to finish, before he would speak to any of them. But at last he set down his utensils, stood up, and walked around his desk to face his fruitless hirelings. While not tall, he was physically imposing merely for his girth: the result of his incessant training. His dark brown hair was always neat, his mustache and short beard always perfectly trimmed; all were flecked with gray. His face was deceptively kind, as if he were a creature of the deep that wore a pleasant visage until it bit the head off its prey without warning.

"Gentlemen," he said, as if he meant it. His voice was one of unquestioned command. "I'm disappointed."

Disappointment was Gareth's most dangerous mood. Enraged, he might try to calm himself down and respond in a way that was rather reasonable. Bemused, he showed mercy. Sad, he put problems aside. Happy, he was everyone's best friend, a giver of gifts and a speaker of kind words. Envy he kept to himself; none had ever seen it in him. But disappointed, he was crueler than any beast that walked the abandoned paths of the Elder Kingdom that he knew—from tales and books alone—so well. A smart man would rather die trying than disappoint Gareth St. James.

He paced before each man individually, looking them all in the eye. Brenish had been subjected to that treatment on several occasions, but this time he was unfazed. He felt calm. Death meant nothing now. Gareth lingered an extra moment on his face, but moved on.

Gareth, finished with his inspection, stood back and spread his hands. He acted as though he expected one of them to speak, but they all knew better.

"Explanations?" he said.

"The first wagon was the decoy," Harry said. Brenish doubted he believed that anymore; Tibs was an excellent tracker, and Harry was enough of a hunter himself to see the difference in the ruts. Harry tried to sell it as best he could, but he lacked Brenish's gift. It might work well enough, if he didn't expect Tibs to crack like a bad wheel.

Gareth acted like this was news to him; Jase had practically raced to deliver their explanation the moment they arrived on the grounds. Now Jase stood smugly to one side, watching them squirm.

"You were told otherwise," said Gareth.

Harry, who had been standing at attention like the others, relaxed and turned his head to meet Gareth's eye. "I know," he said slowly.

If Gareth was bothered by Harry's attitude, he didn't show it. He smiled and laughed under his breath in an amused *same-old-Harry* way. His tone was less of a dressing down than the correction of a simple but well-meaning nephew. He was thirty-two; Harry had a few more years on him. "Funny, isn't it? How these misunderstandings happen."

"I laughed myself poor," Harry said, completely deadpan.

Gareth laughed again, but genuinely; he was caught off guard by the remark and it tickled his humor. The laugh cut off sharply.

"The *second* wagon was the decoy, just as you were told."

"We found naught but straw and refuse. And a mouse."

"Then why, Harry, did the first wagon arrive safely in the city with a load of coins?" Gareth clasped his hands together earnestly. Like prayer, Brenish thought. He wondered if Gareth really did pray, and if so to what. Whatever was listening to him, it seemed to be working out so far.

"Word came an hour before you got here," Gareth added. "Did you think I wouldn't hear about it?"

"That's why we came to tell you," Harry said.

"The *first* wagon carried the gold, Harry."

"That's because when it got there, it *was* the first wagon. The second wagon came through while we were still detaining the first. Your source didn't know that."

Gareth shook his head gravely. "He did. He said that the first wagon to *arrive* was the decoy. When the other wagon arrived, the drivers were badly shaken up. They had been waylaid by bandits on the road, they said: Alfie and his men. But it was *their* wagon that had the gold."

"I tell you it was crates of rubbish."

Gareth's eyes flashed anger now. He turned to strike. The blow would be delivered in words, but whatever he said would be as deadly as anything hanging from his wall. Brenish intervened before Gareth could finish taking a breath.

"'Tis my fault," Brenish said.

Gareth froze, surprised out of his fury, like a man about to kick down a door only to see it was open the whole time. Something like wicked mirth played on his lips. There was some anger at the interruption, but his plain curiosity overpowered all else. What wild story would Brenish try to tell off the cuff to get them all out of this? How far would he be willing to believe it? If the story was entertaining enough, would he be willing to let a part of this go? Similar tactics had worked before.

"I checked the boxes," Brenish said. "I found naught but refuse, as Harry said. And the mouse. I showed him one of the boxes. If they had a hidden compartment, I missed it."

Half truths were Brenish's specialty. Gareth knew as much. He stopped and gave the thief another good long look in the eye. Brenish returned his gaze and held it, unwavering.

Gareth stepped back again and frowned, almost in concern. "What's got into you?" he said.

"'Twas my mistake."

Brenish could hear Naman breathing beside him, and in each breath a silent, desperate plea to shut up. He didn't take his eyes off of Gareth, but in the corner of his eye he saw Gareth's man Bob shift a bit, reacting to some other tension in the room. Bob was the biggest man in the entire village; his brother was a close second.

"Nay," said Gareth, slowly. "Nay, I don't think you can take all the blame. Much though you seem to want to." He seemed perplexed, unseated by the idea that whatever gambit Brenish had thrown at him, it wasn't one he had been prepared to accept. "You didn't check all the crates, did you?"

"Nay. Checking each one would have dragged on too long. I gave up the search and told the others it was empty. I was sure it was the decoy."

Gareth turned to one of his henchmen, off to Brenish's right. "Think he's being completely honest with me, Raden?"

Brenish glanced in time to see the man shrug his massive shoulders. "It's Brenish."

But Gareth only looked back at the thief again. "I'm not so sure of that, today." He paused in thought, then walked back behind his desk and sat. "No matter. The blame rests at least as much on Harry. My instructions were clear. Contents of the *first* wagon to be delivered."

"We were unprepared to bring back a hundred worthless cases of straw," said Harry.

"Opening each one and finding just the ones with gold would have been sufficient. 'Twas a simple trick. You of all people should have seen through it."

"If I may, sir," said Brenish, "that's more my area."

Gareth ignored him. "I'm at a loss. Tell me what I should do, Harry, because I can't simply let this go unanswered. I have friends who know I had something to do with this. Today I'm a laughingstock.

"The guild's friendship means a lot to me; I'm loath to simply have you all killed. I might make an example, but you know how I hate waste. And that Alfie fiction of yours, Harry, was a masterstroke of ingenuity. I need a man like you working the road. I need the rest of your team almost as much. I just need it done competently. You understand my dilemma."

Brenish was surprised by Gareth's honesty; it was incredibly frank of him. It was easy to forget, under the whip-crack changes in the man's mood or his casual meanness, that he could be charming and self-effacing. Yet even Brenish knew political gain required no less. And everyone knew there were other reasons Gareth could only punish Harry so far.

"Let's get down to figures. That wagon contained 2,700p. That's a lot of money I should have received, that I never did. What is that split four ways, Jase?"

"675p," Jase said without hesitation. Brenish looked his way. Jase was good with figures, but he had probably calculated that the minute he learned of their debacle. The tall, glorified clerk wore a self-satisfied smirk above his black goatee. Brenish always wanted to compare Jase to a weasel, but truth be told he was handsome in an irritatingly all-too-natural way that made ladies swoon. A pretty weasel, then.

"That's not round enough," said Gareth.

"700."

"That's better."

"Less our cut, of course," said Harry. Gareth plainly didn't like him speaking up to say it, but Harry pressed on anyway. "Less the cut we would have had, had the gold been delivered. That would be..."

"375," said Tibs, quietly. Harry took forever with numbers.

"375p. Had we found the gold, that's what you would have got. Split four ways."

Gareth sneered as if this was the stupidest notion ever suggested in history. "Nay," he said, his indignation expressed in a high, nasal note of derision. "700. Each."

Harry knew better than to argue further. "All right," he said. "I understand."

"I don't think you do, Harry. I don't think you understand at all. Did I not use the word 'laughingstock'? I did, didn't I, Turk?"

"Aye, boss," said Turk. He was behind the thieves; Brenish couldn't see him. Turk was a man of few words and fewer expressions; he knew there wasn't much to miss.

"And an extra..." Harry began.

"325," said Tibs.

"...325, from each of us, should compensate for that. It's almost double."

Naman finally broke posture and gave Harry a long-suffering look. Harry seemed to know it was a mistake the minute that left his mouth.

Gareth slapped his desk. "Now *that's* an idea. That's what I like about you, Harry. You're the brain of this operation; I've always said so. *Double.* That's a nice word. How much would that be, Jase?"

"1,400."

"Why, so it is. That's almost as much as I would have made from the entire venture. *Each.* That's a good way to make recompense, don't you think?" Jase nodded back to him. "I like that. Well done, Harry. Well done indeed. You've solved my dilemma. And we can all be friends again."

"We'll never be able to pay that back," said Naman. "It'll take years."

Gareth put a hand to his mouth, mockingly. "Oh. Oh, you're quite right, Naman. It probably *will* take years. But I think I'm going to do something kind for you men, since you've all gone out of your way to try and make this right. I'll let you pay it back over time. Aye, that's what I'll do. You can pay me as you go along. No less than, oh, 200p a year. And only a tithe of the balance each year, for interest. You can save up an extra 200p a year. That's a fair deal, isn't it?"

The thieves didn't dare say anything else. Gareth was just warming up.

"But I forgot: Brenish, you still owe me a considerable sum. About 100p, wasn't it?"

"83, sir," said Brenish. But it may as well be an even hundred, he thought. It may as well be a million.

"Yes, that's right. But it is at a higher rate. So I'll fold 100 into what you owe, and we can call it an even… 1,500."

The tragedy of it all was that Gareth actually *was* being more than fair, at least concerning the existing debt. A tithe was a manageable rate. But 1,500p was well beyond what he would have expected Cirawyn's father to demand of him come spring.

"Of course," Gareth said, "if the elusive Alfie and his boys want to get a bit more creative, I'm sure that debt will be paid off much faster. A few pay wagons come through in winter. And there are other roads and cities. Why should a man as talented as that limit himself to a small area? I know I'll have bigger jobs to come, and I know that in the *future*, they'll be done right."

Harry nodded in defeat. Gareth seemed pleased with himself, more than Brenish had seen in a long time. It was wise to take advantage of a mood like that. And Brenish knew he had only one hope left.

"Sir," he said, "as long as I'm in your debt, may I ask one thing?"

Naman stared, in total disbelief. The look on Gareth's face was similar, but painted with gaudy splashes of fascination. No child had ever stared at a traveling acrobat before the climax of the act in such wonder, waiting to find out what could possibly top everything he had already seen.

"I'm listening," Gareth said, his smile wide and merry.

Brenish looked him in the eye. "You own us now. It will take years to pay that back, and we're yours. But I can be of even greater value to you off the road. Send me to cities to do your bidding and put my skills to good use. Let me track down lore for you; you know I'm good at finding it. But I beg you, lend me 800p more, on top of that debt, to use before the month is out. All the longer I'll be yours, and I will be loyal."

Gareth was nearly beside himself with silent laughter. It was clear to see he could hardly believe the thief's audacity, first for claiming all the blame and then for asking a favor. How could he deny someone who made him feel such pure joy? His sides shook until he held them, and then the merriment found his voice, seized it, and bellowed out in great deep braying puffs. When he finally mastered himself, he wiped away a tear.

"I knew something got into you," he said. "I haven't laughed so hard in a mighty long time. I'll make it 100, for your gall."

"I'm sorry, sir," said Brenish, "but I need 800. I am quite serious."

"Nay," said Gareth. "Nay, I won't give you 800p. If I did that you'd flee the village. You might even elude me for a long time, if the guild aided you. You're not worth that kind of trouble."

"I was already planning to leave for the winter. I needed to save as much money as I could before spring. That's hopeless now. I'm begging you, Gareth. If you won't give me the money, then pay it for me. Pay 800p, or less if he'll accept it, and leave me on the hook for the whole sum. Leave me on the hook for a thousand. I don't care. I'm your man, and I'll honor my debt, and when you've paid that sum you'll understand why I'll never flee."

Gareth was quite taken aback by Brenish's apparent earnestness. Not that he hadn't seen such things before: Brenish layered his deceptions like dozens of onion skins over a horse puck, with artistry unequaled south of the mountains. All Brenish could hope was that even knowing that, Gareth would accept this sincere offer at face value, and give him a chance to prove himself. That same artistry could be put to work in Gareth's favor, and he obviously knew it.

"This is madness, Brenish," said Naman, before Gareth could even make up his mind. "We'll find another way."

"There *is* no other way, and I'm out of time."

"You have till spring."

Gareth leaned forward in his chair, looking between the two thieves. "This has been a lively show so far," he said, "but if you're as desperate as you say, I can't trust you not to go Fell."

"He has," said Bob.

That drew the attention of everyone else in the room, Brenish included. He had never told Bob any such thing.

"The other night, Naman and Brenish were at the inn. They spoke quietly, but I heard Naman whisper something about going Fell."

Brenish looked to Naman, who was too pale to conceal his shock. Leave it to Bob, he thought, to trip over a dangerous subject.

"Did he now?" said Gareth.

"Brenish was excited, so I thought he might be right. But after that, I thought it seemed Naman had talked sense back into him."

"That's right," Naman said, too quickly. Brenish kept his own reaction under control; he wished Naman would let him handle this. "I told Brenish he should get a job in the city, and the guild would help him."

Now Gareth scanned Naman's eyes. He looked briefly into Brenish's, but Gareth was too smart to believe he'd find anything there.

"To earn 800p in one winter?" said Gareth. "Nay. Something's amiss."

Brenish wanted to mention the rest of the actual plan, that he and Cirawyn had intended to work towards a common goal, but he felt it best to leave her out of it until Gareth agreed to the debt. But first he had to salvage this situation. "It would have been a start, at least," he said.

Bob raised a finger. "There was more to it. Naman spoke of a map."

Gareth flinched in surprise. For an instant Brenish dropped his guard, and that was enough for Gareth to see that Bob had torn open a hornets' nest. This subject had never been meant for his ears, and now he knew it.

"What map?" said Gareth. But he asked Bob, leaving Brenish the space of a moment to come up with an answer.

"I know not. I bent an ear, but that was all I heard. They spoke of other things after that."

"'Tis unimportant," Brenish said. He was grateful Bob had heard no more, especially that Willy's name hadn't reached him. It left him more space to work. "I have other prospects that might have made up the difference if I found work in the city. Perhaps they'll work out, perhaps not, but not quick enough. Even if they still do, I'm your man for a good long time. If an extra thousand isn't enough, just name your price."

"*Not* this way, Brenish," Naman hissed. "It's not worth it."

"If you want my favor, Brenish," said Gareth, "you'll answer my question."

Brenish hesitated, but hid it behind a show of consideration. "'Twould be of no use to you. It points to certain valuables in Northhill and how to reach them. Nothing more. It has some value to the right thief, perhaps a traveler."

He could see that either Gareth wasn't taking the bait, or he wanted to punch a hole in the story. "And how did you acquire it? From another wagon, perhaps? That would belong to me."

"Nay! I—"

"He found Visak's map," Naman snapped. "He had half a mind to go after the treasure himself, but I told him to sell it. The guild would find him a buyer."

The die was cast now. Brenish understood why Naman had spoken; forestalling Gareth any longer was impossible, and they both knew it. Now there was nothing for it but to play along. "Why would you say that?" he said.

"This is no time to play games. He was on the scent already. Besides, maybe he'd be your buyer. You could pay the debt for us. 'Tis the least you could do."

"I told you," said Brenish, feigning anger and ignoring Gareth's stare a moment longer, "I know not if it's authentic. Not with surety." He faced Gareth. "You know me too well to buy such a thing from me, or I'd have brought it up myself. I'd no intention of involving you."

Gareth looked deep into Brenish's eyes, trying hopelessly to penetrate the fog. "Did you not? Perhaps you thought to find the treasure yourself?"

"He had a plan," Naman said. "He was going to get an investor to buy him supplies, including a teleportation orb so he could bring back all the treasure at once. I told him 'twas a stupid risk."

There was no more denying it, at least that part. Brenish felt as if perhaps he'd had an unclean influence on Naman, for the man to try lying to Gareth in such a fashion. Naman was nearly the last man Gareth would expect to deceive him.

"Aye, and he was right," Brenish said. "I'm no fool. Better to sell it to someone else, and get a small piece, than risk everything myself."

Gareth licked his lips, but he took a minute to consider the opportunity before him. "You think me *your* fool, then?" he said. But in that moment Brenish thought that was entirely possible. Gareth needed this story to be true.

"Nay. You're the last person I would expect to buy it—especially from me. I told Naman that very thing."

"I don't even buy that you *have* it," said Jase.

"'Tis a strange tale," Brenish said. He mustered his courage, all his skill. "I was in the city in June, you remember. Guild business. I stayed in the old inn where Visak used to tell his stories. You remember the one?" He looked at Gareth. "Howlett's Horsehead."

"Of course."

"Howlett's son, he doesn't keep it as tidy. He's not lettered, neither. Those books in his back room were just gathering dust. Thought if I could swap 'em out for blanks, make 'em just as dusty, he'd never know the difference."

"And?" Gareth's eyebrow went up. Brenish had him on the hook.

"I never made the swap. When I looked at the books to see if they were even worth it, I found a paper tucked between the pages of a big volume. I think, maybe Visak knew people would try to find it in his home. 'Twasn't safe there. But old Howlett, he wasn't lettered any more than his son. The books were just for show. Remember he used to keep them up on the mantel? I think Visak just stuck it in there one day when no one was looking. That's why he always went back there. Had to keep an eye on it, in case anyone went after his gold."

"I don't believe you."

"*I* don't believe me," said Brenish. "I spent the rest of the summer trying to find anything I could to verify it. I remember what the old man's hand looked like. I couldn't prove it was the real map, but I studied it." Which he had, but only for a few days. "I think perhaps it's real, but 'tis a learnèd guess."

Gareth did his best to resist. He was at war now with his desire. Even for a man so stern with himself, this pull was too great. Every man had a lever. "Even with the guild's help," he said, "no one will believe that story."

"That's why I would have gone myself, if I could find an investor and some steady men to help. 'Twould be hard to find someone to buy the map outright from a crook like me. If I put my own life on it, they might go in for a stake. But Naman talked me out of it. He was worried I'd gone Fell. And he's right; 'tis too risky. So I planned to let the guild sell it instead."

There was anger underneath Gareth's face. "I see your game," he said. "Do you mean to tell me that you just *begged* me for 800p, so you could spend it on equipment and go into the ruins? A dead man can't pay me back."

"I gave up on that, Gareth. I swear to God, it wasn't for that. 800 isn't enough for that plan; you know as well as I what an orb would cost. That's why I said you can pay the 800 for me. You'd see for yourself what I needed, and you'd be satisfied that I'd work off my debt. And even if I can sell that map, if that gave me the coin to pay you all I owed, I'd still work for you. I'll stay with you for seven years, guaranteed. *Seven years*, Gareth."

Gareth shared a look with Jase, the kind that asked what he should do with a man this mad. Jase went right on smirking.

"Where is this map now?" said Gareth. "I'd like to see it."

"Forget the map. I mean not to sell it to you. I just want to borrow enough for—" He stopped, choked off his words before he said something stupid.

"Suppose I might be interested. If it *is* real, I'd feel plenty foolish for letting it slip through my fingers. Besides, you asked me for a loan on top of a loan, and a generous one at that. I need some collateral."

Brenish pressed his question, still hoping to push the map aside somehow. "Then you'll lend the 800?"

"I've made no decision yet. I've half a mind to kill you for trying to sell me that story."

"If the loan's off the table then go ahead," Brenish said. "There's nothing for me here."

Gareth got out of his chair and went to Bob, holding out a hand for a sword. Bob drew his blade and handed it by the hilt to his boss. It was always hard to tell what Bob was thinking or how he would react in any given situation; he was a good enough man as Gareth's henchmen went, but loyal to a fault. Gareth accepted the weapon and carried it over to the thieves, holding the honed and polished iron up to Brenish's throat. Brenish didn't flinch.

"I've truly never seen this in you, Brenish. I don't like dealing with the unexpected, especially when it comes to people. You've always been slippery to trust, but you were an open book till now. What do you need that 800p for, anyway?"

"I know," said Turk.

Gareth looked over Brenish's shoulder to his unkempt thug. "You think he's being straight with me?"

"'Bout the loan." The voice shrugged for him. Brenish couldn't see the man's shoulders behind him, but he knew Turk enough to guess they probably never moved. He was wooden as an apple cart. Most of the village knew where Brenish stood with Cirawyn's dad, but Turk was almost family in an odd way; he was married to Pernilla's sister.

A slow smile crossed Gareth's face as he put the pieces together. "I'll consider it, Brenish. Aye, I may even do you better than that. I guess that depends on whether I like what I see."

Brenish felt a sliver of relief at that, but he saw something else in Gareth's eyes besides the man's usual glee at having the upper hand. It was a light, an old hunger stoked to life: monsters, lost treasures, and ancient cities cut into the bedrock. The sight of it in Gareth's face made him ill. Was that what Naman had talked him out of? Had he looked like *that*?

Gareth was taken. All those days spent in his tower, staring at the Gate from afar. The books, and the weapons. His need was greater than his distrust.

"I think I'll have a look at that map, if you please."

The Expert

Gareth had taken to calling the thieves his "employees" in the last day since their new arrangement. They had ever been, but now they were forced into his service by debt rather than scarcity. Harry, Tibs, and Naman were allowed to go their own ways, but warned to stay close. At first Gareth wanted to keep them all on the estate, but Jase reminded him they'd have to be fed. Tibs in particular showed great relief, because he had a wife and a little girl to look after.

Brenish, on the other hand, only left the grounds once: in the company of the brothers Bob and Raden, to show them the cache where he kept the map. He talked them out of taking the rest of his things back to Gareth, arguing that he still needed his means of support for winter and Gareth would want him to live long enough to pay him back. They knew Brenish enough not to sway easily, but at the bottom they were decent fellows, and reasonable.

Half the reason Gareth sent them, Brenish suspected, was because Brenish respected them on a personal level above the other henchmen and wouldn't try to pull too many fast ones. Finch would have been an even better choice, but he was away on an errand. At least he didn't send Dex, who was hated even by the easy-going Tibs.

Two days passed. Brenish was fed somewhat well in Gareth's house, kept under constant guard in a wing reserved for servants. The servants had no idea what he was doing there, and at times he overheard them gossiping about whether he was in trouble or Gareth regarded him as an asset. The consensus was that Gareth himself didn't know, as was likely the truth.

On the evening of the third day after the robbery, Jase came to the little room where Brenish slept: his "cell" as it were, though it was nicer than his own bunk back at the boarding house. "You've been summoned," said Jase.

Brenish followed without a word. He couldn't place the look on the lackey's face, whether it was bemusement or scorn. He supposed that was more or less Jase's default mood. It was hard, therefore, to tell if he was going to be in danger when he met with Gareth.

They went back to the office, where the contents of Gareth's desk had been laid aside, the map spread across its surface. The room was dazzlingly bright, though the windows were closed and it was evening. Four great spell lamps hung from the ceiling, casting a sunny glow. The sum of their light was probably little more than Willy used in his work shed, but after being cooped in a dark room with just a few candles it was hard for Brenish's eyes to adjust.

The most important thing he noted, while Jase closed and locked the door behind them, was the fourth man in the room: a wizened scholar, back bent over the desk as he examined the map. He held a magnifier to his eye, the kind jewelers used in the city. Brenish recognized the man at once. Years ago he had seemed like a moneychanger, a gentleman of finance, who appeared whenever there were papers to authenticate, merchandise to inspect. The man was dapper then, but time had since molded his looks to fit his reputation. Now he was the Expert, the man entrusted by the wealthy to appraise everything they owned or hoped to own. Brenish never knew the man's full name, except that he had once heard something like Sealy, or Steely, because for the last decade the Expert was all the guild ever called him.

The guild regarded the Expert as a nuisance, a worthy rival, and a valued appraiser all in one. They had too much respect for his work to consider him anything less, and often enough engaged his services for their own ends. Yet Brenish knew he was a good part of the reason Willy Alder was in lockup. The Expert had become Willy's nemesis in recent years, and vice-versa, each delighting in one-upping the other until their gamesmanship went too far. Brenish wondered if he regretted that Willy was out of commission, if only on a sporting basis.

"Come closer, Brenish," said Gareth. "You remember Sully."

Way off. Brenish nodded a respectful greeting.

"This is quite the discovery, Brenish," Sully said. His voice was dry and crackly, like the husk of a wasps' nest. In years past it had been authoritative in a more classical way; now it was suffused with the confidence that came with years of being the best of his kind. "You say you found this in June?"

"Aye."

"Surprised you didn't come see me then," he said.

"I would have done, if I could afford it," said Brenish. "I had to be sure myself before I took it to the guild. They would have hired you before I sold it, or used it myself. Now I suppose we'll just have to reimburse Gareth." He looked up at the boss's raised eyebrows. "Plus a reasonable fee, of course."

"What makes you think, Brenish," said Gareth, "that this map is still yours to sell?"

"You'd take it in payment, then?" said Brenish. "Everyone knows you're a fair man. For what you'd get for this, 2,300p would hardly make a dent in your profit."

Gareth smiled in spite of himself, at the thief's boldness. "Supposing it's genuine."

"From where I found it, I wouldn't expect otherwise," Brenish said. Moments like these were the best times to reinforce the original story. "But Sully will know best. If it's fake, the guild can still find a way to sell it. You'll still be reimbursed."

Jase, who now stood to one side of the desk where he had the other day, frowned back at Brenish in distrust. The usual distrust, nothing fancy. Fancy distrust he reserved for dice night at the inn, every other Wednesday, and when it wasn't in use he kept it under the bed next to his payday smirk.

"I was a friend of Visak's, you know," Sully said to Brenish. "A more interesting fellow than you probably knew. Back then you were just a runty lad, when your dad ran cart grabs with Obray every winter."

"And does this look like his handwriting?" said Gareth.

"Looks like, yes. The lettering is right. Here's his exaggerated L, and the flourish at the end of his S. And see these smudges: here, and here."

"What of them?"

"Left-handed. Not many people knew that."

"Why is it all broken up like this?" Gareth said. "I recognize a few of these from other charts, but why aren't they all together?"

"The riddles connect the pieces," Sully said. "Look here. What's the answer to that one?"

Gareth gave himself a minute to think it through. "A bird."

"A raven, specifically. You'll find one here, in this symbol."

Gareth nodded his best nonchalant oh-I-see, but Brenish saw the real look in his eyes: the delight of a child seeing an unopened gift, with a tag bearing their name. Doubtless Gareth had seen more than his share of those already.

"You've studied this, Brenish," he said. "Have you solved all the riddles?"

"Most of them." That was the absolute truth. The riddles weren't easy, but they were tailored to a shrewd mind. Brenish had had just a few days to look at them, not the two or three months he claimed. Visak could have penned such things in his sleep; it must have taken Willy a year of preparation before he ever set ink to this paper. Perchance some of them even were Visak's, copied from his other writings.

"I know you'll need more time with this, Sully," said Gareth, "but what's your first impression?"

Old Sully the Expert smiled, as if he could see back into another time when Visak still held court in the Horsehead, the great storyteller and his rapt audience. "Visak had... a *way*. He loved a good joke, especially the kind it took a week to understand. I can't find the right words to explain this, but this paper... it has his way."

"Truly he was a trickster," said Brenish. "Are you sure he didn't make this just to fool someone?"

Gareth gave him a strange look, amazed Brenish of all people would dare disturb the fantasy. But if he hadn't asked that question, Gareth certainly would have. All the better to establish his credibility. Besides, if the Expert ruled the map was a forgery, which he guessed was about as good as a coin flip, Brenish would be in a much better position to feign surprise. He hoped in a way that the fraud would be discovered, the better to talk Gareth out of keeping the map; it might be enough to put his winter plans back on the right road.

"Sure?" said Sully, sound of dry leaves rubbing together in a partial laugh. "There's no way to ever be sure. But I think if he made one fake to fool a ne'er-do-well, he'd make more. It would have tickled him to see so many hapless boobs run after a new map, year after year. Makes me wish I could turn back the clock and give him the idea. Oh how he'd laugh..."

Gareth looked at the old man without impatience, with real warmth. Something human in him was touched by the Expert's reverie. Perhaps it was his own memories of the wizard.

"Forgive me," Sully said. "The mind does wander. This even smells like his old study, from the herbs he dried there. I think he liked the two of you best of all, you know, of the children who hung on his tales. Making little gifts make their way to the folks who he wanted to have them, gifts they didn't know he gave them: that was part of his way too. Maybe in some way you were meant to see this."

"Think you it's real, then?" said Gareth. His lust for the underground was a tangible thing, a spirit of wonder that practically stood in the room with them.

"Give me a few more hours to be sure," the Expert said. "But if I had to decide right now, I'd say it's the real thing."

And Gareth looked at Brenish in a way the thief had never seen. A wide smile that touched his eyes, an excitement for adventure, the way a boy might look at his kid brother before both of them ran off to the woods, fighting imaginary dragons and Viking raiders until the sun went down. The look startled Brenish, but he smiled back in a way he hoped was just as excited, not at all smugly vindicated.

Jase eyed them both warily, more distrustful of the thief than ever. As far as Jase was concerned, clearly whatever spell Brenish had worked with his honeyed tongue, it had spread to the mind of old Sully somehow.

But Brenish didn't care what Jase thought; his only concern was getting out from under it. If he could manage that in a way that left him the means to winter in the city as planned and spring Willy from lockup, all the better. Yet watching Gareth's giddy expression, his modest dreams seemed more than ever to be slipping away. Gareth had no intention of selling the map. And that look... it meant wherever Gareth was going, Brenish would be along for the trip.

Later that night, Finch came to collect Brenish and escorted him back to the office. As a rule Brenish seldom spoke to Finch, who was often dour and intimidating at the best of times. His height alone was imposing enough, but Gareth trusted him above all his other men for much better reasons. It was unwise to ever cross Finch, even unintentionally.

It was dark outside. Brenish and the servants had eaten hours ago, but Gareth had part of a chicken at his desk that he appeared to be picking at. Papers were strewn everywhere. The lights were turned down very low, as if Gareth was trying to acclimatize himself to gloom. It was a bad sign.

Finch didn't exactly release Brenish's arm when they arrived; he merely loosened his grip. Unlike Jase, he didn't prefer to stand elsewhere.

"We were just going over what to purchase," said Gareth.

"Purchase for what?" His voice trembled. He didn't really want to know the answer.

"This was your idea, Brenish. It's clever. For a treasure this size, the cost of an orb is nothing. We'll be the first to try it."

"We?"

"You wanted an investor, did you not?"

Brenish tried to swallow his own tongue. It didn't work out.

"I'm surprised at your reticence. You've been a changed man lately. Do you know how many years this map has been a legend? It was legend *before* Visak's death. Since then it's become much, much bigger. Men have dreamed of a chance like this, except until a few years ago they had a wizard to contend with. Now there's nothing in the way: No heir, no claimant. Just us. *We* are Visak's heirs, Brenish."

If that were true, Brenish was getting shafted in the will. But there might be a way to make it work, if he could keep Gareth above ground.

"Gareth, can I be blunt?"

Finch snickered. Gareth upturned the corner of his mouth. "The question remains open," Gareth said. "Say your piece."

"My plan was to go into the ruins myself, only with men I trusted, and assume all of the risk. And you have good men. I don't doubt Raden, and Bob, even Finch here. But I don't trust them with my own life. No offense, Finch."

"None taken."

"But it's more than that," Brenish said, before Gareth could respond. "You and me, we're the closest there is to experts. We breathed this ever since we were little. We can't both go down there. We'll be butting heads, second-guessing each other. That's no way for a team to operate.

"Look, this *was* my plan, to go down there myself. Naman talked me out of it. You said yourself I'm a changed man. This is why. I've been studying that map since summer and I'll level with you: I'm *terrified*. The closer I got to an expedition being real, the scareder I got.

"But I know I'm in deep to you," Brenish continued. "I'll do this, if it's my only way out. But we need to stick to my plan. I can't be down there with men I can't trust, and the two of us can't work as a team without the whole thing blowing up in our faces. I'll get this treasure for you, I will. I'll come through."

"Do you truly expect me to pass this up?" said Gareth.

Brenish squirmed in place, and slouched. Finch's grip around his arm felt tighter, as if he feared the thief might faint. Brenish wasn't so sure he was wrong about that.

"Nay," said Brenish, quietly. "I suppose not."

"I'm glad you see it my way."

"All right, then." Brenish tried to step forward but was held back. He jerked his arm out of Finch's grasp, or tried to; Finch chose to let him go. "I don't think it can work with the two of us down there. All I ask is that when you come back with the treasure, please forgive our debts. That's nothing next to what you'll bring back. Your men will be happier for it, too. More for them."

"Are you mad, Brenish? You said yourself that if you got an investor, you'd shoulder the risk. I'm willing to take on *my* fair share. I won't let you walk away with none at all. Besides, this is a two-expert job. You've seen how big that map is. I'd judge it's a journey of at least two days to the hoard; maybe three or four. It seems to be through charted territory, but this map takes skill to work with, and we'll be going in deep. I'll need your wits as much as you'll need mine."

"But—"

"We'll make it work, Brenish. All we need is a clear chain of command. One of us has to be in charge at all times. Why don't we pick now? We'll even put it to a vote. All three of us. Who do you vote for as leader?"

"Can I be blunt again?"

"No."

"Then it's unanimous."

"Excellent. 'Tis a fine day for democracy. The Greeks would be very proud."

Brenish held up a finger. "But," he said, "you did say *chain* of command."

"And you want to be second in charge?" Gareth said. He seemed to want to belly laugh again.

"Concerning strategy and how to make the best use of supplies, yes."

Gareth barked gleefully. "You are brazen, Brenish, I'll give you that. I doubt any of my men would take orders from you."

"That's my point. I know 'tis little more than symbolic with you around, but 'twas you who said you needed my wits. What if you send me out as a scout with Jase? If we run into trouble, who would you rather have in charge?"

Gareth smiled again, but half-heartedly because he obviously knew Brenish was right. "Ed?" he said.

"Brenish is a deceitful little knob," said Finch. "No offense."

"None taken," said Brenish.

"But he's right in this. I wouldn't go down there without a guide. Next to you he's the best. Only a fool fails to heed his guide."

Brenish thought he was actually somewhat better. Even though Gareth was quite a bit older, his lore was only *as* deep, no deeper. Both had plumbed the well of knowledge to the stony bottom. It was the edges, the shape of that well, that Brenish felt he knew best.

"Fair enough, Brenish. Now you did raise another concern, which I think is fair too. You said you didn't entirely trust my men. Obviously we'll need some more men you *can* trust."

"That won't be nec—"

"Oh, 'tis entirely necessary. The more men we have down there, the better. This will be a long journey. We'll need all our skills. Besides, I have brand new employees. What better way for them to earn my trust back? Right?"

"And repay our debts," said Brenish. "Naturally we'll get a cut."

He felt Finch tense. Whatever Finch expected Gareth's reaction to be, a wry smile wasn't it.

"Aye, Brenish," Gareth said. "You're absolutely right. You'll all get a cut. *A* cut. Less what you owe, of course."

"That's fair," said Brenish.

"Quite," said Gareth. "Then everyone will know what it takes to make me happy again after a disappointment. And no one will be laughing, except the lot of us."

With a treasure the size of Visak's, it was moot anyway; a four-way split of one cut would be enough to set them up for the rest of their lives.

Then again, he had to remind himself they weren't actually going to find Visak's treasure. They were going to find a completely different one that Brenish would have to talk Gareth into thinking was the real thing. Or, there would be an unpleasant bloodbath. The latter was looking more and more likely.

Finch took his hand off of Brenish and stepped around the desk to whisper in Gareth's ear. It didn't seem like it could possibly be a friendly chat. Finch kept his features locked, his eyes giving away nothing, the entire time he spoke. His lips barely moved. His voice was too soft for Brenish to hear, even so close. Gareth looked at him, at Brenish, and back to Finch again.

"Hmm, aye," said Gareth. "Petty, though, don't you think?"

"Aye."

"All right. I agree with you. Make the arrangements."

Finch nodded and left the room. After being guarded so closely earlier, Brenish wondered what had changed. He doubted it was anything good.

"Now," said Gareth, "back to purchases. I was looking over these notes of yours."

He hadn't been able to keep Raden and Bob from taking a few papers he had kept alongside the map, brief lists and ideas he had made for his original plan. They were borderline incriminating.

"Why did you want so much goldsense with you? We have a map. Besides, Visak's overlook spell would keep you from sensing his hoard even if you drank enough to drown in it."

"Insurance," said Brenish. "I was worried that if something went very wrong, or the treasure were guarded, I might have to leave empty-handed. An investor wouldn't take kindly to that. There are other treasures enough that I could convince them to accept."

"Or talk them into thinking that was all there was," Gareth said. "Do you still think I would've been willing to let you go without me?"

Not after going Fell, Brenish thought. But he didn't say it.

"To tell you the truth," he said, although he wasn't, "I had my own doubts about the map before talking to Sully."

"Aye," said Gareth, musing on some old thought. "Well, enough of that. I think we can do without the goldsense."

"It has defensive uses," Brenish said quickly. "Goblins carry gold, for one. And they're not the only ones. Best to have someone keep sipping, don't you think?"

"Not at the price I was quoted. We'll skip the goldsense. Know you any spells?"

"What, by memory?" said Brenish. Gareth nodded back. "Nay."

"Nor I. No sense in ordering tokens, then. Scrolls will do. I have a few in mind already. I liked a few of your choices. Any new ideas?"

"Silence," said Brenish. "Muffling our movements would be helpful in a tight spot."

"Agreed, but casting a silence spell with words is somewhat self-defeating."

"A charm would do. A big enough charm—"

"No time. We checked with the binders, discreetly as possible. They have naught that would muffle the lot of us, and not enough for each of us. A custom order would take too long."

This talk of checking prices and inventory meant Gareth had already been preparing before he summoned the Expert. Likely, Finch had sought that information in the city yesterday.

"Spell lights?" said Brenish.

"We have enough. We'll rely more on torches. More fuel can be found down there, if need be, but we'll carry enough with us. *Esen* isn't as cheap. Two torches each, so we have a spare. Food we'll need, and water, for a few days. Those are easy enough. We can go a bit light on the water, since we'll be crossing the deep river and there will be other sources wholesome enough to drink from. I trust you can carry a heavy pack, though."

"I can. What about armor?"

"You all wear leather and heavy cloaks on the job," said Gareth. "That will do. Bob wants light chain; there was no arguing with him."

"Weapons?" said Brenish.

"Assorted. You're good enough with a sword, and a knife. We'll all have bows or crossbows, but in your case you'll just be carrying a spare for someone who can shoot. How are you with spears?"

"Dreadful."

"Thought as much."

"I'd still like proper vambraces and greaves," Brenish said. "For all of us. It's just a good investment. Out of our cut, naturally. Nothing fancy, but something that can deflect a hit or two. The longer we stay alive, the more good we'll do you."

"I'll consider it," said Gareth. "You had a great many bindings on your list. The teleportation orb is quite expensive enough, but some of these are absurd."

"It was a wish list," Brenish said. "Money was no object."

"Aye. Well, I like the way you were thinking, but I had to strike a few of these. Some were just too expensive. But you also overestimated the inventory of the binders' shops."

"I expected a month or more to prepare."

"I've made some substitutions. Your potion list was reasonable, apart from the goldsense. You left out any jewelry."

"Overrated, and too expensive. There are better ways to do anything a bracelet would do, except what you've already ruled out."

"Maybe, and maybe not. Ever hear of a fellow named Lew Pieter? He came out before you were born, so maybe you never heard the story."

"He had a ring that told him where all the monsters were," said Brenish. "Anything with a mind that might track him. Worked a treat right up till his friend got eaten by a crawling vine. No mind for the ring to show him. As I said, they're overrated."

"He still came back himself. But so be it," said Gareth, returning to the list. "We'll pass those over. I didn't love the idea anyway. No wands?"

"For me?" He almost felt insulted Gareth thought he could aim one.

"You would have had companions. I assumed you'd give some to them."

"Unreliable," Brenish said. "Limited. No good in an emergency."

"Mmm. Well, I disagree with you on that score. I'll stick with my choices."

Bob came into the room. "Finch said you wanted to see me?"

"Just to escort Brenish back to his quarters. We're finished in here. Unless there's anything else you'd like to discuss, Brenish?"

"Bandages and salves," he said. "Otherwise I think we covered everything."

Going over the list had felt like the playful gabbing he did as a kid, about what it would be like to go down there. But now he had the awful realization that no matter what, he was stuck going into the ruins with Gareth. His friends, through no fault of their own, had gotten dragged into it along with him. That was already bad enough, but Brenish had built up his lie so much he kept falling under the spell of believing it himself. There was no hope of a difficult but ultimately successful adventure. They weren't merely going into danger; they were going into certain death. When Gareth found out the map was a forgery, he would stake them to the walls with meat around their necks and teleport home.

"Good, good," said Gareth. "Bob, tell the others to make sure Brenish gets plenty of time in the practice room tomorrow. The rest of you, too."

"Aye, sir," said Bob.

"And get some rest. After tomorrow, we have a long night ahead of us."

Asaph's Gate

Most of the expedition was assembled in a cluster of short little hills about half a mile north of the river. A few trees had made a token effort at colonizing the area, but for the most part the hills and the spaces between them were covered with short, springy grass and the occasional boulder.

The boulders were odd things, tumbled down from the mountains in ages past until the landscape grew in around them, so that they seemed to rise up out of the earth. The densest parts of the forests around Ilyenis still had boulders like these, where the trees had simply moved in later; but in the fields, the village, and the roads, any other boulders had long since been cleared. To a village native, the boulders were a sign of the absence of civilization.

Finch had stationed their party in a little nook surrounded by four of those boulders, one standing by itself near the path. The stones were arranged roughly in a circle, as if a giant had done it long ago and simply forgot to add the last few on one side. The river was just barely visible through gaps in the hills.

Naman and Tibs sat on the ground; Harry and Brenish stood. None of the other thieves looked pleased about their situation. For Brenish's part, he felt glad just to feel the sun on his face again, however briefly. He was more concerned with the rest of the group. Bob and Raden were late, as was Gareth. Gareth had evidently decided to go in with six of his henchmen, and the four thieves, for a party of eleven. Few expeditions in modern times had ever taken that many, with the exception of punitive attacks on the goblins—though those were less about treasure hunting than straight-out war. Brenish wondered if the hefty size of the party would work for or against them.

Jase seemed the least comfortable out of all of Gareth's men. He was impatient, fidgeting, pacing the clearing, sitting, standing again. Twice he tripped over Tibs' pack while paying no attention to where he was going, and blamed Tibs for it. Once he tripped on Harry's, and said nothing.

Turk was inert, like one of the stones but in desperate need of a comb. His short-trimmed beard and mustache were about his only pretensions to grooming. The man's face was always a difficult read, because he looked bored when he was happy, bored when he was sad, bored when he was angry, bored when he was bored, and vaguely human when he was excited. Some people, Brenish mused, always seemed to have much more going on in their head than they let on. Turk had never struck him as one of them. Right now he looked a little bit listless.

Dex was the happiest of the lot, unashamedly leering over the thieves with a twisted smile that accentuated the scar on his left cheek. He was an unpleasant greasy sort, ill-liked in town and given a short leash whenever he was at the inn, even though Darius the innkeeper feared Gareth; Dex was apt not to keep his hands to himself. Naman had once joked that on a hot enough day, the oil on Dex's head could be used to fry an egg and the hen it came from; the joke had made it back to Dex, who hadn't forgotten. Dex spent most of his morning running about whooping like a maniac, swinging his knife through empty air.

Finch was in charge during Gareth's absence, though it had never been said. It never had to be. He leaned against one of the big rocks and smoked his pipe, calm as a lazy winter afternoon. Tall, wiry, agile, he was known as a terror with bow, blade, and staff. His face was clean-shaven, neat, never showing any stubble. When he moved it was with precision, every action crisp. A less informed man might think he was the son of a military officer, or had had training as such, but Finch was an ordinary village boy—though from a different village. He and Harry both hailed from Ferngarth. He was older than Gareth, and had worked for Gareth's father almost as long as he could remember.

"I can't believe we're doing this," said Jase. "This is mad." Tibs nodded, as if agreement would gain him an ally.

"You scared of the dark, Jase?" said Naman.

"Not hardly. Just death."

Dex swung about in one of his merry prances to kick Naman in the side. He didn't normally get a lot of opportunities to abuse him,

Naman being much bigger and always happy for an excuse to strike back. Harry grunted and shot a glance to Finch.

"Dex," said Finch. Dex looked up at him. Finch's only other words on the matter weren't words: He simply shook his head, just so, barely even moving it. He put the pipe back in his mouth as if to say both that the matter was closed and that he resented the interruption.

"At least you're getting a full cut," said Tibs, to Jase. "You're gonna come out of this a rich man. So are we all, but you're gonna be a lot richer than us. You should be excited."

"Oh?" said Jase. "Are you? Who's gonna do for your family if you snuff it down there?"

Tibs closed his mouth, chastised, but then thought better of it and opened it again. "I have to stay positive about this. You can grouse if you want. Just remember you're one of Gareth's favored men, and that's more than a lot of people can say. And remember this was all his idea."

Brenish smiled. He liked seeing Tibs on the attack for once. The meaning was perfectly clear: If Jase kept on saying this was mad, he knew who he was really insulting.

He caught Harry glaring at him.

"What?" said Brenish.

"I can't believe you dragged us into this."

"This wasn't my idea."

"Of course it's your idea," said Harry. "You always wanted to do this. Maybe not with Gareth, but at least you get your wish. Why didn't you tell me about that stupid map?"

"The stupid map was none of your business," Brenish said. He caught a glimpse of Dex enjoying the argument.

"Leave him be, Harry," said Naman. "If you want to blame anyone for dragging us into this, blame me for not keeping my voice down enough. Damn Bob's ears."

"Aye, and his mouth."

Tibs nudged Naman with his elbow, the old *cheer-up* maneuver. "Hey, at least you'll come out of this free and clear. No more wagon jobs."

Naman just turned and glared, as if that was the silliest thing Tibs ever said. But Tibs had no idea what he was saying; as far as he knew, they had a good shot at surviving this. Naman seemed to remember that anew.

"Brenish," he said, "a word."

"As you like."

Naman stood up, prompting Dex to advance a step. He ignored the goon, which seemed to bruise Dex's ego.

"Don't go far," said Finch.

"You'd just shoot us if we did," said Brenish.

He and Naman walked around the boulder beside the path, where they were out of view of the others.

Naman kept his voice extremely low, barely even a whisper. "I hope you're thinking of a way out of this, because if you don't we're all going to die down there. You understand that, don't you?"

"Quite," said Brenish, just as quietly.

"I know I'm at fault for this too."

"I never thought anything of it. Who knew Bob could hear us at all in that din? At least he heard no more."

"Nay, for telling Gareth the map was Visak's."

"I didn't say a word of blame. You did well. He knew there was a map. One of us had to say something. Better 'twas you."

"Thank you for saying so. But we need to focus on what's ahead. We're outnumbered five to four, whenever Gareth shows up."

"Seven to four. Bob's coming for sure, so his brother is too. They're just late."

"My point. The odds won't get any better down there."

Brenish shook his head. "Gareth has everything figured up here. The ruins reset us to a clean slate. We can take advantage if we act when the time is right."

"Well we're the only two who know we have to do that."

"I suggest we leave it that way," said Brenish. "Tibs might loosen his lips in a pinch, and Harry would kill both of us himself."

"Aye, but we can at least tell them to be alert. Let them know we plan to act before it's too late."

"Same problem. Harry's not about to go in on that without cause. Just give them the notion Gareth won't keep his word, and be sure they keep it to themselves. Might be true enough anyway."

They were about to go back when they turned and saw Gareth coming up the path, dragging a handcart behind him. Gareth had an iron helmet with a nose guard, even though it was already a little warm to be wearing it, armor of thick banded leather, and a shield slung behind his back. The cart looked to be all of two hundred pounds, but he pulled it with aplomb.

"That twisted whoreson is *whistling*," said Naman.

Brenish shrugged. "We might as well be cordial." He waved, as if Gareth were a close friend.

"I respect you a bit less right now."

"Aye," Brenish sighed. "Me too."

They stood where they were while Gareth lumbered gaily up the path. Neither bothered to offer him a hand when he got close, but he didn't seem to mind.

"Good morning, men," he said. "Have you rested well?"

"Nay," said Naman.

"Nay."

"I couldn't sleep either," said Gareth. Their irritation, though plain, escaped him completely. "A few days from now, we'll all look back on this journey fondly. We'll have stories to tell our grandchildren."

"When are the bruiser brothers getting here?" Naman said.

"They'll be along shortly. I saw them not too far behind me. Let's join the others."

Gareth, to their surprise, kept pulling the cart behind him rather than asking either of them to do it. His mood was extraordinarily buoyant. The cart held a few packs and, Brenish noted, some inexpensive but decent leather armor pieces.

When they returned to the clearing they found Tibs and Harry leaning against the other side of their boulder, and Jase sitting against another. Jase sat up straight when he saw Gareth. Finch and Turk acknowledged him but didn't move.

"Morning, boss," said Dex. He was sharpening his sword with a stone he had obviously just picked up. The stone wasn't even wet or suited for sharpening; all he was doing was making a bunch of sparks, apparently for show. Brenish had figured out some years ago that Dex liked to appear simpler than he truly was, which he often did through capricious acts of malice. The raw stupidity was show, but the rest wasn't.

"Good morning, Dexter," Gareth said amiably. "Jase. Turk. Ed. How are we all getting along?"

"Just fine," said Finch. He obviously didn't want Dex to get a word out first.

Gareth turned to Harry and Tibs. "Cheer up, Harry. You'll be free of your debt in a few days, and you can hang up the legend of Alfie for good. This is a great adventure."

Harry shrugged. Gareth, in good humor, laughed it off.

"When are we leaving?" said Harry.

"As soon as the rest of our group arrives. They won't be long now. I had to send them on an errand before we left."

"Are those their packs?" said Tibs.

"Yes, and mine as well. Oh, and I almost forgot, a little bonus Brenish negotiated for you."

Gareth reached into the cart and started tossing out armor. Tibs, Brenish, and Naman caught most of their pieces easily, but Harry dropped a couple, hindered by having just one eye. The pieces were mixed, so the thieves had to trade. Altogether they came to four pairs each of vambraces and greaves.

"How much is this costing our share?" said Harry. His tone implied that the armor couldn't have cost Gareth very much, yet he expected to be charged ridiculously for them anyway.

"I did some thinking about that last night," said Gareth, "and I decided to be charitable about it."

"Why?" said Dex.

"This will come out of the general expense pool, before all the shares are divided," Gareth explained. "Why quibble?"

"Because they're crap at banditry and owe you a ton of coin?" said Dex.

"Oh, I know all that, but look at this from their perspective. Only Brenish truly wanted to come along on this journey. The others only came out of obligation. They're none too happy about being here today. Right, Harry?"

"Right enough," Harry said.

"And their day isn't realistically going to get any better. So for many reasons, a peace offering was in order. A gesture of good faith, as it were. You're familiar with the carrot and the stick, Dexter?"

"Aye."

"There you go. Now as you all know, I've agreed that Brenish should be in charge—after myself—in any matter of direction or survival. He knows what we'll be dealing with down there. I'm repeating this now so that's understood. In an emergency, his orders are second only to my own."

Turk and Dex grumbled somewhat, wordlessly, but signaled their understanding in their own ways. Dex nodded; Turk merely stood rigid. Jase alone felt it was worth speaking up.

"What's to keep him getting big ideas in there?" he said.

Gareth smiled and was about to reply, when the sound of grunting men came up the path. "What fortunate timing. Your answer arrives."

Bob and Raden appeared. The two together each carried an end of a large sack, the kind used to carry big bundles of straw or potatoes. Bob had a shallow cut across his right cheek that appeared to have recently stopped bleeding. They finished the hike up the trail and came to a halt next to Gareth's cart. Bob set down his end first and Raden pushed it upright; it seemed to want to fold itself over when he set it down, forcing him to pull it back up a few times.

"Do you need something for that cut, Bob?" said Gareth.

"I'm fine."

"Very well."

Gareth found the edge of the sack and opened it up, pulling it down around what was inside. The first thing that popped out was black hair, with a braid across the top. Brenish clenched his fists.

Cirawyn was bound by ropes around her ankles, knees, and her forearms that were tied to her sides. A piece of cloth was bound around her mouth. She stared murder at Gareth. Dex clapped and hooted; Jase took out his payday smirk for the occasion.

Brenish looked first at Cirawyn to be sure she was unhurt, but then skipped right past Gareth's face.

"Now you—" Gareth began.

Brenish cut him off and glared directly at Finch. "*Petty*, don't you think?" he said viciously, understanding now what he had whispered.

Finch pulled his pipe from his mouth again, something about his movement conveying both mild contempt and amusement. "Aye," he said.

Gareth gave up on whatever he had been about to say. He took out a knife and cut Cirawyn loose himself, starting with the ropes at the bottom and saving the gag for last. When he removed the gag she looked him right in the eye and said nothing. Both were silent for the better part of a minute.

She finally turned back to Bob and Raden. "*Shame* on you," she said.

"Boss's orders, I told you," said Bob.

"*Shame*," she repeated.

"I guess that explains the fourth pack," said Tibs. Brenish looked where he was gesturing, into the cart: there were clearly four.

"Packs?" said Cirawyn.

Gareth beamed. "We're going on an *adventure*. Turk finally explained to me why Brenish was so desperate to borrow 800p off me."

"*Thanks*, Turk," said Brenish.

"Don't mention it."

"So I thought I'd do him a favor," said Gareth. "After all, he was so kind as to bring me the map. And he'll be my second guide in this endeavor. Now he has a little bit *more* incentive to be helpful, and attentive to my wishes, beyond just the money he stands to make for doing a good job. I know we'll all get along terrifically now, won't we, Brenish?"

Brenish met his eye and searched for an adequate reply. "Blunt?" he said.

"Not on your life."

"Best of friends," Brenish said in monotone.

"Wonderful," Gareth said. "This is going to be grand. Men, here are your packs. My dear, I've brought one special for you, too. I'm sure you'll have time to thank your beau later. This trip was his idea, after all."

"What about her armor?" said Brenish. Cirawyn wore only a simple white blouse, cobalt blue skirt, and light leather shoes. It was hardly an ensemble fit for the ruins.

"Afterthought. I suppose we'll have to be extra careful." Gareth's sarcasm was never funny.

"Here," said Brenish, beginning to take off a vambrace. "You can have mine."

"Leave it," said Gareth. "You're worth more to me than she is."

"And she's worth more to me than I am," said Brenish, "or she wouldn't be here."

"Chain of command." Gareth said it jokingly, his usual kind of joke that meant he was dead serious and the matter should be dropped. "Let's move."

He took the lead, letting a few of his men take the rear while the thieves and Cirawyn were in the middle. He marched them a few hundred yards out of the clearing to a grassy mound that stood beside the path. It was an artificial hill, little bigger than the two-story boarding house where Brenish lived. Its side by the road seemed to have been cut away, exposing a wall of thick, ancient brick. The brickwork contained a reinforced arched doorway, within which stood a great black iron gate, ten feet high.

Gareth took the last few steps by himself, resting a hand on the Gate. He leaned forward and bowed his head against it.

"Almighty save us," Cirawyn whispered. From the dangers in the ruins or Gareth's obsession, she didn't clarify.

Below the world of light, somewhere off to the west if legend held true, the spell concealing Visak's treasure waited for the word to break it. It waited, Brenish thought, for a password that would never come.

Gareth reached into the Gate with both hands, and took hold of the levers to open it. Simple-minded creatures couldn't operate the mechanism; brighter ones stayed far away. The levers creaked ominously, echoes from the deep spilling back into the bright autumn morning like black smoke from the lungs of a ghost.

The double doors of Asaph's Gate swung open.

Gareth stepped past the threshold, never pausing, and plunged into darkness.

Raden, Bob, and Dex followed. Behind them came Brenish, then Cirawyn, then the other thieves as their courage allowed. Finally Turk, Jase, and Finch brought up the rear.

The entry was bright enough to see without torches. The short landing beyond the gate gave way to a broad staircase, which Brenish and the others followed. The light faded quickly as they descended, forty steps down. The stairs showed no sign of long wear; they were even and straight.

By the time Brenish reached the bottom, his eyes seemed to have adapted partway to the relative dark. The room was actually quite bright, considering, for the light from above came down the stairway. They were in a rectangular space smaller than the inn's great room, but taller, where the bottom of the stairway jutted from the northern wall. Each of the other walls had a single door, each with a brick arch identical to the one over the Gate.

Finch came down the stairs as Gareth unslung his pack and lit his torch, which was at the end of a long iron rod formed from two interlocking sections. The torches could double as weapons in a pinch, a detail Brenish had to admit was extremely clever. Brenish would have expected Gareth to carry a spell lamp, but wondered if the flickering flame appealed to something deep inside the man—as it did in himself.

"The gate is secure?" Gareth said.

"Secure," said Finch. He put out his pipe and stowed it away.

"Good. Light your torches, gentlemen. And lady. Weapons at the ready. Welcome to the Elder Kingdom."

Part II
The Elder Kingdom

Day III: The lizard beasts are unwilling to part with their idol. They have blocked our return to the Gate, and killed Purlett. We will go east to Asaph's Gate and return home over land.

Day VI: The fuel is almost gone. I must be brief. We now carry but one torch. I have trimmed it to keep the flame low, although the low light may hinder our progress and make us more vulnerable. Though the danger is great, we have resolved to sleep in darkness. One of us will stay on guard, if only to hear something approaching.

Day VII: We found a small bottle of oil. It will be enough to sustain us a few more days. John killed a large rodent whose meat has stretched our rations. We have not yet crossed the deep river.

Day XI: After the light failed yesterday, we groped in the dark and followed the air as best we could. We would have come to grief if not for two men who came recently from Asaph's Gate. They were unfriendly and refused to provide us enough oil to reach the Gate, nor guide us there themselves, though it was but a mile away. We came to blows, and the strangers were slain. God forgive us this desperate thing, and forgive them the evil for which they have already paid.

Gatetown

"Which way?" said Naman.

"West," said Jase. He used his torch pole to point toward the doorway on that side. The end of his pole held one of the party's three spell lamps, gleaming sunny white; Tibs and Finch had the other two. Gareth wasn't the sort of man to rely on only one form of light.

"Why not use the map?" said Brenish.

"From my reading of the map, we won't need it at all until we reach the old aqueducts," Gareth said. "Do you concur?"

Brenish thought the matter over, relying on memory alone. "I believe so. I think it would be wise for both of us to study the map further, the deeper we go in."

"Agreed. Until then, we'll follow other charts. Jase has been studying those extensively, as have I. Our course appears to take us towards Shatterhelm or Deepwater. I daresay you know the way."

"I could use a refresher," Brenish said, "but I think I remember well enough too."

"Good. Then this is what we'll do: I'd like two of my special employees on point. Let's say Harry and Brenish to start, and Edward and Bob can be up front with them. Tibs, Naman, Dex, and Raden: You'll be the rear guard for now. We have a lot of ground to cover."

"Would an explanation first be too much to ask?" said Cirawyn.

Gareth seemed surprised by that. "You mean your beloved didn't tell you what he'd found?" She shook her head.

"I told you I wasn't even sure myself," said Brenish. "Not till Sully confirmed it. I didn't want her to think I'd gone Fell."

"And none of the others told you? They must have told you where Brenish was the last few days."

"Naman said he was with you," Cirawyn said, "but he didn't say why."

"Same reason," said Naman. "Besides, I thought you'd leave her out of it."

Gareth gave a nod of acceptance, but said, "Best sharpen your wits, then. You'll need them down here."

"Quite."

"We're going after Visak's hoard," Gareth said to Cirawyn. "Brenish practically stumbled onto the map this summer, and didn't have the good form to tell me. As you can well imagine, that hurt my feelings a bit."

She turned to Brenish. "Is this true?"

What was he supposed to say? Nay? That wouldn't go over particularly well at this point. Fortunately he was adept at twisting questions until the meaning was wrung out entirely, and giving answers to match. "Probably not that last part," he said. Although he wasn't even sure of that; he had been offended that Duggle never told him about taking a big chunk of Visak's work, and in many ways he and Duggle understood each other much less than he and Gareth.

"Yes, well," said Harry, "can we just get on with it? The sooner we get started, the sooner we can all go home."

"Well said, Harry," said Gareth. "Let's go."

Torches in hand, weapons ready to grab on a moment's notice, they set off. The Gate room was at the heart of a small fortified complex, at one time perhaps a manned sentry post of the Elder Kingdom. The western door led to a short hallway with rooms to either side: barracks, armories, larders, assembly halls, mess halls, and kitchens. Almost no original equipment was left. A few heavily rusted iron bars and scraps of chain could be seen, and some cracked pieces of pottery.

They were utterly alone; most other living things avoided the Gatehouse. There was no food for vermin, and the ironwork of the Gate prevented bats easy entry. Bats were known in other parts of the ruins where caves gave them access through ceiling shafts, but the entrance was clean. Anything much smarter than a bat knew to stay away from the Gate altogether. It wasn't unheard of even in modern times for a small party to venture in a short way, kill everything they laid eyes on, and return. In this way men kept the fear of the Gate intact.

The hallway ended in a small circular room, like the interior of a tower. The walls were gray brick, not hewn stone, but had no windows. Brenish knew this was not true of all towers in the ruins: many had windows overlooking wide caverns. The party followed a wide spiral staircase, keeping torches out to look for cracks and chips that might cause a stumble, and descended another story.

On the lower level the hallway ran through the tower, to a wide arched door in the west that had been besieged long ages ago. Bent iron stubs, once thick bars, emerged from the heavy brick on either side. The arch had partially crumbled, yet the roof stood. The vanguard, instructed by Jase from behind, led them under the fallen arch and out: into a wider corridor, a street, from which other streets branched away. They followed the road straight along its westerly course.

Brenish, torch held high so his vision was unobstructed by bright light, was unsure which of many feelings was dominant. It was not, he decided, boyhood wonder, his dream of old finally made real; that would come to blossom later, once he could manage to feel only one thing at a time. It was not fear; that too would wait its proper turn. Nor did he concern himself overmuch with deciding how to outsmart Gareth and get out alive, which would require long and clear thought. Concern for his friends, or even Cirawyn, was not at the fore of his attention. Yet his anger with Gareth for bringing her here was all that remained, and that had happened in another world: a bright fall morning on green grass, in another man's life.

It was, strangely, hard to stay mad at Gareth. Not for any of the reasons he would have thought, but for all the things his heart tried to feel at once.

"This is bigger than the village," said Bob, the first besides Jase to break their silence. He obviously only meant the village proper, the little cluster of buildings at the center of town. The residents were scattered over a much wider area.

"Not quite," said Gareth. "This town is about the same size. It only looks bigger."

Though they kept their voices low, the sound didn't seem to carry as far as Brenish expected it would. Echoes died quicker than between the hills, but for no reason he could explain. No other traveler had ever mentioned that, as far as he was aware. Brenish reminded himself to make a note of that later, should he ever come out alive. He kept with him a little book that was once blank, now partially filled with drawings and musings, and a charcoal pencil.

"How do you suppose they grew crops?" Tibs said from the back. "I always wondered."

"Spell lamps, most like," Brenish replied. If Gareth had been about to answer, he didn't say. "From here they could grow above ground if they wanted. A few places get sun. Deeper in, most of the Kingdom must have been lit by magic."

There were no other sounds about them. They were still too close to the Gate, perhaps, to expect anything different. Brenish had heard many tales of the cries of beasts, cracking stones, water dripping, and many unexplainable noises that kept adventurers alert. Here they heard naught but their own voices and footfalls, the crackling of torches, and breath.

In spite of the sights before his eyes, Brenish attuned his hearing to those noises. His own stride and his heartbeat he ignored. Bob was closest, heavy of foot and jingling faintly with each step. Finch walked with steady purpose, gracefully, his steps seldom falling out of rhythm. Harry was next to Finch, keeping up pace but not confidence, often letting his feet drag slightly against the stone floor. Further back, the walk and sway of each of the company grew clearer in his mind. Cirawyn walked beside Gareth, away from the flank of the troop, her skirt swishing softly. On the left flank behind Brenish was Jase, who nervously mumbled a tune just at the threshold of hearing. From walking in the dark with them so many times, he recognized where Tibs and Naman walked at the rear, with Raden's heavy steps between them. Dex's jaunty lop, subdued but not wholly tamed, gave his place away behind Jase. Only Turk, who by process of elimination must have been next to Gareth on the right flank, seemed to be truly silent.

At length the little town around the Gatehouse came to a gradual end. Openings in the tunnel to either side grew fewer. They were simple houses of one or two rooms, or alcoves containing water wells. The remains of iron hinges sometimes were visible, suggesting wooden doors were common in the Elder Kingdom—and by the hinges' size, those doors were not thin. Nothing wooden remained, perhaps having been taken for fuel and burned long ago. In the deep that was less often true, depending somewhat on how many men ever reached a given place alive. But wood could still rot, and in many parts of the ruins it already had.

Signs of brickwork in the tunnel faded, except for occasional arches spanning its width. The arches might have been built for support, or decoration, but not for defense. None of them seemed to have ever held a gate or a door. Some were not fully intact.

As the tunnel marched on its width wavered: never so narrow that it wouldn't have been possible to drive two wagons abreast, with ample room to spare. The arches alone stayed consistent, any extra width blocked by walls, which suggested they were built using forms just as in modern times. Occasionally one of the walls beside an arch was wide enough to have a small window, or a doorway. In one place the tunnel was so wide to their right that the arch had an attached building resembling a guard house. Yet though the width varied, as did the height to a lesser extent, the floor was perfectly level. If the shaping of the road had been natural in part, its floor had been painstakingly cut away and smoothed by craft beyond the use of pickaxes.

No one knew how the Elder Kingdom had been excavated. Some portions were obviously done by nature, not man. But Brenish had always suspected some kind of billowing directed magic, like the plume of flame from a fire-eater's mouth. How else could one explain why the cities were so well laid-out, but generally the farther one got from them, the rougher the cutting became? Many of the roads, he felt, must have been built with greater attention paid to speed than to detail. Finally seeing one of those roads for himself, he was sure of it.

Whatever spell they had used, it was most likely lost to man since the fall of the Elder Kingdom. The few digging spells Brenish knew about had side effects that would have been a big problem underground. He had never heard of others. Then again, his knowledge of spells came almost entirely from stories, a lot of them from Visak.

"It's too quiet down here," Finch said. They had just passed the sixth arch outside of the Gate town; the arches were, Brenish thought, about a furlong apart. "Were we expecting this?"

"Aye," said Brenish. "But it's still eerie. I expect it won't stay quiet for long."

The group walked on in silence for half an hour more, which at their slow pace covered little more than a mile under the earth. The silence was only in the absence of their voices, for Brenish was proved right even sooner than he thought. It began with little furtive sounds, the scrabbling of tiny creatures far off, so faint that it seemed like his imagination. These became more frequent, less easy to dismiss. Hissing sighs came next, from gusts of wind blown down from above or the slithering of snakes across the ancient stone. These too developed into real things the more the party went on. Then came the step-step noises of four-legged things, size unguessable, walking in the dark, and the shrill distant twitters of bats.

The ruins were not unlike a part of nature, Brenish thought. They had their sounds, their rhythms, like any forest. He didn't have a lot of basis for comparison; forest, meadow, cleared field, marsh, and river were about the only things he really knew. He had heard of many others, some from tales halfway across the world, but he was not himself well-traveled.

He and Finch stopped as something became visible just up ahead, lying in the road at the edge of the torchlight. Bob and Harry each got in another step before halting. The rest of the group nearly crashed into them from behind.

"What is it?" said Gareth.

Brenish decided to take a risk and advance a few steps further. "I'm not sure," he said. "It doesn't look like an animal."

The leaders advanced on the object to see what it might be. It was dark in color, black or rich brown. When they got up close, it appeared to be no more than a piece of leather, shredded like a rag.

"'Tis a boot," said Harry. "Or 'twas."

The others came up to join them. "Tibs," said Brenish. He looked back and saw the looks on his companions' faces. Gareth seemed both curious and anxious to get on. Tibs shouldered past Cirawyn, deliberately bumping Jase, to come up to the front.

"Aye, 'tis a boot," said Tibs.

"No kidding," said Bob. "Looks like it got torn up by an animal."

"Doubtless it was." Tibs stooped to pick it up. A few chunks of bone fell out, rotten meat and toenails still clinging to them. Jase turned aside and retched.

"How long ago was it?" said Brenish.

"Hard to say. No earlier than spring. Whoever he was, he obviously didn't make it very far."

"Keep a sharp eye," Gareth said. "Whatever took that boot dragged it out this far. Back in formation, everybody. Let's keep going."

Tibs tossed the boot aside and returned to the back, while the front pressed on.

Two more arches went by. Nothing else appeared in the road, until they passed the last arch and the road ended abruptly. The final arch in the road was no mere wall; it was deeper than any they had seen since leaving the city, ten yards of barrel-vaulted tunnel with a brick wall to either side.

The party emerged into a wide area, a domed chamber with many exits. The room was divided into two levels. On the ground floor it was ringed with stalls that looked like old shops, divided by walls and roofed over. Another tunnel led onward to the west, and a third to the south. At the diagonals of the room, stairs led up to the second story. The outer ring above the shops was lined with stone posts that had once been joined by iron chains, but now many of the posts had toppled over and the chains were missing or broken.

"We turn north here," said Jase. The exit was to their right, on the level above.

"Found more of our friend," said Finch. He pointed ahead where, tossed to the side of the room near one of the fallen posts, a torso and part of a pelvis were still attached to a backpack. It was mostly bones, most of them broken.

Brenish went up alone to take a closer look. He had to lean down to see enough detail in the low light. "This poor fellow's dead, all right." He turned the body over to get at the pack, unfastening it with his free hand. It seemed to still be full, a promising sign.

Without waiting for permission, Brenish rummaged through the dead man's things. "Spare clothes," he said. "Think they've gone to mold." He threw the rags away. "Fire striker. Lamp oil." The last item to come out jingled, and felt like leather.

Brenish pulled out a little pouch, tied shut, with a ram branded into its side. He untied the pouch and counted out a few Pieces inside. "Heh," he said. "90p. Wish I'd taken this off him when I had the chance, the poor fool."

"Told you it was stupid not to," said Harry.

Brenish stood and carried the gold back to Gareth, dropping it in his upturned hand. "Remember the fellow with the tattoo on his forearm?" he said to Naman.

"From May?" Naman said. "Tried to take liberties with Thelia?"

"*Tried?*" said Dex. "And failed? Small wonder he couldn't cut it down here. I knew that lackwit was hopeless."

"Show a little respect, Dex."

"Aye," Tibs said. "The man's dead."

"I meant for Thelia," said Naman. "Or women at all. But for anybody would be something."

Brenish snapped his fingers. "Dobber. That was his name."

"Should we say a few words?" said Bob.

"Are you kidding?" Gareth said. "We can't stop and get gooey every time we see a corpse down here. It's a shame he's dead, but that's all there is to say about it."

A snarl broke their discussion. Under the western arch, an emaciated dog—or wolf—bared its teeth and growled at the group. The light was more than enough to see its fur was patched, matted, and unhealthy. The group turned their weapons toward it at once.

The wolf was not alone. While it stood there, threatening, two more trotted out of the archway and joined it in the abandoned marketplace. The pack's snarls and barks grew louder, egging each other on. The standoff went on as the mongrels tried to work themselves up to attack. Their cries brought a fourth member, and finally a fifth. With the late arrivals bolstering their numbers, they began to howl. Their barking took on a threatening edge, a voice of anger and hunger that had given up on saying "I'm warning you to back off" and moved straight to "I'm going to tear you to shreds in the next five seconds."

"Piss off, ya mutts," Naman shouted. "You're outnumbered this time. Move along."

Finch lost all patience with them, and fired a bolt into the pack leader. His injury set the pack wild; they pounced as if they had nothing to live for but revenge.

Brenish blocked the first dog to reach them with his sword, but nerves got the better of him and he missed the killing blow, slicing it along its muzzle instead and forcing it to the ground. Harry took the head clean off a second. Dex unexpectedly rushed into the fray to deal with a third dog, which jumped at his throat. He seemed to understand the beast's intention and slid to the ground, disemboweling it from below. The fourth was taken out by Bob. His wolf had tried to leap for his neck as well, but he grabbed it by the throat in midair and slammed it to the ground with such force that no one was surprised when it didn't get up again.

Three of the wolves lay dying; Bob's and Harry's were most certainly dead. Brenish finished the one he had injured. Dex stood over his own victim, gloating silently; his armor had very little blood on it, much less than Harry's. Naman did the honorable thing and put the thing out of its misery. Finch, who had begun walking toward the pack leader even before the last of its allies felt steel, pulled the crossbow bolt out of its twitching neck and replaced it temporarily with the point of his sword.

"We got 'em for you, Dobber," said Naman.

"Fine work, men," said Gareth. "Let's get a move on."

The fighters cleaned off their weapons and their persons as best they could. There was no point trying to dispose any better of the dogs' corpses, even though they would attract scavengers in the months to come. At least, Brenish thought, most of those months would be winter and early spring, and the party themselves wouldn't be coming back here. They would all teleport out together using the orb Gareth had purchased, right after they found—

He checked himself. He *had* to stop doing that.

"Up there," Jase pointed, to the northern exit on the second level.

"They only seem to have killed the one man," Tibs said, as they made their way to the nearest staircase on their right. "We should look for any others who were with him."

"Enzo and Pines," said Brenish. "Decent fellows, if a bit thick. Who's to say which way they went from here?"

"The Wide Road is as good a guess as any," said Gareth. "I expect we'll run into them ere long."

"Alive?" said Bob.

"Heavens no."

Before passing through the north arch, Brenish took a peek back down into the old market. It looked like an arena, in the aftermath of a pitched and epic battle fought for a crowd of zero. Most of Dobber's bones were already scattered far. It was a common fate, down here.

Down here, he thought. A strange feeling of elation gurgled up from his gut, heedless of his common sense or his fear. For a moment all other concerns escaped him. Nothing had changed at all and the danger was no less; his resentment that Gareth dragged Cirawyn along was no less, either. But apart from all those things he was glad, in some small way, to finally be here.

Harry smacked him across the back of the head and physically pointed him to the exit.

"Thanks," Brenish said. He rubbed the back of his skull to try and ease the ache, but he actually was grateful. With that, he followed Harry and Finch onto the northern road.

Paddystock

Gareth was impatient for them to move on. The marketplace was barely south of the village; Visak's treasure lay somewhere far to the northwest, at least a day beyond the aqueducts, but those were many miles away themselves. He hoped to reach the aqueducts by nightfall, and occasionally consulted a pocket timepiece—the work of a master binder, and one of his most prized possessions—to confirm the time. Without it, time would have no meaning at all in the ruins. Some travelers even believed it flowed differently there.

Brenish had heard of a cult, one of many that sprang up from time to time to worship the Elder Kingdom, that believed the Kingdom had been excavated, settled, and fallen into long decay in a period of no less than a hundred years of the world above. The Church stamped them out in due time just as they had all the others, but they enjoyed far more support from the populace with that lot because the Order of the Hundred Centuries was more annoying than most. Visak once gave his listeners a gleeful story of a time after he emerged filthy rich, when he challenged the head of their order to a public debate about the nature of the ruins. The debate ended in their utter humiliation. The old wizard had laughed like a boy, telling that one.

Still, Brenish thought, the Order might have had a point. The ruins seemed impossibly old, yet their technology was at a level not far off from that he encountered every day. Could it be that the ruins were little older than the Roman Empire, its people from a generation when the Greeks ruled the seas? Or were the ruins much, much older, the product of a civilization that had advanced far beyond their contemporaries in both craft and magic?

The northern road came to an intersection about a mile away from the marketplace. There it met the Wide Road, a long tunnel running from beyond the aqueducts in the west to far-flung cities in the east. The eastern ruins, like the northern ones, were poorly explored. As the north had been claimed by goblins, the east was the domain of much darker evils: haggard beings that brewed elixirs of long but youthless, desiccated life from healthy blood. Another cult once thought those creatures were a remnant of the Elder Kingdom itself, still alive but with their memory utterly ravaged by time and the indignities of extreme age. Brenish wasn't certain he disagreed with that theory.

As the party reached the Road, Brenish turned to look that way. The Stone Gate, he remembered, was far away above the eastern ruins. It had been buried long ago, and in the centuries since the people of that region deliberately forgot about it. It was hardly the only Gate that had been buried; an even nearer one was simply known as the Buried Gate. Although its burial was fresher and the memory of it was intact, it had never been given a proper name.

Jase ordered them to proceed west. Brenish heeded him little; he very well knew the way to the aqueducts, and probably the great cities of the northwest, from books.

The Road was a tunnel at first, uninterrupted by side passages. Though their path from the Gate city had been stone reinforced with brick, the Wide Road was brick throughout, except for the floor. The floor was barely mounded, so that any water would drain into a ditch that ran along each wall—not that rain was a problem the builders would have faced. Along with the other sounds of the ruins, which only came from ahead and behind once they were in the new tunnel, they heard the babble of water as it moved along the ditches in their direction of travel. For the Wide Road sloped downward to the west, very gradually. Roman surveyors said it had a grade of one foot to a thousand.

After half a mile they reached another arch, and the tunnel opened up into a great chasm. Sunlight from above reached the chamber somehow, filtered through minerals in the ceiling. It was augmented with a few spell lights forever burning in the gloom, affixed to high, inaccessible places in ages past. No one knew where they got their fuel, but Brenish always thought a big enough collector would do the trick. The light was enough to give them a guess at the size of the cavern, which stretched hundreds of feet across and went down beyond the range of any chart. The Road was a bridge here, thick and utterly enduring, with a high parapet. The drainage ditches ended in little waterfalls where the bridge began.

Brenish stepped a short way out of the arch and leaned over the edge of the bridge to look below. A second, identical bridge crossed the chasm from north to south. He wasn't the only curious one: Bob, Gareth, and even Dex showed an interest in the view. A few of the others looked less comfortable with the idea of looking down. Naman, who didn't like high places, pulled in closer from the edge, and Raden seemed likewise put out. Jase stayed away too, and crossed his arms as if he was cold.

In spite of the welcome feeling of open air, which seemed much fresher in the pit, no one much wanted to linger there. The sounds of the ruins were amplified all around them, delivered waiting to the travelers to hear. The acoustics of the rock brought the cries of hundreds of beasts, and hundreds more bats that circled about ceaselessly. Metal struck metal far away, its direction difficult to determine. Faintly, Brenish thought he heard iron boots clomping against stone.

The bridge was surprisingly clean. Its brick surface had a dusty appearance, but there was no guano except in little patches. Each place they found bat droppings, they found many thousands of crawling insects surrounding the pile, carrying it away bit by bit.

At the end of the span, the bridge passed under another arch and became a tunnel again. On this far side, however, there were occasional doorways beside the road. The only denizen they met in one was a rat, not large but considerably better-fed than the wolves they had encountered earlier. The side chambers were spaced at regular intervals, but as they went on the stonework started to show signs of alteration. Where one generation had planned the original Road, later residents had broken through the stout brick to add wider doorways and more of them, along with windows. Thin rusty rods protruded from above one of those windows, suggesting they had once held a sign or banner. The brick around the changes looked as solid as the original, but in a few places the bricks were tinted just a bit redder.

The Road here was clearly the outskirts of another town, which the party reached a short time later. Brenish reckoned they were still not that far west of Ilyenis, somewhere beneath the outer forest where many local huntsmen made their homes.

They entered another wide cavern, its floor cut smooth, whose sides were hidden everywhere by buildings. The ceiling, high above, cast a dim but serviceable light by veins of spellbound crystal, pulling their energy from no one knew where—perhaps from the rock itself, channeled maybe by untapped veins of ore. The entire chamber was terraced structures all around, buildings clustered together alongside narrow streets. Stairs and doorways and windows and roofs of black glass tiles stared back at the travelers. The town square contained a wide well, but the bucket and ropes were long gone.

"Paddystock," said Gareth. He was nothing but smiles today. "We've made it here in pretty good time."

"Wave to your mum," Brenish said, indicating Naman.

Naman looked straight up to the ceiling. "How far up is she?"

"Forty yards, give or take," said Brenish. "I might be half a mile off. No way to be sure."

Naman kept looking up, as if he might see her through the rock. A frown crossed his face. "Wonder what she'll do without me," he said.

Brenish felt a renewed pang of guilt, reminding him they needed to come up with a plan for handling Gareth before it was too late. Naman hadn't had an opportunity to pass the word to Tibs or Harry to start thinking of alternatives. For that matter, Cirawyn should know too. Or perhaps not; she might worry. She was no snowflake, but he was unsure how much worry she could handle. In the ruins nobody's temperament could be counted on to stay wholly the same.

Jase slapped Naman's arm. "It's just a few days. Get off the teat already."

"I did," said Naman, "and before I was six." Jase scowled and shut his mouth. "I just wonder about if the worst should happen."

"It won't," said Gareth. "Not if we all do our jobs. No one comes down here in numbers like ours, except for a raid. We'll fight, we'll survive, and we'll come out again just fine. Have a little faith."

Naman waited for Gareth to go back to looking around in wonder before shooting Brenish a dubious look. Brenish shrugged.

"Shield," said Cirawyn.

"Hmm?" Brenish said. He looked to the shield hanging from Gareth's arm, though it didn't seem to be the one she meant.

"A shield." She pointed behind the well.

Brenish went forward with Tibs to see what was there. Two halves of a round wooden shield were on the ground, one face up and the other face down. It was painted with red and yellow diamonds. The paint was scuffed away in many places or cut. The wood had split along the grain. There was no arm in it, so the owner must have thrown it away.

"Franco," said Brenish.

"How do you remember their names?" said Jase.

"Someone has to. Besides, I remember him well because he made it out. Without his shield. That was last year."

A high, shrill voice tore the air. "Hoy!" The voice was Naman's.

Brenish looked where Naman was pointing, and saw a brown spider with a body the size of a man's head and thick, knobby legs, covered all over in spiky bristles. It trundled out of a doorway and advanced on the group. Each leg was about a foot and a half long, and each was in motion. Its many beady black eyes faced the invaders. This explained Naman's pitch: he was terrified of the things at just about any size.

With the emergence of the first spider, time seemed to slip out of control and many things happened at once. About half a dozen more spiders came out, of the same breed and size, crawling down from the upper levels, ascending stairs out of basements, hopping out of windows. They picked up speed and rushed the party, forcing quick action. At the same time weapons were drawn, and Brenish got a glimpse of Dex grabbing Naman's shoulders from behind, pushing him toward the giant hungry bugs.

Tibs' whip appeared in his hand so fast it seemed like magic, searing the air and driving several of the creatures back. Harry and Raden dove at them, while Finch fired at—and incredibly, missed—another. Brenish tried slashing at them with his sword, but it only convinced them to back up a step whenever he got the blade near, so that he never managed to hit one and they kept coming. One of the beasts finally made a jump at his leg, but he was able to bat it away with the butt of his torch; as he did so, another came too close, where he was finally able to put a sword through it. First blood was not his to claim, however, because Tibs had slashed one open along the hairy abdomen.

Brenish turned to help the others, just in time to see a spider make a mighty leap onto Turk's face. Turk grabbed it with both hands to push its fangs away, but the creature's claws dug in deep around his head. As this happened, even more spiders spilled out of the town.

Gareth swung a mace at the spider attacking Turk, hitting its abdomen full on: a perfect blow. The critter finally lost the strength in its legs as its innards fell out of the mangled body, like the bottom of a wet sack giving way. Turk calmly peeled the rest of it off.

Brenish made a stand there beside Gareth, watching more of the accursed things come at them. Gareth tossed the mace into the air and swept out his sword, catching the mace in his off hand. Both swung freely at the monsters that ran at them. Brenish felled two more; Gareth took out four.

Behind them, Harry and Bob finished off others. Finch had switched to his sword and twirled madly through a group that surrounded him, cutting them apart with awe-inspiring speed. Brenish ran to catch up to Jase, who was brandishing his sword at a single foe, and killed that spider on the run so he could help Naman.

Naman faced down three spiders himself, but his sword swung completely wild; the only thing that kept them at bay was the speed with which he did it. Dex stayed well clear of Naman's blade, trying to goad the others into it; he lunged at one and skewered it enough to leave it wounded before taking out a second with a clean strike. Before Brenish could jump in to help them, however, he saw Raden fall to the ground with another spider looming over him.

He changed direction to assist, but a crossbow bolt went clean through its maw and knocked it off the large man. All Brenish was good for was helping Raden get up.

The party seemed to have gained the upper hand. Finch and Harry now stood back to back, the spiders focusing most of their attention on the movement they generated, while Tibs drove others toward them for the slaughter. Bob threw nearby corpses into the fray, confusing the living spiders long enough to make easy pincushions. Brenish looked to Naman and Dex, but their battle was over: Dex was grinning at having finished off the last of his prey, while Naman tried to ignore him and gather courage to help the others. There was no need: Harry and Finch were efficient killers, dispatching the rest with ease.

No more spiders came. The attack was over. Everyone seemed to catch their breath, trying to return to a semblance of normal. Finch and Harry slapped hands together in mutual commendation, which gave Brenish pause to smile. He looked for Cirawyn, and found her yanking a bolt out of a spider. Raden, by his side, seemed to have trouble calming down, shaking visibly. Tibs was ecstatic. He turned around and saw Gareth applying a bandage roll to Turk's head. Jase seemed about to burst into nervous giggles.

As their combat posture dropped and their emotions cooled, Tibs looked around and did his best to count the bodies. "Twenty-one," he said. "Or twenty-two."

"What a team we make," said Gareth. "You men were magnificent. How does that feel, Turk?"

"Fine," Turk said. "Thanks, boss."

"Anytime. Raden? Raden, you don't look so good."

Raden was still shaking. "Give me a minute."

"Gladly. Now I just have one question, Brenish."

The tone was less congratulatory than Brenish expected, given Gareth's reaction to the outcome of the battle. "Yes?" he said, cautiously.

"Explain *this.*"

Gareth was pointing to Cirawyn and the crossbow in her right hand. She held the used bolt, which she had cleaned, in the other.

"I know how much you hate waste," Brenish said, trying for all the world to sound sincere rather than flippant. "I'm no good with it, and I thought we'd be stronger with twelve fighters than eleven. She got that spider off Raden. Pretty good shot, too."

Gareth looked Cirawyn in the eye; she didn't act especially defiant about it, but she showed no interest in giving back the crossbow. He looked back at Raden, still quivering in place. Finally he gave up and shrugged. "Eh," he said. "Good thinking. If she can shoot like that, all the better."

"Need any help with that, darling?" said Jase, pointing to the bolt she was still holding.

Cirawyn never broke eye contact with him while she drew back the string, a very hard pull, and latched it into place. "Nay," she said. The barked laugh that followed at Jase's expense came from the unlikeliest of sources: Turk.

"Well, men, we've made good progress so far, and we've just fought hard for our place in this little town. Let's take a rest here."

The party all readily agreed to that, but Brenish, looking about the empty doorways and windows of Paddystock, decided to draw from the well of good advice he had collected over hundreds of stories. He motioned to Gareth for a word in private.

Away from the group, Gareth said: "Yes?"

"Franco's shield got me thinking. This is the kind of place a lot of people come through. It's the kind of place things get left. With these spiders around, maybe people died here."

"We came here for a very specific treasure," said Gareth. "Hunting for anything else is a waste of time."

"I understand, but two times out of three, the men I've talked to who made it out alive found something of value to help them down here. We may be well-equipped, but me, I like to hedge my bets. Let me poke around a little. I can take Tibs, and we'll scout for a bit."

"Hmm. A lucky find does often make the difference between life and death, 'twould seem. And you did find me that gold earlier. I'll tell you what: I trust your judgment here. But take Harry with you. Harry's got a better eye."

"Tibs has two."

"Humor me."

"Harry it is," said Brenish.

He returned to the group and explained the idea to Harry. Harry, sitting on the ground and in the middle of sharing a laugh with Finch, didn't seem too keen on the notion, but he got up and agreed to help anyway.

"I wanna look too," said Dex. It was an unexpected bit of initiative from him.

"Not alone," said Gareth.

"Bob, you wanna do some exploring?"

Bob looked at his brother, who had stopped shaking but looked ill. He turned to Gareth.

"It's all right, Bob," Gareth said. "We'll look after him."

"All right."

"Hell," said Tibs, "I'm in too. Naman, you wanna take a look around with me?"

"Nay," Naman said flatly. He obviously didn't want anything to do with the spider dens, even if the residents were good and dead.

"I'll do it," Turk offered. His tone was still perfectly even, but getting so many words out of him in a short time was a serious change. The ruins seemed to bring out the best in him. If he kept this vivacious streak up, he might pass for human eventually.

"All right," said Gareth. "The rest of us will wait here."

"Explain why we're doing this," said Harry.

"Resourcefulness," Brenish replied. He stuck his head and torch into a doorway. "There's an art to traversing the Elder Kingdom. Bah, this one's empty too."

"They're probably all empty."

"People are always surprised what they find down here. It pays to look. Empty."

"I think you're just making this up. Honestly, I've always thought you were touched in the head when it came to this stuff."

Brenish leaned into another doorway and set his torch to a set of fuzzy white spheres hanging within. "You'd hardly be the first to think so. But I know what I'm doing, at least as much as Gareth does."

"That's not as reassuring as you think it sounds."

"Ooh, hello," said Brenish. He stepped into the room while the last bits of spider gunk flamed out. "We have a friend."

A skeleton lay on the far end of the room against the wall. Its clothes and armor had rotted away, save for an iron helm that lay by its side, and a shattered breastplate. The skull was surprisingly intact. Whatever had killed the poor fellow had rent a hole in the plate, probably piercing a vital organ. He had a pack by his side, wide open, and a rusty sword in his hand.

"Well now, I'm sorry things ended so badly for you," Brenish said to the corpse, "but you might do us a lot of good." He stooped and reached into the pack. There was no food left. He found only an empty glass bottle with a cork stopper, a little coin purse, and most importantly: a scroll and a wand.

Brenish unfurled the scroll, but it was gibberish to him. The runes meant nothing to the uneducated, which meant he had no way to tell what it was supposed to do. The only way to make use of it would be to read it aloud. The ink was derived from *esen* and the spell paper was imbued with a tremendous store of energy. Runes written that way had a way of imparting themselves to the mind when read aloud, a fact that made scrolls quite useful tools to ruin crawlers like Brenish.

"You don't read mage runes, do you?" he said.

"Nay."

"Pity. Oh, well. We'll bring it to Gareth."

"What do you suppose the wand does?"

"No idea." Brenish slid the wand into a pocket hidden behind the lining of his leather chest armor, along the bottom seam. It was one of several, meant to sheath a dagger or tools. He had always found it useful, but now it would serve a different purpose. The wand didn't show when he moved, thanks to the stiffness of the armor.

"You're taking a stupid risk," said Harry.

"I want options," Brenish said. "As long as we're both being so honest, I should tell you that Naman and I are working out how to deal with Gareth."

"Why? You think he'd double-cross us? He has no reason to do that."

Brenish shook his head. "You're being overly generous."

"He's always kept his word before."

"Indeed he has. But imagine Gareth hits a stumbling block while decoding the rest of the map. I wasn't able to fully decode it myself."

"You'll manage. If there's one thing I can trust, it's that one of you will find a way to get what you want."

He had a point, but Brenish knew he had to get through to him somehow, convince him of the necessity of making a plan. "Look, I've had misgivings about the map from the beginning. I was rushed into this. Sully allayed some of my fears, but what if Visak did something devious? Something we can't figure out on our own? You know *exactly* what Gareth's gonna do then. And when that happens—"

"*If* that happens," said Harry.

"Whatever the case, if we don't get that treasure, we'll need to act, and fast. I just want you to know that's a real possibility. Can I count on you then, if that happens?"

Harry was somewhat angered by that. "You're asking *me* if I can be relied on?"

"In this specific case, yes."

"Of course. What I'm truly concerned with is what I'll tell Gareth when he finds that wand on you."

"Come on, Harry," Brenish said. "You're plenty good enough to figure that out. But if you want a good story, just tell him I distracted you with something else and I must've taken it when you weren't looking. You didn't get a good look in this fellow's pack, did you?"

"Nay."

"Which means you didn't know it was in there. You didn't see me take it, so you knew naught of it."

"And the gold?"

"Oh, we'll absolutely bring him the gold," Brenish said.

"And then we pretend all's well, right up until we find the treasure or Gareth goes mad."

"Right *before* Gareth goes mad. What say you?"

Harry hissed a laugh from the side of his mouth, as if an especially funny joke had hit him unexpectedly. "You're different here," he said. "Aye, we're in agreement. Just one thing I'd like to point out to you, before we go."

Brenish felt bolstered by Harry's vote of confidence. "What's that?"

"That fellow you've been talking to," he said, pointing to the skeleton. "Take a look at his teeth."

Brenish did. He leaned in close to get a better view at the skull, its shape, and the way the teeth were arranged. The mouth was similar to a man's, but it had eight fangs instead of four—or would have, if one wasn't missing—and they were a tad larger. The skull itself had an odd angular quality that was extremely subtle, and the opening for the nose was extra wide.

"Goblin," Brenish said. "They're not supposed to come down this far. Not for ages, they haven't."

"Even I knew that," said Harry. "But this one didn't get the message."

Brenish straightened up, but kept staring. "He looks like a scout, or maybe a courier. Simple armor, good equipment. Looks like he was on his own. Ran into a spot of trouble and died here."

"Well spotted."

"But what's he *doing* here?"

Dex and Bob were already back. Most of the men were seated or otherwise relaxed, having gathered around the old well. A few nibbled on their provisions. Finch puffed on his pipe. Brenish had heard smoking calmed the nerves, but Finch was never visibly anxious; indeed he seemed incapable of nervousness at all.

"What've you got there?" said Gareth.

"Gifts from our friends to the north," Brenish said. He tossed the purse, which Gareth caught in one hand.

"Did you count this?"

"Nay. Thought you'd find this more interesting." Brenish came closer and handed him the scroll. "I don't know what it does. Anyone here know runes?"

Several heads shook, including Gareth's. "My granddad was a mage," Bob offered.

"Did he teach you the runes?"

"Nay."

"Then why bring it up?" said Jase. "Dust off your wits."

Bob looked embarrassed, but Brenish shrugged. He hadn't expected anyone to know, so he was surprised when a voice said, "Give it here," and the voice belonged to Dex.

Dex accepted the scroll from Gareth and gave it a long look.

"I found this, too," said Brenish, holding up the bottle. "Mind if I keep it?"

"As you like," Gareth said. "What did you mean about friends from the north?"

"Goblin scout," said Harry. "Been dead here for a few years, maybe."

"You're fooling."

"Wish I was. Anyone have use for his helmet?"

Brenish hadn't even noticed Harry take it, or paid heed to him holding it; maybe he was slipping. Jase held up a hand and snatched the iron helm out of the air when it was thrown. He sniffed dubiously at the inside, nodded, and put it on his own head. It was a decent enough fit.

"I don't know all these runes," Dex said, "but I think it's for replenishing a volitional spellbind."

"Such as... a wand?" said Bob. Brenish cursed silently and tried not to show his annoyance.

"Aye."

Finch blew a puff of smoke from his pipe. "That would imply he had one," he said.

Gareth raised his eyebrows at Brenish.

"There was refuse all over the floor," Brenish said. This was true, but it was true of just about every building in Paddystock. They had found endless scatterings of dirt, ancient droppings that had turned to dirt, bits of debris, stone chips, flaked rust, and fragments of bone. "If he had a wand it might've exploded. Probably he got desperate at the end, or it broke and blew up when he fell. Not sure what killed him, except whatever it was went through his armor."

"He had naught else with a binding?" said Gareth. "Nothing to use that scroll for?"

"None that I found. Whatever killed him wasn't interested in looting, either."

Gareth took the scroll back from Dex and unslung his pack to store it inside, along with the purse. While he was stowing them a little golden light spilled out: the spellglow of the orb. The light was otherworldly, wholly unlike the false sun of their spell lamps or the warmth of the torch flames.

Tibs and Turk had reappeared somewhere in the middle of the conversation. "How concerned should we be about goblins?" said Tibs. "Do you think they've spread out enough to be a problem for us?"

"No telling," said Gareth. "We'll have to risk it. You lads should get something to eat. We have a long way to go yet today."

Brenish took off his pack and sat down next to Cirawyn. She had waited for him to eat, and now pulled out some journey wafers, dried fruits, a stick of dried meat, and a water bottle. He put the goblin's empty bottle away and took out a portion of food for himself.

"I'm sorry, love," he said quietly.

"This isn't your fault."

"Oh," he sighed, "there's too many faults to go round. I made my share."

"I don't care."

She seemed more cheerful than she should be under the circumstances. He did his best to throw off his guilt and set into the food.

"These wafers aren't half bad," said Tibs. "Who made these?"

"Perrin's," Gareth said. "Best bakery in the city. Worth the expense."

"I'll say."

"I like 'em too," said Brenish, "but this mutton is top rate. Don't tell me Perrin's smokes and cures meat now."

"Maddie put it up," Finch said. "She's a marvel with curing. Gets her spices from the east."

"My compliments."

"I'll pass it on. You should've tasted that boar she roasted last year."

"Ohhh," Harry said wistfully.

"Eddie caught it in the woods when Harry took him out hunting. Huge animal. Best thing I ate in a long time."

Drawing out Finch's chummy side was making Brenish a little uncomfortable. It seemed to have the same effect on Naman, who changed the subject.

"Why do you suppose they call it Paddystock?" he said.

"Paddy Shoemaker," Brenish and Gareth answered, practically at once. Gareth took over the rest. "He was an explorer, way back. Back before my granddad was born. Charted all kinds of places, from the Gatehouse to the mines. Some places, he just made better maps than what came before. No one had named this place, so when he made the first good map of it, his friends called it Paddystock. It stuck."

"Do all the towns have names?" said Bob.

"Nay. But many do."

Brenish just nodded along to confirm Gareth's word. He took a look about the group to gauge their moods. Jase seemed deep in thought. Turk was expressionless, and beginning to bleed through his bandages; he acted like his wounds didn't bother him. Tibs seemed interested in studying the town, as did Bob. Most of the group looked in good spirits overall, but Raden was still unseated. Raden ate quietly and kept his eyes on the floor.

"Oi," Brenish said. "Raden. You all right?"

"A bit better, thanks," he said.

"It's not the spider, is it? I've seen that look before."

Raden nodded and kept eating.

"Take deep breaths, from your belly. I heard it helps."

"Aye."

"Switch torches with Jase, too."

"What?" said Jase.

"Spell light," Brenish explained. "It's closer to sunlight than the torches. Better choice for someone with the deepsick."

"Why not Tibs?" Jase scowled.

If Jase had any humility, Brenish thought, he would have admitted he wasn't too far behind Raden. Brenish chided himself for not seeing it sooner; it was obvious to look at him that the man wasn't his usual irascible self.

"Sure," Tibs said. "I don't need it, except sometimes for tracking." The only other spell lamp belonged to Finch, who was using it to help light the vanguard a little better than the torches could manage alone.

"I'd rather he kept it for that purpose," Gareth said. "Jase, you can switch off with Raden awhile."

Jase hid his unhappiness with that arrangement rather well. There wasn't a good percentage in gainsaying Gareth. "Aye, sir," he said.

"Eat up, everyone, and be sure to get plenty of water. We can refill our bottles tomorrow. We'll get moving again soon.

The Forgotten Garden

As they got back on the Road, Raden switched places with Bob, putting two spell lamps at the head of the party. Brenish also wanted to make sure he was close by in case he needed to talk him through another rough spot, so Raden was between himself and Finch. Some combination of these reassurances seemed to be enough. Raden stayed on about the same keel as they left Paddystock, even as the tunnel around the Road seemed to close in a bit much even for Brenish's liking.

Brenish was less sure about Jase, now. He didn't like the idea of a man on a tight trigger being right behind him, let alone next to Cirawyn.

West of Paddystock the ruins seemed livelier, as if the town marked an invisible border most creatures didn't care to cross. Rats were seen more frequently, sharing their domain with small lizards, and occasionally ants the size of grapes. The Elder Kingdom felt less like a place abandoned by its builders than one inhabited by its intended residents, as if the Road and its offshoot streets had been made with the vermin in mind.

Overall, Brenish felt that the party was in better spirits since taking their lunch together. In spite of what had already happened, he felt more kindly disposed toward most of Gareth's men, even Gareth himself. It was all too easy to forget the true depth of trouble he was in; his mind wandered off of it and stayed focused on the halls in front of him, the endless brick and stone.

Perhaps it was because Gareth saw the gloom and the enclosure weighing on his men, or it might have been something the ruins stirred inside him; whatever the reason, Gareth began to sing. He sang a slow, rolling melody that was more tune than words at first, like a lullaby or a dirge. It lilted in places and in others seemed to drift mournfully. The music reminded Brenish of the hills above, of grassy expanses in summer and the autumn trees somewhere overhead, yet it seemed to belong here, too, as though it had been written by the Elder Kingdom's founders for just that purpose. The sound seemed to give the Road meaning, life, though nothing like it had been heard there in many centuries.

In his own mind Brenish could almost imagine how the Wide Road had looked in its day: well-lit by spell lamps above, traveled frequently by carts, and men on foot, and horse-drawn wagons, bringing goods and news between the cities. Trees must have once bloomed in places around Paddystock, wheat and barley harvested in great caverns now desolate. Children were born here, grew up, married, had children of their own, and died after full lives, perhaps many having never seen the sky. Nor rain, nor snow.

All was dark and quiet now.

Gareth's voice faded, his song finished. The darkness seemed to close around even more.

"The stones remember," Brenish said, "but they keep their secrets." It was an ancient proverb.

"Hold," said Finch. He held up a hand and the party came to a stop.

"What is it, Ed?" said Gareth.

"I'm not sure. Lower your torches. Crossbowmen, cover me, but watch your aim."

Finch brought his spell lamp down and held it out like the point of a staff, and advanced a little way ahead. When he was sure he saw no threat, he held a hand over his light. He peered into the darkness for several minutes in silence; Brenish pictured him squinting. Finally Finch straightened and returned to the others. He pointed the lamp behind himself to illuminate any threat that might come after him, and never once looked back.

"Well?" said Gareth.

"There's light ahead. Very faint. A little way down this road there's a chamber, and a staircase going up. The light's coming from there."

"We know there are working lights in this place," Gareth said, "though not many."

"'Tisn't a spell light," said Brenish.

Jase gave him a slap across the back, not threateningly but not the kind that spoke of friendship. "How would you know?" he said.

"You studied the maps of this region," Brenish said. "Don't you remember where we are?"

"We're coming up on Stone's End," said Jase, "a little settlement west of Paddystock."

"Do you know why they call it that? I bet Gareth does."

Jase shook his head. Brenish turned to Gareth but found that he, too, was surprised.

"No?" said Brenish.

Gareth gestured emptily, less a shrug than an eagerness to know more. "All I've read of Stone's End is that it's a small complex with several levels, like an old palace. You know something more?"

"There's something I think you'll want to see."

Gareth grinned. "All right, Brenish. Lead on."

The group continued along the Road a short way. At first they saw nothing but more tunnel fading to blackness in the distance, but after about a hundred yards there was no doubt about what Finch had seen: a glimmer of white light, very dim but noticeable, spilling down a staircase within a larger room. Though there were no doorways in the roadside like those that usually appeared near a settlement, they could tell they were approaching the end of the tunnel by the change in sound alone. Where the tunnel's mouth opened into the room, there was a break in the brickwork that was obviously the slot for a portcullis; but the portcullis itself was gone.

The leaders stepped through the gateway and cautiously entered the room. Brenish smiled broadly, seeing the main hall of Stone's End for the first time. The room in which they stood was supported by pillars, not vaults, which from what they had seen so far was unusual. There were six of those, each one square in cross section, decorated in relief that had mostly been worn away by time. At the far end of the chamber and just to the left, a staircase much like the one under Asaph's Gate—partially cut into a wall—was the obvious focal point, being so well lit. Right beside it, another gated arch opened onto the Wide Road; its portcullis was missing as well.

While Stone's End was oft compared to a palace, to Brenish's eyes it looked very different from the way travelers had described it. It had an organic, haphazard architecture that reminded him more of the guild's great house in the city, altered over many generations. The arched doorways into other rooms were placed almost randomly, without regard to symmetry, and came in two distinct shapes: one style tall with a shallow arch, one closer standard door height, wider, with a circular arch. In testament to its builders' disdain for standards the room's downward stair, though also along the western wall, ran parallel to it, a completely different angle from the upward stair. The down stair wasn't close to the western gate at all, and was obviously narrower. The main room was like the demented result of a drunken argument between two bitterly opposed architects who could agree on nothing but its supports. Brenish imagined that many of the other rooms would be similar.

"Another Gate!" said Raden.

"Doubtful," Gareth said.

Brenish kept walking, stopping only long enough to lay his hands on a pillar and take a look at its carvings. Men and beasts, reduced to vagueness. Monsters, perhaps, real as the ruins or imagined wholesale by a culture that vanished long ago. Myth was different in the ruins, rendering true what many believed to be purely fanciful. In the darkness, grains of truth in old wives' tales could be witnessed with a man's own eyes. Some men who left never slept well again, forever doubting any faith they ever had in the very foundations of the world. Their malady was called Fellheart; for some there was no cure.

Sighing deeply, Brenish led the party to the stairs, and up. The steps were littered with old pine needles, and the brittle remains of tiny leaves of former years. He saw an ant carry a maple seed pod down, following some established route its sisters had laid out.

The upper level of Stone's End began in a little anteroom with exits on all sides. In front of the group, however, was a very large arch, the source of the light. Beyond that arch they saw an enormous vaulted chamber, brightly lit, thick with greenery. Brenish felt the joy of his childhood self as he stepped inside.

The room was a disheveled garden, a flowing pattern of interlaced walkways surrounded by raised soil beds, each wide enough across to support a sturdy tree or more. A few scrawny maples and oaks had made their home there, their leaves already changed and ready to fall. They surrounded much older trees, hoary and grotesque but still living, like the fearsome landmarks of a witches' wood. The trees' roots overflowed their bounds and in some places had broken through the stone around them, spilling out into the aisles. Vines and ivy grew thickly on every vertical surface. Undergrowth was dense about the bottoms of the trees, both shrubbery and wildflowers that were no longer in bloom.

The room's vaulting was unlike anything Brenish had seen in the world above: common groin vaults were reinforced with ribs. The ceiling seemed to be made from a mineral that shone and reflected light, or perhaps was painted so, amplifying the sunlight that came through from the four great skylights above: cylindrical chimneys that ended in huge stone grates. The light was weak, but it was enough to sustain life. The blue sky seen through the grates was painfully bright by comparison, almost white to their eyes.

"What is this place?" said Gareth.

"You know it not?" said Brenish.

"Nay."

"This is the only part of the ruins I had ever seen, before today. I've been to the woods up there. A few travelers have spoken of it. Most just pass through. Shows a sad lack of curiosity, if you ask me."

Most of the party were awed with the garden, a truly beautiful place in a world long lost. Whenever it was made, it must have been just as wondrous, the jewel of Stone's End—or whatever its makers called it. The group spread out among the plants, oblivious to anything else, touching leaves and vine shoots, a frail connection to the world above that they could physically hold onto. Raden stared up at the grates.

"Brenish," said Naman, "I hate to intrude on this nice little moment you're having, but there's someone here who'd like to say hello."

"Hmm?" Brenish said. He turned away from the sights to look at Naman, then where Naman was pointing.

"Enzo."

"Oh, rot," said Brenish. His joy at finding the garden instantly evaporated.

"Lack of curiosity, you were saying?" said Harry.

Dobber's friends had come this way after all, but Enzo didn't make it any further; all that was left of him lay beyond one of the great clusters of tree roots blocking a path. He and Pines must have seen the light and investigated for themselves. Enzo's remains were mostly just his clothing and bones. He had worn a garish quilted cloak, which was now torn and stained but easily recognizable. Whatever flesh hadn't been picked at by animals was all but rotted away. His skull was shattered.

With the horror of another explorer's demise right in front of his face, Brenish took a harder look at the place he had been so awed by in childhood. Enzo's was not the only skeleton in the room. Bones of men and animals were visible almost everywhere he looked: a partial skull peeking from behind a bush, a femur behind a tree, vertebrae like nightmare flowers scattered on a bed of moss and half-hidden under leaves.

"He bought me a drink," Naman said. "I offered to burn that cloak for him."

Tibs went in for a closer look, but kept a watchful eye. He stooped to grab Enzo's pack and dragged it over the roots, to where he could sift through it.

"Probably tried to climb a tree to get out or call for help," said Jase. "Then he fell and broke his neck, and wild animals got the rest."

"I doubt it," said Brenish. "Any fool can tell the trees don't reach those grates. Maybe they could've built a ladder."

"Aye," Gareth said. "I never met these fellows, but falling from a tree is a pretty stupid way to die."

"Wouldn't be the first," said Jase.

"Anything of value in that pack?"

"Oil and a stone," said Tibs. "No gold."

"What kind of stone?"

"River rock. It's engraved."

Gareth held out his hand and took the oval stone, wrapping his fingers around it. The stone was less than two inches long, and rather flat. The engraving was a circle with an arrow through it. "Hmm. Bearing stone. You don't see many of these anymore. They're more reliable than lodestone, but too expensive. Binding's worn on this one. He probably got it cheap. It's worthless."

Gareth tossed it back to Tibs and turned away. Brenish signaled that he wanted it, so Tibs threw it to him. Even a weakened bearing stone wasn't entirely useless, and weak bindings could be revived.

"That's all?" said Dex.

"Aye, that was all," Tibs said. "Dig through it yourself if you want." He tossed the bag with great speed and greater annoyance, forcing Dex to act fast to keep it from hitting his face. Gareth didn't intervene.

Dex, for his part, didn't react. He just dropped the pack again. "What about his pockets? Bet you already checked those, eh?"

"Aye, and found naught. Likely his friend made off with the rest."

"Likely?" Dex raised an eyebrow. Tibs snarled.

"Hey," Turk said, "there's coins here."

Brenish turned around; Turk was pointing into the bushes, and actually smiling. And another memory came back, along with the sudden realization of what must have happened to Enzo. Turk leaned in for a closer look.

"Turk," Brenish said, "I don't think—"

In that split second, something impossibly large lunged out of the bushes and pulled Turk's entire head into its mouth.

The group exploded into action, not all of it helpful. Turk screamed for help, with the monster clamped around him. It had a good pinch on his neck and was trying to get a better grip. Some of the men drew their weapons, but some spent a few moments fumbling in panic first. Bob, who stood closest, tried to grab the jaws and pry them open, but cut his hand on the sharp teeth.

The creature's eyes were big and black, reflecting the light as a bright bronze sheen from deep within its pupils, and they were set apart in the wide head like a snake's. Yet in spite of the snakelike head and neck—it had a very long neck—it looked more like an otter or a beaver, or perhaps a giant weasel. The monster had dark, sleek brown fur that was coarse like an aquatic animal's, yet there was little water in the garden but what dripped from above.

Harry and Dex tried to grab the beast and choke it. Dex used just one hand and punched it with the other, repeatedly and rapidly without stopping. Tibs ran in close, showing impressive speed, and got his whip to wrap around the neck a couple of times. The combined restraint helped keep it from pulling its head back into the brush, taking Turk with it. With all the resistance it faced, it stepped out of the underbrush, revealing it had a much larger body than they would have thought possible. It had legs with the power of a bear, oversized paws and claws digging into the soil and then scrabbling on the bricks around the bed.

Finch got in a good shot near the monster's left eye. Cirawyn hit it between the eyes, but the bolt bounced off hard bone and into the brush. Brenish tried poking it in the eye with his torch, but the head moved around too much, so he settled for stabbing at it with the fire, singeing it wherever he could get close enough. Gareth had gotten in even closer, along with Raden and Naman, who all took swords to its hide. The creature however was enraged by the injury; it thrashed and threw off several of its attackers, sending Harry and Raden flying. Naman fell into the bushes. Brenish was pushed back to land hard on his butt; his pack kept his back from hitting the floor, but it gave him whiplash as his head kept moving.

Dazed, Brenish tried to sit up. He didn't feel any injury with so much still going on. During the ongoing scuffle the creature clamped down harder on its prey. Blood flowed freer from Turk's neck where a fang pierced it; his screams became choking sounds.

In a last desperate act, Dex stopped punching and used his free hand to draw a knife. He plunged it into the monster's throat, registering some surprise when the knife sank deep into its flesh. With a smooth, disturbingly practiced motion he pulled the blade towards himself, slitting the neck wide open. The monster's blood gushed out, and it lost all fight. Its neck slumped and the head fell.

Bob finally managed to pry the creature's jaws apart far enough to pull Turk out. Turk was about done for, spewing blood from his wounds and gurgling in his throat. Gareth wasted no time; he threw down his pack and flung it open.

Perhaps Gareth had practiced for a situation like this, or he was simply that good at thinking on his feet, but he had pulled a potion out of the pack in about a second flat. He made it to Turk in two long steps, pulling out the stopper with his teeth on the run, and pushed Bob away from his clumsy ministrations. With a flick of his wrist he poured a tiny amount of the potion into Turk's mouth.

"Swallow," Gareth said. He stoppered the bottle and tossed it to Jase, who tried to catch it but bobbled a few times before gaining control. The liquid within fizzed; it was a bright green, like spring leaves. Gareth knelt and put both hands, now free, around Turk's neck to apply pressure. "Swallow," he commanded.

Turk did his best to swallow, sputtering as he did. But in moments his pain seemed to stop. The sounds of choking and gasping ceased, though he began to cough. His face had become pale as the blood drained from it; now life returned, a rosy flush. Gareth took his hands away.

Brenish stood, and felt the pain in his neck for the first time. As he turned his head back and forth to assess how badly he was hurt, he caught movement back where Gareth left his pack, and saw Jase stowing the potion—or trying to, with unsteady hands. He cursed himself for not taking a look inside when he had the chance; he wondered what other equipment Gareth had chosen to bring.

Gareth got up to give Turk room to breathe. Turk rolled onto his side and coughed out about half a pint of blood.

"Easy now," Gareth said. "That draft should fully restore you in a few minutes. You won't need those bandages anymore."

"Thanks, boss," Turk wheezed.

"Good work there, Dexter. Is anyone else hurt badly? Bob, how's your hand?"

Bob was already going through his pack, grabbing his bandages. "I've had worse," he said.

"Nay, hold up there, Bob. You might get an infection from that thing's teeth. I have a salve for that. Jase, grab me the herbal salve."

But Jase was completely overthrown. Still kneeling by Gareth's pack, he tried to open it again, but his hands no longer wanted to obey. His arms shook uncontrollably.

Brenish rushed over and pulled Jase away. "Come on," he said. "I'll take care of it."

"Back!" Gareth shouted, harshly enough for Brenish to whip his head around and instantly regret the motion. "What do you think you're doing?"

"Jase is undone," Brenish said. "I'm just trying to help."

"I'll thank you to stay out of my pack anyway."

"What if it's an emergency?"

"Then I'll tell you so."

Brenish straightened up and stood, letting Finch step in. "All right," he said. "Seeing as you're carrying all our emergency supplies, might I make a suggestion?"

"No," said Gareth.

"In the interest of group safety."

"No."

"I have an empty bottle. We could—"

"*Enough.*"

The standoff attracted everyone's attention. Only Finch went about his business, handing the salve to Bob. Jase was still trying to pull himself together.

Dex walked over to Gareth and subtly jerked his head toward Cirawyn with a depraved leer. It was a question of some kind, a continuation of some earlier conversation Brenish hadn't been privy to. Knowing Dex, the meaning was clear enough. Brenish had trouble holding his mouth shut. Dex gave someone else a gloating look while Gareth made up his mind; Brenish thought it was probably aimed at Tibs, but didn't want to turn his head again to find out.

"This isn't quite the situation I had in mind," Gareth said, in a detached voice like he was figuring out a puzzle. "You were quite a help with the weasel thing, though."

"You said if he tried to overstep you, I could."

"I said perhaps."

Dex fixed his eyes firmly on Cirawyn now. She didn't have a bolt ready in her crossbow, but the way her fingers twitched said enough. Naman's knuckles around his sword hilt were white.

Brenish was outraged, but he choked it back. Anything else risked escalating the situation, and Gareth was never the one to back down first. Indeed finding a way to threaten Cirawyn besides death was just the kind of thing that would appeal to Gareth's sense of thrift, because the same threat could be used again. Brenish spoke quickly. "I apologize. This should have been a private conversation. I spoke out of turn."

Gareth narrowed his eyes. "Quite."

Whatever feeling of group unity Brenish had felt after Paddystock, it was gone now. Judging by the looks of discomfort on some of the faces of Gareth's men, though, not everyone was prepared to go along with the implied threat. Even Turk, still recovering from the edge of death, had a twitch of disgust on his otherwise blank countenance. But counting on him to step in, or on Bob and Raden who were mostly honorable enough, was not a bet Brenish was willing to take.

"Well," said Gareth, "I suppose you've been quite helpful yourself. What think you, Ed?"

"Last resort," said Finch, without hesitation or blinking. He didn't even look up from what he was doing.

"All right, then. Apology accepted. We'll put this little unpleasantness behind us and move on. I'm glad I saw this place after all, in spite of the difficulties we had here. Let's all take a moment to catch our breath and move along."

Dex was obviously disappointed, but he masked it by going to the creature's skull and cutting out some of the teeth as kill trophies. Brenish had never much liked Dex, but until now he hadn't really understood the depth of loathing most people had for the man. He'd heard of atrocities committed by the occasional wicked drifter or sometimes by men at war, and of course the Vikings were still a legend of dread, but he had always thought his fellow villagers, even Dex for all his faults, above that sort of thing. No more.

While everyone was collecting themselves, Cirawyn stole a moment to come closer to Brenish. She took hold of his arm. "More caution, love," she whispered. There was no accusation in her tone.

"Aye," said Brenish. "For a while there I forgot who we were dealing with."

"I haven't forgotten," said Tibs, keeping his voice just as low and pretending to rummage in his pack without looking their way. His tone had gone to ice. "Naman said you had some misgivings."

"I need options," Brenish whispered. "And time."

"Next to the wand," Tibs replied. He walked away.

Lowcastle

It took a while for Gareth to convince Jase to go back down, away from the sight of sky. In the end he swapped his light back from Raden, and that was just enough. Raden seemed much recovered, either by seeing the sunlight again or by being in combat. The deepsick was like that: It could come and go, and sometimes took several days to set in. Brenish knew enough to keep his eye on the others. The only ones he didn't worry about were Gareth and Finch. Maybe Harry, too.

In the long walk from Stone's End, very little was said. A fog of distrust had settled over everyone. Harry and Finch had the easiest time bridging the gap between the two sides, and showed no outward change in their behavior. Raden stayed up front; he seemed to respect Brenish's space a bit more than he had previously. But they were the exceptions. Gareth didn't sing.

Several hours passed in near silence. The Road seemed unchanging for many long stretches, but then it would fan out into a little settlement briefly, at which times everyone was on their guard. There was no challenge in those places, however, just empty streets and dark doorways. None of the settlements were as big as Paddystock. A few places they passed along the way didn't even leave the tunnel. Here and there, four or five doorways had been knocked into the side of the road in a little cluster, and then the tunnel walls resumed, unbroken again for a long distance.

Rats and bugs shared the Road with them happily, completely uninterested in their company. The tunnel was, however, devoid of bats. And further along, even the rats thinned out, seemingly uninterested in straying far from the nicer parts of the ruins.

After some time, fresher air currents came from up ahead instead of behind them. Tibs spoke of the change, but no one else commented on it. Gareth was apparently too busy with his own thoughts, as was Brenish with his. There was no talk that it might be another Gate; it was more likely a ventilation shaft or a cave somewhere nearby. Had Gareth had the opportunity to use another

Gate closer to their destination as the entry point, even he surely would have. Hanfore's Gate was arguably a little closer, or the Marsh Gate, but both would take days to reach over land and offered additional challenges, and they were well off of the route half-described on the map.

Eventually the monotony proved too much for Jase. "Oi," he said, "somebody say something, will you?" His voice seemed steadier now; the spell light was helping, and perhaps the fresh air too.

A moment of awkward hesitation went by, and finally Turk said, "That goblin helmet looks silly."

Bob snorted in the back row, followed by a giggle from Cirawyn in the middle. The tension seemed to be broken, at least momentarily.

"Thanks, Turk," Jase said.

"Where are we, boss?" said Dex.

"We're quite a few miles west of the village now," Gareth said. "A couple miles south of Ferngarth, I'd guess."

"I've never been," said Naman. "Always wanted to. That's where you're from, eh, Harry?"

"Aye," Finch replied for him. "It's a bit sleepy off the main roads, though. It doesn't see much traffic from the cities, except Acherton."

"Always thought I might settle there someday," Naman said. "Or in the city."

"Acherton?"

"Nay, Eswell. Maybe as a guild elder, if I earned the position."

"No doubt they'll make you one," said Gareth. "Never knew the guild to turn down good coin."

"Aye," Naman said, though he knew that was never going to happen. Not unless Brenish somehow pulled off a miracle and got Gareth to sign off on his plan to go after a treasure pit.

Brenish wondered what Tibs could have slipped into his hidden pocket back in the garden. He hadn't even known Tibs knew about the pocket to begin with. At the front of the party, there was no way for him to check what was there, but it must have come from Enzo's pack. Dex alone had suspected more was there than Tibs said, but it seemed strange that Dex would be the first to think so. Whether Tibs was acting on Naman's warning to keep on his toes, or he had been doing so all along, he was at his very best right now. As well he needed to be: Of all Gareth's reluctant guests, Tibs had the most to lose if things went badly.

Quite a lot of the men had families to look out for, actually. Bob had a son; his brother was childless, but only recently married. Jase was rumored to have fathered a son in the city. Turk had a boy and a girl; Brenish had only met them a few times, but the boy was his father's son, a walking stone, and the girl was an unquenchable bundle of energy. Then of course there was Finch. Gareth had no wife and no child, and no apparent aspirations toward acquiring either just yet. Brenish had trouble picturing the man staying that way forever, so it was probably a matter of attaining some personal milestone first: such as enough money to buy out the whole city.

"I think I'm getting used to this place," Raden said. "It's not quite what I expected."

"Which was?" said Cirawyn.

"I guess something more like the place where we came in. Lots of little rooms. Or caves, maybe. More of the big cities, or that pit we crossed earlier. It's not like in the stories, where it's all treasure and monsters and wonders."

"Never liked those stories," said Harry.

Brenish wasn't entirely surprised by that, but he still found it difficult to accept that anyone could be completely indifferent to tales of the ruins, let alone dislike them. "Ever meet Visak?" he said.

"Aye, a few times. But I never heard him tell a story."

"Pity. Maybe you'd feel different, if you did."

"Doubt it."

"His stories," said Gareth, but he trailed off and thought a moment. "His stories were like spells. Long, winding spells, the kind a binder uses. His words got in deep and wrapped around your heart. Never met another man who could do that, except my father. Or Brenish, sometimes."

"Thanks, Gareth," Brenish said.

"I'm not sure I meant it as a compliment, but take it as you like."

Brenish felt a certain pride in that. He had never thought of himself as the wizard's equal in any way. And he held the old man's storytelling in such high regard, he couldn't help but take any comparison in a kind light. Surely Gareth saw it the same way, whatever he said. The same spell had worked on them both. It very much *was* a binding, one that used a much more ancient yet accessible kind of magic.

Did that make Brenish a wizard of that magic, or a binder?

"Whatever happened to wintering in the city?" Cirawyn said.

Brenish actually stopped walking, so struck was he by the question. The rest of the group stopped with him, though not all at once.

"Keep going," said Gareth. With a little prodding he got the march underway again.

"I would have done," Brenish said. "I was all set to do it till that wagon job went bad. Didn't Naman tell you?"

"Not a word," said Cirawyn.

"I didn't want her to worry," Naman said.

"Well I was gonna sell the map," Brenish explained. "I didn't think I could do that before spring anyway. I needed the guild's help."

He didn't even try to sell her the story that he wasn't sure of what he had until the Expert proclaimed it genuine. Cirawyn saw through him; she always had. The only lies he could ever slip by her were ones of omission, and even then with difficulty. He was certain she knew he was holding something back, yet confident she would recognize his sincerity about the rest.

"'Tis better this way," said Gareth. "The guild isn't in the middle, and Brenish will walk away with a lot more than he would have from a sale. Everyone gets something out of this. And a lot of good stories, to boot."

"Papa," said Tibs in a mock child's voice, "tell us about when you got chomped on by a huge mink."

Naman sputtered, as did Bob. Jase and Dex laughed outright. Brenish couldn't be sure, but he thought he heard Turk snicker as well.

The cordial mood was restored, but Brenish could no longer forget his jeopardy. For the next hour, which was kept lively by occasional bursts of song, jokes, and chatter, he reengaged the part of his mind that worked best when it was up against impossible odds. How, he thought, could he talk his way out of this trip alive?

When he failed to decode the entire map and find the treasure, Gareth would be disappointed. He would be angry like nothing Brenish had ever seen—like nothing *anyone* had ever seen—if he actually knew it was fake. That kind of anger might not be one he would hold back, especially as it would be rooted in the same disappointment. Getting out of the situation then would be like befriending a bear in springtime.

But if seeds could be sown to *temper* that disappointment, maybe he could channel it into the idea he first pitched to Naman. He had already been thinking along those lines. The problem was that they had no goldsense; Gareth said he intended to buy none, and Brenish had no reason to doubt his word. Finding a treasure pit without goldsense would be a terrible challenge—not impossible, he knew, but difficult. Since the ruins were abandoned there had only ever been so many pits. Unless the goblins or other creatures were creating caches, as he sometimes suspected, that number dwindled every time an adventurer emptied one.

In practice, of course, the pits didn't get emptied very often. Most explorers lacked the gear to transport a large amount of solid gold home. That was the genius of the orb idea: he would have been able to clear out an entire pit, all at once. Anyone who got out with part of one usually didn't bother to come back. Non-mages disliked teleporting as a rule, and buying two scrolls per trip was a silly expense. As a result there were actually at least three pits whose locations he had heard about, that were not empty and might even contain significant loot, that he thought he could possibly find without goldsense.

In theory, of course. Brenish had memorized the locations of those pits, but actually finding them would be chancy. Two, at least, were somewhere near the route they were taking, so he had that in his favor.

Unless someone threw him a miracle, those pits might be his only chance to assuage Gareth. If he wanted to make a convincing case to go after them, he had to start building it now. Building a rationale to convince Gareth would take all the time he had.

The increased frequency of doorways indicated outgrowth from a city. After four hours of long travel from Stone's End, the Road broke into a city the likes of which none of the travelers had yet seen. The tunnel didn't widen at first, where the easternmost buildings in the city abutted the corridor, but the space above them opened up. The city roof was not visible by the light they carried; its buildings seemed instead to march up into blackness. Only after they passed the first cross street did they get a little more room to either side, where sidewalks were paved in brick with a pink hue.

Unlike the terraces of Paddystock, this city was built straight up; it reminded the company of a much more modern city, though taller. Every building was at least four stories high. They were supported and interconnected by a series of arched bridges, one of which had crumbled long ago. There was no uniformity to any of them, bridge or home. Doorways and windows carried some architectural similarities, but they varied a great deal in size, type, and construction. The faces of each building were a little different, many carrying design elements not seen on any other structure. Where one edifice might have recessed niches all in a row, another had intricate scrollwork, or a façade of arches and pillars. Some of the places they passed shared little courtyards behind tall archways, or had staircases going down from the sidewalk to "basement" levels. It was a startling reminder of just how many people had *lived* here, each making their mark on the place.

"We'll find a place to rest in one of these buildings," said Gareth. "Preferably a house. Ed, Brenish: Find us a good spot."

The place they found was a tiny one-room shop on a side street, a place probably no one had seen since it was abandoned. The floor was covered in coarse grit, a few flakes of stone, and decayed fibrous material that Brenish thought to be rubbish from the old civilization. With enough magic to light the city, a steady supply of food, and a few minutes with a broom, humans could easily live here again. It made the emptiness so much more difficult to comprehend. Centuries of speculation had left mankind nowhere near an answer as to why the Elder Kingdom vanished.

Brenish sat with Cirawyn, Tibs, and Naman, a little distance apart from Gareth's men. The little room had a low counter—almost a bench—that helped break up the sound, but it also helped obstruct the view. It was a perfect place for their group to be. Brenish couldn't decide if Harry chose to sit apart because he regarded himself as the inside man in Gareth's group, or if he felt some distance from his guild brothers. Harry was with Finch in the doorway, the two of them chatting freely while Finch took another smoke. Bob and Raden had formed a little cluster with Turk; the other men were with Gareth.

"How are you holding up?" Brenish said, more to Cirawyn than the others.

"A little better now," she replied. "The balm helps."

As they sat and started breaking out their food and water, Gareth had passed around a round wooden container of healing balm for blisters. Brenish had to admit he had naïvely overlooked that himself; Gareth had outplanned him. He had thought of the need for healing, but not of injuries from the sheer distance they had to travel on foot.

"It's been a long day, though," she added. "I'll be glad when we stop for the night."

"I won't. I don't like staying still too long down here."

"Visak did it," said Tibs.

"Aye, but it left a mark on him. He told me about it, once. 'Twas late one night at the Horsehead. My dad had stayed out pretty late and I had to sup at the inn. All the other kids went home after dark, but Visak told Howlett he'd look after me awhile."

"You never mentioned that," said Cirawyn. She smiled. "You truly knew the old man well, didn't you?"

"Well? Nay, love, I wouldn't say so. But he was a kindly soul. Guess he could afford to be. I was trying not to fall asleep by the fire, lest I miss my dad coming back, and he started into one of his stories in the middle like he did. Like he was already telling it in his head and forgot himself. It's how he was.

"'I was on my feet well into the night,' said he, 'and I could stay awake no longer. The wyrm had waited a few hundred years; it could wait a few more. But a man without his sleep is no better than a rabbit in a wolf's den, and that's as true of wizards as farmers. Mark that, lad,' he said. So I did.

"I asked him how he found a safe place, and he laughed. 'Weren't any safe place, so I tucked up in a hole in the wall and put out a fear spell and a ward. Best I could do.' And when I asked if he was afraid, he laughed again. 'Aye,' he said. 'Sometimes I still am.'"

"Did he sound like that?" said Cirawyn.

"That's how I remember his voice."

"Maybe it's no coincidence you found his map," said Tibs.

"The Expert said about the same. Said Visak had a *way*."

He took a quick glance at the rest of the room to be sure everyone was busy. The conversations had risen in volume enough that he felt comfortable opening another subject. He reached into his hidden pocket and pulled out the item Tibs had stowed there, next to the goblin's wooden wand.

"Discretion, please," he said, just above a whisper.

When he opened his hand and looked down, he found a little wooden charm, about three inches tall. It was birch, carved in the likeness of an owl, polished, and covered in a clear coating that was hard to the touch.

"What's this then?" he said to Tibs.

"You tell me," his pudgy friend said with a shrug. Tibs adjusted his glasses to get another look at it. "Some kind of unk."

If an object was obviously spellbound but its purpose or provenance was a mystery, it was customary to call it an *unk*. When such a thing was found in the ruins it was usually a powerful talisman, often found in the hoard of a deadly monster or on the person of a high-ranking manthing like a goblin captain. In the world they knew, however, unks were far more common and seldom worth much. Most unks were the castoff early works of apprentice binders practicing their craft, or else they came from the efforts of gifted amateurs who practiced on their own: often in secret lest they offend the binders' guild.

"Obviously an unk," said Brenish. Birch was a good wood for binding, and the shape, while owlish enough, had enough resemblance to a collection jar that it could probably replenish its power over time. "But I wonder what kind. I never saw this when they showed me their gear."

"Who?" said Cirawyn.

"Enzo and the others. They wanted my opinion on their supplies. I told them they were ill prepared. Pines had a few scrolls, and Enzo had the bearing stone. But naught like this."

"Maybe they picked it up down here," said Naman.

"Unlikely. They didn't get very far. I wonder if Enzo took my words to heart and tried to improve their chances."

"They crossed the Gate the day after we met them. They didn't have time to go to the city and back first."

"Aye," Brenish agreed, "which means they bought it in the village."

"But we have no binders," said Tibs. "Collectors, only."

"I've never seen it either," Cirawyn said. "I doubt they got it from Gareth. So you can rule out a collector, I think."

"Aye, love," said Brenish, although he wondered why her never having seen it was relevant. If she knew of another collector he didn't, it was news to him. "So if we want to know what it does, we'll have to ask the fellow who made it." He jerked his eyes toward the only man in the party who seemed to know much about magic.

"You're not serious," said Naman. "Please tell me so."

"The way he pressed the question of Enzo's pockets? Aye, I'm quite serious."

"I don't like where this is going," Naman said, "but if it gets us out of this, do what you have to."

"Please do," said Tibs. "Gareth keeps his word, but this whole situation has me on a knife's edge."

"You're not the only one," Cirawyn added.

"I know," Brenish said, sighing. "You know I would never have allowed—"

"That's not what I meant. But I know. I meant something's wrong here. We haven't been challenged since we left the garden. Don't you think that's odd?"

Brenish looked around the room, his imagination trying to see through the walls. "Not necessarily," he said, but with hesitation.

"Around Lowcastle men have fought scorpions and wolf-lizards. We haven't seen any. We haven't seen so much as a *cat* in hours."

She was right. Rats were the dominant creature here, but they shouldn't have been. Brenish was deeply unsettled by the realization, as much by the fact itself as that he wasn't the first to see it.

He stood with his torch and walked over to Gareth, who was listening with some fascination to Jase's and Dex's banter about mathematics. Gareth looked up. "Yes?"

Brenish again watched his tone to be sure he delivered his question the right way: "Can we have a chat outside?"

Gareth took a moment to interpret what that might mean, then stood. "Aye."

They stepped out past Finch and Harry, into the dead street that intersected the Road. The quiet was more disturbing now than when they had first arrived; Brenish wondered if there was any chance he too was afflicted by the deepsick, experiencing its early symptoms. But no, the fact of being under stone and so far from the world of light didn't bother him so much as this newest unease.

"I have a concern," Brenish said, very quietly.

"I'm listening."

"This is quiet for Lowcastle. 'Twas Cirawyn who said so, but she's right."

Gareth looked about the streets. Even the rats kept a low profile, but not in a way that suggested they were afraid of anything. "Hmm. Yes, though it does happen."

"We haven't seen any predators in some time. You're a hunter; you know more about these things than me. Does this seem natural to you, or should we worry?"

The question seemed to trouble Gareth more than he wanted to let on. He stroked the hair on his chin a few times, deep in thought. Brenish thought he was comparing the ruins to other places he had known, patterns that animals followed in their native environments.

"Nay," he said, "you're right. There should be predators."

"Could this be a sign the goblins have spread out farther?"

"Perhaps. But anywhere they spread far enough to eliminate predators, they should have an outpost. I would have expected to find them here if that were the case, but we've seen no sign of them."

Brenish wasn't so sure; he couldn't dismiss the scout he had found so easily. "This would be rather far east for them, but perhaps we should be more cautious on the Road."

"Far east, and far south, but you're right," said Gareth. "More caution is warranted either way. But I don't think it's goblins."

"What, then?"

"Something simpler. Not unlike a forest after a wildfire. There's been a disaster here; who's to say how long ago."

"Wildfire would be a trick," said Brenish. "What is there to burn?"

"That's the wrong question. The right questions are: What form did the fire take, and how was it put out?"

A Gauntlet of Jelly

After taking time to refresh and attend to other needs, the team was ready to depart. Gareth felt they were a little behind schedule and was anxious to get back on the road. He urged more caution to everyone, but didn't speak of Brenish's concern. Perhaps, Brenish thought, that was for the best. It looked like the deepsick cases were finally getting under control; he hated to make them worse, let alone spur on any new ones.

They came back to the main street and eventually picked their way through the debris of the bridge that had fallen. The streets remained fairly quiet, with no sign of goblins or even other adventurers who had perished here. Not that Brenish had ever heard of fatalities in Lowcastle, but he expected there had been a few. Usually if people ran into trouble it wasn't in the tunnels; it was in places like this. Yet Cirawyn was right: Nothing was lurking about that would endanger them. There wasn't even any scat, except for droppings from the few rats and lesser scurrying creatures.

The city ended in another tunnel, but the Road here made a curious change. After the usual set of outbuildings and roadside delvings whenever they were close to a settlement, the brickwork around the tunnel began to fade away. At first this came as gaps in the work. Here and there a section of tunnel wall seemed to have been left incomplete, exposing the roughly excavated rock behind. Wherever there would have been space behind the brick, it was filled in with some kind of spackle. Perhaps these gaps were places where a cross street had been intended but never dug, but there was no way to know. In these sections there was no roof either; nothing could have supported the arch.

During the next hour's travel the gaps became extremely frequent, to the point that in many places any brickwork to either side was halfheartedly done, ending just above head height where the builders would have had to prepare forms for the arched ceiling they never finished. The floor, too, had a rougher texture, as though it hadn't gone through as many passes of whatever art was used to smooth it. The ditches running alongside were often more suggestion than fact.

Brenish had known about this from lore, but now it made him seriously wonder: Was the finishing of the Wide Road merely an afterthought? No one could agree on where the heart of the Elder Kingdom lay, but it was widely believed to be to their west, or perhaps northwest where the goblins had taken over. There were some scholars of course who believed the Kingdom had its heart far in the east where the blood-drinking manthings—or twisted men—held sway. Yet the prevailing theory was that the ruins had not one heart, but several, and that being the case the closest was probably somewhere in the vicinity of the goblin realm.

Even so it made no sense to build nicer roads between cities at the edge of their territory, yet leave so much of the heartland untouched. Clearly the Kingdom had undergone centuries of development, experienced dramatic upheavals and shifts of power over generations. In spite of their love of stone they had recorded none of their history in any enduring medium; all that remained were the masonry and a few cryptic reliefs.

The rats didn't seem to like the change. Brenish noted fewer of them as they went on; the insects as well. Bats could be heard some distance ahead, probably in another tunnel or a ventilation shaft that was providing the air and, if it could be called that, the breeze that blew on their faces. The air was not stagnant, though it was warm.

The warmth made him think of other tales he had heard, gathered from distant places and only half-believed by those who told them. It had been said that some parts of the ruins were lit by fires in the earth itself, where deep chasms looked down onto lakes of fire that spat up toxic smoke, and heat that could kill from great distances. Though Brenish was educated enough to know what a volcano was, he knew there were none near him, which made it almost certain he would never see such a sight—even if he survived this trip. But it was also said that many of those places had since been blocked by flows of molten stone that hardened into black glass, closing off some pieces of the Elder Kingdom forever. The thought of missing out on them, no one seeing them ever again as even more of the Kingdom's history was erased, saddened him.

Over an hour from the city, the brickwork began to fail altogether. There was nothing like even the simple rib-like arches that they had seen when they arrived. The tunnel remained wide, the floor relatively even, but everything was rougher here.

"Do you ever wonder if the people who made this place weren't men?" said Bob.

"Not much," Gareth said.

"I thought since there are all sorts of manthings down here, maybe they made it."

"Any carvings that have been found always depicted men."

"Maybe the manthings are just crap artists, and men came later."

"Aye," said Gareth, "but that would still mean men lived here at some point."

"Oh." Bob thought about that for a few moments. "Guess you're right."

Gareth reached ahead to give his shoulder a sturdy pat. "'Twas an interesting idea, though. There was a philosopher who thought it might be true, but too much evidence stacked up against him. Then he was caught worshipping the goddess *Khamrol* and he got put to death."

Brenish had heard something of that, but he couldn't remember who had told him. He didn't know which was sillier: that a man would venerate the goblins and their false gods, or that the Church would bother dealing with him so harshly. Just because it was heresy didn't mean it was *effective* heresy. Besides, if a man was willing to jeopardize his soul that way, it was his own business.

Many mages—though not most—were heretics of one kind or another: One of their more popular beliefs was that the Creator made the world and set it on its way, intervening not at all in the affairs of men. One sect strongly believed that rifts in the void, connecting many worlds, were the key to understanding everything; though Brenish had never heard of a riftborn who was anything but human. Not of those who made a permanent home in this world, at any rate. Most Fae found the world of men uncomfortable on a deep level, and most men liked Faerie about as well. There were realms much stranger than Faerie, but little was known about them.

"Do you think our finding that scout was just a fluke?" said Harry. "We haven't seen any other goblins along the way. If they were expanding I'd expect we'd've seen more by now."

"That skeleton was a few years old," Brenish said. "Maybe they made a push, but pulled back."

"Wonder why," said Finch.

"Whatever it is," Harry said, "maybe it has something to do with why all the wildlife are spooked. Have you noticed that, Brenish?"

"We discussed it," Gareth said, not giving Brenish a chance to answer. "Something drove out the animals here a few years ago. They're all coming back. Maybe it was the goblins, maybe not."

"Is that what you think too, Brenish?" said Dex.

Now that was an odd comment, Brenish thought, from one of Gareth's men. Almost like calling the boss out. If the question offended Gareth, he didn't make a sound to show it, but Brenish would have to turn around to see his face.

"I'm no expert when it comes to wildlife," Brenish said. "Gareth and Harry would know better."

"I'm in agreement," said Harry. "Except I think something is still spooking them. How many rats have you seen in the last half hour?"

"A few," said Jase.

"Not as many as before," Finch said.

"Then keep sharp," said Gareth. "Whatever's spooking them, we're gonna spook it right back."

About four miles west of Lowcastle, Finch called for a halt.

"What is it?" said Gareth.

"A new smell on the wind. I can't place it."

Wind was a bit of a misnomer, but Brenish overlooked it. He sniffed the air himself. There was naught but the odors of men, the dusty, ancient scent of the ruins, the faint fragrance of Cirawyn's oils, and a hint of pipe smoke still wafting from Finch nearby. "Hmm," he said. "I don't smell anything."

"Anyone else got a good nose?" said Finch.

"Aye," Cirawyn said.

She stepped forward. Finch handed her his spell lamp as she walked by, and gave her room to get out in front of the party. Brenish felt his heart jump, in fear for her safety.

Cirawyn stood out ahead for a minute and breathed deeply. No one else spoke, as if she were listening rather than smelling. The air moving down the tunnel was by no means swift, and not even enough to really warrant calling it a breeze. It was a simple, slow current carried from above. A fell current, Brenish thought bemusedly. After it came down through a shaft somewhere, it mingled with the air in the caverns. Whatever new scent Finch had detected must be coming from somewhere ahead, unless it was just the smell of autumn leaves carried with the fresh draft. But then, Finch was woodcrafty and would have known that.

"Ed's right," she said, "but it's very faint."

"What does it smell like?" said Jase.

"It's… a little like herbs, but unpleasant. It reminds me a bit of eastern spices, but… nay. Perhaps an alchemist's shop. It smells a little like potionry, but not like boiling cauldrons, if you follow. There's a bite to it."

"Acrid," said Gareth. Brenish turned around and saw that his face was grave. Gareth and he had come to the same conclusion. "Like lye."

"Aye," she said, her voice brightening. "Not exactly lye, but 'tis close. Lye and spices."

"Damn," Brenish said. "Come back."

Cirawyn returned to the group and took back her torch. She didn't like the look on Brenish's face any more than the one on Gareth's. Everyone else seemed to wait for an explanation from one of their guides.

"Well," said Brenish, "there's your wildfire."

"They've no business in these parts," Gareth said. "I don't understand it."

"Nor I, but that's our lot. What do you want to do about it? Do we go around south through poorly charted areas, or north through goblin country? Either way we'll have to backtrack."

"No. We go through. I will *not* be turned away by that. A detour is too dangerous, and I won't risk going too far off the map."

"Uh," said Jase, "care to let us in on what's going on?"

"Something's up here that doesn't belong," said Brenish. "That's all you want to know. But I think 'tis best I take your spell lamp, for now. We'll need them at the head of the party."

Cirawyn showed sudden understanding. "Oh, damn," she said. She unslung her pack.

"What are you doing?" said Gareth.

"I'm getting out the spare torch. I'll keep it ready to light. Crossbows are no use here anyway."

Gareth smiled in true amusement. "Aye," he said. "Men, do just as the lady said. Except... Ed, Harry, Bob, and Naman. You four keep your swords out. Swords are of some value. The rest of you, be ready to draw swords if need be, but have an eye on your torches first. And no short blades."

"What about my whip?" said Tibs.

"Absolutely not," said Brenish. "Keep it stowed."

"So you'll not tell us what we're up against, then?" said Raden. "How'm I to know what to look out for?"

"You'll know."

Gareth was fixated on Cirawyn, to the point where he hadn't yet bothered taking out his spare torch. It wasn't attraction, just fascination. She was a puzzle to him, where he hadn't seen one before. "You seem to have learned a lot from your paramour," he said.

"We don't talk much about the ruins," she said.

"Oh? Dabble in lore yourself, do you?"

"Not as such."

Brenish tried to hide his grin at seeing Gareth's questions shut down. He didn't know himself whence Cirawyn knew of these things, but it was enough for Gareth to be piqued. Gareth resigned himself to not knowing, and slung his shield behind his back. It was partly metal, but the wood and leather parts would make it useless ahead.

Jase put his pack back on and traded his primary torch with Brenish. "Any other instructions we need before we head to our certain death?" he said.

"You could cinch up your cod," Turk said. Harry snickered.

"Aye," said Dex, "show some backbone."

"I'd just like to know what I'm dealing with," Jase protested. "No," said Cirawyn. "You wouldn't."

For half an hour they advanced, cautiously, the whiter gleam of the spell lights blazing their trail. The party was mostly silent. Aside from their fear, the air seemed to be getting worse. Whatever smell the wind had carried, it was the kind that could get lost over distances; closer to the source, it gradually became an irritant. The alchemical reek lodged in their throats, sucking the moisture away in a dust storm of pepper and cinnamon. Naman was the first to begin coughing involuntarily, trying to expel the noxious odor from his lungs, but it did no good.

There were no more rats, nor bugs, nor any other living thing. The road was dead, wiped clean.

As the smell became almost unbearable, the tunnel began to split off. Forks appeared off the main branch, almost as wide as the road itself. The tunnel walls widened, and soon they found the first of many open chambers, like a domed cave with many exits rayed out like a star. The first cavern was empty. It looked as if it was meant to simulate the appearance of a natural cave, but everything still had the hallmarks of being dug out by the same magic used to make the road. It was a primitive place, yet almost deceptively so, as if it had been dug for ritualistic purposes.

The western path of the Road was still clear; the exit on that side was bigger than all the others. The vanguard pressed on.

Two more star caverns lay along their route. At the end of the third, a sigil glowed blue where their lights hit it. The symbol was positioned on the cave wall next to the western exit, and was obviously a warning. The rough outline of a flame stood above a wide X: an admonition for travelers to light fire here. Whoever put it there must have done so only in the last few years, if Gareth was right, which limited the possibilities somewhat. Some adventurers were the type to pass along warnings to any who might follow; others minded themselves only.

Brenish turned and lit his spare torch with Jase's. "Light up," he said. "Think bright thoughts."

"I wish we were home," said Tibs. He lit his own spare as he saw others doing the same.

"Different bright. Anyone want to say us a prayer?"

"God doesn't listen to the likes of us, Brenish," said Gareth.

"I sure hope you're wrong."

Cirawyn looked up. "Lord Almighty," she said, "cleave us a path."

Several in the party crossed themselves. "Right," said Finch. "Let's go."

The last segment of tunnel was only about twenty yards long; it seemed like a mile. As they neared its end, the leaders saw vague movement in the cavern beyond. Brenish took the lead, insisting the others stay back. At the very end of the corridor, he thrust out the spell lamp and his spare torch, waving them back and forth, high in the air, then low to the ground in broad swoops. More movement followed, a slow scurrying that was hard to see.

The rest of the leaders joined him at the edge and mimicked his movements in the limited space.

"What are those?" said Raden.

"Keep aiming the light high if you can," said Brenish. "We don't just want to clear the floor."

The last cavern in the network had only two exits. Its floor, walls, and dome were covered with clear, shiny globs, each about pint-sized. They stood apart from one another, and they were alive: as the light neared them they backed away. The entire cavern seemed to be in motion, but the blobs nearest the travelers receded with haste.

Cautiously, fearfully, Brenish stepped inside. The others followed: first Raden, Finch, and Harry, then the others behind. The stench of spicy poison soap was everywhere.

"Clearly these are terrifying," said Jase. "It's moving snot."

"They're usually called jellies," Brenish said, "or puddings if you like. I always preferred puddings."

"And I'm a fritter man myself. What's so scary about them?"

"We may not meet a more dangerous creature on our entire journey. They usually only live in the deepest reaches of the Elder Kingdom, and they're seldom seen. I've heard stories about them you'll never want to know. They're aggressive, and relentless, but they do hate the light. And fire."

The party was still very near the doorway, moving only slowly. The puddings still oozed out of their way, dividing ahead of them. The ones on the ceiling seemed to avoid them as well, scattering to either side. It helped that some held their lights high, thanks to the iron poles the torches and lamps were built into.

"If they only live in the deep," said Bob, "what are they doing up here?"

"An excellent question," said Gareth. "I've been giving it some thought. Remember the drought we had three years ago?"

"Aye," Cirawyn said.

"I think it affected the flow of the deep river. That could have disturbed the puddings' food sources in the lower levels. One of them made its way up here, and they formed a nest. With so much to eat up here, their population exploded. Now they're declining again. Some may be migrating back to the deep. The rest are probably slowly dying off."

"That's great," said Jase. "How about we use the orb and come back next year, then?"

"They're moving aside," said Gareth. "Patience."

It took some time, but the company was able to make their way steadily forward, toward the far exit. The jellies that had parted for them closed back in behind, not so much in a menacing way as simply returning to their default positions. The adventurers had formed a loose circle, Cirawyn and Gareth still in the middle, with torches facing outward and in constant motion on all sides.

"Don't forget to keep the light over our heads, too," said Brenish. "The last thing we want is one of them dropping on us. Make sure they get out of the way before we get too far ahead."

"Why'd you want me to stow the whip?" said Tibs.

"They'll eat it."

Either the slow progress or the danger seemed to have roused the storyteller in Gareth. "There was a mage named Largus," he said, "who went into the ruins alone. Not recommended. He went south of the Gate, into the old mines. Deep into the mines, where there's still seams of gold to be had, for anyone mad enough to go. He met a jelly down there. He'd never seen one before, but he felt it was coming after him. It swallowed up his cloak he had left on the ground, and it got bigger.

"It split, and there were two jellies. It split again, and again. And they all came at him. He found out his sword would hurt them, but nothing worked better than fire. In desperation, he cast a spell. All his food was burned up, along with all his supplies. It took him five days to get home. He barely survived."

"Sounds like he did all right," said Bob. "The worst they did was eat his cloak."

"There are other tales," Brenish said. "They get darker."

Cirawyn nodded. "Morleth," she said.

"Aye."

"Do I wanna ask who Morleth was?" said Raden.

"Nay," said Gareth.

Jase sword under his breath. "We're gonna be rich," he muttered. "Rich rich rich. It'll all be worth it."

"They're following," said Naman. "No question. Getting out of this cave isn't gonna be enough."

"I hope Dobber's buddy didn't come this way," said Tibs.

"If he didn't turn around when Enzo bought it," Dex said, "he's a fool. I told him they were in over their heads."

"Surprised you even remember them."

"How could I forget? Dobber was hopeless with dice. Enzo was the only one of those fellows with a brain."

"Aye," Brenish sighed. "That's about right. You couldn't talk them out of going either, huh?"

"They were too eager. All I could do was try and part them from some coin."

That confirmed it for Brenish: Dex clearly knew something about the unk. "I never have the heart. How'd you fare with Enzo and Pines?"

Dex snorted. "Are you writing a book or something?"

"Thought I might."

"Just keep the snots back on your end. We got our hands full back here."

Brenish clenched his teeth in frustration. His guess had to be right, but Dex was too cautious to let his secrets go. Getting the truth out of him would take some time. Doing it without Gareth getting suspicious would be a thorny problem indeed.

"We're almost clear," said Finch.

A shout came from the back of the group. Naman's voice, not his girlish spider scream but a shout of surprise and anger.

Brenish couldn't turn to look; even if he did he wouldn't be able to see much past the others. "What's wrong?"

"They're none too happy with us leaving," Naman said. "I had to hit one with the torch."

"It isn't dead," said Bob. "Bubbly and slow though. It looks hurt."

"They can be killed," said Gareth. "It isn't easy. I'm just glad our torches are iron."

Raden was the first to make it to the relative safety of the western tunnel. When he was inside, he rushed forward to get out of the way of the others, allowing the remainder of the party to quickly escape. The rear guard kept their torches focused on the jellies, which were clustering thickly behind, risking injury.

Gareth took off his pack and dug out Dobber's oil bottle. "Ed, Brenish," he said. "More oil."

Brenish passed back a bottle of his own. "What I wouldn't give for a daybreak scroll," he said.

"Waste not," said Gareth.

Once he had collected enough oil, he stepped into the fray between Naman and Bob, kneeling down within the wall of torches. He poured out the oil in a line, making it as thick as possible. When the middle section went down he tackled the left side of the tunnel, then the right, until there was an unbroken line of oil from wall to wall, running a bit as it followed channels in the rock.

"All right," he said, standing and getting out of the way. "Light it, and let's double-time out."

Bob got his torch to the oil first. The rear guard all jumped back as a wall of flame came up. No pudding would dare cross it.

"Douse your spares," Gareth said. "Let's move."

The Aqueducts

Gareth's urging to a faster pace was a waste of breath. Everyone knew the firewall wouldn't last long and they wanted to be far, far away from the puddings when it went out. Brenish was concerned that they were still upwind of the things, but he had never heard of puddings stalking prey over long distances. With any luck, they would keep to their cave.

Beyond the cave, the Wide Road was but a hastily dug tunnel for a mile or more. The party crossed only one intersecting tunnel along that stretch, and then they were hemmed in again, their only options to go forward or back. No one would have opted to go back, even if Gareth were amenable to the idea.

Somewhere above, in a field or forest, the sun was setting. It was a depressing thought, even to Brenish. He tried to avoid thinking about it.

Eventually, signs of order and construction appeared again. An arch loomed ahead, and underneath it they found the Road looked much as it ever had. It was as if the star caves were a horrible sort of park, intentionally left fallow, between Lowcastle and the great aqueducts. The memory of the bare caverns that should have been proper road left a bad taste in Brenish's mouth, a feeling he had never felt before for the original denizens of the Elder Kingdom. It was something like contempt. It seemed wrong that anyone who could build this place would leave any of it unfinished, except perhaps at the periphery (if there was such a thing).

Gareth took the change as a good omen, and allowed the company to slow down to a normal pace. Several of the men took deep breaths. A sense of relief broke over the lot, though Gareth ordered the rear guard to keep watching for trouble anyway. He had allowed everyone to stow their spare torches, which had cooled, while still on the move; this involved a lot of passing things back and forth so people could get two hands free.

The fresher air was another source of relief. After attaining even a short distance from the cave, the sharp aroma of the blobs faded. Now it was a memory only. The air on their faces was scented with notes of dank, of mustiness, guano, rat musk, all the things they had come to expect, under the ever-present smell of antiquity that came from the brick and mortar and the foundations of the earth itself.

These tunnels were just as empty of vermin as the ones leading up to the caves, as though the creatures of the area had some knowledge of the danger behind and stayed away. The air currents didn't favor such a thing. It lent credence to Gareth's theory that the immediate vicinity had been decimated by the jellies, and other creatures were only slowly moving back in. This part of the Road, Brenish thought, farther from any food source for rodents and offering little for ants, must not have been reclaimed yet.

A new settlement appeared. It had no outskirts, opening suddenly from the tunnel. The only sign that it was almost upon them was a change in the shape of the tunnel itself. The barrel vault above became a series of groin vaults. Arches lined the tunnel walls to either side, so that it had become an open colonnade. Where the colonnade began, the stone floor was replaced with wide pavers in a diamond pattern of many different shades.

The front of the group approached cautiously, concerned that anything might still be living in this place, although the absence of rats was a good sign. Brenish peeked out into the darkness, and took a careful few steps off the road to his left. He was grateful to still have the spell lamp for better light.

The pavers continued out on both sides, a flat expanse that served as a town square. Though it was difficult to see far, he was able to barely make out a number of buildings to the south. Around its edges this city was built like Paddystock, but on a grander scale. Nearer at hand, other buildings of ancient brick were laid out in a rayed network of streets that all terminated in the square. The street construction didn't reach up to the distant cavern ceiling as in Lowcastle. As for the ceiling itself, Brenish didn't know if it was natural stone or if it had been cut into ribbed arches like in the garden, which seemed to support much bigger spaces. No one had ever seen the ceiling here at all, as far as he was aware.

Three round towers stood away from the colonnade, marching alongside it, and they were joined to it and to each other with enormous arches. He could see three towers along the north side as well. The tower furthest to the west from where he stood was damaged; its top and the upper part of a wall had crumbled. A number of stray bricks had fallen to the ground and cracked the pavers where they landed.

The air here was much fresher, fed by ventilation shafts somewhere nearby, though a steady current still came from the west.

"What is this place?" said Raden.

"Wootenghast," Brenish and Gareth said at once.

"Is that 'cause a man named Wooten croaked here?" said Bob.

"Aye," Brenish said.

"'Tisn't truly haunted, is it?"

Brenish looked back to see if Bob was joking, but by the look on his face it was a serious question. "Nay. There's no such thing as ghosts, Bob."

"So say you."

"Aye, Brenish," said another voice, hushed and with a tone of dread. Surprisingly it was Finch's. "Stick to what you know."

"I know there's no such thing as a ghost," Brenish insisted.

"You never were out in the forest much," Finch said. "There's things in the woods you don't know about."

"Aye," said Harry, with the same note of fear. "But we'll not speak of it."

"No indeed."

"Gareth?" said Brenish.

"I don't believe in ghosts either," he said, "but Ed's not one for flights of fancy, nor leaping to conclusions. If he says there are ghosts, he has good reason to. Still, it's safe to say there are no ghosts *here*."

"That's a relief," said Bob.

"Some places you find shimmers, though," Brenish said. "This is the kind of place they'd like. They play at being ghosts, but mostly they're harmless."

"I suppose we don't want to know what a shimmer is, either," said Jase.

"It's a wispy floating creature," Cirawyn said. "Like lots of strands of spider silk, in a loose netting. It eats dust and midges out of the air. It prefers dark, open places, and glows a little bit."

Bob piped up again. "You've seen one?"

"Nay."

"I don't see any here, either," said Brenish. "I imagine they'd be safe enough from puddings, if they didn't drift into one, but there don't seem to be any of them here now."

"What a sad place," Raden said. "How many people do you suppose lived here?"

"Thousands, most like," said Gareth. "Five or six thousands could live here easily enough, if they had the food."

"What about water?"

"Closer than you think."

Brenish took a last look and came back to the colonnade. "Shall we continue?" he said.

"Yes. We're behind schedule already."

The sight of real architecture had raised Brenish's spirits again. He felt confident in the front of the pack, although he was back to using a torch now. Jase, though no longer deepsick, had taken back his spell lamp. Now that he was back in his element, Brenish tried to turn his mind back to the tangled puzzle of how to deal with Gareth.

Very soon, Gareth would start relying on the map more, thinking ahead to the last puzzles it held and trying to work those out for himself. Brenish had never determined what Willy did to frustrate the map reader at that point, but he guessed it would involve going in circles or seeking a hidden door that wasn't there. The latter was likely; it was well in line with what Visak would have done. He believed, too, that there were several gaps in the map, places where the transition from point A to point B was little more than a bearing and a shrug. He would have to get a look at it again to be sure, but they had probably already passed quite a few of those gaps. The presence of familiar landmarks, making the gaps moot, would be enough to reassure most people.

All of this meant that eventually, the map would fail. Willy, after all, had no more idea where the treasure was nor the password to unlock Visak's overlook spell than anyone else. At best Willy might be able to make an educated guess at a password from the notes

Duggle gave him. The *general* location of the hoard was also something Visak had mentioned freely, though not often: somewhere in or around a city about a day or two west of the aqueducts. The city was suspected to be Shatterhelm, a known dragon warren in the past, but no one had been there in many years. Deepwater, a few miles north of there but much further down, was another popular theory. The map did seem to lead in their direction; Willy had done his research.

A part of Brenish hoped, against all reason, that Willy might have stumbled onto the right password by a combination of intense study, intuition, and dumb luck. Finding a place in a city where a dragon might have brooded might be easy enough that they could simply call out the password and the treasure room would reveal itself. Although Gareth would be annoyed that Visak had ostensibly screwed up the last part of the map, he wouldn't care with the treasure in his hands. It would solve so many problems if that were true.

Fatigue had set in among the party: not just their tired legs and feet, but the weariness of a long day. The Wide Road continued two more miles after Wootenghast, but those miles felt much longer, especially after the fast pace they took out of the star caves. Brenish heard Raden next to him breathing heavily, the big man's endurance flagging. Even Finch seemed to have lost a little pep. Conversation was minimal. Cirawyn commented about a mile along that she smelled water.

Water there was. It babbled softly somewhere up ahead, at first so quietly that it seemed another trick of their wandering imaginations in the dark. Harry was the first to confirm that he could truly hear it. After that it became persistent, a constant noise that while faint, almost seemed to disappear from sheer familiarity.

The tunnel came to an end. A dark wide space lay beyond.

The vanguard emerged into a great room. The lights they carried were feeble against the darkness here, but not wholly ineffective. Brenish could see much better than he could in Wootenghast where the walls were very far away. Their torches and spell lamps revealed two great waterways running north to south, at a very slight but visible grade.

Each aqueduct was two levels, supported on marching pairs of square columns joined by arches. The columns were easily four feet wide apiece, with several yards between them. The bricks they were made of were thicker than the bricks of the tunnels. Several huge arched spans joined the two aqueducts. Above the second level the pillars continued all the way to the ceiling, helping to support the space.

They were near the southern end of the chamber. Its northern end was lost in the dark. The only other exit Brenish could currently see was a doorway on the south wall, only barely visible, that was right between the middle two lines of columns.

The rest of the party shuffled in, staring in awe at the great aqueducts, which grew brighter as more torches arrived.

"Here we are at last," Gareth said. "A little late, but none the worse for it." If his words sounded disappointed, his voice was anything but. Brenish heard the edge of the Fell Current there, that same madness that hinted he saw this place as a child sees a sparse forest: a playground. "These are the great aqueducts of the Elder Kingdom, one of the most famous landmarks known to man. This is where I intend to make camp."

"Aren't we a little exposed here?" said Harry. "Meaning no disrespect," he added.

"Perhaps a little, but this is traditionally regarded as a safer place than most. We won't find any better place to rest for some time. Here at least we can see trouble coming. Naturally we'll set a watch."

Though sore and tired, no one seemed eager to set down their packs and rest just yet. Everyone's attention was on the huge stone structure, which captured their attention much more than the cities they had passed through so far. Perhaps it was the sound of the running water, perfectly clear now and impossible to ignore, reminding some of the river. It might have been the appearance of its massive bricks, which were made of a type of unpolished marble that was completely foreign to the region; it gave the aqueducts an alien quality.

"I don't even know what to think about this," said Bob.

"Me neither," Naman agreed. "I'll never forget this as long as I live. Not that I was in a rush to see it."

"Aye," Gareth beamed, oblivious to the rest of Naman's comment. "There's a wonder here. Stirs something deep down inside you. Till I saw this I didn't realize how badly I longed for it. 'Tis beautiful. Beautiful."

Naman gave Brenish a look of pure exasperation. Brenish understood his feeling about it, but he was just as moved by Gareth's words himself. And even Naman couldn't take his eyes off the spectacle for more than a few seconds; as soon as Brenish acknowledged him, he went right back to staring at the lines of the water channel.

Nobody was unmoved. Turk was rapt, lost in wonder. Harry slapped Finch on the back as they both took in the structure's tremendous scale. Jase, smirkless, stood next to Bob and Raden; though taller than they, he looked like the runt of the litter. Cirawyn walked up to one of the pillars and ran her hand along it, seeming distant. Brenish turned to his left as Tibs walked up; Tibs put an arm around his shoulder.

"'Tis truly something, isn't it?" Brenish said.

Tibs had a calm smile. "'Tis," he said. "I'll definitely want to remember this place."

Brenish smiled back, but it faded. There was something wrong about this moment between them. Something was off, he realized, about Tibs' demeanor. There was a coldness he had never known. His friend's hand on his shoulder felt jittery. For a moment he wondered if a spell might be taking hold of the party, something left as a booby trap by a powerful mage. He looked to the others, but their awe seemed genuine; the spell, if it was one, had a completely different effect on Tibs. That didn't seem right, either.

"Torch ready," Tibs whispered.

Brenish didn't have time to ask why. He didn't have to; a flash of understanding shot through his mind, and he knew what was about to happen. His brain was too slow to come to grips with the truth and decide on a course of action. Before he had even fully processed the situation, he caught the scent, suddenly strong in his nostrils: lye, and spices. And then the screaming began.

Dex howled at the top of his lungs, as a wild beast caught in a trap. He flung open his hands; a small shiny object fell out of one, his torch out of the other. He scrambled to pick the torch back up.

A pudding had crawled up his left leg, over the rim of his boot.

The entire party scrambled to action, turning their torches to the invaders. The puddings had formed into several larger masses, and were now separating again as they swarmed out of the tunnel. They moved quicker now than they had in the cave, as though their hunger had been stoked and could no longer be ignored.

Brenish drew his sword, at the same time thrusting his torch into one of the puddings. The beast bubbled and sizzled, and drew back wounded. Naman came up beside him; both hewed at the approaching jellies with their blades. The bite of the swords left lines of damage through the creatures' bodies, visible scars that seemed to slow them down, but blades weren't as effective as fire. The touch of flame, or spell light, left blisters and pockets of air and smoke. Others rushed up to help.

Dex's wail went up an octave and turned to a horrifying screech, as the pudding attacking his leg traveled upward and began to turn red, while at the same time it burned through the boot. Bob, in desperation, tried to attack it with his torch, but the pudding just shrugged off the flame; when feeding it was too difficult to kill. Jase got in close with the spell lamp, which seemed to work a little better, but the pudding had the upper hand—rather the upper thigh.

The attack pressed in hard, moving around the thin crescent of flames and threatening to flank the group. Raden and Turk tried to hold them back on the left, while Tibs and Finch did a little better containing them on the right. The only real advantage the men had was that they controlled the fire, and this time they were going for the kill.

Brenish finished off the first pudding he had burned, reducing it to a membrane that collapsed in on itself as the puddle inside thinned beyond its ability to stand up. Cirawyn hit them with quick jabs that did massive damage, one at a time, driving them back ferociously. Harry defended the middle, boiling anything that tried to come near Dex, who had fallen to the ground. More of them fell to the fires, but they kept coming, almost without end. It seemed the entire cave had emptied to follow them: hundreds of puddings, transparent with near-starvation and more than ready for a meal. And all the while, Dex kept screaming in mindless agony.

"Gareth!" Brenish shouted. "Do something!"

Gareth was already on top of the situation. Behind the line, Brenish heard him speaking in another tongue. He risked a brief glimpse back to see the leader of their expedition holding open a scroll. As the words were intoned the air grew brighter, like the glow of a distant forge. The sounds from Gareth's tongue took on a life beyond simple words. Reality bent inward, shifted, and was about to break.

There was a flash in the darkness. The scroll burnt up its energy, committing everything to the spell.

A light broke in the east, from the walls of the aqueduct chamber and even down the tunnel where the slime monsters were still coming out. But with the appearance of that light, they hesitated. It grew rapidly brighter, as a rising sun, until it was unbearable to the dark-adapted eyes of the company, and still it grew.

The puddings roiled and bubbled, like living soup that had jumped from the kettle too late. Their color went from clear to unhealthy yellow. Several of them popped violently, sending bursts of fluid out a short distance. Others were rent asunder like eggs left too long in the pot, shuddering and gasping steam, yet unlike eggs they spilled liquid innards out along the cavern floor and continued to cook.

The creature attacking Dex turned from red goo to brown goo, then splotchy black, as it gave up its essence along with its meal in the glaring light of day. Dex still screamed. Blood trickled from his open mouth.

Gareth was back in his pack, searching for the healing potion. But he was too late. Dex's cries stopped. His body, arched from spasms, went limp. His head lolled to the side.

"Don't bother," said Bob. Gareth had the bottle in his hand and was already getting up, but he stopped, frozen. He looked back as if waiting for confirmation.

Finch assessed the carnage of the battle, and took a long look at Dex. There was nothing to be done. "He's dead."

Part III

Greenskins

There are two kinds of creatures in the ruins: Some are bred for darkness, and have no use for light. For some of them it's fatal. But then there are those who need the light. Manthings among them: they use fire or spells when they can. Aye, lad, spells.

Both are dangerous. The dark creatures are at home there where you would not be. If your light goes out, woe to you. Most are unknown to us, and the unknown is a great threat.

But the other kind is deadlier still. For the animal you know under the sun may behave quite different under stone. Manthings are worse; the ones you must fear most are little different from men. Some may be smarter than you. If you challenge them on their own ground, they surely are.

The Day Watch

The aftermath was too much for Jase. He stood up and tried to get away from the rest of the party, to end up spewing across the smoking remains of the puddings. Turk put a hand to his heart in farewell. Even Naman and Harry seemed moved. Jase tried to wipe his mouth as his lungs began to make a series of whooping gasps, not sobs but raw panic. Cirawyn alone was stone-faced.

"Why wasn't anyone watching our rear?" Finch roared. "This shouldn't have happened." He glared at Tibs, who had a tear in his eye. Brenish tried not to scowl, wondering how much of that tear was rehearsed and how much was guilt.

"No, Ed," said Gareth, calmly. "No, let's not start that. Dexter was in the rear guard himself. There's blame enough to go round. And it's as much mine as anyone else's."

"Nay," said Tibs, "I'll take the blame."

"Pipe down, Tibolt. 'Twas my fault. I should've cast daybreak back in the cave. If I had done, none of this would have happened. And I brought him down here." Gareth faced Brenish. "You can say you told me so, this once. I won't take offense."

"It was only a suggestion. I didn't even know you had the scroll till you said as much back there. It was on my wish list, but you never told me what you bought. And besides, I agreed with your decision at the time. I'd have done the same."

"Forget about recriminations," said Finch. "I don't care whose fault it is. This cannot happen again. The only reason Dex is dead is that nobody was looking when someone should have been. We can do better than that."

"Aye," said Gareth. "And we will." He blew out his torch. The others took that as a signal to do likewise. There was no need for the extra light, with full daylight upon them.

Brenish looked back to the aqueducts, saw them shining gloriously in the false morning sunlight. The pillars cast long shadows to the west. The rest of the room was fully visible now. There were eight exits: one in the south that he had already seen, one on the far north wall, and three each on the west and east. The bauble Dex had dropped had rolled away toward the arches: a small glass ball about the size of a shooter marble or an eyeball.

Turk noticed the object too, and bent to pick it up. "What's this, then?" he said.

"Dex dropped it," said Brenish.

"Give us a look," Gareth said. Turk handed the item over. Gareth took it and held it out in the light, turning it round and round with his fingers. "Hmm. It's quite smooth. Obviously glass. It looks like a scrysake, but if it is it's unbound. I don't see an image here."

"That was my thought too."

"Seems an odd thing to hold in his hand. Perhaps it was only for luck."

Bob choked a sound of disgust from his throat. "Fie," he said. "What a waste."

"Aye," said Tibs, though only Brenish caught the intended double meaning in his swift agreement.

"We can't leave him here like this," Naman said.

"I'm afraid we'll have to leave him here," said Gareth, "but at least we can get him out of the open."

"I'll take him behind one of those pillars," said Tibs, pointing towards the southern exit. "Least I can do."

"Good idea. Leave his pack here. We'll divvy up his supplies."

Tibs nodded and pulled the straps off of Dex's heavy, limp shoulders. He tried to pick him up under the arms and struggled.

"Here," Brenish said, "I'll help."

"Thanks," said Tibs.

Each of them took an arm and dragged the corpse along the stone floor. A trail of blood and slime was left behind, oozing from the ruined leg, that thinned out as they got closer to their goal. They heard Jase start up his uncontrollable whoop again.

Brenish judged they were out of earshot enough when they neared the southernmost set of pillars. "Explain yourself," he hissed.

"Nay," Tibs said quietly, grunting with the weight. "I think I won't."

"I know the man was a blight and I knew you hated him, but he did *not* deserve that. And you put us all in danger to see it done."

With Tibs and Dex at the rear even after they arrived, all Tibs had to do was look back to see the puddings following. Dex had been closest to the tunnel still. It was easy to see how the opportunity had presented itself, but it must have taken only a moment for Tibs to choose silence. Brenish had never thought Tibs capable of killing anyone in cold blood, let alone in the space of a wink.

They rounded the first pillar and kept going, deeper into shadow. "I knew we could handle it," said Tibs. "And he did deserve it. Have you forgotten what he tried to do back in the garden?"

Brenish looked down at the man's face. It was not the face of a peaceful death. "God help me, I did," he said. "But he never got the chance."

"He never got the chance *this* time," Tibs spat. "You didn't know the half of what he was. If you did you'd shut your damned know–it–all mouth and call me a hero. Justice was done upon him. My conscience is clear. And I just gave *you* more options, so by St. George you're welcome."

Tibs had never spoken to him that way before. He'd never spoken to anyone that way before. Brenish refrained from saying anything else that might upset him.

They finally set down their load between the third and fourth pillars, where he would hopefully stay in shadow. They propped him up against the stone as if he were sitting. Brenish closed his eyes and mouth, and tried to rearrange his features into something a little less horrified; somehow he felt he should do that much.

"Most of his armor's good," said Tibs.

Brenish looked the man over. "Aye," he said. "The boots are a loss, and the greaves. But these will do." He started to remove the vambraces.

Tibs went right for the chest armor, pulling it off over Dex's head and interrupting Brenish's work temporarily. Brenish waited for him to finish; Tibs was in a mood that couldn't be argued with. This was a new side to his friend, an ugly one, yet he didn't doubt Tibs spoke true about having a worthy motive.

It was still murder. If Dex had gotten his way in the garden, perhaps everyone would have come to blows then. It would have been a massacre. But at least then it would have been provoked.

But nay, he decided, he had to let it go. Tibs was a good man. And in his place, Cirawyn would have done exactly the same thing. Brenish struggled with the thought that perhaps he should have entertained the notion himself, had he known about the puddings. The idea made him feel deeply unclean, like Dex's hair.

The armor finally removed, Brenish took off the right vambrace, then the left. Tibs held out a hand. "Options," he said.

The two objects in Tibs' hand looked like coins. They were dark blue and translucent, with ten flat sides instead of being completely rounded, and each had a round hole in the center. Brenish didn't take them. "I don't know any spells," he said.

"Doesn't much matter," said Tibs. He closed his hand, but Brenish was sure the spell tokens would find their way into one of his hidden pockets before the two men returned to the rest of the group. Tibs had no use for them, and probably trusted him to find a use himself.

They stood and rejoined the party. Jase had collected himself enough to go through Dex's pack, separating the supplies into neat little piles. Two things Brenish hadn't expected to see were a small vial of amber liquid and a scroll. Finch looked unhappy at the sight of Brenish and Tibs carrying Dex's upper body armor; Gareth didn't look any happier.

"What's this?" Gareth said.

"Shame to waste it," said Brenish.

Gareth merely grunted and turned back to Jase. His mind was elsewhere.

"I am not wearing that," said Cirawyn.

"Sorry, love, but you're unprotected. If I could find you greaves and proper boots I'd get those too, but this will have to do."

Cirawyn nodded to this, accepting it was the smarter choice, but she didn't like it.

Gareth still stared at the items in Dex's pack. "Aye, put them on," he said, not even looking. Cirawyn responded by rolling her eyes and, out of his view, biting her thumb.

"Who else is carrying scrolls?" said Brenish. "And which ones? This would be useful to know."

"None but me," Gareth said. "I *thought*. Ed's carrying a few items of use, but no scrolls."

"What do you suppose he needed a bottle of *esen* for?" said Jase. He was still emptying the pack, which at this point was only food and spare clothes. "He wasn't carrying a spell lamp."

"Indeed. Is the scroll labeled?"

Jase stopped pulling out clothing and picked it up to examine it. There was a wide white ribbon around it, with thin lettering. "Shop label," he said. "Mass protection."

"Well that would have come in handy," said Gareth. "Though it still might."

"That bag there," said Brenish, pointing to the pile. A little blue cloth bag with a black cord stuck out from under a thick woolen sock. "What's in it?"

Jase uncovered the bag and looked inside. "Empty." He looked over both sides. "Probably just a spare purse."

"Nay, I think it's a mending bag. That's what the *esen* is for."

"Mending bag for what?" said Gareth.

"The scrysake. To keep it intact. That's why it was in his hand when he died. He was trying to bind an image of the aqueducts to it. He wanted a memento."

"Dex was a fishmonger's son. He was a good fighter and a decent gambler, but he wasn't a spellbinder."

"Not in the guild, nay," Brenish said. "Before Dobber and Enzo came down here, I saw him sell something to Enzo. Wasn't on him when he died, but it was some kind of charm. I always wondered where he came by it and what it was. Now I think he made it."

Gareth squinted, perhaps in mild distrust. "You say Enzo didn't have it?"

"Nay. It was a little wood thing. Didn't get too good a look. Dex obviously expected Enzo would still have it on him, but Pines must have it."

Naman was trying not to stare, or pass it off as incredulity at the idea of Dex being an amateur spellbinder. (Although, Brenish thought, incredulity was probably a big part of it.) Brenish was back in form, spinning his maze of half-truths. His friends, except Harry who presumably knew nothing of the unk, understood perfectly what was going on. Hopefully Tibs understood, too, that this was an indictment of his decision to up and kill the man. Now Brenish would never know what the little owl unk was for, unless he stumbled on how to use it. It was only a guess that Dex had sold it to Enzo, but there was no other good explanation for it.

"Hmm," said Gareth. "It seems I underestimated Dexter. More's the pity. Maybe with an education he could have bound us something a lot more useful. Or saved me some money on the orb."

"I think we all underestimated him," said Brenish, "though you'll forgive me if I don't say it fondly. Seems he died loyal, at least. That must be worth something."

"Aye."

And that was it. No one else wanted much to speak of it, for differing reasons. Most of Gareth's men, Brenish guessed, didn't like Dex all that much either. There was a feeling—something he hoped he was reading in their body language rather than projecting onto them out of his own bias—that if anyone had to die, it may as well have been him. It wasn't a very comforting thought; if Dex was viewed as the most expendable, surely there must be a second-most. With all the time they'd had to think about it, no doubt everyone had a list in their mind of who they'd be willing to let go of, first to last, with themselves at the very end. Brenish thought he and Cirawyn might be the only exceptions, each putting themselves next to last.

"Nighttime," Jase grumbled. "We were supposed to stop for sleep. Now we have this spell overhead. We'll have to hole up somewhere else for the night."

"And waste all our fuel?" said Gareth. "Nay, we can sleep here, with our eyes covered. The watch will have a clear view this way. We'll rest here till sundown."

"This spell will last a good twelve hours."

"A bit less. But the better rested we'll be."

Jase walked away, dragging his pack toward the columns holding up the aqueducts. Gareth shook his head, perhaps out of consternation.

Brenish found Cirawyn laying out a bedroll, partly in the shadow of the pillars. She seemed to be neutrally affected, but he knew it for an act. He couldn't tell if that meant she was suppressing glee or anger, or some mix of both.

"Sorry, love," he said quietly.

"Sorry for what?" she replied. "For me being here? You said that already. If anyone's to blame for that it's Gareth."

"Or Finch, or Bob and Raden," said Brenish. "But I meant sorry that what just happened wasn't my idea."

"You wouldn't have done it unless you had to," she said. "I know that. You're too practical. We needed him down here."

"Aye."

"But I'm not sorry he's gone."

Brenish sighed. "Nor I."

Gareth decreed that watch shifts would be two hours. They drew lots, but in two sets: One for him and his men, one for his new employees (and hostage). That left one of the thieves having to double up, which turned out to be Naman on first watch. Gareth's men swapped places freely, Finch choosing to switch with Bob so he'd be on watch with Harry. Gareth made a swap himself, to watch with Brenish on the fifth shift, apparently not trusting any of his men alone with his silver tongue for two hours.

Sleep did not come easy. Brenish used his cloak as a cover for his own head and for Cirawyn's, to block out the light, and a blanket from his pack as a pillow. Yet it was warmer in the ruins than above ground, where the autumn had already begun to turn cool; the spell warmed them like a hot summer day. After so many hours of walking, the heat was perhaps most unpleasant of all. He kept his water bottle by his head and took a stale, lukewarm sip whenever he woke.

When Harry roused him for the watch, he saw that the light had shifted a great deal. The shadows of the aqueducts were facing east, and shorter than they had been. It was around mid-afternoon in spell time. Daybreak was only as long as an actual day; in summer it was stronger than in winter. High wizards of great renown had dedicated volumes of study to figuring out why, yet after a century they were little closer to an answer.

Brenish left his cloak over Cirawyn; as armor it might be moderately effective on him, but this was a watch, not a melee. He joined Gareth away from the others and sat with his back to him.

Gareth watched the southwest, Brenish the northeast. It was a reasonable arrangement.

For the first half hour they said little to one another. Brenish needed an opening if he hoped to draw Gareth into a stratagem; his employer—former employer, no matter how it went—was too canny by far to take him seriously otherwise. But this was his chance to plant some seeds, to get Gareth thinking along lines he could handle. *When* the map failed, he would have something to work with other than an enraged madman. Since Gareth wasn't talking, he took the time to go over the possibilities in his mind, to make the lies truth.

That was the key for Brenish: Whatever he said had to be true, somewhere. His mastery of artifice was less about outright deceit than stepping into another character, a different Brenish whose world happened to be more amenable to what he preferred the truth to be. There were thousands of him. Right now he only cared about a handful, each of whom had truly found Visak's map hidden in an old book, who would encounter different outcomes depending on how close their map was to the real thing.

"You've been quiet," Gareth said.

"Pondering," said Brenish. "What think you of the ruins so far?"

Gareth let out a long breath. It wasn't such an easy question for him. "I can't say. A man can only prepare himself so much. It's everything I expected, I suppose, but it's more real, down here. I never doubted the hugeness of this place, but to see it with my own eyes... 'tis humbling."

"Aye. It gives me a whole new respect for our benefactor. And to come here alone, that's brave almost to the point of madness. I miss the old man."

"I too. I'm sure he'd love to hear our tales."

"Wouldn't be so pleased about us taking his gold, though. But now that he's gone, part of me feels maybe he left it to us. We were the ones who took his words most to heart."

"'Tis a nice thought," Gareth agreed.

"Old Sully said he had a way. Maybe he meant for me to find the map, and you to finance our way down. What better way to bring his two best students together?"

"The same idea came to me. I never much believed in coincidences. But some say Visak was a seer."

"Wouldn't have figured you to believe in seers," said Brenish.

"Eh. I keep an open mind. Met a riftborn once who claimed it was rubbish, but he said his world belonged to a different time. If rifts can cross time, why not a man's mind?"

"A rift inside a mind would be mighty fatal," Brenish mused. "You know, I'd bet there's some down here. Maybe that's where the Elder Kingdom went."

"Or where the deep monsters come from. Nasty thought."

"Aye. Well, if Visak knew what he was doing, I'm sure we'll figure out the rest of the map without any trouble. Have you made any new discoveries?"

"No time. I want to sit with you and work on it later. A few riddles were giving me trouble."

Brenish put a thoughtful nod into his voice. "You're not alone there. Even if he did mean for us to have it, we're gonna have to work for it. Visak was too sneaky. I have a bad feeling he threw in a little joke or two to keep us guessing."

"Aye, that would be like him. Still, I'm sure we'll crack it."

"Aye."

Brenish let the notions simmer for a minute. Gareth needed a little time to take them in, but the best way to force a lie down was to wait for just the wrong moment and *choke* it down. He knew Gareth didn't completely trust him, because Gareth wasn't a fool. He couldn't approach this entirely from a friendly angle.

"Back in the garden," Brenish said. "Did you truly entertain Dex's suggestion?"

Gareth took his time replying. "You know I have to keep you on a leash," he said. "I won't tell you the thought never crossed my mind, even before he said anything."

"It wouldn't have gone well."

"Nay. Most of my men were against the idea. You handled it well. Gave us both an out that we could live with."

Brenish smiled. Except for taking blame for Dex's death, this was as close as Gareth usually came to admitting wrong.

"Of course," Gareth added, "I'll do whatever I feel I need to. As long as that leash stays slack, I won't need to do anything. I prefer we get along here."

"The point was well taken."

"Then we'll speak no more of it."

But he would think of it. That was the point. Gareth had to be unsure, always, which Brenish out of the multitude he might really be dealing with. If the question of keeping the thieves in line consumed him, the truth of the map would not.

They went back to long stretches of silence, broken mostly by idle questions or spot checks to see if the other was still awake. Brenish took out his little book and started writing down the events of the day, the things they had encountered, and his impressions of the ruins so far; he felt he owed it to the next generation. Another hour passed without incident, and their watch together drew near its end. Gareth kept pulling out his expensive timepiece to check, as if he was unsure of his own ability to keep time.

"Wait," Brenish said suddenly. He sat up straighter and shook his head.

"What do you see?"

"Nothing. But..."

Gareth waited for him to say something else. "But what?"

Brenish shook it again, more vigorously, but the feeling remained. There was a pressure from outside: something that made him want to pop his ears, and his navel. "It's a twisty feeling. Do you feel it?"

"Nay. All seems well to me."

"Something's wrong. Just to be safe, we should—"

Pop.

A powerful jolt shook the room, not physically but on a level that could be felt only with the mind. Gareth reacted too, seeming to feel the event itself even if the build-up was lost on him. And the invisible sun, the daybreak spell, raced untimely toward the horizon that wasn't there.

Spellbreaker

"The torches!" Brenish shouted.

Gareth was already two steps ahead of him, running for his pack. The light failed completely before either of them got there.

"What's going on?" said Finch. He sounded annoyed but not groggy.

"Spellbreak," Gareth said. "Find your packs, light the torches. We need to move, *now*."

Brenish tripped over someone in the dark and landed hard on the floor. He heard an *oof* that sounded like Jase. The sudden pain in his arms and the stinging scrapes on his hands seemed worth it.

"I can't see a blessed thing," said Naman.

"Find a torch and light it," said Finch.

"I'm not a cat."

Gareth managed to find his pack; this was evident immediately when he flung it open and weak light came out. Brenish was just standing up when this happened, and got a brief look inside the top compartment. (Gareth's pack had three.) There were several potion bottles, two of which gave off very faint spellglow in rose and gray-violet. The most powerful spellglow came from the teleportation orb, a glassy sphere about the size of an apple, which gleamed yellow-white through mottled, slowly moving swirls beneath its surface. The pack contained several scrolls, though no wands; Gareth must have kept any wands on his person, which made good sense. The only other item Brenish could see was a piece of folded spell paper with Visak's handwriting. It looked like the map, but it was not; the writing was little more than geometric diagrams with short annotations, absolutely nothing like the writing and drawings on the map.

No wonder Gareth hadn't wanted him getting into his pack. There would have been no reason to worry about Brenish stealing from him when he would obviously be caught, but he clearly didn't want those notes discovered.

Brenish turned away before Gareth noticed, and found his own pack in the dim light. It was enough to get out his own torch. By the time he managed, Finch had lit his own spell lamp. Gareth shut his pack. A few torches lit up. The party was in chaos; some were only just waking up.

One of the early torch-lighters was Cirawyn. She brought Brenish his cloak just as he lit his own torch. "What happened?" she said.

"Spellbreak."

"Spells don't break on their own."

"Indeed."

Finch moved into a position where he could monitor the north entrance. "Nothing yet," he said. Brenish doubted he could see any light there, but it was the most logical direction an attack could come from. An unfamiliar object was in his weapon hand: some kind of censer. It couldn't possibly be any use for seeing foes far-off.

"Pack up," Gareth said. "Be quick about it. We leave through the near western door. Ed, Harry, take the rear guard with Bob. Tibs, Naman, you're up front now."

"Aye," said Tibs. He rubbed his head sleepily and tried to hurry packing up his bedroll. "What broke the spell?"

"Goblins, most like," Jase said. "Though this is outside their territory."

Gareth pointed to Jase's own bedroll. "Pack faster."

Brenish tried to make himself useful by helping Tibs with the rest of his things. "Spellbreaking isn't scout's work. They must have a mage with them."

"Aye, which means a large party. They must be close, to have seen the light."

Tibs pulled on his cloak and Brenish handed him the pack.

"All right," Brenish said, "Naman, Tibs, Raden, follow me."

Brenish ran headlong for the near arch before waiting for anyone else. The tunnel outside the aqueduct chamber was still the Wide Road, a familiar sight of brick walls and a vaulted ceiling running straight as far as his torch would show. He kept going for a long way, far enough to get some distance from the chamber. Gareth and the others, he knew, wouldn't be far behind.

Raden caught up to him first, then Naman, followed by Tibs who was out of breath. "Why are we stopping?" said Raden.

"We'll wait for the others."

He turned around and saw more lights coming up the tunnel. Cirawyn and Gareth were the next up, with Jase jogging behind briskly. Behind them he could see four lights in the distance, but couldn't tell who they belonged to except that Finch's spell lamp was pulling up the rear.

"We're here," Gareth said. "Hold a moment."

Harry and Bob came at a dead run, just behind Turk. The three men practically crashed into the rest of the group, stopping short. Finch followed with no less speed but stopped a few yards back.

Working quickly, Finch did something to the censer that caused it to belch forth a thick black smoke. The smoke spread rapidly out as he swung the censer in wide circles. He reached to one side of the tunnel and held the censer there, where the smoke seemed to want to cling to the walls, and then began to move it through a huge arc, reaching as high to the ceiling as he could. When he was finished, the smoke in the middle already seemed to have formed into a smooth surface, a wall of cloud.

Gareth kept his hand up for silence until Finch was done. The fog became denser as it settled, and the wall of fog became one of pure black nothingness. Light didn't penetrate it at all. Nor, Brenish knew, would sound or scent.

"How many?" said Gareth.

"Not sure," Finch said. He sounded rattled, though not winded. "They didn't get to the chamber by the time we left. With any luck the mist will keep them off our trail for a short while. It won't hold them long, especially if a mage breaks the mist too. We need to move."

"Aye. Double-time forward."

The party needed very little encouragement. They set off as fast as they could, almost running, as they had when escaping the puddings. Unsuccessfully escaping, Brenish reminded himself. Goblins—they all assumed it was goblins—were smarter. The dullest of their kind might be fooled long, but it was unlikely the expedition would have taken any exit but two: the southernmost door to the west along the Wide Road, or the door running south to follow the aqueducts. A concealment mist wouldn't be enough to stop a determined group of greenskins.

There was every reason to believe the goblins would follow. It was their nature. The ill-tempered manthings were territorial and extremely violent, even when dealing with each other. Against anything that wasn't a goblin, they were ten times worse. Although tales and fables exaggerated and ascribed the worst traits to any creature considered a foe, Brenish had heard enough stories to understand there was more than a glimmer of truth to such things.

Their run slowed to a jog rather quickly as they tired. Gareth let them continue so, for fifteen minutes. Then he called a brief halt.

Finch took out a silver pendant flute with too many holes. He placed it to his lips without covering any of the holes, and blew loudly into the mouthpiece. A jarring note played: a sound of pipe-horns and screaming infants and badly tuned lutes, of stone scraping across glass, of crows gone shrill and ghosts cackling right behind the listener's head. Brenish set his teeth. He glanced at Naman and felt a dim desire to strike him with the torch, but it passed as soon as it came. It wasn't meant for him.

When the spell passed over him, Brenish felt relief—not least because it would protect them, but because it was one of his ideas that Gareth had accepted. A discord organ was the perfect way to deal with a rabble of goblins, or indeed any significant number of foes. The enchantment would settle into the tunnels behind them, an invisible menace until the nasty creatures turned on one another. Hopefully the carnage would be severe before the goblins managed to break that spell too; or better still, perhaps their mage would die in the melee.

Finch put the instrument away, and Gareth ordered them to resume their jog.

They made it about another mile before everyone began to tire, and their pace slowed. Side tunnels appeared again before long, a chance for some misdirection. Finch laid down another wall of mist in a southbound street, far enough that it might be convincing but close enough that it would seem suspicious to the passing goblins. Much further ahead, he made the mist again.

Another hour they walked, tired from their earlier exertion but unwilling to take a rest. Finch had low expectations for the mist, and said so. Gareth and Brenish were in agreement. Running wasn't much of a choice, but so far it was the only good one they had. Their best hope was that the goblins would eventually be satisfied they had chased the invaders off, and go back to their business.

But, Brenish thought, what business could that have been?

"Gareth," he said, "why would a goblin mage travel as far south as the aqueducts? I can't shake that thought."

"Nor I," said Cirawyn.

"More scouts, perhaps?" said Gareth. "None of the likely answers seem encouraging."

"We knew they sent out a scout to Paddystock," Harry said. "What's so strange about a mage at the aqueducts? We're closer to their territory now than we were."

"Closer, but not within it," Brenish explained. "Not unless much has changed in the past few years. Yet the pudding outbreak should have held them back."

"Perhaps they're sending larger parties," Naman offered.

"Goblins only gather in numbers when on the attack," Cirawyn said, "or when safe in their own realm. Their mages have always been few; those would be protected, not used in an advance guard."

Again Gareth shot her a quizzical look. Her body of knowledge made little sense if she hadn't learned these things from Brenish, but Brenish had told the truth about that: they discussed the ruins little.

"A binding, then," said Jase. He didn't sound like he believed it. "If a scout had a tool that allowed him to break spells without being a mage himself…"

"I've never heard of such a thing," Gareth said. "Spellbreaking is an art. Maybe a cluster-fire approach would handle most common spells, but it would be expensive to revive a binding like that. There's no question we escaped a mage."

Bob *hmphed*. "Would that we had one," he said.

"We practically did," said Naman.

After a minute's brooding silence among the group, Turk spoke. "Is there a death benefit?"

"Pardon?" said Gareth.

"If any of us don't make it. What happens to our kin?"

Gareth took a moment to respond, as if he hadn't thought of this before. Brenish thought that extremely unlikely, given Gareth's planning so far, but then again Gareth's chief concern had been survival. To move Turk to more than two words, it had to weigh heavily on his mind—a fact even Gareth could appreciate.

"Half a share," Gareth said. "But Dexter had no family."

"Settling his debts would be enough," Naman suggested.

"Indeed."

"I've no family either," said Jase, "but I left a will before I came. It's in my room back at the manor."

"Then I'll honor it, if it comes to that," Gareth said.

"Thank you."

"It won't come to that. But we have to get away from this madness first. I fear we could be driven off our route by these blasted greenskins. I had hoped to consult with Brenish on the map long before we reached our destination. Indeed I had planned it even before we left the aqueducts."

"They haven't given us a lot of choice yet," said Brenish, "but the time will come soon when we'll need a better plan, unless they give up the chase."

"How far do we have to go before that's likely?" said Raden.

"Ever wondered what it would be like to see Vinland?"

"Aye." It was rare in Eswell, and rarer still in Ilyenis, even to meet anyone who had been to the Vikings' far land across the sea. After a few seconds, in which Raden apparently waited for Brenish to say something else, he finally got it. "Oh."

"Hopefully once we get to Candlestead we can review our options," Gareth said. "I'd prefer to avoid a fight if we can, but maybe that isn't possible."

The heart of Candlestead was little more than a small complex at a waymeet. It was a building with several levels above and below the road, serving as a marketplace or plaza in a past age. The main chamber was a perfect square, and its center was open space for more than three levels up. An elaborate chandelier had once hung from the ceiling, but now it was nothing but old black iron, a skeleton of its former glory. The eastern tunnel emerged under a covered walkway that ran the room's perimeter, held up by groin vaults supported by thick square pillars. The arches these formed were repeated on the second level, and on the third. The town must have been impressive in its day.

The only thing in the square, besides a scattering of bones, was a raised pedestal that might have held a statue once; it was empty now. This place had once been bustling, but now its only visitors were manthings, explorers, and the beasts that preyed on them both. The town was silent. The only noises they heard came from further onward in the ruins, through the western and northern exits.

"All right," Gareth said, "let's take a moment. If we can hide somewhere around here for a few hours, the goblins might pass us by or go home. I hate the delay, but better to be safe.

"Brenish, take Bob and Turk and explore the lower levels. Be quick. Be back here in five minutes with your report. Harry, Raden, you do the same as a separate team. Third team will be Cirawyn and Jase."

"What?" said Jase.

"I don't work for you," Cirawyn said.

"Just get it done. You obviously know aught about the ruins. If you want to risk someone you care about getting hurt, you go right ahead and do as you please."

She gave him a loud, exasperated sigh and rolled her eyes, but grabbed Jase by the collar and pointed where she wanted him to go. Brenish smiled, but he wasted no more time.

Inside the walkway there were frequent doorways and empty shop stalls. Stairwells were easy to find; there were several of them, each with a spiral design. Brenish led his team down the first one he spotted, which emptied into a long hallway with many rooms on either side. After the tunnels they had traveled so far, this hallway, no smaller than many he had known in the city, felt close and confining. The Wide Road had been built for horses; these alleys below Candlestead were built for men alone.

He kept a silent count as he went from room to room, a trick his father had taught him. Thirty seconds. Thirty-one seconds. Bob's chain mail tinkled softly in the dark. Forty-three seconds. He found the broken remains of a chest, looted long ago. Seventy-one seconds. More empty rooms. One like a small house, two little rooms clearly meant for habitation. It might do.

"What are we looking for?" said Bob.

"Any place they're not likely to look," said Brenish. "Big enough to hold us, big enough that a concealment mist won't be easy to spot from the hallway." He was already headed to the next room, wider than some of the others he had seen so far.

"Was this a table?" Bob said, pointing to some wooden debris.

"Good eye. And that was a hearth. This was a kitchen."

"Still is," Turk said.

Brenish was about to leave the room, but he turned back around. "What?"

"Those ashes are fresh."

He went to the old hearth to take a closer look. There were ashes in it, but they could have been quite old. They were cold, at any rate. But he put his nose up to the shallow pit and sniffed: the smell of a fire was still there.

One hundred sixty-nine seconds. One hundred seventy.

"No one's been down here in weeks," Brenish said. "This smells fresher than that. Maybe just a few days old. I wish I had Tibs here, or Harry. They could tell us for sure."

"So not Pines, then?" said Bob.

"Nay. Nor Giacomo, Henri, Tanner, or any of the others who came since. A man didn't make this fire."

He looked around the room a little more and found some old bones shoved in a corner: Large lizards, a few rats. Dried-out piles of filth were close to them.

"They've been eating here. This must be a frequent travel stop. It just makes no sen—"

A loud, shuddering scream cut him off. A man's voice, being ripped from his body.

Bob and Turk were up the stairs ahead of Brenish, looking out for the danger. When they all got back up to the main level, he saw Cirawyn and Jase coming out of another archway, looking perplexed. Finch and Gareth ran into a third stairwell. Brenish sprinted past his companions to follow them. Another voice screamed repeatedly from that same direction, but not in pain.

The bottom of that stairwell was not a hallway, but a hall. It was not unlike the great room back at the guild's headquarters, except that it was empty and undecorated. Yet its walls to the left or right weren't there; it was as a very wide city street, curved away from the stairs so that it seemed to go on in a circle around a large building in the center. Through that building's door, Brenish saw a torch and a spell lamp, and followed them.

The building was some kind of temple, a place of worship. Stone benches fanned out on both sides of a wide aisle. The benches were cut from the same stone as the chamber, in one piece, and shaped to high precision. The only brickwork at all was in the doorway behind him. He kept following the light, up a few steps at the room's far end, and on into a smaller doorway that led into a short hallway. There he saw four lights, but one was on the ground.

He passed the doorways to either side and came up right behind Gareth, whose helmet and shield were recognizable even from far off. Gareth had a hand on Raden's broad shoulder to steady it; he could see Raden was shaking again. For a minute Brenish thought it might be the deepsick returning, but then he saw Finch's spell lamp drop to the floor, and understood.

Finch wept, and his grief was a terrible racking bellow such as Candlestead had probably never heard. It passed over Brenish like the hot blast of a furnace, an angry mountain wind, or a sheet of solid rain in a great summer storm. But nature was nothing next to Edward Finch, and deep below the earth no fury was his equal.

Brenish shouldered his way past Gareth to see what had happened. The entrance to the small chamber at the end of the hallway was half-blocked with five vertical spears, heavy spikes that had come down from above, through the bricks in the door's arch. It was no artifice of the Elder Kingdom, but a goblin trap through and through. And at the floor, pinned to the ground and stuck through three points of his body, was Harry Card.

"'Zwounds," Brenish said, nearly choking on the lump in his throat.

Finch went wild with rage. As he mastered his grief enough to stand, he sheathed his sword and pulled from his pack—without first unslinging it—a hand-axe with an edge that gleamed like diamond. He hacked at the iron bars of the trap, cutting each one away from its housing near the top. The bars came away cleanly, glowing yellow at the tips where they had been sliced. Finch pulled out the ones that had impaled Harry, and flung them aside.

Gareth put a hand on Brenish's shoulder now, as if to warn him not to intervene. He needed no such warning.

Finch snatched up the spell lamp and barged into the chamber. In the light it was clear enough what it was: a shrine to one of the goblins' heathen gods. An idol of polished stone stood silent there, wide mouth grinning back with doubled fangs and an expression that humans would interpret as clownish, though it was probably meant to be fearsome. Brenish didn't know the thing's name nor what powers it was supposed to have in the goblins' chief religion. Perhaps none; maybe the goblins who had put it here were heretics among their own kind. Why else would they have a shrine out in the middle of nowhere? Then again, why did the goblins do anything they did?

The hand-axe flew. Again and again Finch hewed at the abomination that had brought about Harry's death. Sparks and embers scattered throughout the room, and barely would they land before more joined them on the floor. Great chunks of rock broke asunder, cleaving away from the bulk of the idol as Finch sloppily dismembered it and hacked its trunk to bits. Were the idol an actual god, Brenish thought, it would have fared no better against him.

Whatever the axe had been intended for, Brenish was sure this wasn't it. The spellbinding that made it so sharp against metal and stone was being used up, slowly, for what Gareth would consider a trivial purpose, yet the boss didn't dare say a word about it.

At last the shrine was dashed to pieces, a strewing of rubble whose pieces hardly resembled its original form. Finch's rage seemed to abate a little.

"We found evidence the goblins have been coming here regular," Brenish said. "This must be why."

"Indeed," said Gareth.

"You know what this means, though."

"Aye. It means we're not dealing with a mage. We're dealing with a priest. God help us."

"God *will* help us," said Finch. He walked out of the shrine room with his anger on simmer, bubbling at the surface but cooling no further than it already had. "They've naught left to help them."

Brenish looked to Raden and saw he was pale and sick, trying to pull himself back together. It wasn't the deepsick, just shock. He felt for the man.

"I suppose we can't hide now," Gareth said. "They'll be furious when they find their shrine has been desecrated."

"Well," Brenish said, "we probably have a few minutes to come up with a plan. Not much more than that."

"I already got a plan," Finch said.

"Will I like it?" said Gareth.

"You were concerned they'd chase us off our course. I'll solve that problem for us. Good enough?"

Whatever Gareth's feelings about being spoken to that way, he always gave Finch special license. A lot of that was the man's unrivaled competence. The rest might be his age; at thirty-six, Finch was older than Gareth. The boss's response was soft-spoken, even kind.

"You have my full support, Ed," he said. "Just so long as we don't forget why we came here. Don't let it be in vain."

"Aye," said Finch, exhaling part of his anger with it. He took in another deep breath, and let it out just as slowly. "Aye."

Vengeance

The enemy had been on their heels the whole time. That much was clear now, for their arrival came less than a minute after Finch declared all was ready. Their throaty, phlegmy voices gargled their way noisily into the ringed street outside the temple, even before the manthings reached Candlestead's square. It was impossible for Brenish to count the voices; it could have been as few as half a dozen, as many as a score. They all sounded alike, lots of *glob-glob-glob* and *chark wark shark* that was unintelligible to any but the most learned linguists—although he supposed a tonguestone would do the trick.

There were a few variations in the voices to be sure; these became clearer as the goblins advanced. Some were gruffer and drier, some smooth and sharp, some wet like stomping in muddy rain puddles. In pitch they ranged from bearlike to burly. Several of the voices were joined in a single chant, over which a lone voice intoned a crooked kind of song, always seeming flat or sharp to Brenish's ears.

The voices got closer. Flickers of light appeared in the stairwell. Brenish, hood drawn down to the point that he could barely see, watched from the darkness of a side room. He felt especially vulnerable, for he could still see himself, Tibs, and Finch as clearly as he could see anyone else. The small sip of glowing rosy potion that Gareth had granted each of the forayers was enough to make them fully invisible, but not for very long. Gareth gave them their doses with a little cup he had been carrying around, then put the bottle away and extinguished the last spell lamp the moment they heard voices. At this rate the effect might last another twenty minutes or so, after which the men would slowly fade back over the next hour.

Even though Brenish had seen Tibs and Finch disappear, and saw them reappear after he took the potion himself, he still worried they could be seen. Perhaps, he thought, it was because some creatures of the deep had voidsight. Such gifts could be bestowed any number of ways: by potion, by spell, by spellbound jewelry or garments, even (he had heard) by diet.

Being an expert in ruins lore meant having a little bit of knowledge about all sorts of disciplines: potionry, weaponry, armor, the types of spells used in scrolls, spellbinding, basic survival, and—useful to the moment—creature lore. Goblins weren't known for voidsight, but a goblin priest was a rare and unknown challenge; they were seldom seen by adventurers who lived to tell about them, and even more seldom challenged and defeated. In the past century, only three parties had reported dealing with them; two escaped detection, and only the third risked battle and won.

It was largely for his understanding of goblins that Gareth chose Brenish for the mission. That, and as a thief he knew aught of moving silently. With his smaller size he stood a better chance of getting in close without detection than Naman, who was heavier in his footfalls even when sneaking about. Tibs' proficiency at maintaining silence was never questioned; Gareth knew his skill set.

The first of the goblins to appear were clearly guards. They came two by two, weapons sheathed and talking quietly among themselves. Evidently the priest didn't require their silence. They wore iron chain mail, high leather boots, plated vambraces, and iron helmets. The few places their skin was exposed it was gray-green and rather hairy, though no hair but eyebrows grew on their faces. The guards carried only light packs. They walked casually into the dark street at the bottom of the stairs, and continued into the temple without stopping.

Just behind them came the priest. His station was clear from his robes, which were fiery red and magnificent dark blue, embroidered in gold-colored thread with a great turtle as seen from above. The turtle's back had a hollowed-out oval space, where there was a large and many-branched tree. This was something Brenish had heard of, but scholars he had asked about the goblins had never been able to tell him much. It laid to rest the idea that they were heretics among their people, though; he at least knew that the tree-turtle was a common religious symbol, and this group's finery and riches alone said they enjoyed strong support back home.

The priest carried a long wooden staff, overlaid with gold in a pattern like tree roots that grew thicker as it neared the top. The head of the staff was solid gold but for its very tip, where it encaged an emerald the size of Dex's scrysake. The emerald alone would set a man like Brenish up for life, especially without needing to be fenced. He knew the staff was basically just decorative, unless it had been bound with a specific spell like a wand. Wizards loved to carry staves mostly for three simple reasons: Staves helped them aim directional spells; they were a mark of the profession; and they looked intimidating. This wasn't a well-known fact to the layperson.

Visak had never used a staff. *It's beneath me. Not worth the weight to carry, and I got better things to do than look fancy. Fanciness is for second-raters, lad. Mark that.*

After the priest there were clerics, or acolytes: four of them. Brenish preferred to think of them as a religious flavor of lackey, the Bob or Jase to their Gareth; he wasn't sure which group came out worse in that comparison. The chanting lackeys wore simple hooded robes in a gold color, with leather belts. They had no other armor.

Behind them were three large goblins carrying supplies in heavy packs, wearing only light armor. And then there was the rear guard, only two more like the bruisers in front.

The final count did not come out in the party's favor.

Tibs was the first to leave the safety of the side room, before the back of the procession had even made it into the temple. He crept up silently behind the rear guard and readied his first crossbow; he carried a second so he could get another shot off quickly. Finch was right behind with two crossbows, and had a wand in his pocket. Brenish followed last, with only his short knife in one hand and a charm hanging by a thong around his neck; no one trusted him with a crossbow.

The priest yelled in swift anger. He could not have seen the damage done by Finch, but what he did see well enough was another concealment mist halfway down the little hallway behind the dais. Goblins being a touch thick on the best of days, even the priest would think the adventurers were hiding behind it. The idea that they were in there, defiling his holy place, stoked his temper.

Brenish had only moments to rush into the temple. The six guards, roused by their master's ire and the imminent threat, ran up the stairs to the dais and into the hallway to help. He followed as quickly as his feet would take him without making a sound. He was halfway to the steps when he heard the priest raise his voice again, this time in command and power. At the steps, and the words of the spell wrapped their hold around the air. The three baggage carriers rested on the steps or on the benches, oblivious to his presence but concerned at what might be going on. Again Brenish felt the sense of something about to tear, as he ascended the last of the short steps and got a clear view down the hallway.

For a very long second his gaze was fixed at the torchlight and its bearers, as if time had slowed. His invisibility would withstand the spellbreak, being potion-induced, but he shivered in anticipation all the same. The guards and the acolytes waited, weapons ready, to press the attack against whomever was behind the barrier as soon as it went down. Rushing through a concealment mist would deaden their senses briefly, if they tried it; it was usually considered unwise, even by goblin standards. They dared not fire any weapons through the mist, however, because their shrine was there. Therefore no attack could begin until the priest finished his spell. It ended on a high, striking note of power.

The concealment mist disappeared in a puff. Behind it, torches shone out at the goblins.

Brenish put the discord organ to his lips, and blew into the hallway with the force of a gale—or so his lungs felt. The layered notes of distrust, fear, resentment, jealousy, bitterness, greed, contempt, misery, and blind hatred pounded down the tunnel and stampeded everything in their path. The spell shattered senses where it went, burned tempers down to the core, and called all swords to action. The priest, utterly apoplectic with fury at seeing his beloved god of goofy sneers demolished, was too slow to stop it.

He heard a crossbow bolt fly and hit its target behind him, then another. As he watched, the goblins before him tore into each other. The priest tried desperately to master himself while fending off his own kind. Brenish blew into the silver instrument once more. Loyalties were rent, oaths broken, familial ties cast aside in madness as the horrid music thundered upon them. The note was sustained and powerful, as cruel to the ears as to the soul. Even Brenish had a hard time listening to it, but he was protected from the spell itself by virtue of wielding the organ.

With that last long burst, the binding gave out. The magic within the organ fell apart and all that remained was a shrill whistle, which he ceased.

He stepped away from the tunnel and turned to deal with any surviving pack mules, but all three lay dead. Finch and Tibs hopped onto the dais to join him, and observed the chaos beyond.

One of the goblin guards nearest them seemed to be holding his own, so Tibs let fly his whip long enough to stun the brute, who was then stabbed in the eye by a cleric. The cleric was in turn run through by another guard, who turned back around to deal with the others. Yet in the inner chamber, the priest was no slouch in battle: He held his fellows at bay with his staff and a sword, and despite his great anger he recognized what was happening. After all, they had encountered the discord spell before.

The weighty growl of the spellcaster's voice rose up to begin his incantation.

Finch drew the wand from his pocket and fired down the hallway. A long jet of flame burst out of it, searing any who remained in the tunnel. Those who survived the blast still tried to fight each other, badly burned though most of them were. The voice broke momentarily.

Though the counterspell was aborted, the priest was not one to give up easily. He shouted a single word that hit sharply like a cracking stone, and whatever that did broke the discord as effectively as his original plan. The goblins snapped out of their fit of violence and reacted at first in shock.

Finch fired the wand a second time. All that remained now were the priest, and whoever had been fighting him in the inner sanctum. Brenish caught a glimpses of them as they peeked into the hallway long enough to see who might be attacking them. They obviously saw nothing. It was a single acolyte, and maybe one or two guards.

Suddenly there was a flash of red and blue: the priest. Brenish, Tibs, and Finch all dove aside just in time. A powerful bolt of lighting shot out of the hallway and into the temple, barely missing them. For a moment Finch considered firing back, but another bolt tore at them and he was forced to back away.

"Now what?" Tibs said.

He and Finch were on the left side of the archway, Brenish across from them on the right. Finch reloaded both crossbows while he crouched, and tapped Tibs to let him know he should do the same.

A third bolt erupted. It was hard to tell if its origin was any closer, or if the priest was just taking random shots from the doorway at the far end.

"Why are you asking me?" said Brenish. "This is his plan."

"Shut up, both of you," said Finch. "Let me think a minute."

Brenish didn't actually hear the last part, and had to fill it in within his head. The discharges still came at them. The other goblins could be using the gaps between lightning bolts to advance into the hallway, using the little rooms to either side as cover. Finch was a strategist, and had to know that too.

Finch and Brenish stood at the same time, having the same idea. They readied themselves to run.

The next blast came. Both men leaped into the tunnel.

One of the guards was on the move. Finch shot him down.

As soon as he reached an opening, Brenish ran inside. The cleric was there, hiding behind the doorway and waiting for another chance to move. He seemed to hear Brenish's footsteps come in, but saw nothing. Acting boldly and quickly, Brenish stabbed him in the throat and sprang back. The cleric fell dead.

He looked back through the open doorway and saw the last guard on the opposite side. The guard cried out in surprise and turned to run back down the hall toward the priest. The lightning had stopped. While he decided whether to give chase, he heard a sound like an arrow in flight, and a heavy thump. Tibs appeared in the hallway.

"Come on," said Tibs.

Brenish followed him out, both walking unimpeded now to the end of the hall. The priest couldn't stop them anymore; he wasn't dead, but pinned down on the ground. He grappled with Finch's unseen hand around his throat. Every time the priest tried to grab his staff or any weapon, Finch used his free hand to wrench the crossbow bolt that was lodged in the goblin's shoulder. If the priest tried to speak, Finch tightened his grip and twisted the bolt again.

"Aren't you going to finish him?" said Brenish.

"Get me one of those rods," Finch commanded.

Tibs ran to the back of the chamber and found one of the sharp iron spikes. It still had Harry's blood on it. This didn't seem to bother Finch, who accepted it gladly. Still holding the priest by the neck, he dragged his quarry around the floor till he found a good spot, then jammed the dull end of the rod into a seam between two stones leftover from the base of the shrine.

Finch was stronger than he looked, and his hatred gave him a strength mortal man wasn't privy to. He lifted up the goblin by its neck, forcing it to stand. When it stood he jerked the manthing from its feet and raised it over his head, as though the goblin weighed practically nothing. The force of his rage brought the priest down onto the same spike that had murdered Harry, impaling the screaming manthing from the crotch to the upper chest.

The goblin made wet choking sounds. Its head lolled forward. Silence fell.

Brenish was afraid to let out his breath, lest he disturb that moment. Finally Finch let out a breath as well, softly through his nose, and they knew their mission was complete.

"Give Gareth the all-clear," Finch said.

Tibs ran from the room to give the others the good news. Or to get away from the carnage. Brenish wanted to join him. He turned his gaze from the mangled goblin to Harry's body, lying still behind the remains of the shrine where they had dragged it.

Finch began systematically stripping the goblin's corpse of all its jewelry. That wasn't going to go into the common treasure pool—not that there was ever going to be one anyway, Brenish reminded himself. Anything of value, except the robes and the ruined garments, Finch took. Doubtless he intended to keep the staff as well. Doubtless Gareth would do nothing to stand in his way. He looked at the priest's face and paused in contemplation.

"Have you any pliers?" said Finch.

Brenish felt as if the blood had drained from his face. "Nay."

"Guess I'll have to do this the hard way."

"Good work, men," Gareth said. He was looking at the wrong part of the room, trying to guess where Finch and Brenish were. Evidently the items Finch had taken had been absorbed into the spell that hid him. Tibs was near the back of the pack where he would be out of everybody's way, since they couldn't see him either. He was holding his spell lamp again, but it illuminated naught but himself.

Finch bent over Harry's body and gently removed his eye patch.

Gareth's eye tracked the movement. "I think Harry will be at peace now," he said. "We should gather up his supplies and anything we can find off these swine, and get moving."

"Aye," said Brenish.

Finch opened Harry's pack, resting beside his body, and looked inside. "Blood's got to the food, and his water bottle's punctured. Still has lamp oil."

"That's too bad about the food," Gareth said.

"I don't suppose we can salvage the cloak," said Brenish. Gareth looked vaguely in his direction. "But his greaves will do. Fi— Ed, do you mind?"

"Go ahead," said Finch.

On his way over, Brenish saw that Tibs was busy looting the corpses before the others could get to them, out of view of the rest of the party, tucking his trophies away inside his armor where they would fade almost instantly. He guessed Finch was too busy to notice what Tibs was up to, and didn't have a good enough view to see anyway. Having an invisible master pickpocket seemed like a wasted opportunity; besides Finch, only Gareth was likely to be carrying anything else of interest, and they'd both know if something went missing.

The greaves came off without too much trouble. None of Harry's blood had reached them; it had basically all pooled in the cloak and soaked into his clothing. The boots wouldn't fit Cirawyn, though.

"I think Cirawyn should take his crossbow too," Brenish said. "That way she'll have a spare."

"As you like," said Gareth.

Most of the party diligently searched the dead. Brenish watched them as he returned. He felt that if anyone was likely to have anything useful besides the priest, it would be one of the clerics. Of course the supply carriers might have all kinds of goodies, but he expected to find mostly food and water. The water would be too heavy to carry but they could at least replenish their own supplies with it. Goblin food would probably be inedible.

"Wow," said Bob. "Those disappear fast."

Brenish guessed by Bob's eyes that he meant the objects in his hand. "Huh. I thought 'twould take longer."

He walked carefully to Cirawyn, trying to avoid bumping into Jase, and took hold of her hand. She let out a startled gasp but quickly realized it was him. He placed both of the greaves in one hand, and then took hold of the other and gave her Harry's crossbow.

"Put those on once you can see them," he said.

"Aye."

"I found a potion," Turk said. He pulled a glass vial from the body of a badly charred acolyte. "It's blue."

Gareth took hold of it, uncorked the bottle, and sniffed. It was blue, but dull, like the sky after sunset. Bubbles erupted beneath its surface, rose, and popped, without end. "Interesting," he said. He took a sip, as a gamble; it was unlikely a goblin cleric would carry poison. His eyes turned right to Finch, then to Brenish. "Heh! It's voidsight."

Brenish burst out in laughter. The sound carried with it the release of all the horrible tension he had built up since before the battle. Even with the bloodied, toothless body of the priest gaping nearby, he felt relief in the humor.

"What's so funny?" said Turk.

"He didn't use it," Brenish said. "It might've ruined our whole attack if he did."

"Here," said Gareth. "Take a little sip."

Turk wasn't one to pass up a free drink, so he did as he was told. When he handed the bottle back to Gareth he exclaimed, "Oh!"

Brenish smiled. It was amusing seeing Turk with an expression on his face, though it lasted all of a blink.

"You look like ghosts," Turk said.

"If you drank more you'd see us clearly," said Brenish.

Gareth noticed the wand sticking out of Finch's pocket. "How are our tools?" he said.

"Used two shots on the wand," said Finch. "Organ's dead."

"Pity. That'll be difficult to restore."

"You have that scroll," Jase suggested.

"Only if we need it. Though 'twould be fitting that an unintended gift from the goblins should revive it." He seemed to take stock of the priest's staff for the first time. "That staff is quite a treasure," he said.

"I'm giving it to Eddie," Finch said. "It'll be an heirloom."

"That's a good idea," Gareth replied, without hesitation.

"Does that mean we get trophies for the goblins we killed, too?" said Tibs.

"Are you asking my permission to keep what you've already taken? I'm not a fool, Tibolt. But consider permission given. Whatever you found, keep it."

Tibs swallowed meekly. "Thanks."

"I don't think this is very fair," said Jase.

"Quit whining, Jase," Naman said. "You already got something."

"A lousy helmet!"

"A lousy *silly-looking* helmet," Turk said. "Was it truly *lousy*?"

"What? Nay, of course not. Any lice would've been long-dead."

"Why are you itching your head?"

"Shut up, Turk." Jase didn't like that he was so suggestible.

"All right, enough," said Gareth. "Let's get moving. Anything else useful on the bodies?"

"Naught on the priest but his robes and jewelry," said Finch.

"I found a knife I like," Raden offered.

"All right, then we're done here. Let's grab the rest of their supplies and get out of Candlestead. We'll leave Harry to his rest."

Jarrett's Folly

The party had to be rearranged again. Finch stayed on the rear guard, trying to keep out of the way of Bob and Naman until they could see him again. Tibs remained with the vanguard. For the time being however, Brenish and Tibs kept well ahead of the others, and Turk was temporarily up with Raden to make sure he could warn the others if the invisible thieves came to a halt. The potion was stronger than Brenish or Gareth had anticipated: Half an hour after the dose, everyone who took it was still unseen.

Gareth's next immediate goal was to get everyone to a relatively safe place where they could rest properly and take lunch. Or breakfast. Except for the battle, everyone had been on the move since suddenly waking just a few hours before. No one had taken the time for a meal. Brenish felt his insides rumbling a little, but that might just have been nerves. He didn't feel all that hungry.

In spite of the fact that their pursuers had been annihilated, Gareth was restless. It wasn't just his lust for the treasure driving him on. He knew, as Brenish did, that if goblins were comfortable traveling in these parts and kept an active shrine, the priest might be discovered at any time. If so, every goblin in their vicinity would rise against them. These particular manthings had ways of passing news that befuddled even great scholars; there was a small chance that others already knew what had happened.

Even if they didn't have that to worry about, ordinary greenskin travelers could still pose a threat. So far they had been lucky, and seen none. But the faster they gained distance from goblin territory, the better off they would all be.

The only living thing they saw after they left the town was a ravenous furry beast like a tusked boar crossed with a jackal, that ran at the party from up ahead in the tunnel. It didn't see Tibs, or his whip, both of which were still invisible. It yelped once and then fell still. The rest of the party walked around it as it bled out of the wound in its neck. Scavengers and bugs would carry off its remains; the large tunnel ants were incredibly efficient. Hopefully they would do that quickly, lest the party leave a trail for any avenging goblins to follow.

"What do you think of our options now?" Tibs whispered. Being so far away from the main group, he and Brenish had a rare opportunity to talk.

Brenish had already been wondering this for some time. With Harry counted among their group, Gareth might have taken a lighter hand when he inevitably found out he was never going to get Visak's gold. The best-case scenario Brenish had been musing on was that he could talk Gareth into going after a treasure pit, in exchange for merely wiping out their debts but giving them no share of the treasure. The latter would have been made to seem like Gareth's idea. Without Harry that was a lot harder to sell; Gareth had much less reason to be lenient with the others. And even if Gareth could be talked out of anger, Finch was another problem entirely.

"We're in pretty bad trouble," Brenish said back, keeping his voice down so Turk or Raden couldn't hear.

"Why?"

"Because I couldn't figure out the whole map. I don't think Gareth can either. Maybe we'll strike some luck in Shatterhelm, but the city doesn't exactly have a reputation for that. Deepwater's no better."

"I doubt we'll ever be in a better position to act than we were back there. I don't especially want this to come down to a fight, though."

"You and me both," said Brenish. "I just wish I could get a good look at Gareth's notes."

"What notes?"

"He has some of Visak's writings in his pack. I only got a quick peek back at the aqueducts. Maybe there's a clue there. Whatever it is, he obviously doesn't want me going near it."

"I'm sure he's just protecting his potions and scrolls."

"I think you're wrong," said Brenish. "Too bad I can't get more than a glimpse of what he's keeping in there."

"I wish you'd've said something earlier. I could've done something right after the battle."

"It wouldn't have done much good anyway. I need to study those notes, not just peek at them. I'd need at least a few minutes to memorize what I saw. Without those papers I'm not sure we can complete the riddles on the map. With them, I might be able to come up with another option."

"Maybe you're not giving yourself enough credit," Tibs said. "You and Gareth are both pretty smart. If that map was meant for you, I'm sure you'll get it. I mean, I think you're worrying over a fallback plan for nothing."

"Naman would disagree."

"Cirawyn wouldn't. She has faith in you."

"Aye. Makes me finally realize why her dad didn't want me around."

Tibs had nothing more to say. He'd have to think of more ideas on his own, but Brenish didn't put a lot of hope in him coming up with anything new. Tibs was still under the delusion he would leave the ruins a rich man. That was such a hard notion to shake, even Brenish had to keep reminding himself over and over that the whole expedition was a sham. All he could do was stall, but stalling hadn't done anything so far but get two men killed.

Brenish tried to push his problems to the back of his mind again. When he wasn't trying to lie on the spot, he did his best thinking there. He focused on the Road instead.

There were large sections now with no bricks at all, and in these places bunches of mushrooms appeared along either side of the tunnel. There must be water nearby, he reasoned, but they were some distance from the aqueducts and farther still from the deep river. Another stream, a tributary of the river perhaps, must have run above or below them. The walls and floor didn't seem especially moist, though.

Once, a furry scavenger appeared in the road. It was about as big as a cat, but looked disturbingly like the giant thing that had attacked Turk in the garden. It startled at the company's approach, and took off running when Brenish drew near. It could see him.

"I know everyone's hungry," Gareth said. "Jarrett's Folly is near. We'll stop there and take a rest."

"Do I wanna know?" said Bob.

"Nay," said Cirawyn. "Though I've a mind to tell you anyway."

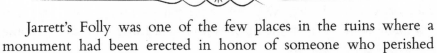

Jarrett's Folly was one of the few places in the ruins where a monument had been erected in honor of someone who perished there. It was usually difficult to scribe anything that would endure, as that required a chisel, a hammer, and time. Someone had taken a shortcut long ago with a spellbound stonecutter's pencil, etching out the unfortunate story on a square pillar with a pyramid spire, about twice as tall as a man.

The only writing readily visible on the obelisk, as originally carved, was the name Jarrett Fell-Hand. A depiction of his final battle showed a mighty swordsman overmatched by a beast taller than himself by half. It had claws like a scorpion, three eye-stalks, ten legs, and a long spiked tail. No one had seen a creature like it before, or since. In lore it was simply called the Aberration, or Jarrett's Bane, regarded by some as more myth than fact. Brenish knew better than to discount such myths. No one had seen a monster that size in these parts for generations, but their experience with the jellies proved they could take nothing for granted.

The monument stood in the center of a cavern that was dug out as a large space, partially finished by the Elder Kingdom's builders, then left alone. Half of the room was crude, the other half cut smoothly, its doorways lined with perfect brick arches. Gareth pointed to one of those as their temporary rest site.

Brenish was too busy studying the standing stone. Up close, it seemed more people had scrawled on it. Graffiti going back a few hundreds of years was etched into each side. He went around in a circle, trying to make out the names of—

Visak.

"Oi, Gareth," he said. "Have a look."

Gareth, whose curiosity was easier to arouse than his greed and could be depended on to overrule his stomach, came right over. He looked right where Brenish was pointing.

"W and G?" Gareth said.

"Nay, next to it. Here." Brenish stabbed his finger toward the stone again, at a faintly luminous symbol, a semicircle crossed by a bisected angle.

"There's naught there."

"I see it plain as day. It's Visak's mark."

"I see it too," said Tibs. "See? This is a good sign."

"Did the voidsight wear off already?" said Brenish.

Gareth shrugged. "It must have. You've been about half here the whole time. Do you see it too, Ed?"

"Aye," said Finch. He came closer and leaned in with his staff, the spell lamp affixed to it with leather thongs taken from the goblins.

Brenish nodded to himself. So the mark was written in some kind of magic that was only visible to the invisible, or those gifted with voidsight.

Many thoughts crashed upon him. First, Visak had once come this way. It wasn't much of a surprise, but it was reassuring. Second, knowing it was here would further convince Gareth that the map was the genuine article. He couldn't have prayed for a better piece of evidence. But best of all, the fact that only the unseen could see it gave him the seeds he needed to sow in Gareth's mind.

"I wonder if we missed any other marks like this," he said. He put his hand on the rune. Seeing it reminded him of the old man as he had known him.

Gareth waved a hand. "Not important. We have the map."

"Maybe the map makes reference to them. These marks could be a vital clue to the last riddles. What if we miss one? What if we've *already* missed one?"

"You aren't seriously suggesting we backtrack all the way to the Gate, are you?"

"Nay, of course not. But now I'm concerned. I wish I'd been able to solve the rest before we came."

"We'll have another look at it before we leave here," Gareth said. "I'd like us to share our insights from here out."

"Aye," said Brenish. He took his hand off the stone and walked away.

He followed the others who were already headed into the doorway Gareth had chosen; Jase and Naman led the way. Cirawyn came up beside him and gave his arm a squeeze. He looked at her and smiled. She smiled back, but he saw in her eyes that she still saw through him. She knew he was holding something back, and the fear of missing invisible markings along the way was partly false. Only partly, because just then he believed his own words more than not. If Visak had placed any other marks around, it could be enough to make a lucky guess at the hoard's true location. All Cirawyn knew was that he had told Gareth another partial lie; she didn't know why. He was determined to withhold that as long as possible, lest she worry.

The room Gareth picked was actually a two-room house, with a hearth that was no longer in use. The back room was occupied by a large lizard who was none too happy to leave, but nevertheless did so without a fight after Naman slapped it with the broad side of his sword a few times. Everyone was in a hurry to get out the food; Brenish felt his own stomach rumbling and realized it had been a while since he'd eaten anything. Gareth insisted they all eat in the same room, using the back as a latrine only. In spite of that the seating wasn't crowded at all. Brenish sat by Cirawyn and his friends again.

The meal was much better than any they had had so far in the ruins, for the goblins were better stocked than they had anticipated. The greenskins' supplies had included several bottles of rather excellent red wine, which might have been intended for sacraments. (Brenish of course wondered where they grew the grapes.) The party had also acquired a few wheels of semi-soft cheese coated in wax, a bag of apples, hearty brown bread, butter, and a jar of honey.

The relief of finally sating their hunger improved the company's mood. It was almost too easy to lay aside the frantic morning, or the disaster in Candlestead. Brenish found it harder than most to let go of those events, having participated in the counterstrike. But nobody seemed to take it harder than Finch, who had only a little wooden plate full of plundered food and his own bottle of wine as a consolation. Brenish felt sorry for the man; having grown up envious of Finch's relative success in everything else, this was new.

"Good to see you two again," Naman said.

Brenish turned to face him. "Hmm?"

"I can see you. You haven't faded back all the way, but you're getting there. What's it like being invisible?"

"The same as being visible," Tibs said, "except everyone bumps into you. Bob hit me in the jaw with his big elbow."

Bob reached over and slapped a hand on Tibs' shoulder. "Sorry, mate," he said.

"'Tis well. You couldn't help it."

Turk laughed at something Raden said. Bob turned around again, perhaps in surprise.

Brenish grabbed his group's wine bottle and took a swig. It paired deliciously with the cheese. The cheese had a very mild flavor, but was saltier than many he'd eaten. It was quite good, considering its origins. Perhaps if the goblins opened up trade routes, he thought, there could be peace with them. Then again, they probably wouldn't forgive the destruction of their shrine anytime soon.

"I can't wait to see real daylight again," said Cirawyn. "What think you, perhaps one more night here?"

The direct question caught Brenish off guard, but he tried to field it well enough that she wouldn't see any hesitation. He nodded, lips still around the bottle, and put the bottle down. "Aye," he said. "I think we're headed for Shatterhelm. We can probably reach that by tomorrow. Hopefully we'll rest before anything else."

"Aye," said Tibs. "I could sleep again already."

Naman didn't say anything. It was better that way; he looked bitter about the position they were in, especially that he had to keep hiding it from Tibs and Cirawyn.

At least, Brenish thought ruefully, there was no more need to wonder how Harry would take it when he found out.

He turned around to look at Finch. No one sat with him, whether out of habit or fear he didn't know. He decided to change that. Perhaps this was an opportunity to gain an ally. He stood up, and planted himself again by the senior henchman.

"I'm sorry about Harry," Brenish said quietly.

"Leave me alone."

Brenish didn't get up again. He took a bite of an apple and waited Finch out. Half the time that was all it took. Getting someone to accept a brazen story often required getting them to open up a bit first. Silence could be as effective as words in those times.

Finch was more patient than most, but eventually he decided to try harder to make Brenish go away. "Harry never liked you."

"Aye, he was pretty vocal about it. But for what it's worth I liked him. I respected him. He always found us work."

Finch grunted and ate some more. Maybe that was some kind of acceptance. He chewed in silence for a minute or so, taking another pull off the bottle and a couple of mouthfuls of bread and honey. But something in the man's will bent, and he paused in the middle of a bite. It took a moment to recover, before he swallowed and spoke.

"I don't know how to tell Maddie," Finch said.

"She grew up with you both, didn't she?" Brenish said.

"Aye. Aye, she did. We were inseparable, at your age." He took another drink and wiped his mouth. "I think Eddie will understand. I hope he will."

"He's a good lad. How old is he now? Eight?"

"Nine. Three weeks ago. Harry made him a bow. They were gonna go hunting again, when the deer got thick."

Finch was about to say something else, but it choked off. He clenched his empty fist. His breath stopped briefly, then came out in a slow exhale with a single silent hiccup.

"I'd be happy to go with him," Brenish said. "Perhaps he could teach me to shoot straight."

Finch's answer was hoarse, but there was a partial laugh somewhere in it. "Can't nobody teach you."

"You're probably right."

Finch downed another mouthful of food, and sighed. "I didn't tell anyone yet, except Harry, but Maddie's expecting again."

"No kidding? Congratulations."

"It's a difficult birth at her age. At least we can afford a doctor and medicine if things go wrong."

"Are you hoping for another boy?"

"Old Hilda says it'll be a girl. She's never been wrong."

"Well that's great, Ed. Another child is a lot to be thankful for."

"Aye. Except she'll never know..." He stopped, and clenched his fist again.

"I'm sure Eddie will tell her all about Uncle Harry," said Brenish. "Good stories. She'll get to feel like she knew him."

"I hope so. He'd've liked that."

Brenish slapped Finch's arm and got up to return to the others. He smiled at Cirawyn when he sat down.

"This is what I like most about you," she said.

Naman worked a belch into a grunt, with an intentional sour note. "He's a regular saint." Cirawyn gave him a look of mock-disdain and stuck out her tongue in response, but the extra helping of sarcasm wasn't lost on Brenish.

Cirawyn pulled out one of the candles from her pack, a thick red one. "Can you spare me a leaf of your book, love?" she said.

"I tore some rags from the goblins' clothes," said Brenish. "Let me get one out."

"Not for the privy. I want to make a rubbing from the stone before we leave here."

The notion baffled him. A rubbing would be of more interest to a man like himself, or a scholar collecting material for a book, than to her. "What for?"

"Never you mind," she said slyly. "Will you give me a leaf or no?"

"If not for love, for curiosity alone," said Brenish. He took out his little book and turned to the end, where the pages were all blank. "Have as much as you need."

Cirawyn pulled a single leaf free of the spine. "I need only one."

She stood and headed for the door, but Gareth spoke up. "Oi," he said. "Where do you think you're going?"

"Just to the stone."

"Use the back room."

"Nay, for a rubbing." She moved the candle back and forth across the paper.

"Not alone. Jase, go with her."

Jase froze with his hand in his mouth, apparently hoping that if Gareth saw he was eating he'd withdraw the order.

"I'll go," said Turk.

Jase finished his bite and then pretended his mouth was too full, slapping Turk on the leg as he walked by.

"When you're done eating," Gareth said to Brenish, "we should look over the map."

"Let's have a look now."

"All right. Outside."

Brenish walked out first. It would give Gareth a chance to get the map out from wherever he was hiding it, and therefore one less reason to distrust him. But he knew he had to get another look at Gareth's extra notes. Obviously those were papers Willy hadn't had access to. If they weren't enough to reveal any clues, at the very least Brenish would know what information Gareth was working with. He hoped he might learn something to his advantage. Gareth obviously was concerned enough with that possibility to keep the notes guarded.

While he waited for Gareth, he saw Cirawyn make a rubbing against the pillar while Turk held both of their torches. She seemed interested in some of the graffiti. She looked over long enough to flash him a smile, so he returned it.

"Here we are," said Gareth. He held the folded map in one hand and a spell lamp in another. It made sense to use the better light for reading. He leaned his lamp pole against the stone and unfolded the paper.

"I haven't seen this in a few days," Brenish said. "It might take a minute to get my bearings."

"We're here," Gareth pointed. "See the stone here? Now the next few riddles should jump us to this piece here, and here, so we're headed west along the cavelands. Tonight, perhaps tomorrow, we should cross the deep river in time to head north into Shatterhelm. This looks like the entrance to the city over here."

"I agree."

"From there it gets tricky. I see the route taking us partway into the city, but then I'm stuck on this: 'The bird under stone flies home all alone, but roosts in the gables in pairs.' That's cryptic even for Visak. What does it mean?"

Brenish shrugged. What it meant was that there probably was no answer. "You don't have a map of Shatterhelm, do you?"

"Nay. Why?"

"Because it seems to me like the riddle will make more sense once we get there. There must be something specific he's pointing out."

"But the rest of the map has been straightforward. Solve a riddle, it tells you which piece to look at next."

Brenish raised an eyebrow. "And you think Visak wouldn't change the rules?"

Gareth grinned a little back at him. "I suppose he might."

"Perchance he wrote about that somewhere else."

"I've looked all over the map and haven't seen any indication. Not that he'd feel a need to coddle us. He preferred his 'students' solve things on their own."

He hadn't taken the bait. Gareth was determined to remain tight-lipped about those notes. Brenish only nodded to his statement, and didn't let his disappointment show. There had to be another way to crack the man's defenses. Nobody kept secrets perfectly.

Brenish tried to memorize the rest of the map as best he could while he had the chance. He was usually very good at remembering things, but it was helpful to have a refresher. The next time he saw it might be in Shatterhelm, and by then he would need to have a plan mostly ready.

Cirawyn and Turk joined them. She looked rather pleased, carrying her torch in one hand and the paper and candle in another. "I got what I came for," she said.

She handed the page to Brenish. Gareth's curiosity was too great not to look. In the negative image left by the red wax, there was a name and a date. The date was nearly thirty years ago, when Gareth was just a toddler; the name was Hamish Bowman.

Gareth spoke before Brenish could clear his befuddlement. "Ha!" he said. "So that's where you come by all your lore. I didn't know your dad came down here."

"Aye," she said. "It was long ago, before he married."

"Which expedition did he go with? Was it one I'd know?"

She shrugged. "Maybe. He went with four other men. Only one other made it back."

"I can't believe it," Brenish said. "I knew the man hated me, but I had no idea how much till now. Why else wouldn't he tell me about this?"

"He doesn't hate you, m'love," said Cirawyn. Her voice was musical as if she meant to say "silly" in there somewhere, but she seemed to notice he genuinely believed her father had it in for him. She took hold of his hand with the two fingers she had free. "He worries about you going Fell."

"Welp," Turk said, "dodged that arrow, didn't he?"

Gareth snorted a laugh. Cirawyn and Brenish laughed right after. It was strange, Brenish thought, getting to realize Turk had an actual personality and was even something of a dry humorist. If only he'd start using a comb, he might be all right.

Cirawyn got hold of her amusement and looked Brenish in the eye. "His pals left widows," Cirawyn said. "He didn't want that for me. That's why he's been trying to marry me off."

"I thought it was mostly because he didn't approve of me being a thief."

"Just an unsuccessful one," she said. "He said being a highwayman working for Gareth was beneath you. Meaning no disrespect, Gareth."

Gareth waved his hand dismissively and said *pssh*. "He's right. Brenish is a crap bandit. He should be running scams for the guild in the city."

"And I would have done, if this hadn't come up," said Brenish.

"But you were late in coming to it. You could've secured a good living in the city if you started years ago. You stayed here for the tales."

Brenish couldn't argue; Gareth was entirely right. He'd had the opportunity to take on a larger role in the guild three years ago, and he'd turned it down. The folly of that decision was plain to him now. Harry had even encouraged him to go, and he realized now it wasn't because the elder thief didn't like him; he wanted Brenish to get out of whatever trap he'd fallen into himself, years before. All that good advice went to waste in Brenish's youthful arrogance.

"Let's get back inside," said Gareth. "We should get on the move again soon. The quicker we get to the trail's end, the sooner we can go home."

"Aren't you going to scribe your name on the stone?" said Brenish.

Gareth looked at the monument, over Brenish's shoulder. "Nay," he said. "I know I was here. When I have children of my own they'll know it too." And he went back inside without another word. Turk followed.

"What about you, love?" said Cirawyn.

He turned to see it for himself. The obelisk was dim in the light of their two torches. The mark of Visak was visible from where they stood, but only barely so anymore; Brenish guessed the potion's effect on him must be nearly gone. So many names had been carved into that stone, but only one really mattered: Jarrett Fell-Hand. His legend was one of brashness and good fortune, right up until he met the Aberration.

"Nay, m'love," Brenish said. His voice sounded small, drained of bravado. "Gareth is the wiser. I've made a mess of everything so far. I'll leave it be, and hope we have our own children to tell about it someday."

"Of course we will," she said brightly.

But her confidence faltered, seeing some of the turmoil in him. The secret wouldn't keep much longer. Sooner or later he had to share his concerns with her, at least, as he had with Tibs, but Cirawyn was smart enough to put together the puzzle on her own. Once the doubt was there, she would look for its source.

Cirawyn glanced back at the doorway briefly, and spoke in a near-whisper. "What aren't you telling me, love?"

She always knew. He swallowed hard and put his walls back up. "Same thing I'm not tellin' him."

The Winding Trail

With everyone fully visible, they departed with a more normal formation: Three men in front, three in back. Raden left Turk in the front and took his place next to Gareth.

Less than half a mile from the obelisk chamber, Brenish saw a glint of something reflective in the ditch beside the road. It turned out to be a broken bottle, pieces strewn for a few yards along the trench as if they'd been swept there. Not long after, he saw a wishbone from a large bird: a chicken or goose, perhaps. He pointed both out to Gareth, who only urged them to continue.

A full mile away, the grade of the tunnel steepened noticeably. Though it still looked fairly level, their gradual descent could be felt subtly in the way their weight hit the ground, the way the pressure on the toe seemed slightly more than that on the heel. Before that point, it was all but impossible to tell without surveyors' tools.

Another curious change came, which was that the road bent very slowly to the right. As much as he had expected it, this bothered Brenish; unless Gareth had a lodestone (which he might), they would have to rely on landmarks to tell when their direction had changed. They had been traveling more or less due west. Brenish had no way to know how far the curve of the tunnel had taken them into a northerly direction; Enzo's bearing stone was worn out.

They came to a crossing where six ways met instead of the usual four. There, old cobwebs clung to the ceiling and to a lesser extent the walls. It seemed to have once been a web for spiders like the kind they had seen in Paddystock, but the spiders were long gone. Not long enough, or the cobwebs would have disintegrated from age. The nest might have been a few months or a few years gone, but probably no more. Naman made a shivery sound of disgust as they passed through, which Jase repeated in a mocking tone.

Brenish was now convinced they were within an outer margin of goblin territory. There were no settlements nearby, it seemed, yet their foot traffic was evident. If a priest felt safe enough to come to a shrine there, albeit in an armed party, it had to at least be patrolled from time to time. The goblins would want to keep their area clear of any serious trouble. Perhaps they hadn't known about the puddings, or decided their cave was far enough away from the traffic routes not to bother finishing them off. The creatures had, in a way, formed a natural line of defense against possible marauding humans.

But the clearing of the webs, that was goblins' work. The removal of what remained was both too thorough and too sloppy to be anyone else. A wild beast might have won a fight against the spiders and trampled its way through. Humans would have burned off the remnants of the nest instead of leaving a few tatters to waft in the light tunnel breeze. That left greenskins, who would reclaim the waymeet and clear it out, but in a slapdash way.

This, too, couldn't have been lost on Gareth.

The tunnel brickwork came to an end beyond the spider nest, as if the builders had just given up. They had ended it in a regular arched doorway in a wall, but the space beyond was nothing but more tunnel. Here the excavation was wider, roomier, letting the party spread out more but keeping them ever more on guard in case a side passage might appear.

The tunnel's rightward drift straightened out, but soon became just as subtle a curve to the left. Still it descended. They could only guess which direction they were really facing now, or how far below the surface they were. The others had stopped asking what part of the world was overhead quite some time ago; Brenish couldn't even remember the subject coming up since the aqueducts.

Reckoning in the ruins was done mostly by landmark. Charts were notoriously loose with distances, some claiming a particular stretch was a mile while others might say a mile and a half, two miles, or five. Willy's map was made the same way, with barely a care given to such things. All that really mattered was time, and by time—though for most visitors even that, too, was hard to measure—the distance from Asaph's Gate to Shatterhelm was roughly two and a half days. It was maybe another few hours to reach Deepwater.

Noon might have passed already; or it might not have, for they were chased off early by the spellbreak, and much less time had passed since then than it truly seemed. Brenish was fairly good at reckoning time, but Gareth, with his timepiece, would know for certain.

The tunnel turned right again, and Brenish heard a groan. It was hard to be sure, but the voice sounded like Bob's. Perhaps it was his turn to get the deepsick, after his brother had—at least for now—overcome it. It wasn't like Bob to complain. Perhaps he was tiring, but that was his own fault for wearing chain.

"How about another song?" said Tibs.

"Not here," Gareth said. "The winding tunnel has an ill reputation as it is."

"Oh come on, now," said Naman. "Your singing wasn't *that* bad."

The quip actually got a snicker out of Finch, but Gareth ignored it completely. "Keep checking behind us. If we run into trouble I'd prefer we see it coming."

"What kind of trouble are you expecting from the rear?"

"Don't be thick, Naman. Use your imagination. You're the senior member of your group now."

"Aye," said Jase. "And you have *two* eyes to work with, so use 'em and you might fare better."

Brenish didn't see what happened next, but there was a scuffle behind him, with Jase saying *hey* and *what* a lot. He turned around and saw that Finch had broken rank and had pushed Jase backward toward the wall, his hand on the smaller man's throat.

At the tunnel's edge, Finch slammed Jase against it hard enough to give him a good bump on the head, even through the helmet.

"Say another word," Finch said. "*One* word."

"This isn't helping anything, Ed," said Gareth.

"He should show some respect." But Finch released him.

Jase rubbed at his neck. Brenish doubted Finch had really done anything to hurt him, though a wash of his undergarments wouldn't go amiss. Although that was probably true of most of them.

"Sorry," said Jase. "I thought a light jest might help a little."

"If that's your sense of humor then keep it to yourself."

"Have it your way. But I didn't see you getting all misty when Dex died."

"That's because Dex was a hog-smelling little troll. Harry was my *brother*."

"No kidding?" said Bob. "I didn't know you—"

"Not by blood, Bob." Finch turned to look at him, if only for the sake of a withering stare. "But that's what he meant to me. And I won't let some sluggard arse-pated stoat dishonor his memory before the body's even cold."

Jase didn't take insults lying down. "Harry was no saint," he said, "even to you."

Naman dropped his head into his hand and shook it there. Raden groaned, and Brenish stared in frozen horror at Jase's gaffe. He spared a glance at Cirawyn, who was utterly agape. There were certain lines that were never crossed, things never said, especially in a small community like Ilyenis.

Finch turned back and glared fire at Jase, but Jase wasn't done. "You think just because he's your best friend you knew him so well, but—"

Jase's words cut short as Finch grabbed his neck and slammed him against the wall again, and once more for good measure. "Go on," Finch said. The menace in his voice was pure acid. "You were saying something about what I don't know? Tell me, little man, what you think I don't know. Tell me what you think my *son* doesn't know."

If there was a right answer, Jase didn't know it, so for once he did the wiser thing and kept quiet. It was all he could do anyway to keep from being strangled. Brenish looked at Gareth; he watched with the intensity of a sporting judge, waiting to see if the situation turned so ugly that he would be forced to intervene.

Finch grabbed Jase's head and looked him in the eye, holding him in his gaze like a snake holds a mouse. "If you should ever find yourself a woman who'll put up with your ways for more than half an hour, I'll give you some free advice. When someone you love wants something so badly it tears up their heart, year after year, a real man finds a way to do something about it. So don't you get the wrong ideas in that pretty skull-cavern. And don't you *dare* speak ill of Harry Card in my presence or out, or so help me I'll feed you your own tongue."

Brenish understood, as soon as Jase did, how badly he had misjudged the situation between Harry and Finch's family. He knew Harry had loved Maddie, and that it cut both ways, but now it was all clear. Maddie didn't have a child until she was late in her twenties, an age where most people already had several children. She was about thirty-four or thirty-five now, still comely but beginning to gray, when most mothers would have a few children already full-grown. And she had told him once her many sisters all had large families. At the time he'd thought nothing of it.

Jase squeaked out, "Sorry," and Finch finally let him go. Jase slumped to the floor.

"We'll not speak of it again," Finch said. "Any of us."

Jase nodded. Finch didn't look around to see if the others agreed. Brenish saw a number of heads nod anyway. With Finch, it was well implied that if this ever made its way into village gossip, heads would literally roll. Still it was a shame; the truth was so much more flattering than the gossip they already had.

Finch resumed his place at the rear, satisfied his point was made.

"Get up, Jase," said Gareth. The tone in his voice made Brenish wonder if he had truly ever intended to step in. He acted as though Finch's revelation was not news to him. "Let's get moving."

The party got on again without much fuss, but in relative silence. Jase's knack for turning an ordinary conversation into an altercation had shut down all will to make small talk awhile. It gave Brenish a chance to think some more. He felt he should at least have some plausible answers to the bird riddle.

Turk spied some more trash by the road: shards of pottery, and a few more animal bones the scavengers hadn't cleaned up. Brenish found fragments of a sword, an arrowhead, and even a pile of dung that was being devoured by flies. The excrement might have been the most disturbing find of all, because Tibs judged it less than two days old, and it looked as though it could have come from a man or a manthing. The amount of debris seemed to be increasing, as if they were traveling further into goblin realms rather than away. Yet to Brenish's eye, the garbage had a decidedly militaristic flavor, even for goblins; he began to wonder if this tunnel was more than just a patrol route.

For another hour their path continued to wind and descend. Wherever it crossed another route, the party would stop and proceed with greater caution, but they encountered no other intelligent creatures or any beasts to challenge them along the way. At one junction they were extra wary, because the road intersecting theirs was given proper archways on either side, and in the gloom they could see it was properly finished with brick and mortar. The Elder Kingdom had some use for that route which, in this area, had once made it more important than what was left of the Wide Road. As usual the vanguard inspected the crossing, and the group hurried past.

"Ach," said Bob, "is there no end to all these *tunnels?*"

"You're not getting the deepsick too, are you?" said Naman.

"I have the reins on it. I just remind myself this is for my family. I hope they're all well."

"I asked Sara to go stay with them," Raden said. "She could use the company anyway."

"Thank you," Bob said. "That's a comfort."

"To her as well. Gets drafty in the house alone."

"No one fed the animals," said Cirawyn.

Brenish stopped and turned around. "What?"

"I feed the animals every morning."

"I sent a hand to take care of that," said Gareth. "I planned ahead."

Gareth had odd notions of kindness. Kidnapping Cirawyn and forcing her to join the expedition as a threat to hold over Brenish was perfectly fine by him, but he wasn't about to let her dad's farm suffer. But then there was plenty of flexible morality to go round.

"Oh," Cirawyn said. She seemed distant, preoccupied. "Thank you."

"Don't mention it." He waved a hand toward Brenish. "Keep walking."

They resumed their long course down the meandering tunnel, but barely a hundred yards later, Turk pointed.

"There's another broken shield," he said.

"Aye," said Gareth. "We know the goblins use this route from time to time."

"But it's not the type they use."

He stopped the group again and bent low over the ditch on their right-hand side. He grabbed what he saw there and pulled it out. At the same time a snake, startled by his arrival, reached out and bit him right between the eyes.

"Gah!" Turk said, and swiped the snake away. It left two dripping red marks in his forehead. The shield he'd picked up fell to the ground.

"Oh, for the love of…" said Gareth. He pulled off his pack and rummaged within without lifting the top flap.

"I'm not hurt," said Turk.

"You could be poisoned. I'll give you a sip just in case."

Tibs lashed his whip at the retreating snake, severing its head. If he ever wanted to go into honest work, Brenish thought, the city would find no better flogger.

While Gareth administered the potion, Brenish found the shield and picked it up. It was small, not meant for human arms. The shield itself was solid iron, yet its convex surface was polished to a mirror finish, bearing no heraldry. Its shape was a standard heater style, with a flat top. Just below the arm straps, one of which was torn, the thin iron had been rent and twisted inward.

"This is no goblin shield," Brenish said.

Gareth was already putting the potion away. Two little rivulets of blood dripped down Turk's face, but the holes that had made them were gone. "Let me see," Gareth said. He hoisted his pack again and took the shield from Brenish.

"Maybe it's for a goblin squire, or apprentice," Raden suggested.

"Mmm," said Gareth. "Not a bad first guess, but nay. There's no coat of arms here. Goblins mark their shields as we do. This shield is polished, but not painted." He turned it over and over, looking at every detail. "'Tisn't of goblin make, either. What think you, Brenish?"

Brenish only had muddled half-guesses to go on. The creature who wielded that shield had to be small, maybe only three feet tall. It had to be good with metalworking and crafts to create the shield. It had to be daft enough to come anywhere near goblin territory.

"Gremlins," he said.

"My thought as well. But how came it here?"

Brenish pointed. "A goblin blade would make that gash well enough. Half the rubbish we've found is broken weapons or equipment. If you want my guess, I'd say it's a war."

Bob swore under his breath; Jase swore over it. Gareth merely turned the shield around a few more times.

"Aye, you may be right," Gareth said. "Not that it changes much. We have to get through this tunnel."

"I'm fine with greenskins killing each other," said Raden, "but do we have to be on the road where they like to do it best? Can't we take another way round?"

"Nay. I was unwilling to risk it when we started, when we knew the best ways to go. This far in, we're too likely to lose track of where we are along the map. We press on. If we run into anyone at all, it's apt to be a small party either way. We have the numbers to handle that. Just keep your eyes open."

Brenish agreed with Gareth's logic, so he said nothing more, but he was deeply worried that the party had unwittingly crossed into a war zone. Willy couldn't have planned for disaster on the map-holder's part any better. It was strange to him that both the goblins and the gremlins should be trying to expand their territory, especially into the same dead space. Perhaps these crisscrossing tunnels were a network of some strategic importance beyond his understanding. Or maybe there was more to it; the puddings coming up from the deep shouldn't have happened either, yet it had. The drought could have had an enormous impact on all parts of the ruins.

In spite of the road clearly being well-traveled—by the standards of the abandoned Elder Kingdom—they saw no creatures on the road bigger than foxes, and those they saw ran off. The cast-off gear, spent ammunition, and broken blades kept coming as they walked.

Nothing they found was worth salvaging. Dex's mending bag wouldn't help. It was only made for a small object, even smaller than a knife; and the object had to imprint on it intact before it could be mended. There were spells that could function somewhat for repairs without imprinting, but Brenish didn't know them. Dex might well have.

"This place reminds me of a dungeon," said Turk.

"That's why some people call it the dungeons," Jase said.

"I mean it's like lockup. Except the food's better."

"Aye," Naman said.

"I see it," said Bob. "I only went in a few days, though."

"Never had the pleasure, myself," said Brenish. "Never care to."

Jase gave him the Wednesday night dice smirk. "Talked your way out of it, I'd wager."

"Aye. More than once."

"What you men said before," said Turk, "it got me thinking. Hope someone looks in on my missus while I'm gone. It was hard on her, last time I was in lockup. Her sister's in the same fix now, bless her."

Brenish's throat tightened up. Ilyenis being such a small town meant a lot of people were related, if not by blood then by marriage. He had taken that kinship for granted so long he had forgotten there was any danger of Willy coming up in conversation. But then, Turk had never been much for conversation before.

"You've probably said more in two days than the whole time I've known you," said Naman. Brenish thought it might be Naman's way of changing the subject. Naman knew perfectly well who Elspeth's sister was.

"The mind wanders here," Turk said.

"What's wrong with her sis?" said Bob.

Maybe Bob was making conversation to stave off the deepsick, or he could have just been bored or curious. Yet he so often managed to say the wrong thing at the wrong time, it seemed like the work of a powerful curse. Brenish could say nothing.

"He's in lockup again," said Turk. "The guild's doing for her, though."

"That's good," Bob said.

"Aye. Oh, that reminds me."

Seemingly without provocation, Turk reached past Tibs and slapped Brenish upside the back of the head.

"Ow. What was that for?"

"All summer my kids got scared from stories their cousins told them. Promised the wife I'd hit you."

"I guess that's fair, then."

Maybe this was better. Brenish knew he'd have to throw Willy's name past Gareth eventually anyway, in casual conversation, just to disrupt any inklings forming in his head. Avoiding the subject entirely would do nothing to allay suspicion, but embracing it as a meaningless connection probably would. Sometimes a little brash honesty worked best.

Jase cackled, watching Brenish rub his head. "Oi, boss," he said.

"Nay," Gareth replied.

"Aww."

"If you're bored, you can chew on a riddle for me. The bird under stone flies home all alone, but roosts in the gables in pairs. Figure out what that means and you get a bonus."

Bob raised a hand. "I'm good at riddles."

"No you're not," said Finch.

"I am so. It just takes me a while. We've plenty of time."

"Naman's good with riddles too," said Tibs. "Can we get a bonus if we figure it out?"

"Oh, why not," said Gareth. "Have at it. Brenish is stuck too."

Jase snapped his fingers. "Gargoyles. I bet it's gargoyles."

"Hmm. Well that's an interesting notion. I never heard of gargoyles in the ruins, but it could be something like that. There were animal carvings in Lowcastle."

"Ha! I bet I'm right."

"I hope so," said Brenish. "If you're right, we get closer to the treasure. But you have to be *proven* right."

"Indeed," said Gareth. "Any other guesses? We'll make a game of it."

"I say it's scrollwork that looks like birds," said Bob. "You know, the fancy kind like you see in the city."

"Where there's nests there's eggs," Raden suggested. "Look for eggs."

Bob nudged Naman. "What's your guess?" he said.

"I have none," said Naman, who knew perfectly well that if there was an answer, it wasn't going to get him any closer to being rich. "Just thinking about birds makes me hungry. I can practically smell Christmas goose right now."

Brenish smirked, but kept it hidden. It was both another clever change of topic, and a dig at Brenish himself. Naman's wit had a fine edge; many a man had walked away without realizing he'd been cut with it until the wound festered.

"Luckily we have more than one expert," said Gareth. "Isn't that right?"

Cirawyn didn't answer right away. This surprised Brenish enough that he turned around, but saw the others had stopped.

She lurched out of formation toward Jase. Though he tried to stop her, she pushed him aside with ease. She didn't even make it all the way to the wall, or the ditch, before she retched. She heaved twice, dropped to her knees, and heaved several times more until there was nothing left.

"Oh grand," Jase said. "Just when I get over the deepsick, she goes and gets it."

Cirawyn shook, tremors rippling through her small body like a flag flapping in steady wind. Brenish tried to rush to her side, but Jase stood in the way and tried to block him with both arms. It was an obnoxious move, and Brenish responded in kind. Without breaking stride he brought a knee up into his groin, grabbed Jase by the shoulders when he doubled over, and threw him to the ground as easily as a tailor's dummy.

Brenish squatted next to Cirawyn and tried to get her attention. She shivered as if cold, but the tunnel was quite warm.

"Love, look at me," he said. "Look at me."

She finally turned her head. Her eyes were glassy and panic-stricken. Whatever words she tried to form, they failed and broke apart on her lips. All she could do was make strangled, fearful cries.

"It's all right," said Brenish. He put his arms on her shoulders. "It's all right. We're going to be fine."

Naman made an expression of guttural dismay that sounded something like *Unfh*. He knew what Brenish knew: Cirawyn was too smart. The mention of Willy was all it took for her to put the rest together.

Gareth scratched his head just under the helmet. "This is the worst case yet."

"We'll get out of this just fine," Brenish said again. "Don't I always find a way out of trouble? We can handle this."

Cirawyn trembled but reluctantly nodded. She didn't seem particularly reassured.

"Here," he said, "let me get out a rag and we'll clean you up."

"Oaf," said Tibs. He tapped Brenish on the shoulder and handed him a much cleaner piece of cloth, dyed a dark blue. "How many times have I told you to carry a proper handkerchief?"

"Thanks."

He took the handkerchief and handed it to Cirawyn, since he knew she'd hate to have someone else do for her what she could do perfectly well herself. Having something to hold, and a small task to focus on, seemed to help her. She wiped carefully around her mouth. It took a minute for her to get a handle on the job, but her hands steadied and her arms stopped rattling quite so badly.

"Th-thanks, Tibs," she said.

She offered him the cloth back, but Tibs waved her away. "Hold onto that. Just in case."

"Brenish," Jase wheezed, "I'm going to—"

Brenish didn't even look over. "You're gonna lie there and take it, Jase. You had the deepsick yourself not too long ago, and you could have shown a little compassion. Down here I answer to Gareth, but you answer to me."

Gareth didn't say a word in contradiction. Nor should he have, for he had accepted the arrangement that Brenish was effectively second in command, but it wouldn't have been unexpected for him to reconsider. This was, after all, the first time it had truly come up.

Cirawyn allowed Brenish to help her up. She looked in his eyes again and held him there a long moment.

"We'll rest soon," Gareth said. "The end of the tunnel should be near. Do you need a spell lamp?"

She shook her head. "I can keep going. Just give me a minute."

"Take your time. Not too much, of course, but catch your breath."

"'Tis so stuffy down here." And now Brenish saw *she* was the one lying. Her mind was too quick. She was already using the deepsick as a cover for her reaction.

"Jase," Brenish said, "you're up in front in my place till we take our rest." Again no word from Gareth; he had ordered the party all by himself up to this point. Perhaps he saw the wisdom in Brenish being next to Cirawyn until she calmed down, or else he was just amused by the thief playing with his authority.

"Nice," said Jase. "Kick a man when he's down."

"Don't tempt me." He turned to Cirawyn. "Better now?"

She nodded. "Better."

"You have an iron will," Raden said. "You'll push through."

"Thanks."

"Maybe once you've settled," said Bob, "you can solve the riddle. It might take your mind off."

"Aye," she said. But Brenish knew, as Naman did, as she herself did, that she had already solved one. "Aye, 'tis quite the riddle. I'll try and help."

The Keep on the Cliff

For the remainder of the winding road, Brenish resisted the constant urge to whack Jase, who was right in front of him, on the head with his torch and ring his goblin helmet like a bell. Gareth encouraged light conversation to try and lift everyone's spirits back up. Tensions were still quite high.

Cirawyn, for the most part, mastered her fright as quickly as could be expected in her situation. Naman had had days to realize that he was going to be dragged down here. But for Cirawyn, the realization that there was no easy way out was like the hand of Death tapping her on the shoulder. If Brenish failed to appease Gareth, she was in the line of fire; maybe she was equally concerned for his safety, too. That was a difficult fear to calm down from so soon after acquiring it, and it showed in her ongoing nervousness.

The road ended in a bridge over a deep chasm. Unlike those they had crossed on their way to Paddystock, this bridge was more roughly built. It had no curb, but it was very wide, and showed no sign of crumbling. The ravine below was not (seemingly) bottomless; it was merely a nasty drop. In that huge cleft, a forest of enormous mushrooms grew. Their scent was strong but not unpleasant, mixed with smells the travelers would expect around a stream.

The far end of the bridge was a castle. The walls were stepped like a ziggurat, every two levels having a wide ledge with a parapet. Its windows were narrow, save for a few. The bricks around the main gate were considerably different from those of the castle itself, and even differed amongst each other, suggesting it had been destroyed and rebuilt several times. The archway was whole, now, but there was no gate left in it; somebody had obviously given up on defending this place.

"Do they call this the mushroom castle?" said Bob.

"Aye," said Brenish.

"Truly?"

"Aye."

"Huzzah! I finally guessed one!"

Jase pointed ahead with his lamp. "Should we be worried this place might be watched? It's on a patrol route between two warring races. Seems like it would be strategically valuable."

"You're looking at the lion's share of its defenses," said Gareth. "'Twould be useless to the goblins for defending from the west. And gremlins, 'tis said, don't like places like this. They prefer to live in tight clusters, in warrens with fewer access routes."

"Why would the Elder Kingdom build it to face east, then?" said Raden. "It's facing *into* the heart of their realm."

"Answer that question and you'll be a rich man, with or without a share of Visak's gold. But don't be so sure we've passed through the heart. Deepwater is a bigger city than Lowcastle or Wootenghast, and Shatterhelm is bigger still."

Brenish mumbled his own agreement. He was a proponent of the theory that the Elder Kingdom was more than just one kingdom: it was many. Perhaps it had been a single realm in the beginning, but fractured as it spread outward. There was ample evidence that different parts of the ruins were built during different time periods. The Order of the Hundred Centuries might not have been so wrong about that part, though they were still mad cultists.

No challenge came from the gates, the windows, or the ledges above. Tibs, Turk, and Jase led the party through the remains of the not-so-old gate, into a wide corridor and then a spacious hall.

Rather unlike the palace at Stone's End, planning had gone into this place. Everything was built in a consistent and eye-pleasing manner. Stairs were where they expected to find them. There was a sense of order in the mushroom castle that none of them could truly claim to have seen since leaving the aqueducts.

Inside the building, Jase took charge of the vanguard. He must have seen a map of this place, Brenish thought, as he had of many of the other places they had visited. Still, it seemed as though it would be difficult to get lost here. Jase led them up three flights of stairs, pausing on each landing to inspect the premises for danger. On the uppermost floor he turned left, crossed through two small rooms, and turned right again into a wide hallway.

The structure reminded Brenish very much of the Gatehouse. Once this had been a living, working keep with a large force of men;

now it was a home for vermin and occasional visitors from the deep. Though it might have been a perfect place to rest, Gareth seemed especially unwilling to do so here; when Brenish asked, once, if it might be a good idea, Gareth gave him a stiff nay.

There was a very old rumor that the mushroom castle was haunted, or cursed. Maybe that was what made Gareth push on. He wasn't known as a superstitious man, but he and Brenish both knew that when a traveler got out alive and claimed a place was haunted, that usually meant it was inhabited or frequented by something no sane person would wish to encounter. The halls and archways were large enough for something like the Aberration to move about with ease. And besides, the builders liked to put structures like this at intersections; there might well be another road leading here from the north or south. The castle had never been fully explored.

The western side of the castle was almost indefensible compared to the eastern side. They saw first a large, open room with three archways opening onto a wide balcony. The team passed through the middle arch, into the huge "outdoor" chamber beyond, almost a courtyard but with no far wall to enclose it.

The walkway atop the castle's western wall had a low parapet, only waist-high. It looked out over an enormous natural cavern, which could be accessed by a relatively narrow stairway to their right. That stairway hugged the northern rock wall, which was fairly straight until further west the cavern curved away in that direction. To the south there was no wall, and no floor either. The ceiling there sloped gradually downward until it faded from sight; the cavern floor on that side ended in a cliff. There was no way, from where they stood, to see how sheer that cliff might be.

Gareth ordered them down the stairs. These they could traverse only two abreast, with very little elbow room, going down two stories in one long descent. Once everyone was safely down, he pointed toward the high castle wall—which had no windows on this side—to indicate this was where he intended to stop.

The party spread out along the base of the wall, dropping packs and sitting down, though not all alike. Brenish kept walking with Cirawyn toward the cliff, though she was the one leading him. He looked back and saw Gareth hadn't yet had a chance to sit, because

Finch had taken him aside near the base of the stairs for a discussion. He saw Finch pointing to the rampart and the arches beyond; it had to be out of concern for their defensive position. Gareth nodded along but, Brenish knew from experience, wasn't about to budge.

Cirawyn squeezed his hand to get his attention. Brenish turned to face her.

"Who else knows?" she said.

"Just Naman. I told him about it right after I got it."

"What was your plan?"

"Before coming here, it was just what I told you. Except I also planned to sell it through the guild."

"What about now?"

"I'm still working on it." He tried to point his eyes toward Gareth without drawing attention. "Gareth knows more than he's said about our course. He has some of Visak's papers in his pack. There might be a clue there we can use to find the real password to the spell."

"Perhaps 'tis no more than survival tips for this place," she said.

"Perhaps. Either way I need to see them. I can't keep this bluff up if I don't know everything he knows."

"Well good luck with that. What have you told Tibs?"

"Same as I told Harry, to help me look for options."

"You should tell him."

"He might let it slip. Probably best not to."

Cirawyn frowned. "You don't give Tibs enough credit. He's more capable than you think."

"Of many things," said Brenish.

She cocked an eyebrow. "Is that what this is about? You don't trust him? If you knew what Dex did you'd understand."

"He said the same. But how'd you know what Tibs did?"

"You were angry with him at the aqueducts," she said. "You pretended not to be."

She *always* knew.

"I was just as angry with myself," Brenish said. "I should've killed Dex in the garden, consequences be damned. But once Tibs got me that unk I wanted to find out what it did. Made me start looking at Dex like an asset. Just like Gareth."

She smiled reassuringly. "You're not like Gareth, love. You'll see that soon enough. You may have the same passion but your hearts are different. Trust that."

"Aye. But that difference could get us killed. I'd go easy on us, in his place. I'd take me up on my fallback plan."

"You'll work it out," she said.

Before he could protest, she walked away. She sat next to Tibs, which was a polite way of saying everything had been said that needed to, and he should get to work on finding a solution instead of arguing their impending doom any further. It was his job now to squirm out from under the boot, as he always did.

Since their previous meal break had been long overdue, the whole party was hungry enough to eat again after only a few hours on the march. Everyone who was already seated had their packs open, and munched merrily on what was left of the goblins' provisions, combined with a little of their own rations. Brenish sat by Cirawyn and Tibs. Naman sat with Bob and Raden this time, a surprising change. Gareth and Finch were seated in the corner between the stairs and the wall, still deep in conference. And Jase and Turk were in a discussion of their own, one where Jase's side was heated and full of big arm gestures while Turk barely even moved his head.

"What do you suppose they're on about?" said Cirawyn.

Tibs snorted. "Blah blah blah *unfair* blah blah—"

"I meant Finch and Gareth."

"Planning how we'll go forward from here," said Brenish. "I think Finch is still on edge from losing Harry."

"Me too," said Tibs.

"Gareth knows the ruins better, but I think Finch is the better strategist."

"Shouldn't you be part of that conversation, then?"

"If they wanted me they'd have asked. I assume they're also discussing how to keep me under control, after what happened in the tunnel."

"Aye."

"They both agreed I should be second in command down here, but I don't think Gareth ever got past the idea that Finch should be in that spot."

"Well at least," Tibs said, "this time tomorrow it won't matter anymore. Eh? Cheer up."

"I'll try," Brenish said, "but I still have my concerns."

"Don't worry about that. It'll sort out. Just keep us alive till—"

He broke off in the middle of his sentence and cocked his head.

"Till?" said Cirawyn. But Tibs shushed her and kept listening. Brenish saw Finch take notice.

Tibs stood up, and shushed the rest of the group. He slowly turned around, stepping outward from the wall until he had a view of the arches leading back into the keep.

"Goblins," he said, as quietly as he could.

A scramble of activity began. Everyone reached for their packs; they made fighting harder but retreating without them would be suicide. Brenish put his on in a hurry and ran to Gareth. "We can't hide here. We're too exposed and we daren't douse our torches."

"I told you," Finch said.

Gareth replied with a terse bow, conceding the point. "Very well. We'll fight it out. 'Tis probably a small party."

"I wouldn't hear them this far off if they were," said Tibs. Brenish hadn't seen him come up. Tibs' talents sometimes spilled over into his everyday habits like that.

Gareth pulled a wand from one of the many pockets on his chest armor. "In that case, we'll fight harder."

"Gareth," Brenish said, "use Dex's scroll. Right now, while there's time."

Gareth nodded. He darted an eye to Finch, who retrieved the scroll from Gareth's pack; it was already on his back. Finch seemed to find the right scroll without having to look.

"Here," said Finch. He handed the scroll to Brenish. "You take care of it. We'll muster up."

"Gather everyone close, then."

Brenish turned. Naman was already conferring with Tibs. Jase had his sword and crossbow out. Turk and Raden checked each other's equipment, while Bob busily cocked a few crossbows that hadn't been ready. Cirawyn had found a way to tuck her torch slantwise through the straps in her pack, where the flame was far enough away so as not to burn her but she could be mobile with two hands free; each of those hands had a crossbow, one of which had been Harry's.

Taking one last look at the ribbon on the mass protection scroll, put there by the shop that sold it to Dex, Brenish slid it off and unfurled the spell paper. The others formed up around him as close as they could, Finch acting as sheep dog for the exercise by waving his arms around in command. Brenish cleared his throat, looked at the words on the page, and tried to speak them aloud.

Though he didn't know the runes, they passed through his mind and his mouth moved on its own. He felt a sense that the process still hung on his volition, required his intent to stay in motion. The spell energy coursed through him—a truly strange sensation, one he had never experienced. The tug of warped nature was all around, feeling at its core as if gusts of wind were passing through his body in all directions. The magic grew more intense, where it felt as if it could shoot out his eyes if he kept going. Still he read on, in an even cadence.

On the last rune a key turned. A gate opened on the world, and a powerful shock rushed over him and all his companions. The scroll crumbled into dust, smoke, and ash, its *esen* and ink completely spent.

Brenish felt subtly different. His body and clothes seemed encased in a thin film, a coating thin as a spider web but with even more of its deceptive strength. The sensation passed, seeming to melt into his being. He briefly caught sight of bluish halos around the others, or imagined them there, but those faded too.

"Not bad, little mage," said Finch, but he wasn't talking to Brenish. It was a sort of respectful send-off to Dex.

The spell, Brenish suddenly realized, was still in his mind. So too was the daybreak spell; it had never really gone away. He felt certain he could cast them with one of the spell tokens, if he was so inclined. He had always known this about magic, that it stayed with the spellcaster, or sometimes hearers, for a long time. But until now, he had never really taken that knowledge to heart. Hearing spells cast had never imprinted them so firmly to his memory before, but perhaps the act of casting gave them new life in his mind. He tried to remember others from the past, but they were too dim and distant, their power faded, and there was no time to think harder.

Gareth urged everyone to disperse. The group had no adequate defensive position to take, so they spread out along the floor, keeping their distance from the cliff edge. No one stayed close to the wall. Everyone with a crossbow kept theirs aimed at the archways above. Brenish, however, felt exposed where he was. The best he could hope for was to try and wrest one more weak blurt out of the discord organ, still hanging from his neck, so he stood a little further back from the wall.

"How many?" said Gareth.

"Hard to tell," Tibs said. "Sounds like a fair number. They're getting—"

A shout came down from the castle. The goblins had spotted the light of their torches. At the first call of alarm, the rest of the host bellowed defiance.

Tibs frowned. "A score or more."

The voices rushed closer, like the onslaught of a storm.

"Steady now," Gareth said. He held his left hand high, a wand in his grip.

Lights appeared in the gallery above, reflecting off the roof of the interior room. Firelight, but no spell lamps. The lights brightened as they approached.

In half a moment, a dozen greenskins swarmed the balcony.

Gareth dropped his hand. "Volley!"

But no one waited for his order; as soon as there were targets, they fired. About half the shots found a decent mark, sticking in some point or another and seriously wounding whomever they hit. The rest missed, or struck armor and bounced away. The armor hits stunned their targets, but didn't do any real damage.

Brenish blew into the silver pendant. The note failed, wielding no more power than when the binding first ran out of magic hours ago, except the power to annoy friend and foe alike.

Gareth didn't wait for the others to reload or Brenish to give up on the organ. He fired his wand into the fray, at one of the goblins near the stairs that had escaped the crossbow fire. A purple arc shot out and struck its mark.

The goblin didn't die; he screamed.

While some of his fellows rushed past to take the stairs, others had stopped in fear or in shock at the spectacle in front of them. The struck goblin hunched forward, almost doubled over, as two new arms sprouted from his sides above the waist. His head darkened and developed a pronounced beak. The eyes grew to big black orbs. His body armor and clothing tore and fell away. He dropped his weapon; the hand holding it was now just a single insectile claw. In seconds, all that was left was a giant beetle, eight feet long, its new armor hardened against the weapons of its former allies.

Brenish reeled in shock. Polymorphosis was too dangerous a spell to play with, except as a last resort. Everything he thought he admired about Gareth fell to pieces in an instant. Gareth had bought the wand because he liked the idea of using it, it wasn't *entirely* without strategic value, and using it successfully would earn him an immortal place in song. For all his knowledge, Gareth had never let the sheer stupidity of rolling the dice on creature forms stand in his way.

But the shock was short-lived. Two goblins had made the stairs, and Brenish had to fight them. While most of the others readied their crossbows for another shot, he ran to the stairway and ascended just behind Finch, ready to put his knife to use. Finch however didn't give him the chance, and two more goblins fell.

On the balcony, the beetle blocked off most routes to the stairs; it used its powerful forelegs to grab the other goblins and snap at them with its mouth. The creature was an efficient killer, slaying or maiming three goblins in just that short time.

More goblins boiled through the archway to fight the giant bug. A few of them tried to get around behind, but the beetle opened its massive wings, tossing away any goblins on its flank or else crushing them against the wall or the rampart. One goblin fell over the edge and flipped end over end, a full rotation, in the second it took for him to hit the ground dead. Two of the flankers, however, managed to get in behind the creature and attack from the rear.

Gareth took aim at another goblin on the balcony to keep them busy up there. Another magical bolt hit its target, but this one didn't turn into anything as big or dangerous as the beetle. The goblin shrank until its clothing collapsed around it. Where it had stood, a bright blue bird flew away to the west.

Those who weren't fighting the beetle readied their own crossbows to fire back at the scattered group below. Only a few got off a shot at all, and of those most missed. Jase's helmet got dinged by a direct hit; another bolt hit Turk's sword and was deflected, but knocked him to the side. But the party's second crossbow volley was ready to fire by then, and half a dozen bolts flew to the rampart. Three of the archers there fell, and Cirawyn managed to land an impossible shot on the goblin leading the charge against the beetle.

The insect leaped forward suddenly, throwing all plans into disarray. It plowed into the mass of goblins attacking from the front and grabbed another. But behind it, the way was now clear for more goblins to take the stairs. A few of them came out of the northernmost arch and began their descent.

Finch clashed with a few of the manthings on the stairs, taking one out with his sword but at the risk of nearly being sliced in two by another. With the tide turning against him, he jumped from the stairs so he could defend on the ground level. Brenish had his doubts he could face the remaining goblins on the stairs alone, but Tibs spared him the decision. Right beside Brenish, the whip lashed out and struck his nearest opponent in the arm, forcing it to drop its weapon; Brenish was quick to react and dispatch it. Two more came at him, but Tibs struck again with a biting *crack* and left a horrid weal on the face of the nearest attacker.

Focused entirely on defending the stairs, Brenish didn't know if anyone on the balcony might be targeting him with a crossbow. There was a steady exchange of twanged bowstrings and the whooshes of projectiles in his right ear. But another sound got his attention, crackling through the air along the path of a bright flash. An arc of magic passed over his head and struck the goblin nearest the top of the stairs.

Gareth's third victim liked its transformation no better than the others. The goblin gave a cry of agony, and its neck began to stretch. Its helmet popped off of its head, and the armor broke apart almost instantly as the body grew too large to accommodate it. The arms and legs remained what they were, but the legs grew powerful haunches. Its putty-green skin turned greener, and scaly. A great, whipping tail, easily ten feet long, sprouted from the goblin's backside, and stumpy little wings poked out behind its shoulders. It croaked, for its head was much like that of a bird, though its body was more like unto a dragon. Pale white feathers grew out along its mane, from the neck to the tip of its tail.

A goblin near the top of the stairs fell, though he was only brushed by the creature's tail. When he hit the ground his body shattered into three pieces of stone.

"Cockatrice!" Brenish shouted.

Brenish leapt from the stairs before the whip-wounded goblin in front of him could decide what to do. That goblin turned around too late; the cockatrice bit him and threw him aside. Like his ally, he was stone before he touched the cavern floor.

Tibs was at the bottom of the stairs, casting his whip back and forth to try and keep the creature away.

"Keep it at a distance," Brenish said. "It can touch the whip, but don't let it touch you!"

The crossbow bolts kept flying. One caught his left arm and knocked him off balance, forcing him to his knees. Fortunately the vambrace protected him from serious harm. When he looked up, the beetle was losing the battle of the balcony, yet still a half dozen more goblins issued from the keep.

The cockatrice was now unmolested, unchallenged, on the stairs. The goblins saw that it had become a greater menace to the party than to them, and turned their aim against Tibs. They had fewer crossbowmen at the moment, however, and those had to hide behind the rampart to keep from being picked off by the fighters below.

The cockatrice squawked angrily and lashed its tail. Tibs slowly managed to drive it back, ascending the stairs one step at a time as he did, so that it could once again be a bigger threat to the enemy. A bolt flew mere inches in front of Tibs' face, missing him; this was followed by a bolt flying practically the opposite direction, a gurgling cry from the balcony, and another greenskin falling over the side.

"Keep driving him," Gareth said. "We'll hold off the shooters." He pulled out his wand again.

"God's sake, Gareth," Brenish cried, "stop using that thing!"

Another bolt came from above, and this one found a mark in Tibs' right shoulder. The scroll of mass protection didn't make any of them indestructible. Tibs cried out in pain and fell back.

Finch took charge of the defense. He still had the fire wand, and used it to aim a short burst at the cockatrice in hopes of forcing it back up the stairs.

The cockatrice turned to flee, but it saw that the goblins were holding firm at the top of the stairs. They were every bit as determined to keep it away, and proved that by tearing off pieces of the beetle's carapace—Brenish couldn't tell if it was dead or merely dying—and throwing them at the feathered dragon-thing.

It had only one response: It jumped from the stairs onto the ground below. Naman had just enough time to see it and roll away. Jase, on the other hand, was caught reloading his crossbow, and had to throw it aside and jump back.

Finch tried to roast the beast, but the flames only seemed to aggravate it more. He fired again, but this time at the beetle-hurlers above, where the fire could do more serious damage. Jase swept out his sword.

Naman shouted, "Gareth! Hit it again!"

The beast turned toward the commotion and took a step toward Naman, who was unprepared to take it on, but Jase thwacked it on the leg with his spell lamp. It turned back and took another hit, to the face. As the third strike came in, it swatted the pole away in annoyance, wrenching it out of Jase's grasp.

"Get back, devil!" he screamed. "I'll have your feathers for my bed!"

The sword whirled back and forth, seemingly as effortless as the tip of Tibs' whip had done, dazzling the beast with reflections and movement. Its tail moved ever more furiously, while it flapped its small wings and snapped at Jase, trying to get him to back off.

Another beetle part, thrown from above with impeccable aim, knocked Gareth back before he could act. Jase stood firm, brandishing his sword with an unexpected fluidity. Brenish picked up a piece of beetle shell lying nearby and threw it at the creature, but it barely flinched; it was too focused on Jase. It was a frightening yet epic sight, for Jase looked exactly like a great hero in that moment, lunging forward and thrusting with his blade as he faced down a mighty beast of legend.

Jase drew back his sword and raised it for another swing, just as Gareth sat up and fired his wand at the cockatrice.

The beast wailed, but its transformation took too long to take hold. As it turned to face its new attacker, its tail swung wide.

Jase couldn't have picked a better pose for a statue. His face was determined and hard, one foot before the other, arms up and sword out in mid-swing. Generations would pass, in later years wondering who he was and what he had been fighting, imagining a blow that would never fall.

The cockatrice succumbed to the magical blast, pulling everything in on itself. Its skin turned to an iridescent pink, glistening wet as if it came out of deep water or a pool of oil, and its body was a solid four-foot-wide trunk. A writhing mass of tentacles grew out of it, several dozen at least.

Finch used the wand of fire again; this time the flames stuck. The creature ignited like a dry tree, burning where it stood. A sharp odor of rotten fish and brimstone filled the air.

Bob's voice rose in alarm above the commotion. "Hoy! Watch the rear!"

Brenish turned around and saw a new threat approaching from the west. A small war party of gremlins came at them from around the bend in the cavern, running faster than their little legs should have made possible.

Each gremlin was armed with a sword little bigger than a hunting knife, and a highly polished shield exactly like the one Turk had found in the winding tunnel (though intact). They were no more than three feet high, green, bumpy like lizards, with beady black eyes set into their toad-like faces. None wore any armor. They moved like seed pods in a strong wind, weaving back and forth dizzyingly.

Brenish joined Bob, Raden, and Turk to form a crude line of defense against the gremlins, but the diminutive manthings outnumbered them two to one. They showed every interest in attacking the party, not simply because they stood in the way of their greatest rivals, but because greenskins as a rule had overly simplistic concepts of friend and foe.

The gremlins crashed into the line. Three flowed past the defenders; five engaged. Bob was beset by two enemies, but one of them turned its blade on his thick greaves and he was able to kick it to the side. A purple flash caught it moments later.

Brenish would have cursed Gareth's carelessness with the wand, but he was too busy fighting off his own foe, and only saw what happened out of the corner of his eye. The little ankle-biter repeatedly tried to reach around his legs as if to hamstring him, but he fended it off with his sword. Each time the creature came too close to his left leg, Brenish pivoted around, until he was slowly turning to face the cliff. Bob was behind him.

A crossbow bolt struck Brenish's gremlin in its chest, hurling it a few feet across the cavern floor. Brenish risked a brief glance to see Cirawyn aiming in his direction, sheltered from the goblins above by using Jase as cover. Another gremlin lay dead before her. Satisfied she was well for the moment, he turned his attention back to the other gremlins.

Turk and Raden, he saw, were badly beset. Turk was overwhelmed by his opponent, while Raden was getting pushed back against the cliff edge by the gremlin engaging him. A bright orange flare lit up the cavern again from somewhere out of Brenish's field of vision, with a whoosh of flame.

Brenish ran towards Turk's gremlin at full speed, as if enraged by its mere existence. The gremlin saw the movement and was momentarily distracted. This gave Turk just the right opening to lop off its head, when Brenish was only a few yards away.

Another gremlin wailed in terror as it flew through the air toward the cliff face, evidently launched by Bob. Its knife was gone, but the shield was still strapped to its arm. All its limbs flailed in a desperate attempt to arrest its motion. It overshot the cliff and fell, still screaming, into the chasm beyond.

Brenish ran past Turk to help Raden, but got a pat on the back for his help. Still on the move, he saw another creature go flying, even faster and farther: a turtle.

Raden was overmatched by his foe. He was aware of his position and tried repeatedly to circle around for the advantage, but his gremlin must have been better trained or smarter than the others. The manthing not only wielded its evil little sword effectively, but it used the shield mounted on its arm as a club. Raden fought with his sword in one arm and his torch in another, but whenever he brought his torch's long pole low and tried to sweep it wide, the gremlin neatly jumped over and tried to land a strike.

Finally Raden's luck ran out; the clever gremlin ducked *under* a swing of the torch, and diverted it upward. With Raden stunned, it slammed its shield into his arm and got him to drop the pole. The gremlin kicked the torch away, over the cliff, and lunged at his enemy. The only way for Raden to avoid getting skewered was to jump back, but his feet got too close to the rim, and one slipped off— then the other. He dropped face-down onto the edge, holding his arms out and gripping the stone as best he could to keep from falling.

The gremlin didn't see Brenish until it was too late. As it moved in for the kill, Brenish caught it in the back with his sword.

There was no more time to waste. Brenish let go of his sword and grabbed hold of both of Raden's arms as best he could, trying to get enough of a grip to pull him up. Raden kicked at the cliff face below.

"Help me!" he said.

"Grab my arm," said Brenish. He leaned over the body of the gremlin, hoping it would help anchor him. Raden weighed a good deal more than he did.

Raden was obviously worried about keeping his grip, but he managed to lift up his left arm just enough and grab Brenish just in time. His grip held fast.

Brenish tried to pull. Raden did whatever he could to help, but seemed to have trouble getting his feet to find purchase. The thief strained, and braced a knee against the gremlin for leverage.

It was a mistake; he knew as soon as he did it. The gremlin's arm was still looped through the straps of its shield, and the shield beneath its body became a sled. It shot out from under Brenish's leg. The shift was enough to throw Brenish forward, off balance, but Raden couldn't let go.

Momentum took them. Brenish felt the slide but could do nothing to stop it. The edge of the cliff rushed up, and then it was gone. Empty space greeted him, a black void.

Part IV
The Deep River

It is my opinion, Legate, that we waste our resources charting these caverns. The empire that lived here has departed, and wild beasts are all that remain. Of the men I have not lost, many have lost their minds to the darkness.

There is little to be gained by fighting the creatures that reside in this place, for we know not their number. We know not their strength, nor what kinds of creatures they are. I myself have seen a stoat bigger than ten horses, even though such a thing cannot be. The power of the gods is at work throughout. Some of the men say we explore the outer halls of Orcus itself. I cannot truly say they are wrong.

My men are brave, but many have quailed at the thought of returning to that place. They will follow my orders, as I will follow yours. Until I receive further instructions, I have emptied the ruins of our people. We will return only if you are still resolved in this thing. If my counsel is of value to you, I ask you to confirm my decision and end this mission. I await your reply.

— Publius Galerius (translation by Eldi the Scribe)

Accord

The feel of cold, hard stone stung Brenish's palms. They felt battered, scraped. Sensation returned to those first. Presently he noticed his body ached all over, as if he had been beaten by a gang. A sharper pain emanated from the back of his head, seeming to bounce off the inside of his skull like the ringing of a great church bell. He hardly dared to move.

Eventually there seemed to be nothing critically wrong that he could tell without stirring, so he began to cautiously wiggle his fingers and toes, flex his arms and legs, turn his head. His neck and back hurt rather a lot, but nothing felt broken or too badly sprained. He knew a broken bone should make him sick, but he didn't feel sick.

He opened his eyes and was surprised to see some light, flickery but reddened. His ears seemed to turn on then: it was a torch. The light was only redder in his left eye; the right was fine.

He groaned, and rolled over onto his back. His pack was gone.

"How bad are you hurt?" someone said. He was surprised to hear it was Raden.

"Are we dead?"

"If we are, I'm disappointed. Are you hurt bad?"

"I'm not sure," said Brenish. "I don't think so. You?"

"My leg is broken. I set it. Used my spare torch as a splint."

"You can't walk on it," said Brenish.

"Nay. But my other torch is nearby. I can see it from here. We can use it as a crutch."

"Whose torch is burning, then?"

"Your spare. I needed to go into your pack."

Brenish sat up, slowly. His pack was lying close to him. Raden sat with his own legs stretched out, the right one wrapped tightly with cloth from the first aid supplies. The two pieces of a torch pole stuck out from the wrappings.

The gremlin had followed them down. Brenish's sword was still stuck through its spine. It was a wonder neither man was stabbed with it on the way down. Then again, it was a wonder they had survived the fall at all.

"How'd we live through that?" said Brenish.

"The cliff isn't sheer, just steep. But I think that scroll you read had a lot to do with it."

"Oh. Aye, it probably did."

Brenish got to his feet, but took his time in case a hidden break in his foot or elsewhere revealed itself. One injured man was bad enough; two meant they would surely die here. But nothing felt hurt too badly. His legs took his weight. He turned around to face the cavern wall, the cliff, hoping he could see lights at the top. But all was dark there. The single torch was inadequate even to see the top of the cliff.

"How long have we been down here?" said Brenish. "I'd call for the others but I'm not sure it's a good idea."

"I don't know how long I was out," Raden said. "I've been awake for half an hour, maybe. You stirred a few times, so I knew you weren't dead."

Brenish held his head in both hands. He felt a little dizzy. The back of his head was sticky. "I didn't dream."

"How could you tell? Your dreams must look just like this."

"There's usually more gold involved."

Brenish turned around and reached for his sword, pulling it out of the gremlin's back. He found the other torch and walked over to pick it up.

"Aye, this should do as a crutch, if we wrap it."

"Bring it here, then," said Raden.

He came back and handed off the torch, but kept looking around. "This cavern runs south and east," he said. "I think if we go east we'll just end up in the mushroom canyon. The others would've gone northwest."

"You think they're still alive?"

"No question. I think we'd see traces of them down here if anyone else was killed. We had the goblins mostly beaten. I can't figure the rest of the gremlins were an overwhelming threat."

"Would that I had your outlook."

"I'm sure your brother's well." Brenish kept his gaze on the cavern, looking south. At least he thought it must be south. "I think there's light that way."

"There is," said Raden. "At first I was afraid to light a torch myself, but I decided to risk it. It hasn't gotten stronger."

"Could be sunlight or an old spell light, then," said Brenish. "We should investigate. 'Tis safer than the canyon, and we have to hope there's a way to turn west, then north."

"*Hope?* You don't know where we are?"

"I know exactly where we are. We're at the bottom of the cliff on the west end of the mushroom castle. But no one knows what's down here. We may be the first men to see it since the days of the Elder Kingdom. If not, with any luck we'll be the first to live to tell about it."

Raden patted the cloth wrapping over the head of his original torch, making sure it was able to take his weight. "This may do," he said.

"Excellent. Let's away. The faster we get out of here, the more hope we have of meeting the others in Shatterhelm."

"There's one problem. How do I know you won't use me till I'm no longer valuable, then leave me to die here?"

"Because I'm a good man," said Brenish, "and I'm offended you'd suggest such a thing."

"You're not trustworthy."

"You're a fine one to talk, Raden. Cirawyn wouldn't be here if not for you and Bob."

"We were following orders," he said. "There's no wisdom in disobeying Gareth."

"And that's why I don't trust *you*," said Brenish. "Now that we've come to it, I don't know that I can count on you at all. We'll need every bit of our wits and our supplies to survive here, yet if we make it out, every single thing I say or do will be reported to Gareth. For you're his good and faithful squire, aren't you?"

Raden appeared to be enraged, but he kept his temper in check. He said nothing for about a ten count, then took a breath. "And you, you'll lie to anyone in any way you please. Just because you're the expert here doesn't mean I can count on you any better. Lord help me, I don't even dislike you, but you make it hard on a man."

"I've never swindled you," said Brenish.

"Nay, but you've never been fully truthful, either."

"You want the full truth?"

"Aye. Whenever I ask. And no lies, asked or no."

"I'll agree to that," said Brenish, "on one condition. Whatever I tell you, whatever you see, it stays between us. No sharing with Bob, no telling Gareth. It doesn't get back to him at all. Would you swear to *that*?"

Raden blinked and stared off into the distance, taking a moment to decide. "Aye, I'd swear to that, if you'll swear to mine. I'll meet your terms. I swear it on the soul of my mother."

Brenish hadn't expected him to capitulate, but it was a fair condition. Honesty for secrecy; he could live with it. "And I on mine," he said. He spat in his hand and held it out to shake. Raden did the same, and the deal was struck.

"What now?" said Raden.

"We take inventory. We have only one working torch. One sword. I have a knife, and so does this fellow." He kicked at the gremlin's corpse.

"I have the knife I took after your raid on the goblins."

"Have you a crossbow?"

"Lost."

"And Cirawyn has mine. We should have ample food. Was anything in our packs broken?"

"Nay. You still have the empty bottles. Our water bottles are whole."

"Good, good. That leaves me with a few oddments I've collected. The goblin we found in Paddystock had a wand, but no telling what it does."

"You told Gareth he had none!"

"Aye. I told him I saw Dex selling Enzo an unk, too, but 'twas no more than a guess. Tibs found it on Enzo's body. I'm sure Dex made it, but I've no idea what it does. You don't know any spells, do you?"

Raden shook his head, but then stopped. "Well, my mum had songs she used to sing us. They felt like spells. My granddad, he was a mage, but I never got the hang of channeling magic."

"So much for that, then," Brenish said. "I can cast daybreak or mass protection in a pinch, but we only have two spell tokens."

"How came you by those?"

"Dex."

Raden pursed his lips as if to whistle, but frowned thoughtfully instead. "You've hidden quite a lot from Gareth, 'twould seem."

"Which you've sworn to keep hidden too, now."

"Aye."

"Then we have an understanding. Let me help you up."

The cavern was natural, but not entirely so. Like every part of the Elder Kingdom anyone had ever seen, the builders had left their mark here. At its southern end, past the remains of the gremlin Bob had chucked into the abyss and the cracked carcass of the turtle, the floor leveled out. Mining had been done in this area; veins of silver could still be seen on the walls, and holes where posts from scaffolding had been driven in. But most of the mining zones known in the ruins were further southeast, or down in the lower levels.

Rough, shallow steps led up to a tunnel leaving the chamber. The light from there was faint, reflecting off of the minerals and metals in the rock. It seemed like an afternoon glow, or perhaps something closer to sunset, which would fit about right. Brenish guessed the sun would probably go down in another hour or so, unless perhaps it was setting already.

Raden used his makeshift crutch like a cane, holding it on his left side so he could walk while keeping weight off the right. He was able to move rather well with it, owing to his massive upper body strength. Unlike his brother, he hadn't donned any chain mail that would weigh him down now. He walked only a little slower than his normal pace, letting Brenish go ahead with the torch.

They passed into the tunnel, which was much narrower and smaller than the Wide Road, but still roomy enough for their purposes. A dragon might be unable to slither through, but it was easily wide enough for both men to walk abreast if they wanted to.

"Can you tell where the light's coming from?" Raden said.

"Not yet. But I hear water. 'Tis a good sign."

Brenish suddenly realized as if for the first time that Gareth's eyes weren't upon him, and he could act freely. He pulled the owl figurine from his pocket and turned it about in his hands, examining each whittled groove, every place the birch had been cut and smoothed. The piece had been covered with a thin hard coat like lacquer—not the imported stuff, which was beyond Dex's means, but a cheap alchemical version often used on tables.

"Was Dex fond of birds?" Brenish said.

"Not that I knew. Why?"

"The unk is an owl. The one I think he sold to Enzo. I thought it might mean something."

"Dex kept his secrets," said Raden. "If he was working without a guild, can't say I blame him. I always thought he wanted to look like a worse fool than he was. Helped that the bad parts were mostly true, eh?"

"Aye. But why an owl?"

"Owls are wise. They see in the dark. They hunt. If it's an unk, maybe it helps with one of those things. Think you it's spent?"

"Nay," Brenish said, "it probably holds the full power. The shape seems built to collect magic over time. No one's used it for months."

He tried giving the unk a squeeze but nothing special happened. He didn't expect it to. When that didn't work, he rubbed it along his arm. He shook it, turned it end over end, and clutched it to his heart. There were only so many kinds of unks he knew of, and only so many ways to activate them.

"Well," he said, "I can tell you what it's not. It's not for healing. It's *probably* not for light. It doesn't hide us, and it isn't a bearing stone."

"Don't you already have a bearing stone?"

"Used up."

Brenish tried sticking the unk in his ear next, but it had no effect. The thought of seeing in the dark, or seeing other life from afar as an owl sees its prey, led him to try putting it against his eye. This too failed. Finally in frustration he bonked the owl against his head.

He lurched back.

"What is it?" said Raden.

Brenish put the owl down again. "Huh," he said. "What a fool I've been. If I'd found a way to use this sooner, it might've replenished its power by now."

"What does it do?"

"It's for spellsight. Makes perfect sense now. I've heard of scrolls and spells for this purpose, but never a binding. What a useful tool for someone who might run across another unk."

"My granddad never mentioned spellsight. What is it?"

"The wand I'm carrying is made for lightning. It's good for two or three more blasts, but no more. I saw the bindings on the rest of my things, but they're all depleted."

"What else did you see?"

"Naught else. It lasted only a moment."

Raden gave an appreciative nod. "How long before you can use it again?"

"I've no idea."

Brenish decided to put the owl away, its purpose now clear. Truly Dex had been a genius to make such a thing. A journeyman spellbinder might embark on such a project, to create a new and useful binding to present as a masterwork to his guild. But Dex, guildless and employed as a simple enforcer, had no chance to do so.

Yet maybe it was better the man's talents were gone. Mages and wizards were rumored to engineer "accidents" against students who turned frequently to evil. Binders were less apt to abuse their power, but now and then an ill-favored member of their order would die too. The idea of Dex wielding any kind of magic at all was disturbing. Not all of his ways had been play-acting. Brenish wondered which was worse, if the character had grown from evils already within him or Dex had grown into the character.

It was hard to look at the owl and imagine the deep thought that went into its creation, the skill and the effort and the concentration, set alongside everything else. And it was a reminder that he still wasn't sure how to feel about what Tibs had done. He turned his eyes ahead, down the tunnel, and put the unk away.

Though the corridor looked more natural than the road, it ran perfectly straight and its floor was smooth. The light ahead was brighter now, clear to see rather than half-imagined in the deep dark at the foot of the cliff. Still it was nothing more distinct than a hazy golden glow. Somewhere high above them, a pleasant wood must be basking in that same color, autumn leaves blazing their glorious colors in the rich light of the low sun. They might be close to Northhill by now, but it was a very rough guess; the Buried Gate was somewhere in the mountains north of there.

The tunnel seemed to go on for miles, though Brenish attributed that to their slower pace. Raden breathed hard behind him. He tried to keep just the right speed, and gauge it by those breaths. Too fast, and Raden had to work harder to keep up. Too slow, and just as much work went into standing as walking.

"I think I should have the wand," Raden said. "It's no good to you."

Brenish stopped momentarily. "Aye," he said, and handed it back. Raden didn't seem the type to shoot him in the back, though it wasn't a part of their agreement.

They walked on. The light seemed to carry well from its source, even nearly a mile away as it seemed. Brenish felt this was strange, despite the reflective walls; it should have faded quicker. Nor did it seem to change in color or intensity, except that as they drew closer it grew a little brighter. A late afternoon sun should have turned a richer orange by now, and darker.

There was one branch in the tunnel. It loomed ahead on their right as they approached. There, another tunnel forked off at nearly a right angle, leading into some distant darkness. When they reached the opening the sound of water grew more intense. There was a warm breeze that way, a note of humidity, and the intermingled smells of running streams and dank stone.

"We're not turning?" said Raden.

"Not yet. I want to see whence comes this light."

"Curiosity seems dangerous down here."

"It can also be profitable."

"You think there's treasure ahead?"

"The gold color hasn't changed," Brenish said. "Perchance an old spell lamp still shines on a hoard."

"What if it's a dragon hoard, and there's a dragon with it?"

"No dragon hides underground unless it also hunts above. We haven't had a dragon around for a long time. Besides, any dragon that nested *here* would have been a rival to the one Visak slew. Unless it died a long time ago."

"Maybe there *were* two dragons. Maybe that was the answer to the riddle. Remember 'The bird under stone'?"

"Aye, I remember." But Brenish didn't want to say any more about it, lest Raden ask another direct question.

The light grew steadily stronger. Soon it competed noticeably with Brenish's torch. Only then did they see the light was not solid; it wavered like a flame, or perhaps like many flames, waves of light clashing against each other in a beautiful, chaotic dance. Both men stayed quiet, avoiding as much noise as they could. The torch and the clicky-clack of the iron pole of Raden's crutch seemed much louder. The noise of water and the very distant sounds of animals seemed to fade to almost nothing.

And then the light revealed itself.

"Bless me," Brenish said. Raden, coming up a few more steps, gasped.

A small lake lay before them in the next chamber, not blue nor black, but shining amber.

"What is that?" said Raden.

"Something I've never heard of," Brenish said. His wonder was tinged with caution, but those feelings stayed at the back of his mind. Neither crept into his voice, which came out flat. When facing the unknown, it was better to think quickly than to feel. "No tale ever spoke of this."

The Golden Lake

Brenish walked the rest of the way out of the tunnel. Steps led down into the vast main chamber, which was shaped like a great bottle. The cavern seemed to have been formed partly by nature, but finished by the Elder Kingdom. The base of the room consisted of many concentric terraces, carved with precision and extending down into the lake. The steps marched downward and inward until they reached a wide circle at the base, as if this room had once been an amphitheater. There were several exits around the room, the farthest being perhaps as much as a hundred yards away. Above ground it might have been considered a large pond.

The surface of the amber lake was about six feet below the level of the tunnel. The light welling up through it came from several objects below. Where the light passed through the lake's surface, ever moving in the constant drafts that ran throughout the ruins, it broke apart in a complex netting of shimmer that danced across the walls and the high curved ceiling. The whole room was bathed in a golden glow.

"What is this place?" said Raden.

"I have a guess," Brenish said. He pointed around the room. The walls were not bare. Many earthenware pipes ran along the outer rim, some dribbling in trace amounts of the thin golden ichor. The terraces, too, were interrupted in places by pipes, many of them below the surface of the lake. The lake's surface seemed to coincide with the bottom of one such pipe, suggesting that all the outflow went through there. Clearly this room had never been intended for any other use.

"This is all *esen*?" Raden said.

"Aye. We're in a giant collection bottle. Most of these pipes must be to draw the *esen* away. Probably to farms and cities. Only I think naught's drawing from it now."

Raden scratched his head with his free hand. "Think you, this is why the Elder Kingdom fell?"

Brenish could only shrug. "Who's to say it fell? I doubt the Kingdom ran on just one room like this one."

He looked down into the bottom of the pool. There were objects there—many of them—and bones. He handed his torch to Raden, who took it without asking why, and started to take off his armor piece by piece.

"What in the name of the Saints are you doing?" said Raden.

"Looks like a lot of stuff has washed down here over the years. There are spell lamps down there. I'm gonna get us one."

"You can't swim in *esen*! Have you gone mad?"

"Who says you can't? It's smooth as cream on the skin."

"I wouldn't know. I never put any in my hand."

"You never spilled some filling a wisp? It's expensive, not dangerous."

"No one ever swam in it before. You're risking your life and mine."

Brenish finished slipping off the last of his clothing, leaving only the worn-out discord organ strung around his neck. He met Raden's eye. "Down here, you seize opportunities as they come. Here, I'll show you 'tis safe."

He picked up his cloak and fished out the bearing stone. Holding it, he plunged his hand into the *esen*, and pulled it back out again.

Suddenly he grabbed his wrist with the other hand, and dropped the bearing stone on the step. "Aieee!" he screamed. "It burns! It's burning my hand!" Raden's eyes bugged out. He tried to reach for Brenish's pack, perhaps to find water, but Brenish abruptly stopped screaming. He laughed.

Raden took a moment to realize what had happened. When he did, he was thoroughly unamused. "You poxy tit," he said.

"I had you," said Brenish. He picked up the stone again. "Ha! The binding is refreshed, just as I hoped." He pointed around the room. "That way is due north. We came over a mile down the tunnel, as the bat flies."

He searched in his clothes for the owl, and held out a hand for Raden to hand him the wand. Again he put his hand underneath the amber surface of the lake. He left it there for half a minute before he withdrew.

"There," he said. "I think that... nay. Wait." He put the owl token to his head again. "Nay, the wand is no better off. It can't absorb the *esen* on its own." He handed the wand back to Raden, but dunked the owl one more time. Satisfied he had made his point, he set the charm onto the terrace where he sat, and made ready to dive in.

"Just because your hand fared well, doesn't mean your eyes will," Raden said. "Leave them closed."

"I thought I saw a blade down there. You want me to cut myself?"

"I don't want you to go blind, woolly-wit. If you can't see, we die. Better a cut."

"Your concern is deeply moving. I'll do it your way."

With that, Brenish walked down the terraced steps into the *esen*. It was quite warm, as a shadeless pond in high summer. He swam out into the middle of the lake, keeping his head above the surface. The light came from directly below him.

He took a breath, and dove down.

Diving blind was difficult, but he had dived into ponds with his eyes closed before; this wasn't that much different. The fluid around his body felt like water, but it conveyed a sensation of unreality that seemed to slide down each and every tiny hair on his arms, chest, and legs. The feeling of being surrounded by pure potential, possibilities as countless as the stars, pressed at his mind. The growing pressure in his ears seemed like distant music carried over the wind. In the embrace of so much magic, he felt as if old Visak were sitting nearby in his chair at the Horsehead, still telling his old tales.

"You'll see stranger than that, if you ever go, lad," the wizard's voice seemed to say. He couldn't tell if it was memory. "Mark that. A man can't prepare for everything. Steady now; watch your hand."

The bottom was shallower than he thought. He smacked his hand a little too hard against it, but he was unhurt. The spell lamps were easy to find; he could see the light shining through his eyelids. Only one was a true lamp, mounted in a setting; he found four others that were luminous, but loose, and kept one of them.

The spellbound lights weren't the only items down there. Something had washed them here along with all the bones; perhaps an inflow pipe. The first item he found was indeed a blade, a little dull but seemingly free of rust. He avoided getting cut. It was a sword; unfortunately he had no way to swim with such a heavy thing. Another hand however found purchase on a thin chain, so he grabbed hold and took it. His air was getting harder to hold, the need to breathe becoming stronger.

Pawing around old bones during his last few breaths, Brenish found a small bottle and a wooden disc. There could have been many more items to find, but with his eyes closed and his time running out, he had to give up. He had no way to hold anything more, anyway; it was a struggle to keep hold of the things already in his hands.

He tried to turn away from the light so he could orient himself, but he remembered too late that there were two spell lights in his hands already. Flipping over only confused him more, until he wasn't sure which way was up. The pain in his lungs grew intense. He had to breathe soon or drown.

There was no other choice: He opened his eyes. The *esen* stung a little, but no more than water. Brenish was heedful of Raden's warning however and only left them open long enough to find the floor again. It was enough to plant his foot against it, and push off hard.

Brenish gasped as he breached the surface. The *esen* dripped freely off of his face. He tried hard not to drop anything he had collected, while kicking his feet to return to shore.

Everything was tinted yellow. At first that didn't seem unusual, until he realized the torchlight didn't look right. He also realized, in a sudden panic, that he had swallowed some of the liquid. Having it in his hand was one thing, but he didn't know if it might poison him or worse. Now he regretted his decision to jump into the lake, even though the items in his hands might prove valuable.

He reached the shore at last, dumping his collection on the step. The spell light that was secured in a lamp, a copper cage wound around a collection jar, kept burning happily; but the enchanted hunk of glass beside it dimmed and winked out. The chain he'd discovered was attached to an amulet, a simple silver charm with a pea-sized sapphire in the middle. The wooden disc was some kind of box, engraved with a flower on top. He observed that the bottle was glazed earthenware, not glass, and tightly stoppered with a thick, waxy cork.

"Enjoy your swim?" said Raden.

"It was refreshing. I had to open my eyes though."

"Don't you dare go blind on me."

"I won't. The yellow is fading."

"Good. Put your clothes back on."

Brenish took his time drying off, though, running his hands vigorously through his hair to shed as much *esen* as he could, and letting the rest drip dry for a minute. Eventually though, even in the warm air of the cavern he felt too chilled, so he relented and got dressed.

Raden poked around the new treasures. He found how to open the round wooden box—it only needed a twist—and found a pink salve inside. He sniffed it curiously.

"Spellsight might not tell us what that is," said Brenish. "Unless it's magic."

"I think it is. It smells like... sweaty tea, and overripe apples."

"Sweaty tea? That's disgusting."

"Nay, my granddad had some of this. The other one. I think this is a healing cream, an old kind."

Raden put some of the stuff on his fingers and reached under his wrappings to spread it around.

"You're a brave man," said Brenish. "Or a stupid one. Can't tell."

"You're one to talk." Raden continued rubbing in the salve. His face softened in relief. "Aye, 'tis a healing cream."

"Excellent. Spread it all over."

"I don't think it can mend my leg. Granddad said it wasn't very strong stuff, but it was still good for pain in the joints and stiffness in the muscles. It might hasten the process. Probably best to use it sparingly."

Brenish shrugged. "As you will. You keep it, then. You've the greater need of it."

He didn't have all of his armor back on yet, but his curiosity was too strong to ignore the fruits of his treasure dive any longer. He picked up the amulet and the bottle, and used the owl token again.

The binding around the amulet flashed into his mind; the potion was inert to him. Spellsight should have worked on a potion. Although a potion wasn't bound, it was focused magic, folded into a specific use. Even scrolls could be understood by spellsight. Yet this was a complete mystery.

"Huh," he said.

"I hate when you do that."

"When I say 'Huh'?"

"When you're surprised by anything. That vexes me. You're supposed to know this place like the back of your hand."

Brenish shrugged. "Not everything is known. I said it because this doesn't seem to be a potion."

"Well, what's the amulet do?"

"It's a charm of stealth."

"Perfect for a thief," said Raden.

"Nay, you should take it. You make too much noise with that crutch already."

He tossed the pendant to Raden. Raden grabbed it with his free hand and put it around his own neck, insofar as he had one. Brenish went back to examining the rest of his haul.

"If that's not a potion," Raden said, "what is it?"

Brenish pulled the cork from the bottle. Whatever it was made of held together when he tugged it out, but he had never encountered anything like it before. It was soft and had a little give, but it obviously wasn't wax; a thin seam ran through the center as if it had been pressed together from two pieces. Uncapped, the bottle gave off a sharp alchemical aroma.

"Whoo!" he said. "Whatever this is, I'm not drinking it to find out."

"I'm with you," said Raden. "Close it up again."

Brenish pushed the cap back in and jammed it down tightly. The cork formed a tight seal against the glazed lip. He looked over the bottle and found a kind of label stuck to the bottom, a strip of cloth or paper that was straight on the long sides and frayed on the short ones, less than an inch wide. It was stained from the *esen* and the ink on it was smudged, but it was readable—or would have been, but for the language. The label wasn't proper words, but a sequence of letters and numerals.

"If you're finished here," Raden said, "can you put on the rest of your armor so we can get moving?"

"Just a moment."

Brenish dunked the owl charm once more and returned it to his pocket. He then reached into his pack and found the two empty bottles: one from Dobber, one he had saved from the goblins' wine. He quickly removed the stopper on each and filled them as far as he could, then corked them back up again.

His pack contained more items he had salvaged from their past encounters. One of them was a long leather thong. This he retrieved, and ran it through a loop on the spell lamp. He made a large necklace out of the leather, using his quick fingers to tie a sturdy knot.

"There you go," he said. "Now we'll have proper light."

"What about the other light? What are you going to do with it?"

Brenish picked up the little bead and turned it in his fingers. It felt warm. On contact with the residual moisture on his skin, it glowed dimly. "I don't know yet. Stash it, I suppose. We don't have a collection bottle, but I should have plenty of fuel for it without one. If we find more wire I can make a wick so it won't burn so fast."

He finally got around to putting on his vambraces, greaves, chest armor, and cloak. Putting the bottles away, he closed up his pack and hoisted it.

"I'm ready," he said. "Let's find the river."

The tunnel they had passed earlier seemed noisier than before, after the quiet of the lake. Brenish had to wonder if the *esen* that got into his ears had sharpened his hearing somehow. His vision at least had returned to normal, which was a relief.

Rats ventured willingly into these parts, heading the opposite direction. Perhaps they were going to feast on the remains of the gremlins and the turtle at the bottom of the cliff, or they had errands to keep in the mushroom canyon. He was happy to indulge the idea that they had important lives he should care about, if only to keep himself from thinking about Naman, Tibs, and most of all Cirawyn.

If he survived but she didn't, her dad would kill him. And he'd be grateful to the man for doing it.

The sound of water grew louder as they walked. The deep river, however, was farther away than they had thought. It was about half a mile before the tunnel came to an end. They traversed that distance fairly quickly given Raden's condition, but Brenish was slowly beginning to realize how much time had passed since his fall, and the thought that the others might now be many miles away began to worry him greatly.

Before the battle at the keep, he might have felt a little differently; he'd had more confidence in Gareth's ability to handle the situation then. Now he felt Gareth was too reckless to be trusted. Hopefully Finch's influence would keep his impulsiveness to a minimum, but he couldn't imagine Gareth's composure staying firm once he failed to find anything. Even if Willy's bird riddle had an answer, one of the last few would not.

Where the tunnel ended, there was another running north to south. It was bricked over like the Wide Road, but not as large. The western half of the new tunnel was a trench three feet deep and lined with irregular pavers, but the water running within had a depth of only half a foot. Brenish didn't know if that was supposed to be the river's normal level, or if the flow had split or diminished.

The nearer half of the tunnel was an ordinary cavern floor, smoothed and leveled. Unlike other tunnels they had seen, in this one the walkway was broken into steps. Each step was only a few inches high, but they were many yards apart.

The men turned right, headed upstream. The channel ran straight north by northwest, so said the bearing stone. Raden had a little trouble negotiating the first few steps, even though the ones by the lake hadn't given him any problems. After a while, however, he got the knack of using his crutch effectively and found the right rhythm to always hit each step in stride.

"Where do you suppose this will come out?" Raden said.

"I'm not sure. There's a low bridge over the deep river somewhere upstream, but I think 'tis far northwest of here. The others may have passed it already."

They walked along without speaking for some time. The tunnel held its straight course the entire way; its upward grade was just as steady. The water moved swiftly by beside them. Brenish saw little fish swimming against the current, each one glowing a soft red. In places, little fungal growths like weeds came up between the pavers, but for the most part the channel was in top condition for having been built so long ago—however long that actually was.

Brenish found he was increasingly concerned with the perfect line the channel kept. No river should flow so straight. The Elder Kingdom had tamed the caves, but they had not reshaped them entirely. He had never heard of the deep river having such an artificial course. But then, most people who had crossed the deep river had done so along Gareth's route, or much deeper and further south, or far to the north. The knowledge that he and Raden were probably the first to see this place might have been comforting to part of his mind, but the rest was deeply worried.

The sound of the rushing water grew again, after perhaps half an hour had passed. Time was difficult to gauge here, though Brenish felt fairly sure the sun had already gone down. Would that he had a timepiece like Gareth's, he thought, so he could know how hopeless their attempt to catch up truly was.

"I see something," said Raden. "Something shimmering."

Brenish didn't respond. He kept going uphill until the thing Raden had seen came closer. It was more water, but it reflected the light of Brenish's torch and Raden's spell lamp readily, because it was a vertical stream. The sounds of splashing and bubbling came from there, where the fall hit the channel. It was a heavy torrent that flowed in.

Beyond, there was only a wall.

They approached the fall anyway. The water came in through a large hole in the ceiling above, some kind of channel diverted from the river. In the space behind the waterfall there was only a short empty niche. Within that, the only visible features were two identical holes, one in each side wall, big enough to insert a human arm.

"There was a wheel here," Brenish said. His voice was sad, but he wasn't sure particularly why. It could have been frustration, but he also felt a real sense of loss, a mourning for whatever had once been there.

"What for, I wonder," said Raden.

"Driving a pump, most like. All that lovely *esen* had to go somewhere."

"Mayhap the pump failed, and they closed off this area. And then the wheel rotted away."

"Aye. Or the wheel broke. Or they abandoned this place long before then."

He looked up at the hole. There was no way to climb up, even if the water wasn't pouring in. Two healthy men with a ladder might force a path, but for them it was a dead end.

"Our only hope is downstream," said Brenish.

"Are you're sure we can't go back to where we started? If we can find that ravine with the mushrooms, we can go north through that."

"No one knows where that ravine begins. We could end up at another dead end. The river is better mapped. We just have to pray there's a way back to it."

The Shaft of Jewels

Brenish felt no joy as the two men trudged downstream, but Raden was surprisingly chipper. Perhaps the balm had secondary effects, or else Raden placed far too much faith in his companion as a navigator. He expressed confidence, more than once, that they would get out of this trouble and return to the others safe and sound. Brenish couldn't share his optimism.

In part, it was because the bearing stone said they were going exactly the wrong way. The necessity of going that way didn't do much to counter the constant echo in his mind. A map, too, was forming there, courtesy of the stone. Brenish could tell exact distances, knew with his eyes closed exactly where the *esen* chamber lay. The stone might even be more powerful now than when it was first bound. It was probably a binding made with very low energy to make it cheaper, but the quality of the spell was all that mattered. With that power, the map in his mind grew broader as it drew from his memories (or perhaps its own), gradually piecing together an exact route all the way from Asaph's Gate.

What Brenish felt most was anger, and fear. He was irrationally angry with the builders for letting the path end where it had, with no way up to the main channel from there. That was poor tunnel design. Logically, this path had to lead *somewhere*, or else no one would have built it. It was easier to believe the exit lay ahead to the south than through the wild mushroom canyon, but this too could take them to a dead end. Raden wouldn't be able to continue like this on a broken leg forever, and they'd have to sleep sometime.

The fear was easier to understand. They were getting farther away from the others, traveling in very different directions. He had no way to protect Cirawyn or his friends if he wasn't with them. They would need protection: if not from the dangers of the ruins or from Gareth's brashness, then from Gareth's temper. And he couldn't speak of this fear to Raden, at least not in full.

They passed the side tunnel that brought them here, which brightened Raden's mood but not Brenish's. It only meant they were going deeper into the unknown.

The main tunnel went downstream for two more miles without a change. There were no more passages intersecting the channel. It took most of a long hour to cover that distance. Raden had found his downhill rhythm easily enough, but with the crutch they were hampered. Brenish admired the man's endurance, though. Even with Raden's strength, supporting himself on a crutch and one leg and traveling for several miles at a stretch, while still feeling pain in his other leg and the weariness of a day's travel, must have been brutal.

The first sign of anything different came unexpectedly, with an uptick in insect activity. The tunnel went from harboring very few bugs to very many, in just a short distance. Ants, centipedes, and the occasional small spider crawled about on the floor. A pungent smell came from somewhere up ahead, but the air carrying it smelled otherwise cleaner, more pleasant than it should. Fine grit appeared on the floor, requiring Raden to slow his pace a little lest he slip.

"Smells like bats," Raden said.

"Aye."

"That's good news. It means we're close to the surface."

"Nay. We've been headed downhill for two days."

"But the land slopes down west of the village."

Brenish shook his head. "The river valley does. But our descent was a lot steeper most of today. If there's less than a hundred feet of rock above us, I'll eat a mouse."

"But you can't rule out an exit, can you? A stairway could end down here, easy enough."

"Hanfore's Gate is nowhere near here. I'm not aware of any others in this area that survived."

"Caves."

"Not with accessible entrances to the ruins," Brenish said.

"A secret entrance, then. One no one has ever discovered."

"And if we find such a thing, do you really want to abandon your brother down here? You'd be in a part of the wilderness so inhospitable that no one ever found a secret gate there, you'd still be injured, and you'd be alone because I'm not leaving."

Raden grumbled. "Thanks for being so cheery. I was just looking for something to lift our spirits."

"Fine luck with that. The wine's gone already."

"Have it your way, then. Be miserable. Here I thought *I* was the one with the deepsick."

Brenish brushed him off. But the longer they went on, the more he wondered: *Did* he have the deepsick? Though he had always dreamed of coming to the ruins, two days of darkness and all the stone, stone, stone had worn at his mind. Now that he faced the real possibility of never finding a way out, it seemed as if a slower, more insidious cousin to panic had taken root in his heart. Perhaps that was what the deepsick felt like in its early stages.

"Maybe you're right," he said at length, though it had been easily ten minutes since Raden suggested it. "Perchance 'tis the deepsick."

"Or hunger. I could use a bite, and a rest. Soon."

"Aye."

Sometime during their silence, the dirt on the floor had become a thin layer of guano. There were no bats at hand, probably because it was the time of night for them to feed. If they had access to the open air, they would already be out. Hordes of insects dissected and dragged away a few little skeletons and scattered bones, but otherwise the tunnel was clear.

Before they found the source of the fresh air, they noticed another change. The water that babbled beside them in its channel was noisier than before, though Brenish saw no change in its flow. Even Raden commented on it. The increased debris on the floor should have, if anything, muffled more sound. Brenish's best guess was that there might be a cavern somewhere ahead, causing the sound to resonate and echo more.

Finally, after they had come nearly four miles down the tunnel, they could see its end. The tunnel opened into a small, mostly natural cavern whose floor had been smoothed. The channel ended halfway through the room, diving beneath the floor where the water could continue its journey south. Here a few bats were in residence, and even more of their bodies littered the floor.

Neither man considered stopping here; it was an unpleasant place to try and sit. They crossed over and passed into another cavern to the west, through an opening that appeared to have been widened by the Elder Kingdom.

The sound of water didn't leave them. It was somewhere westward along their current path. Brenish remarked on this with more of a smile in his voice; it was a hopeful sign.

The new cavern was long, snakelike, with a higher ceiling and wider span than the Wide Road. The walls were smooth in a way that told him water had done the work, not magic. Even with their meager light they could see far ahead down its length, which was a bat highway. A deeper darkness could be seen near the far end, before the cavern turned a corner to the north.

"I'm not one to complain," Raden said, "but we need a place to rest soon."

"Aye. As soon as we get past the bats."

The blackness beyond got bigger, untouched by the light they carried. There was no doubt it was the mouth of the hidden caves. The air that flowed toward them was chilly but clean-smelling, with a distant scent of evergreens and autumn leaves. The forest fragrance was almost heartbreaking. Brenish felt a sudden longing to escape the stone prison they were in, to breathe clear air again and see the sky.

Something in the outlet glittered back at them when they came near. Brenish saw that the floor of the cave there had been paved over with bricks in a large raised circle that extended into the darkness. A short brick wall like a rampart had been built across the opening in a perfect semicircle. He felt drawn there, pulled in by the sparkling beauty beyond. For a moment he forgot everything else. He stepped onto the platform and walked to the wall.

He stood on a balcony set into a huge vertical shaft, supported by a rock outcropping below. The shaft went down as far as the light would reach, perhaps to the deepest levels of the ruins and beyond. Upward, it ran straight to the surface. And in either direction, on every side of the enormous chimney, he saw brilliant crystal and gemstone formations in every color he could have imagined. The torchlight, and the sunny light of Raden's approaching spell lamp, sent reflections cascading back and forth in a dazzling, ever-shifting display.

The opening far above seemed tiny; it was black, with no stars. Brenish was almost glad of the blackness; it would have made him all the more homesick. A man would have to scale the razor-sharp walls for twenty-five fathoms or more to ever reach the surface, while hanging over a drop that could easily be a mile.

Raden stood next to him. Brenish didn't hear him come up and only vaguely remembered the light changing, but he couldn't say how long he had stood there.

"I can't find the words," said Raden.

"Aye. What a pity we didn't come here during the day. What a sight that would be." His mind strayed to the spell tokens in his pocket. If he used one here to cast daybreak, he'd still have a spare. But in the open like this, in unknown places, it was a supremely terrible idea. Besides, he had never heard of that spell being cast under open sky, and had no idea what might result.

Raden tried to shrug, but that didn't work with a crutch. "Maybe you'll come back here someday."

"Not on your life."

That was a strange thought, for Brenish. It snapped him out of his trance. The temptation to cast a spell in parting, just to get a quick look, didn't entirely go away, but he no longer felt connected to this place. The scent of the trees was stronger in his heart, and Cirawyn was very far away. Brenish took one more look down, up, and around from left to right.

"Nay," he said. "I'm glad I saw this. I'm glad I had a chance to come down here. But 'tis time to go home."

He turned his back on the shaft, and looked ahead.

The cave turned north here, and from that direction the sound of flowing water was the strongest. The deep river had to be near. Brenish stepped down off the platform and sniffed. If there was water in the air, the inflow from above masked it.

"Come on," he said, "let's find a place to rest."

Raden had trouble tearing himself away from the sight, but he sighed and turned, hobbling back down to the cavern floor. He groaned, once.

They walked on a short way through the remainder of the sinuous cave. The presence of bat droppings and remains dropped off rapidly, as if the bats didn't like this part of the system. The floor was mostly level, but Brenish felt alternately as if they were walking uphill, down again, and back up, on a very slight grade. The cave turned slowly left, back to the west.

He felt the fatigue in his legs now, and a strong hunger in his belly. Soon they should consider sleep. But if they wanted to catch up to the others, they couldn't afford to sleep long. And if they wanted to stay alive, they could ill afford to sleep at the same time.

At last they reached the end of the cave. It emptied out into another, larger tunnel, much larger than the Road. A swift-moving river, about ten feet wide and high enough to reach their knees if they stood in its channel, ran through the center of the floor. This place, like the cave they just left, was mostly natural. But in places it had seen rough excavation to straighten its course or widen the banks, and the floor on either side of the river channel was partially smoothed. There were no steps.

"You were right," said Raden. "This looks like the deep river."

"Aye. Hopefully we'll find no more obstacles." Brenish turned right, upstream, and looked ahead as far as he could. The walls were not solid rock; they were interrupted by numerous passages or little grottos, most little bigger than a doorway, that had been roughly carved out. "We may find a place up here that's safe enough," he said.

Only a little further upstream, the first of the openings led into a chamber the size of the inn's great room. Brenish was surprised to see that the doorway had been chiseled out not by magic, but by actual tools. Two bricks and crumbling mortar stood at one side of the doorway, but no more, as if someone had thought to build an arch here but inexplicably decided to stop with the job barely begun.

"This is a fine place to rest," Brenish said. "We'll stop here."

"Aye," said Raden. "Help me sit."

Brenish tried to take Raden's weight as best he could, so the large man could sit without harm to his broken shin. Raden groaned in grateful relief and stretched out on the floor. Brenish pulled off Raden's pack, and his own as well, and sat down beside him. They faced the doorway, and the river, lest anything try to sneak up on them.

"That's more like it," Raden said. He grabbed the box of balm and smeared another generous helping under his wraps. "Ahh."

Brenish busied himself taking out the food. Raden had some of the goblins' cheese left, and he had some fruit. Both still had several helpings of Maddie Finch's mutton jerky. The water was running low, so he took both of their bottles and ran out briefly to refill them; the deep river was a poor source, but both men had drunk from worse. There were rodents in the tunnel, mice and rats mostly, but not very many. It seemed a half-wild place, a backwater, far from whatever civilization had once existed here. He went back inside quickly, not wanting to linger there alone.

"What time would you say it is?" said Raden.

"I'm not sure. Seven at the earliest. Eight or nine, most like."

Brenish took his seat and discovered Raden had already divided up the cheese and the fruit. Raden had a wooden plate, which they shared. The taste of food was bliss, after going so long since their last meal. Brenish savored every bite, nibbling to prolong the experience.

He wondered if the others had already stopped to rest. That was a mistake; once he started thinking of them, especially of Cirawyn, he couldn't let it go.

"Three down," said Raden, sadly, as if he had similar thoughts.

"Five," said Brenish. "You forgot about us."

"But we'll get back to them. Dex won't. Harry won't. Nor poor Jase."

"Aye. Would that we could move him to the village square."

"What a loss. Jase was a better man than you think. Not always the nicest, but he wasn't bad. Just bad luck."

"Nay," said Brenish. Raden looked askance at him, so he clarified. "Not the fact he's dead. 'Twas tragic, but it had naught to do with luck."

"What had it to do with, then?"

"Gareth. What kind of damned fool brings a polymorph wand down here? I told him I don't trust wands—"

"You can't use them, is why," Raden said. He seemed annoyed that Gareth was blamed for anything.

"But he wanted to bring them anyway. Each man has his own methods, I thought, so I didn't argue. But if he told me he planned to bring a polymorph wand, I'd've talked him out of it."

"Why?"

Brenish indicated by his brows what he thought of the question. "You *saw* why. Sometimes you get a turtle, sometimes you get a cockatrice. He used it to make a goblin turn against its own. Well done with the beetle, but what did that cockatrice give us? Only two dead goblins, and the prettiest statue in all the Elder Kingdom. 'Twas a stupid gamble."

"Everything about this is a gamble," Raden said. "But Gareth has done well by us so far."

"Somewhat. Anyone in his position, with his resources, might have done as well. And I was there to help. You want to know why I was so grumpy earlier? I'm terrified he's gonna do something else stupid without me there."

"Do you blame him for Harry, then? Or Dex?"

"My troth, no. Harry stumbled 'pon a trap. Maybe someone else would have seen it, maybe not, but there's no blame on Gareth for it." He saw a burst of emotion pass across Raden's face, and remembered he had been there too. Odd, that he hadn't thought about that until now. Raden had seen him die. "Nor you," Brenish added, "if you feared anyone thought so. Finch would be the first to say so, if there was blame on anyone."

"Aye." Raden gave a nod, seeming to take Brenish's absolution as some comfort. "Harry wasn't Gareth's fault. Gareth admitted he should have used that scroll sooner, for Dex's sake. But I think you were right not to blame him for that either. 'Twas merely a tragic accident."

Brenish said nothing. Raden turned and stared.

"Merely an accident, then," Raden said.

But again he got no response; Brenish was under oath, and could not casually agree no matter how much he wanted to twist the logic to suggest otherwise.

"Tell me truly, Brenish. Did you arrange for Dex to die?"

"Nay. 'Twas Tibs."

"Oh," Raden said. He frowned in disappointment and shock, but thought on it a moment. Presently he nodded acceptance. "I can understand that."

Brenish wondered if everyone knew Tibs' motives but him. Knowing Dex's character, he didn't want to think on what that could be.

"By our oath," Brenish said, "that truth stays between us."

"Aye. By our oath."

They ate quietly for a little while, listening to the sounds outside. A rat peeked its head in the doorway, but ran away when it saw them. In the ruins even the animals were torn between furtiveness and adventurousness, always needing to find a good meal at great risk. Otherwise nothing disturbed the men. Brenish heard no predators.

"Who'll take the first watch?" said Raden.

"I'll take it, unless you'd rather."

"I care not either way. But how long shall we sleep?"

"Two hours each. No more. It might be enough to catch up. We'll be tired, but better that than alone."

"Aye. Then you take the first watch, if you don't mind. I could drop off right now."

"As you will. I'll wake you in two hours."

The Lost Girl

For the first time in many years, Brenish dreamed of open sky in all its colors: vivid blue, evening violet, sullen autumn gray, deep winter white, black and starry, darkness contrasted with moonlit clouds, and the thousand shades of red, pink, purple, orange, and green that appeared only briefly at sunset. He dreamed of rain on his face, and snow, and hot sun. Wind that was more than a gust of air in a tunnel. The breeze of summer that was already gone. Trees, wheat, birds, and the bustle of a living city haunted him. He asked Visak what these things meant, but the wizard only smiled and smoked his pipe thoughtfully, staring into the hearth fire. He thought he heard the old man snickering under his breath, as if to say *'Twas you who wanted this, lad.*

A hand on his shoulder roused him. "Wake up," said Raden. "It's been about two hours."

He opened his eyes and saw stone, lit only by the torch and the spell lamp. His spirit flinched.

"Very well," Brenish said.

He sat up, still groggy, needing far more sleep than a meager two hours. His body was stiff and reluctant to move. In his mind he shouted at the muscles to obey, the joints to crack and loosen. They were already angry from the punishment they took when he fell, and the soreness was spreading. He reminded himself of the need to catch up to the others, of the danger Cirawyn and Naman and Tibs were in. That was enough, finally, to spur his body to action.

With similar effort of will, he stood and took on his pack. Raden didn't hand him the torch right away, but pointed to the back of the grotto. "Before we get on," Raden said.

"Good thinking." Brenish followed his lead and relieved himself against the back wall. The river might or might not have been a better choice, but these parts seemed free of predators that might sniff out this spot. Brenish even wondered if they could have slept safely at the same time, but he hadn't been willing to risk it.

When he was finished, Raden gave him the torch and they departed. The banks of the river seemed livelier now, as if a shadow of the day and night cycle still existed here. The activity of the animals and insects could be heard more than seen, up and down the length of the tunnel.

"Upstream?" said Raden.

"Upstream."

They set off together along the right bank, against the fast current of the river. Raden seemed slower than before, possibly from fatigue. They were traveling in the middle of the night and on barely a catnap, after all. Brenish counted himself lucky never to have broken a bone, but he had been told the pain was severe. All this travel couldn't be doing Raden's shin bone any favors, even after it had been set and wrapped tightly. Raden barely showed his pain, but Brenish saw it all the same.

"Tell me about your granddad," Brenish said, mostly in the hope of keeping Raden's mind occupied. "On your mum's side, the mage. Did you know him well?"

"We never knew him at all," Raden said. "He died before Bob was born. Mum said the old man was cranky, but kind. She said he thought magic was too stuffy and formal, and all the schools and trappings around it were hogshyte. He liked to say magic was better than that, and everyone should learn how to use it."

"Sounds a lot like Visak, actually."

"Aye. I don't know how well they knew each other, but Granddad did live in the city."

A large brick arch appeared ahead, much like the ones on the road from the Gatehouse but larger and more decrepit. It didn't look like it would crumble for another thousand years, but the surfaces of many bricks were cracked, many corners broken off. Its decay seemed less like the ravages of age than shoddy craftsmanship. There wasn't another arch like it as far as their lights could reach, but after walking a bit further they saw one in the distance. Brenish guessed the arches might be as much as a quarter mile apart. It left their purpose in question, since they couldn't possibly be there for structure.

The only other edifices were brick archways around some of the cave entrances to either side, reminders that they had once been lived in, and the occasional foot bridge with the same half-hearted masonry. What the Elder Kingdom built badly they still built to last, but there was no doubt that Brenish and Raden were in a disused corner of the ruins, perhaps no more than an outlaw settlement in its time. Perhaps some ancient version of Alfie the highwayman once prowled the Wide Road, and wintered in these hovels.

Even the tunnel was rougher than it ought to be. Stalactites had formed all over the ceiling, but had been mostly cleared away— broken off by force—from above the river channel. These, and other formations such as outcroppings or loose boulders that seemed to have been left there by careless giants, grew more common as the men ventured further upstream. The banks were still easily traversable on either side, but the path seemed to regress into savagery. As wild growth might overtake a long-disused road, so the very stone seemed to want to take back the river.

"Why didn't you go Fell before?" said Raden. "We were betting on how long it would take."

"I came close. I was too scared. Maybe too smart. By the time I got my courage half up, it was too late. Coming here would've meant losing Cirawyn. I chose her."

"And you came here anyway."

"So did she."

Raden seemed to want to respond, but Brenish cut him off. "Nay, save your apologies. You're right; you had no choice in it. And though it was Finch's idea, I don't blame him either. 'Tis Gareth's fault she's in danger. I just hope his recklessness doesn't get her killed."

"She'll be well. I know you're learned enough to second-guess his decisions, but—"

"Jase is dead, Raden. Gareth was a fool to bring that wand, and Jase is dead for it. He didn't even learn from his mistake. It won't happen to Cirawyn."

"I'm sure it won't. With time to think about it, he'll understand where it went wrong. You don't understand that about Gareth. He's pained by his mistakes. He does learn from them, though maybe not straight away. I'm sure he's awake right now, wondering how it could have gone different. You needn't fear for Cirawyn tomorrow for what happened today."

"You misunderstand me," Brenish said. "Even if I shared your faith in your boss, accidents happen. If any harm comes to her, that's one mistake I'll be sure he learns from. I promise you that. If she doesn't leave here alive, then by God neither will he."

Raden didn't seem sure how to reply. He held his tongue. Brenish could see he was angry; his loyalty was considerable. Yet since Raden truly believed they would leave the ruins rich, he had to think his employment with Gareth was near its end anyway.

"You strain my oath," Raden finally said.

"As you mine," said Brenish, without animosity.

The deep river was not straight; it wound a little in its southward course. Brenish felt the subtle changes in direction as they made their way upstream over the next two hours, thanks to the bearing stone. They were headed north by northwest again, sometimes almost due northwest, but the turns were so gradual that Brenish felt sure Raden was unaware of them.

As they went on, he felt they were making slightly better time. Raden appeared to feel less pain than when they set off, and kept a constant clacking rhythm between his crutch and his left foot.

Brenish told stories periodically to keep his companion occupied, but he strayed away from tales of disaster. Instead he spoke of the different kinds of creatures that lived here—mostly the harmless ones. He shared survival tips he had read, or had been told by adventurers who returned. Raden listened with either interest or great patience; Brenish knew he could prattle on terribly when he got rolling, worse if he got drunk first. Everyone had told him so.

But the time passed, a few more miles went by, and the deep night deepened still further in the world above as the hours before dawn approached. Raden stopped just once to sit for a few minutes and reapply the balm, and they went on their way again. They felt in good spirits, confident about their chances of catching up to the others, until both heard the sound of splashing in the distance.

The sounds came from something too big to be a little fish, or a rat. It might be something large enough, even hungry enough, to pose them serious danger. With only one sword and a few knives between them, and Raden in no shape to fight, they silenced their idle talk. Brenish however kept advancing and gestured to Raden to do the same. Whatever they had disturbed had seen their lights already, unless it was blind.

One of the narrow little bridges came into view at the edge of their light. As the men drew nearer they saw that something had been in the water close to the bridge, and had left puddles along the west bank, leading behind one of several tall rocks in a rough corner the builders hadn't bothered to clear.

Brenish didn't want to move on and leave the beast to follow behind them, whatever it was. He walked past the spot where it had come out of the water, and crossed the bridge to get a closer look. Raden clacked along behind.

"What is it?" said Raden.

"I know not," Brenish said. "'Twas fishing here. Would that we had Tibs with us to say more." Lacking the skills of a tracker, he ventured a guess anyway. "It moves on two legs. You see the spots here, and here. They look much like footprints, but they're too wet to tell. A manthing, most like."

He looked up and caught a glimpse of straw behind one of the rocks. The creature had already moved. A brief flash of pale pink flew past a gap, to another hiding place.

"'Tis watching us," Brenish said. "Whatever it is, 'tisn't a goblin."

A voice came back from behind the rock. "Come no closer." It was a young woman's voice, fair to the ear yet terrified. In three words she told a whole story of abandonment, loneliness, and desperate survival in a cruel cave.

"As you wish," said Brenish. "Are you human?"

The girl peeked out at them. Her skin was very white, except where it was covered in a thin layer of grime. Her hair was wheat blonde, a hallmark of Viking ancestry that was nevertheless considered exotic and attractive, and grew long yet slightly tangled. She looked about seventeen or eighteen, a grown woman. Her face was quite beautiful even for her unkempt appearance, with a small perfect nose and a delicate chin. She looked back at them with big, doe-like eyes, blue as the near-forgotten sky, that pierced Brenish's heart with feelings of pity.

"Aye," she said, her voice trembling. "Who are you?"

"My name is Brenish, milady, and this is Raden. May we have the pleasure of your name?"

She paused as if trying to remember. "L... Lila."

"We mean you no harm, Lila. Would you step into the light?"

She looked carefully at them, then took a quick glance upstream, before coming out from behind the rock. Lila was short for a woman her age, slender at the waist. Her garments were brown rags, threadbare but still servicing to cover up just enough for the barest modesty. A wide strip of old cloth was bound against her bosom, and another, wider one across her hips that barely reached to her thighs. If she weren't so frightened and alone here, her appearance could be called alluring, or possibly brazen.

"How came you here?" she said.

"We fell off a cliff and were separated from our companions. We're seeking them now."

"Companions?"

"Aye, milady," said Raden. "We've come in search of the wizard Visak's treasure."

"Visak," she said. It wasn't a question, nor a statement, but blank repetition. She blinked, and stuck her tongue barely through the side of her mouth as a nervous tick. She turned her attention back to Brenish and seemed near tears.

"How long have you been here, Lila?" Brenish said.

"I don't know," she said. Her voice was like milk at the rim of a mug, about to spill over. It was grief and terror and long suffering. "There are no days here."

"If you follow the river south, there's a place where you can see the sky."

"I don't go that way. 'Tisn't safe."

"How old were you when you came here?"

She blinked again a few times. "Fifteen," she said, as if it were a guess.

"Maybe three years," said Brenish. "Or a thousand sleeps."

Lila waited a minute, then nodded affirmation. "Aye," she said, and tears seemed ready to fall.

"That's a long time to survive down here," said Raden. "You must be very brave."

"I'm scared here," she said. Her upper lip trembled. She tried to stop it with the tip of her tongue again, and looked Brenish in the eye. "I'm scared all the time."

"Then come with us," Brenish said. "We're armed, and so are our companions. We'll protect you. You can go home with us."

"Home." Her voice broke, and then her resolve. She wept bitterly, barely able to hold up her head.

Brenish let her cry herself out. She took a few shuffling steps toward him, then reached out an arm. Brenish offered her his free hand and took hers in his own. Her skin felt cool to the touch, clammy because it had been wet, but her flesh had a deeper warmth within. She didn't meet his eye. She licked her lips again a few times from the tears, staring at his chest while she composed herself. Once or twice she glanced at Raden as well, perhaps to gauge whether he would be as friendly. Finally she looked up at Brenish—for the top of her head only came up to his chin—with her huge, needful blue eyes, glassy and damp.

"You will help me?" she said. No stray kitten ever mewed so balefully. Help her? He wanted to grow wings and carry her out through the jeweled ventilation shaft, and fly to the sunrise.

"Aye," he said, "we'll get you home. Come with us."

"But," she said. Her lip quivered again. "'Tis dangerous now. There are bad things up the river. This is their feeding time."

"We're armed," said Brenish. He patted his scabbard, and Raden pulled the wand halfway out of his pocket.

Lila did her nervous tick again, letting the tip of her tongue just graze her lower lip, and stared in Raden's direction, sizing up his potential from his legs to his thick neck. Though injured, he must still have looked imposing enough to be formidable in combat. But presently she looked back to Brenish's armor, the silver discord organ hanging by its thong around his neck, then finally his face.

"Rest a bit first," she said. "We'll go when it's safer. I need to gather my things." She blinked again as if to clear the tears, or the river water. "And you look weary."

"Our time is short," Brenish said. "We need to catch up to the others."

"Aye. Just a short time," she said. "Come in with me. Please."

"I could use a short rest myself," Raden said. "How long have we been walking? Two hours?"

"About that," said Brenish, "by my reckoning. All right, Lila, we'll take a short rest while you make ready to go. But feeding time or not, anything that lurks upstream will have us to contend with, and I promise you we'll prove the stronger."

She smiled in great relief. "This way," she said, pointing toward a doorway nearby.

They followed her into the cave. It was larger than the one where they had last rested; it could have been divided into several rooms with the use of curtains. The main chamber was quite spacious. Its ceiling was low but seemed well supported, with two rock columns bearing the load. The room had a mostly level floor except on the side opposite the doorway, where it sloped down into a little pond that continued under the wall through a large rectangular opening. The remains of an iron grate could be seen there, but the bars had been smashed apart by time or force until only their ends were left.

A little fire pit was built into the middle of the room, where wet ashes had burned into the rock until a bowl-like depression formed over time. Lila directed the men to sit around it. She went back into the adjacent room and came out with a wisp in her hand. With its feeble light, combined with that from the two men, she took a few pieces of wood from a pile and twigs from another. She found a loose stone near the fire pit and struck it expertly against the floor, creating a spark and instant flame, as if she didn't notice Brenish carried a torch already.

"Whence came the wood?" said Brenish.

"It washes down the river sometimes," she said. "When it comes, it comes in bunches. I keep whatever I can gather."

"Very resourceful," said Raden. She smiled.

Brenish watched her movements in fascination as she sat down opposite them. This place had become home for her; she seemed much more at ease in these surroundings, even among two strange men. In the firelight she had a sad, lost loveliness. She brushed her hair back with her hand. She was so beautiful, he thought. And he was ashamed with himself, for he felt feelings stir that weren't entirely proper.

"I have fish to eat," she said. "We can cook one."

"Nay, thank you, milady," Brenish said. "We have ample food, and we can't take the time to eat now. But if you have any fish dried, you should pack it to bring with you. Have you a pack?"

Lila nodded. "We needn't hurry. Please, eat a fish. 'Tis fresh."

Raden took out his balm and rubbed more of it into his leg. She looked at the box strangely, as if she hoped it held costly Vinland cocoa. But then, Brenish thought, probably anything would be a step up from eating fish all the time. She caught him looking at her and smiled sheepishly, tucking her tongue back in.

"You say there are others?" she said.

Brenish felt momentarily tripped up. The hopeful look in her face, her sweet smile and big, needy eyes under fluttering lashes, caught him as if in a spell. But the timing of the question, the abrupt change of topic, made him feel for the briefest moment as if he were in a conversation with himself. It was the kind of thing he might do to redirect attention.

"Aye," said Raden, answering for him. "Seven others."

"And they are armed too?"

"And well-equipped. We have a shortcut out of the ruins. We can get you to safety."

She smiled at him and nodded, which seemed to melt his heart a little. Brenish felt the same tug, the need to see her safely to the surface. It was hard to imagine the things this poor girl must have gone through.

"How came you here, Lila?" Brenish asked.

She turned and batted her eyes as she looked into his, as if it could release old memories of light and nature. "We came through a gate," she said slowly. "My father, and others."

"You didn't come through Ilyenis, then. I'd've heard of you."

"Nay," she said.

"Why would a father bring his daughter down here?" said Raden. "You were nearly old enough to marry."

She turned his way, her eyelids in constant motion under the sunny light of his spell lamp. "He was more worried for me, up there," she said. "I wasn't safe there alone."

Lila bowed her head in grief, and wetted her lips again. A moment passed, to compose herself. She turned back to Brenish. "What is that, on your neck?" she said.

It was so easy to talk to her, to tell her the truth. But Brenish's nature resisted. Something deeper, too, pulled at a thread. Perhaps he should tell her no more than she needed, for now. "A keepsake," he said. "'Tis but a poor-sounding instrument."

"Surely a talisman," she said, disbelieving his story. "Is it not?"

Lila's mouth moved, though mostly closed, her tongue sweeping from one side to the other. It never seemed to stay still for long. She turned her eyes to Brenish's armor again, which he thought strange. He tried to track her focus, but she took his gaze again.

"So my father said," said Brenish. "But I never believed him more than half."

He tried to make eye contact with Raden. Raden stared as if he must be mad to deceive this young lady, but fortunately he didn't dare interfere with the lie.

"Who came with you?" she said. It was another shift. Calculated, Brenish began to feel.

"Friends," said Raden. "My brother. And Brenish's beloved."

"Beloved?" she said. She turned back to Brenish as if the idea stung her, closed her eyes sadly and opened them again. "Who?"

"Cirawyn," he said. He felt the name on his lips give him power, a magic beyond magic. Remembering her danger, the threat from Gareth, he abandoned any urge to stay in this cave longer than need be. Cirawyn was capable, but she needed him even more than Lila did.

Lila seemed about to cry again, but not from her own pain. "You love her very much," she said. She seemed overcome with the idea of two people having such love. Brenish nearly felt it, nearly felt moved to compassion for Lila for missing out. But the thought just missed its mark and floated away. Having been reminded of Cirawyn, he seemed shielded from Lila's misery. Nothing else truly mattered.

"Aye, milady. That's why we need to leave this cave. The fire is appreciated, but we should delay no longer. Pack up some food and any gear you have at hand. Your wisp will be handy. And we can carry some wood, as well."

"But," she stammered, "but 'tis dangerous!"

"So is living here for three years," Raden said. "Why wouldn't you want to go?"

She turned to him and teared up. "I'm so scared," she said. She darted her tongue again, and stared at Raden's pocket. She looked up after a moment but didn't meet his eye; she focused on the silver sapphire pendant instead. "So scared."

The spark of distrust in Brenish's brain came to the fore. A librarian lived in his head, a piece of his consciousness ever searching through centuries of collected lore. It was slow to reach conclusions sometimes, and it was held in check by whatever battled Brenish's will to leave, but from the moment he'd spoken Cirawyn's name the librarian had been turned loose. It flipped through page after page, now, ever faster. Possibilities were considered, some discarded.

Raden put his hand on Lila's to reassure her. She smiled again and gave him the sad eyes of a puppy. Watching Raden's reaction alarmed Brenish; this was more than a man showing kindness to a strange girl. She redoubled her pleading look, and incited more than pity and a desire to help; there was something lusty about her, exciting, as deeply enchanting to the body as the heart. Brenish silently urged the librarian to greater speed and in the meantime decided to take command of the situation.

"Sara awaits you," Brenish said.

Raden and Lila both turned. In Raden's eyes there was a moment's confusion, but his will, too, was hardened; he nodded. Lila, however, flashed a hint of anger for no more than the space of a wink. She reverted instantly to fright and woundedness and vulnerability. Her shoulders hunched in unease, the cloth across her chest drooping fractionally lower.

"Aye," Raden said. He raised his crutch and lifted himself up. Brenish followed, grabbing the torch. "Weary though we are, we really must go."

Lila stood and tried to motion them back to the floor with her outstretched hands. "But 'tisn't safe!" she protested.

"From which gate came you?" said Brenish. It was his turn to take over the conversation.

He held Lila's eyes. She blinked repeatedly, uncomfortably, as if that was all she could think to do. And in each blink she was there, peeking around corners in his mind. She left the door open behind her, and he followed it back until he saw what she saw. *Not Asaph's gate.* Blink. *She doesn't look like the sorts who live near Hanfore's Gate.* Blink, blink. *It must be…*

"The Marsh Gate," she said.

"That's quite far from here," said Brenish.

"We were chased from our campsite" Tears came again; she tried to bat them away furiously. The rest of the story that came was as much Brenish's invention as hers; his imagination was doing all the work for her. "My father was killed by the beasts. I ran with my little light. I kept going all the way down the river."

"We came through Asaph's Gate," said Raden. "But we're leaving directly, once we find the treasure."

She looked at Raden dubiously, at Brenish much *more* dubiously, her eyelids moving the whole time.

The librarian closed its books and consulted with the rest of Brenish's mind. He glanced at the pond briefly, then snapped back to her with a catlike stare. She blinked a few more times. Her eyebrows furrowed. The blinking slowed, stopped. Lila licked her lips once more, and looked again at his chest: the pocket with the spell tokens, and the one with the owl.

He knew now. "Have you any goldsense, Lila?"

"Goldsense?" said Raden. "Why would she have such a thing?"

"The water nymph," Brenish said, "can brew it from their spittle."

"I have no potions," said Lila. "Please stay and eat, and I'll go with you. I'll feel better then."

Brenish kept his eyes on her but addressed Raden. "I never told you about nymphs. They won't kill a man outright, but they like valuable things. Shiny things. Woe to the adventurer who meets one, for he'll wake up hours later, alone, with little more than a torch and the clothes on his back. Few men have survived to tell."

"But she…" Raden said.

"She'll have goldsense, I deem," said Brenish. "Check the next chamber."

"*No*," Lila said. She turned and stretched out a hand as if to stop Raden, and held another near Brenish. Near his pocket with the tokens. Her voice slipped into something feral for a mere instant. She looked at Raden sadly, then Brenish. She softened her voice again, sweetened it beyond human measure, and the notes of despair and loss and loneliness were like knives in their hearts. "Please take me with you. Don't leave me here."

"Nay, milady," said Brenish with some effort. "I think you'll be well all on your own." He shot his eyes over to Raden to indicate he should go, then turned his stare back to the girl. He could see wherever she tried to go now, hide away anything she'd look for in his head. He brought out his other selves, the many Brenishes who each lived in a world where their story was the absolute truth. Let her waste her time on that, like a rigged tavern game. His selves danced and juggled for her, speaking first from one mouth, then another, and in mingled groups even he couldn't track.

"But I'll propose a fair deal," he said. "The late spellbinder Dexter the Unctuous, a man of wide renown, bestowed upon me two talismans of great power." He patted his pocket to convince her; she surely knew they were there. "I will trade you one of these tokens, and a bottle of *esen*, in exchange for all of your goldsense, which you can replenish any time you will. What say you?"

He drew the curtains aside for her, just enough to prove he was sincere about the deal. An item of power, and a bottle, would be hers if she accepted. She would be a fool not to accept. Blink blink blink. Anywhere else she tried to turn in his mind, the clowns cavorted and the minstrels played on.

Raden was already off and moving, keeping his crutch as quiet as he could while he hobbled toward the back. Brenish could barely hear him, thanks to the amulet. He kept his eyes locked on Lila. She licked her lips again, repeatedly, and darted her eyes to and fro across his frame. Assessing.

"You have talismans to protect us?" she said, still playing the innocent. "Will you show me?"

"Not here," he said. "If one falls into water, it will explode and kill us all."

She took half a step back. Even though he was half daring her to believe it, the idea of such a thing was too much shock, too great a danger to ignore. Her focus was utterly on Brenish now. Since his mind was a blur of deception, she tried to study his face; it served her no better than anyone who had tried before. "You are surely men of great power," she said. "I'm not afraid anymore. I'll go with you now, to find the others."

"Aye, where there's more to steal. You could try and seduce our boss, with all his scrolls and lovely wands. And the teleport orb, no doubt you'll want that too. But if he sees you not for what you are, I assure you Cirawyn will."

Lila glowered in response, and blinked frequently again. The name seemed to bother her, if only because the very concept of Cirawyn stood between her and her aims. She was searching for an image, so he let her see. And with that glimpse into his heart, at least part of the futility of overpowering Brenish's will sank in. She pointed her chin toward the discord organ hanging down onto his chest.

"What is that, truly?" she said.

"Not for trade," he replied.

She stared pointedly at the lower part of Brenish's armor, near his abdomen.

"Dexter crafted a spellsight charm," he said. "'Tis unique in the world, to my knowledge. A fine addition to any collection, and useful. It will replenish its power over time. I will add it to my price, and that is my final offer."

This seemed to anger Lila, the idea of him bargaining with her when he should be helping her. She was so helpless, defenseless. She was pretty and scared. He had no right to treat her so. So said her face. The outrage inched up her body like froth in an ale. She blinked again, but not her eyelids: a nictitating membrane slid sideways across each eye, almost too fast to see.

"Decide quickly," said Brenish. "If Raden finds your goldsense before you accept, we will take it outright, and anything else you have besides."

Lila's anger boiled over. She dropped the wisp and grabbed hold of Brenish's wrists with both hands. He struggled against her, trying to reach his sword or a knife, but his arms wouldn't budge. The left hand was still clasped around his torch pole, barely able to move. Her grip was like iron forged from the bones of the world, unyielding as the stone.

She leaned toward him and hissed. "Why do you make trouble?" she said. Her voice was still that of the sweet, hurt girl trapped for years under limitless tons of rock, cut off from the sun and moon and sky, but a harsh edge bled into it.

"Because my friends are in danger. My *love* is in danger. You would keep me from helping them. You would leave us both here to die in the dark, if you could."

"*You* steal. You *lie*. I see. You think I don't see. I see."

"We both lie," said Brenish. "I'm better at it. But I've made you a fair offer, and that's the truth. Your time to accept it runs short. Choose quickly."

She blinked again a few times, but then snapped her head back as if struck. She'd ducked around his defenses for just an instant. "You *lie*," she repeated, but almost in astonishment. Her voice fell quiet. "Gareth doesn't see."

"That's why I need your goldsense," Brenish said. "I'll not leave without it. Take my offer or take naught. Make up your mind, nymph."

She gritted her teeth and hissed. Her body drew back, but she kept her grip firm as ever. He tensed, prepared to butt her in the head if she should try to bite.

"I found her stuff," Raden called.

Lila reacted in alarm, having forgotten all about him. She whipped her head back to see. Brenish had no other option: he let the torch pole slide down through his fingers.

She screamed in sudden, apparently intense pain, and released her grip with both hands. The torch had never made it all the way down to her forearm; her arms were both unhurt. Yet scream she did, and the sound was layered across many octaves, in tones both low and high that no human could ever reach.

Brenish pulled away and drew his sword. The torch slipped a little further, singeing his hand, but he barely noticed and merely pushed it back up again. Lila dropped back into a fighting stance, legs wide apart. She was not unarmed; the knife Brenish had taken from the gremlin was in her right hand, snatched away during the split second he wasn't looking. They held each other at bay, while she growled like an animal.

The cave wall seemed to ripple and shimmer behind her, as if it were but a painted cloth and something moved beneath its surface. Back and forth the distortion flicked, small but very fast. She kept the knife in motion, trying to draw his eye there, but she was unskilled as a fighter. He could see this was not a natural position for her to be in, and she was out of her depth.

"Time's up, Lila," Brenish said. "I'm taking everything. And I'll have my knife back, please."

"*Thief*," she hissed. "*Liar!* Filthy liar!"

"That's right, nymph. You hate me. You hate me for lying. Go on and do something about it. You're a worse liar than I am."

She gave him a frustrated growl that sounded entirely human. Rather than move in closer with the knife, she stood back. The irregularity behind her moved up high and suddenly rushed toward his face, but he dodged aside.

"You have a tail," said Brenish. His voice gave away his surprise, but he recovered quickly. "Sneaky girl, hiding your tail like that. Does it have a stinger, like a scorpion? I bet that's why so many men can't remember how they fell asleep when they met your kind. I'm going to pass that on when I leave. You'll find your baubles much harder to come by from now on."

Lila tried to stab him with her tail again, but when he dodged a second time she came in close with the knife. Brenish, however, saw the move coming. She was so used to being able to control her prey's attention that her whole repertoire was built around misdirection. He casually blocked her thrust with his torch. She made the inhuman scream again and jumped aside lest she suffer another burn, even though she didn't even make contact with the flame this time.

"Very clever, Lila, but you forgot one thing."

She seemed almost interested enough to ask, but before she could, Raden cracked her across the back of the head with his crutch. She dropped to the floor, unconscious.

"That was the one thing," Brenish said.

The stress of holding Lila's attention on him, of hiding everything he didn't want her to know, crashed upon his already fatigued brain all at once and caused him to stumble. Brenish took a moment and a deep breath to right himself. The pain in his scorched left hand surfaced now, as if from nowhere. He winced and sucked in air through his teeth.

"So that's a water nymph?" said Raden.

"Aye. She probably has more caves like this one, connected through this waterway." He pointed to the pond and its broken grate.

"What'll we do with her? Kill her?"

Brenish looked down at the girl, seemingly asleep. A trickle of red blood ran down the back of her neck, but it didn't look like too serious a wound. He leaned down to touch her arm; she still had a pulse.

He found the stinger easily, now that it was no longer in motion. It had been burned badly by his torch. Half visible, it started to fade into being more as he held it. The heavy, fleshy limb behind it gained substance, by blurring the image behind it rather than hiding it entirely as before. Brenish picked up the stinger and, with effort, brought it to Lila's leg where he could jam it in. The tip didn't sink very far into the flesh, but when it did some kind of venom pumped along the tail. He waited a few moments and pulled it out again.

"That ought to keep her out," he said. "I haven't the heart to kill her. But she'll wake with a little wound and a nasty headache, no doubt. She'll have a harder time of it now, anyway, unless her tail heals up."

"You didn't know they had tails?" said Raden, pointing. Lila's pale skin was beginning to fade to a darker shade.

"Nay. Not even a guess." Brenish took back his knife, stood, and finally sheathed his sword. "What did you find?" he said.

Raden held out a worn old sack. Brenish took it and began inspecting what lay within. Besides a single bottle, there was a gold-rimmed monocle, a medallion, and about a dozen diverse coins like a collection. He took an interest in the medallion right away, pulling it from the bag to examine. It was silver, with an embossed image of a raven and two crossed spears.

"This belonged to Daniel Whitewood," he said. "I gave it back to him when I was twelve."

"You mean you stole it?"

"Aye, but I gave it back. He went in with a Spaniard. The Spaniard didn't make it out. But Daniel, he came back a week later, half dead. Never did find out what happened to him here."

"Do you suppose he came to this same cave?"

"Nay. But he must have been in this area. I wonder if he went searching for Visak's treasure."

"Visak was still alive then. That would be suicide."

"Indeed." His attention had already moved on. "Odd coins, some of these."

"And the eyeglass?" said Raden.

Brenish examined the monocle. The gold rim was marked with one symbol, a guild mark, which he showed to Raden. Raden frowned at the sight. Brenish put it back in the bag without using his owl, and uncapped the potion bottle.

"Oi," Raden said in sudden concern, "what are you doing?"

"Testing," said Brenish. He took a whiff of the new potion before imbibing, but its effect on his mind gave him confidence in his guess. He took in just a sip, and swallowed.

The ruins came alive around him as points of light formed in his mind. Precious metals, and anything touched by magical power, were clear to him as plain sight. The effect spread out for many miles with even the little bit of potion he took in; further out it faded in intensity, eventually down to nothing.

He was aware of two treasure pits near the horizon of this temporary sense. A few lesser concentrations of items dotted the world around him, and each individual thing had a flavor, or a color, that separated it from others. The *esen* lake and its contents were strangely invisible, as if the liquid shielded his sense. Visak's treasure would of course be impossible to find with goldsense, thanks to the overlook spell he had protecting it. He felt vast wealth a few miles away, above ground, most likely the city of Northhill. The contours of the surface were like a thin film he could trace if he focused.

But the point that most interested Brenish was in the distance north of them, among other, lesser motes. The bearing stone told him exactly how far away it was.

"I see the orb," Brenish said. "Let's away."

"Why didn't you use the spellsight charm?" said Raden.

"I knew the potion had to be goldsense, and that glass is likely useless to us. If we had to replenish the binding before its time, we'd use up some of our *esen* that we might need for something else. Waste not."

Brenish looked down at Lila's sleeping form. Her appearance had changed much in just a few minutes. Her skin was no longer alabaster pink, but a mottled gray shot through with splotches and veins of dim color. The beautiful blonde color of her hair had faded to an iridescent black. Her face and body were mostly human but for the tail, yet without her color-changing talent no one would mistake her for one. Her tail was plain to see, as was its badly blistered tip. He pitied her like this, a real pity not based on any of her tricks.

The mote of the teleportation orb was still in his mind. It reminded him their time was precious.

"Are you ready?" he said.

"Aye."

"Then let's find our friends."

Waterfall

Brenish's hand still stung from the burn, even after applying a little of Raden's salve. The sensations in it kept distracting him from his goal, a point far ahead that he could feel more than see. Raden's pace seemed to improve every time they started off again. Nevertheless, the lack of sleep wore heavily on them both. Every now and again, one of them stumbled.

They were already an hour out from Lila's lair, still following the river. Its course wound a little more here, and grew slower. Occasionally the channel bent more sharply, and where it did there was usually a pool where swirling debris collected. Lila hadn't lied about the wood; some of it could be found along the shore, in various stages of rot. Brenish had already insisted they take along a few logs from Lila's pile, and she was in no condition to object.

Dawn must be near, Brenish thought. Somewhere.

"Would that we had a potion of wakefulness," Raden said. "I've never been so tired."

"We can rest for a short time if you need to," said Brenish.

"Nay. If I rest I won't get up again for a long time. Best we keep moving. But keep talking. It might keep both of us awake longer. What do you plan to do with your cut of the treasure?"

"You mean my cut of a cut? I hadn't thought about it, beyond marriage."

"You must have thought about it all your life. Who hasn't?"

Brenish grumbled, as much to change the subject as in disappointment with himself. How foolish he had been. "Most of those thoughts are worthless now. Only one thing matters anymore."

"Since your cut is so small, you can keep those coins. We wouldn't have got this far without you anyway."

"Thanks," Brenish said. "Actually, I never did get a good look at all of them."

He fished the handful of coins out of his pocket and brought them into the light. About half of them were currency he knew: a few silvers and a gold piece. "Here's about 130p," he said. "The rest of these are a mix. Two of them are Viking make."

"How can you tell?"

"The runes, for one. But this silver one has one of their ships on one side, and a strange-looking man on the other. The copper bears an image of corn and wheat."

"20p says you've never seen corn."

"I have so," said Brenish. "In the market in the city. They grow it aways east. Tasted it once, too. They roast it, then you spread on butter and eat the pips off the core."

"You're making that up."

"Nay, my troth. The pips have skin between that gets stuck in your teeth."

Raden scoffed. He seemed to find Brenish's persistence silly, oath or no.

"I think one of these coins is Fae," Brenish said.

"Fae? You're mad."

"Perhaps. But the writing is most like wizard runes. The face looks Fae. Here, have a look."

He passed the coin over. Raden took it and held it up to the spell lamp around his neck, turning it. "Aye, it does look like Fae. But who brought it here? One of them, or the poor sod who owned that eyeglass?"

The monocle bore the insignia of the riftkeepers' guild. The riftkeepers were respected, but distrusted. For one thing, nobody much liked the idea of getting stranded in another world, which could happen when rifts opened and closed on a cycle. But those who stayed long in other realms tended to come back with vicious plagues, if they came back at all. One of many reasons Fae kept such limited contact with men was that simple influenza had taken a heavy toll on their kind.

"Probably the riftkeeper took it as a souvenir," said Brenish. "Look at these now."

He gave Raden two more coins: one silvery but not actually silver, the other copper. Each had a different man's head on one side. The other side of the copper had an image that looked like two stalks of wheat; the silvery one portrayed a fearsome beast with a great shaggy mane.

"I can't read," said Raden.

"Little good would it do you. Some of that's Latin. Not the rest. I can make out bits of it, but most of the words come together as nonsense."

"Think you they're Roman?"

"Nay. I've seen Roman coins. I knew a collector once, who... never mind." Brenish remembered almost too late that if he told the truth, he was obliged to tell more of it. "But nay, these aren't Roman. The Romans never used numerals. The words would all be Latin, besides."

"Oh," said Raden. "Aye." He handed the coins back.

"Maybe I was right about there being rifts down here. What else would a riftkeeper be doing in the ruins?"

"Dallying with nymphs, 'twould seem."

Brenish snickered. Though truly, it was unlikely that anyone getting too close to Lila would be fully to blame for their actions. She had played a dangerous game, trying to seduce two men at once. Even so she would have won, had she faced an opponent not her equal.

To keep Raden and himself awake, Brenish went back to telling stories. Instead of what he knew of the ruins, he told Raden about things that had happened in the village, in the city, or on the road between as one of "Alfie's" men. Harry had entrusted Brenish to play the role of Alfie once, but was evidently so unimpressed that he had never invited the younger thief to reprise it. Naman usually made a more intimidating Alfie, anyway.

As their talk went on, Raden started to tell of his own history as well. He shared with Brenish some of the adventures he and Bob had had when they were younger, and the tale of how they came into Gareth's employ. There was much about both men that Brenish had never known, something he now realized was his own failing.

Listening to Raden, Brenish felt he should have known more about everyone in town. Had he never taken enough interest, preferring instead to speak with doomed strangers? But then, the gossip network distrusted him for all the usual reasons; he couldn't blame them. Hence why everyone knew what Tibs held against Dex but him. Being an expert liar had made Brenish something of a pariah when it came to sharing secrets. That was the kind of thing even money might never fix.

Not that he was going to walk away with any, he reminded himself again. He still had no plan for dealing with Gareth when the time came. Catching up would be hard enough. But the thought of Gareth did remind him of another problem.

"Gareth doesn't trust me," Brenish said.

"Water is wet."

"He has papers of Visak's in his pack. I saw them when the daybreak spell broke. That's why he was so fiery at the garden. He didn't want me to see them."

"That's silly, Brenish. Why would he hide that from you?"

"He'd have no need," said Brenish. "Not unless he planned to break his word and cut us out. If he did, maybe he'd cut you out too."

"That's unlike Gareth. He keeps his word."

"Till yesterday I thought he was as crafty in the ruins as me, too. He proved me wrong. I trust nothing he says anymore. Better to see those notes for myself."

A thought had been bothering him for some time, that perhaps Gareth knew or suspected the map was false—in spite of the Expert's assurances—but had seized on the opportunity anyway. It wasn't unreasonable. Gareth might even be using Visak's notes for what Brenish himself hoped to do: find just the right clues in those pages to break the overlook spell.

And then a thought so vile came to Brenish, he was half certain it was true. Gareth was a man of his word, but gold had silenced the conscience of better men than he. Brenish made a strangled croak.

"What is it?" said Raden.

"I was thinking," said Brenish, "Gareth might have another plan for those papers. What if they give him a clue without the need for the map? What if he already knows all he needs to find the treasure? He could declare the expedition a failure, tear up the map, and send us all home. Then he could teleport back any time he pleased, trusting on his own craft to survive, and finish the job. Maybe he only needed us to get him this far."

"Nonsense," said Raden. "If he did that, the rest of us would demand our cut when he returned."

"'Twould be a solo venture then."

"But our work for it would be no less. Even if Gareth were the sort of man to break troth, he'd have to answer to all of us. Nay, he'll be true."

"I thought the same," he said, "but there's another possibility. Maybe Gareth intends to leave by himself."

Raden stopped. The thought seemed to shake him. "Why would he do that?"

"Because he can. None of you will be in his employ when this is over. He knows that as well as you. He has most of the tools we would need to survive. Most of what Finch still has is useless. And the odds are against the rest of the party without me there. Even if the rest of us could make it back to the Gate without Gareth, he could set a trap or seal us in. A few weeks later, he could come back. The treasure would be all his, without contest."

What scared Brenish the worst was that this wasn't merely a story he spun to undermine Gareth. Feeding Raden's doubts could only be a good thing, but this idea could well be true. It could just as easily be false. Betraying his men seemed counter to Gareth's nature, but in the ruins, with the treasure firmly in hand, all bets were off. Brenish didn't need to break his oath and stretch the truth to sell this idea to Raden; he needed to find a way to convince himself he must be wrong.

It would be unlike Gareth. But it was the best explanation Brenish could think of for having those papers in the first place.

"Nay," said Raden. "I don't believe it."

"I wish I could say the same. The test will be if he denies having those papers, or he tries to split us into small groups. If he tries to use the orb or a teleport scroll to escape by himself, he'll have a fight on his hands."

Raden shook his head and continued on their course upstream. Brenish sighed and followed, letting him lead awhile. He didn't especially want to get Raden to agree; he wanted reassurance that Raden couldn't give.

A short time later, they came to a feature that was new to both men. The path they followed had so far been mostly one cavern, rougher in some places than others, but with reasonably well-defined banks and a clear channel for the river running right down the middle. But the cavern came to a sudden end ahead, and there the river and its banks divided into three different paths, through three arches: one wide and low for the river, and one on each side big enough for a few men abreast to pass through. The arches were set within a brick wall that looked like the face of a fortress, its sides angled outward from the channel, yet where Brenish would have expected to see a watchtower there was none.

He didn't like the look of the arches, and said so, but there was nothing for it but to keep going as they planned. At least this change seemed to represent a return to more "civilized" parts. The sounds of water ahead were stronger, torrential, as if rapids were contained within.

The western arch led into a structure that reminded Brenish somewhat of the Gatehouse, but seemingly less finished, as if it had never been fully manned and was much longer abandoned. The rooms here were smaller, simpler, but it still appeared to have served an important military purpose at one time. Brenish was silent and kept his own interest sheathed as they went through; the building's secrets were far less important than returning to Cirawyn and the others.

At length they came out on the other side of the keep, emerging into an echoing roar. The building's northern face was a rough cave wall with three brick archways. There the three paths met again, at a small lake—smaller than the lake of *esen*—that pooled in the base of a large, mostly natural cavern. The lake was fed by a waterfall about fifty feet high.

There was no northern shore; that end of the lake appeared to be very deep, where the water came in from above. The western shore was easily wide enough to walk, but was mostly taken up by stairs that had been cut directly from the stone. The stairs led up northward in a great partial spiral stopping at three landings, the highest of which was level with the source of the fall. At each landing was a doorway. The eastern shore was broader, but had no stair; instead it had a doorway leading due east. On the south shore, a wide stone bridge connected the two banks.

They were not alone in the cavern. On the eastern shore near the far end, a great bulk lay quietly, breathing slowly in sleep. Brenish knew it had to be a troll. It looked too much like the drawings he had seen in so many books, the descriptions given by frightened men who only wished to forget. The troll slept soundly.

But that was less disconcerting than what lay nearer at hand. Floating debris had collected in a little pool by the near shore, driven there by swirling currents instead of washing away downriver. This included many pieces of driftwood, a closed bottle of the kind the party used for carrying water, and a shaggy-haired human head encased in light blue crystal.

Raden stopped and crossed himself; Brenish did likewise. He looked at Raden as if to say this proved they were close. But instead of rejoining seven companions, there would be only six at most. Turk, bearing an actual expression of surprise, seemed as shocked by his death as either of them. Whatever the cause of the strange curse upon his head that had followed him from the time they entered the ruins, it had finally won.

Brenish pointed to the troll and put a finger to his lips, indicating with gestures that they should go up the stairs silently. Raden nodded. Brenish showed that Raden should go first, so that he could cover the rear himself—not that his sword was likely to do much against a troll. Yet higher ground might be some minor advantage, anyway.

They went up very cautiously, hardly daring to breathe. Brenish had grown used to hearing the clack of Raden's crutch, even muffled by the stealth spell on the amulet, but now it was silent. They took each step with the utmost quiet. In so doing, they attained the first landing without incident. But halfway up the second stair, the troll rolled over in its sleep. It opened its eyes.

"Wand," said Brenish.

Raden turned around. "What?" he whispered.

Brenish pointed. "Wand."

The troll sat upright in alarm and quickly got to its feet. The creature was easily ten feet tall, thick-limbed, massive, with hide like strong leather. Its head was broad rather than tall, with a huge wide nose and an even wider mouth. It opened that mouth now in a rictus of anger or defiance, and displayed its large, indomitable teeth. From that maw it bellowed in rage, a deep roar with high tones, like swirling winds and thunder both angry with each other. The sound shook the cavern; it echoed off the walls and multiplied itself, like the voices of a hundred trolls in one.

The troll bounded south along the far shore, towards the bridge. Its strides were very great; though lumbering and ungainly, it could easily overtake a man over open ground.

Raden drew the wand and fired true. A bolt of lightning shot past Brenish's head and struck the troll. A thunderclap came at the same time, booming throughout the cavern. The troll screamed its anger, but Brenish couldn't tell if it had been seriously hurt. He blinked repeatedly, momentarily blinded by the flash. His ears rang.

When his vision returned, the troll had reached the bridge. It seemed completely unharmed. Raden fired a second time for good measure, but this time Brenish closed his eyes. He opened them again and saw the troll leaning back, trying to recover its balance, but it was otherwise unfazed. It turned to face them and roared once more.

A third time Raden raised the wand. Brenish didn't see it in time to react, but all he saw were a few stray sparks. The wand fizzled, its power spent. All that remained was locked into its structure, impossible to tap.

Raden looked down to the water. "Can trolls swim?"

"I know not, but we can't. Not with your splint, nor all this gear. And we've nowhere to go but downriver."

The troll resumed its run and seemed to be accelerating.

Brenish acted quickly, relying only on his instincts, his many years of dreaming his way out of tough scenarios, and all his lore. He pulled a bottle from where he had tucked it behind his armor. The potion he had found in the *esen* pool, though seemingly not magic, was too vile to drink. But he had spent enough time around the city, taking in the unfamiliar smells of alchemists at work, to know that the odds favored any such concoction being dangerous.

He lobbed the bottle at the troll as hard as he could. The earthenware vessel broke into pieces against the beast's thick, unyielding hide. The troll was only angered further by this offense, but it was enough of an affront for the creature to stop where it stood near the bottom of the first stair. It leered and shouted at them again, holding its mouth open wide in that awful grin.

The troll cut its scream short, suddenly taking in great whiffs of the devil's brew dripping down its hide. The potion didn't seem to be an acid, but it was noxious in the extreme, throwing heady vapors so unpleasant that even Brenish smelled them strongly. The troll tried to wipe the liquid away but it only spread the vapor more.

"Get back, beast, or you'll get worse!" Brenish said. It was total bluster, but the troll seemed for a fleeting second to believe him. It took one step back down, paused, and shook its head to try and clear the odors out of its nose. Its failure seemed to make it more furious.

"Daybreak!" Raden shouted. "Use one of those tokens!"

"It won't harm a troll," Brenish said. "That's a myth."

The troll, still standing on the stairs below, let loose its mightiest growl yet. It filled the great room like boiling water in a tiny bottle, growing ever louder as it went on. The walls seemed about to topple from its force. But presently the monster's voice broke; it coughed. It coughed again, stronger, but looked all the more enraged for doing so. Again and again it tried to expel the fumes from its enormous lungs.

Brenish reached into his upper pocket and pulled out one of the spell tokens. "Here." He passed it back to Raden without looking. "Try something."

"But I don't know any spells!" Raden protested. "Only the same ones you know!"

"This may be our last chance," Brenish snapped. "Put your heart in it or we may well die here!"

The troll's anger was beyond a rolling boil now; its rage grew in strength every time it coughed, and the rage gave it focus. Even barely able to breathe deeply, it staggered forward, up one step at a time.

"Back, I say!" Brenish screamed. The troll paid him no heed.

Raden raised his voice, but not to speak. What came out of his mouth was not a spell, but a song. His voice was weak with fear and the certainty of imminent death. The words were lighthearted, a tale of a boy who slew imaginary monsters every day before supper. And this, Brenish realized, was how they were to perish: at the hands of an opponent his blade—if he ever found the courage to draw it—would barely scratch, hearing the tale of a dim-witted version of his younger self as he was torn to pieces.

Yet Raden's courage seemed to grow as he sang. The troll stumbled its way nearly to the first landing, and as the men saw it come, Brenish heard his companion's voice harden. A second verse began, in which the boy got lost far from home, but had his toy sword at the ready. Tension built in Brenish's gut, but even so he felt almost hopeful at Raden's new strength, brief though it would last.

Brenish had only one weapon left that might harm the troll, the one reliable thing he had ever heard they feared. He swung the pole of his torch out toward the creature, jerking it to a quick stop. A dash of burning lamp oil shook free of the housing and kept going.

The flame didn't scare the troll; it never had a chance. As soon as the oil came within two feet of the troll's body, it triggered a concussive blast.

A bright flash of orange and purple light tore the darkness. The explosion pushed Brenish back against the second stair, and threw the troll back far enough that it lost its balance completely. Its flesh was on fire, as was part of the stair where the potion had dripped. The troll waved its arms, which only made the flames worse, and toppled back, rolling in two painful thuds toward the bottom.

Raden sang on, almost as if he was oblivious to their victory. The boy encountered a mighty dragon in a cave, and though his heart was brave, there was no escape. Brenish felt his heart sink at the morbid lyrics.

The troll quickly regained its footing at the base of the stairs. Having less of a neck than Raden, there was nothing to break during its fall. The bones of a troll were, in truth, probably harder than the steps. The patches of fire still going along its chest and arms seemed to fuel its anger, and vice-versa. It would be held back no longer. With a continuous yell, it charged up the stairs.

Brenish's stomach tightened further, threatening to wrench itself free in terror. The burning troll might die from its injuries, but not before it ended the both of them. And all he heard were the troll's terrible roar and the determined last stand of the lost boy backed into a corner. There was no more escape for them than for him.

Yet there was more. Raden's voice grew resonant, rich, the chamber seeming to mold itself to his sound more than the troll's. Half-imagined harmonies echoed back from the far walls, the room itself singing in a round. And the twisting feeling in Brenish's insides grew deeper, greater. All of reality began to turn on itself.

The flaming troll reached the landing and ran across it, just steps away from reaching the second stair, two steps more from being able to snatch Brenish up in its hand. But Brenish didn't draw his sword. The boy in the song drew his, and showed the dragon the fire in his eyes, the will of a very mighty man. The dragon, never so challenged before, drew back and felt doubt for the first time in its wicked life.

The troll stumbled on the run and landed on its belly. Brenish grabbed the empty wand from Raden's hand. He didn't fully understand why; it was as much instinct as throwing the potion. The troll looked up with uncertainty, but also still with great anger and pain, and it stood again, ready to make the kill.

But it stopped just short, staring at Raden instead. It felt what Brenish felt, the same sense that the world wanted to turn itself inside out.

In a thundering chorus, a thousand Radens' voices boomed out the moment that the dragon reached down to chomp the boy, and the boy, in all his courage, leapt onto the monster's tongue and drove his little wooden spike right up through the dragon's palate, into the heart of its brain, where the beast's own fire cooked it to death. The boy emerged triumphant, and shouted a mighty challenge to every monster in the world that their time had come.

"Huzzah!" Raden finished.

A heavy thump erupted around them. The twisty feeling in Brenish's innards fled with it. The troll gaped in abject horror, no longer even aware of the fire still burning slowly on its body.

Brenish drew back the wand. "Fetch!" he said, and threw it at the troll.

The troll grabbed the wand out of the air without a thought, but the hand that did it was on fire. The wand ignited.

A second later the wand blew apart into fragments, releasing the last of its magic in a bolus of blue-white light. The troll's left hand was blown completely off. The blast threw the beast down the stairs a second time, tumbling all the way to the bottom.

Though now badly hurt, it raised itself to its feet with barely a moment's pause. But this time, it didn't take the stairs again. It wailed in terror, a thin screech of pain and fear and despair that followed it beyond the arch into the keep, and on into the river cavern beyond.

Brenish caught his breath. "Bless me," he said, "you do your granddad proud."

He turned to look Raden in the eye. Raden was pale, moving his jaw spastically to try and make it form words again.

"'Tis well," Brenish said. "We survived."

"You took on a troll," Raden said. "You might've won all on your own. You took on a troll and you won."

"Nay," Brenish said. "I couldn't have done that alone."

"Forgive me," said Raden. "I never thought much of your lore. Even less so than Gareth. But you're the master here. I'm sorry I ever doubted you."

Raden seemed to get some of his color back. He took a deep breath and unclenched his left fist, palm bitten by his fingernails. When he saw what else was there, he had another shock.

A spell had been cast; neither man doubted it. Brenish guessed it to be a spell of dread, that would move anything inhuman to the kind of mindless fright the troll had experienced. But if the token had powered the spell, it should have evaporated like a scroll.

"'Twould seem," Brenish said, "my doubts were unfounded too."

Part V
Rogue

The beast fell upon us in the open, north of Goldsmith's Crossing. Phillip was slain. Belor and Daniel wanted to slay the beast in turn, but I urged them to leave. For I judged that the creature, for its size, would not eat another man for several days at least. They called me coward and vowed vengeance on the beast. I could not persuade them.

They threw down their packs and drew swords. Belor told me to watch, if I would not fight, and see how a true man responds to the death of his shield-brother.

I picked up the packs and left quietly, with hope the beast would not follow me in anger after it finished them. We were only a few miles from the Gate, and the treasure was not a great burden.

A true man uses the gift of reason.

Aftermath at the Crossing

Brenish and Raden reached a proper road at the top of the waterfall cavern, arched over and brick-paved as neatly as anything else they had seen in the Elder Kingdom. Privately Brenish was terrified that more than just Turk might have fallen. He took another sip of goldsense along the way, and discovered Gareth's orb was still where it had ever been: a few miles to the north, sitting stationary as far as he could tell. That could mean Gareth was dead and being devoured by wild creatures; but in spite of the man's terrible recklessness in choosing a polymorphosis wand, Brenish still gave him more credit than that.

Still, it was hard not to imagine a worst-case scenario in which he and Raden were the sole survivors. Brenish would seek out Hamish Bowman, hand him a knife, and beg him to take revenge for dragging the poor man's only daughter into this mess. Then Naman's mother would die in poverty, as would Hamish. Turk's widow would struggle to keep her children fed, and Tibs' wife and child would be even worse off. Pernilla would have to wait longer for Willy to serve out his time in lockup. Maddie and Eddie would probably live all right on whatever savings Finch had kept from his long employment with Gareth; perhaps Harry had funneled some money their way as well. And Raden would be stuck looking after both his wife and his brother's family, on a gimp leg. Few would be left to remember Jase. Dex's loss would be mourned only by Darius the innkeeper, who hated him but lived in hope the greasy rat's debt would someday be repaid.

Where the road opened onto a large artificial cavern, supported by four huge columns, they saw what had befallen there. The worst seemed a likely outcome.

A veritable army of scaly-skinned lizardmen was scattered on both sides of the river, or in it. All were dead. Patches of pale blue crystal were strewn about the room in a way that spoke of a maniac wielding a wand. But the way most of those patches avoided the lizards, that maniac was evidently not Gareth. Indeed the most solid patch was enclosed about a man, of moderate girth, with glasses and a whip and a pole-mounted spell lamp that had gone dead in the hours since the battle. Another chunk of crystal on the ground contained a human arm; the body it belonged to, missing a head, was draped over the rail of a wide stone footbridge.

There were no scavengers. They might have fled at the approach of the spell protecting the two men.

"Mother of God," Raden exclaimed. "What happened here?"

Brenish held a hand to his heart and was silent. This was the hardest loss yet. Turk had been one of the good ones, and he'd been fond of Harry, but Tibs was one of his closest friends. He was almost unwaveringly cheerful, always quick to lend coin or share a meal with a friend in need, a credit to the village and to the guild. Now he was dead. He died believing he would go home with even a small piece of Visak's treasure.

In time Brenish gathered himself. Nothing could be done for Tibs; he had to think of the others now. He looked among the bodies of the fallen. Some of the manthings had been hit by crossbow bolts. Many were missing limbs or had crushed skulls. Shields had been broken. A patch of ground on the eastern bank was blasted as if by flame. On the west side, one of the creatures in lizard garb was no lizard but rather a large cat, a deadly cousin of the lion with a mix of stripes and spots; some of the other lizardmen nearby had clearly been mauled by it. The crystal clusters grew mostly on the eastern bank, Tibs being one of the few exceptions, or on the bridge. The fighting had been heaviest on the bridge.

He inspected what was left of Turk's body. The pack was empty and both torches missing; he took that as a good sign. There were no other human corpses or limbs at hand.

Looking back to the west bank, Brenish saw one other thing of note: a sigil glowing on a pillar. Semicircle and bisected angle. It was right above where a crossbow bolt had pierced the weapon hand of one of the lizardmen, pinning him there where someone had run him through.

"Visak's mark again," Brenish said.

Raden turned to where he was looking. "Where?"

"On the pillar. That one, there."

"I see naught there."

Brenish scratched his head. His invisibility had faded more than half a day ago. He never had a sip of the voidsight potion they found with the goblins. He had no reason to doubt that Raden couldn't see the symbol, which meant it was invisible. Yet Brenish could see it somehow.

"I don't understand," Brenish said. "But I suppose it doesn't matter." He gave the area another sweep with his eyes. "I think there were only two casualties here. Perhaps there were others before they reached here, but somebody survived. They took Turk's supplies." He pointed about. "We have scorching there, and there, probably not from the wand because I'm quite sure it was used up at the cliff. So the lizardmen had a spellcaster, at least one. When the battle turned against them, one of their leaders took out a wand of encasement. It hit only part of Turk and felled him here. Tibs got the full brunt of a shot. But Gareth used another shot from his polymorph wand over there. That was probably the mage.

"The rest were taken down by our people. Some of those wounds are from Gareth's mace, methinks. Those two were disemboweled, which I hope to be Naman's work. He favors lower swings."

"And Bob is a limb lopper," said Raden. He pointed to more of the bodies.

"Aye, and a shield breaker. Any of the rest could have been Gareth or Finch."

"What about Cirawyn?"

That question had been with Brenish as soon as they found the bodies. He expressed concern with his brows, but he soon found what he was looking for. "Many of the kills on the west side and the bridge were by crossbow. She stayed back and fought at range for as long as she could. Turk's sword is missing. And his scabbard. She might have taken the sword when he fell."

Raden looked among the lizard corpses more himself. "Aye, some of these wounds could have been made from a lesser height. These two here aren't very deep. Cirawyn's a strong woman, but I wager she'd have trouble with a sword."

Brenish walked back over the west side of the bridge, where Tibs stood immobile. Like Jase. The crystal showed signs that someone had tried to hew at it. Some of the marks looked to be made with ordinary blades, but a few deeper cuts reminded Brenish of Finch's spellbound hand axe. Silently he blessed Finch for having heart enough to try.

"So this is encasement?" said Raden. "Seems dangerous as a spell."

"No more than polymorph," said Brenish. "The crystals can be broken."

"But the risk of harming your own fellows would be great."

Brenish only nodded. He tried to hold back tears for his friend.

"This crystal is more magic than nature, is it not?"

"'Tis," Brenish said. "Why?"

"I heard a story once of a man caught in crystal for a hundred years. Just a tale, but—"

"Aye," Brenish said. His face brightened. "Aye!" But his brows furrowed again. "Nay, we have naught to shatter it."

"What have we left?"

"Goldsense. A sword. Three knives. A single torch. Dex's spellsight charm. A spell lamp. The light piece to make another spell lamp. A small bottle of *esen*. A wine bottle with *esen*. Two spell tokens, but no spell we know for this purpose. A riftkeeper's eyepiece. A handful of coins. The stealth charm on your neck."

"And the charm on yours," said Raden.

Brenish held up the discord organ. "To what purpose? To wait for a creature and goad it into breaking the crystal apart rather than attacking us?"

"Nay. Know you nothing of glass? 'Tis said there are singers who can shatter it with their voice alone. One crystal is much like another, is it not?"

"It is not," said Brenish. "Broken glass is unlike crystal. I have seen both." He turned back to look Tibs over. "Yet I recall laying hold of a green crystal goblet once. Tibs showed me how to make it sing, with water on the rim."

"Aye," Raden said. "I know of that trick."

Brenish smiled. "We'll try your idea."

He gestured to Raden to stand back, and he himself stood far back from Tibs. Cautiously, he raised the silver pendant to his lips and blew. He only barely winded the thing, lest he weave too great a spell with it; only now did he regret having restored its binding in the *esen* pool. But then, maybe magic was needed to dispel magic crystal.

A light shimmering kind of sound came back, bounced from another point in the room. Brenish took this as a sign, and tried to change his note on the organ by covering parts of it with his fingers. The shimmering wavered, growing quieter and then louder, then louder still. Tibs seemed to vibrate in place as a hundred different hideous notes attacked him. At least Brenish found what he judged to be the right note, and gave the organ one strong, sustained blast.

The blue crystals broke apart into thousands of pieces, all over the chamber. Tibs fell forward, nearly onto his face, and only barely managed to reach out an arm to cushion his fall. The pole with his spell lamp clattered to the ground in front of him, still extinguished. Thankfully, his eyeglasses were still intact.

Tibs got to his knees and stared at both men with an expression of utter contempt. He jumped to his feet and lashed his whip at Brenish, catching him in the back of the leg where the greaves didn't protect him.

"Have at you!" Tibs shouted.

"Tibs, 'tis the spell!" said Brenish.

Tibs lunged at him and drew the whip back again. "To the Pit with you, liar! I'll take your head!"

But Tibs stopped short before swinging a second time. He paused in confusion. He looked about, seeming lost and troubled.

"Brenish?" he said. "Raden?"

"Aye, Tibs."

"Am I dead?"

"No more than we," said Raden. "But less than poor Turk."

Tibs swiveled about, pivoting to survey the battle. He picked up his spell lamp and shook it, but no more light came out.

"Here," Brenish said. He unslung his pack and fished out the smaller bottle of *esen*. "Take this for your lamp."

Tibs grabbed the bottle and opened up the receptacle in his lamp. That style of lamp would collect its fuel too slowly to burn indefinitely; it had to be replenished from time to time. With more of the magical liquid in its belly, the lamp fired back to life.

"You came back for me," said Tibs. "Thank you."

"'Twas Raden who figured out how to free you," Brenish said. "In truth I thought you were dead as Jase. But we merely found you along our way. We've had a long night coming here."

"Night? How long have I been here?"

Brenish shrugged. "Hours perhaps," he said. "The sun should be up by now. We're both terribly short on sleep. But the others are only a few miles off."

"How would you know that?"

"I found goldsense."

"Oh. Good on you. I was worried the others might have left without us already. 'Tis a long way back to the Gate."

Tibs turned around and looked back the way the main party had come, out through a doorway to the east. He saw Turk's broken trunk and frowned.

"Shame about Turk. He was a decent man."

"Aye," said Raden.

"He was gonna use his share of the treasure to get his brother-in-law out of lockup. Selfless, he was. Maybe Elspeth will still do it with her half share."

Brenish chirped a little laugh, unable to help himself.

"'Tisn't funny," said Tibs.

"Nay, not the loss of Turk," said Brenish.

"Then why'd you laugh? You should want Willy out as much as anyone. He's been a good friend to you."

"Aye, he has. And I've done what I can for his family. But 'tis funny, how things happen. You might not find it so."

Raden seemed annoyed by that answer, or perturbed. Tibs didn't like it any better, but shrugged it away. "What's the plan, then?" said Tibs. "Gareth solved the riddle of the birds, but he's stuck on another."

"That doesn't surprise me."

"It's been a wreck since you two were lost. Bob's got the full deepsick. Cirawyn was bad at first, but she pulled through. She was sure you weren't dead. Been at odds with Gareth the whole time, though. They got into shouting matches, if you believe it. Almost came to blows. She called him a fool for bringing a wand of polymorphosis, and it got worse from there."

"Brenish said much the same," Raden said. "After what I've seen, I'll take his word. He's the expert here, not Gareth."

"Aye," said Tibs. "So what happens next? Raden, if you're with us, then Bob's with us, and that's six against two."

"Whoa there. Just because I think better of Brenish doesn't mean I'm ready to give up on Gareth. He's the leader of this venture. When we get back, I expect he'll still be in charge. I won't stand for a fight."

"You may not have a choice," Brenish said ruefully. "You asked for a plan, Tibs? Here's the one I had before we came down here: We use goldsense to find a treasure pit that still has enough gold to matter, and we all climb down in. Then we use the orb to get home. We'll all be richer for it."

"I know you still have your doubts about the map," Tibs said, "but I don't. Gareth won't settle for a lesser treasure lightly. He has the map, and you said he has more papers of Visak's."

"Aye, Tibs, and 'tis possible those papers have the clues he'll need. If they do, I daresay Gareth might double-cross us, and we're even worse off. *Might.* I hope I'm wrong. But if they don't hold clues, he'll be furious when he doesn't find the treasure. So we'll cut our losses. If we leave with a lesser haul, he'll rob us of our cut, but I think I can talk him into erasing our debt. Those are the stakes I'm playing for. They're what I've played for all along."

Tibs was dumbfounded. Raden seemed equally shocked. But Brenish was resolute. He stood back and looked them both in the eye, one by one.

"You don't think it's real, do you?" said Raden. "Even after Gareth brought in old Sully? Even I've heard of Sully's reputation. And you knew Visak better than anyone here."

"Aye," said Brenish. "Sully had good reason to believe it was real. He would've been convincing if I didn't know better. But I didn't find that map in the Horsehead, like I told Gareth. Naman knew it too, but he had to tell Gareth something once Bob said 'map'. We both knew once Gareth took an interest, he wouldn't take to disappointment."

"Brenish," said Tibs, "what are you saying?"

"Now you know what's so funny. I thought I'd get investors with the map, and find a treasure pit. I'd give a share to Willy, and some to

Duggle for his contributions. But Naman talked me out of it. I was gonna winter in the city, just as I said, and sell the map outright in the spring with the guild's help. That's all Pernilla ever wanted, anyway. Just enough to get him out early."

"Merciful Almighty," said Raden. "What have you done?"

"If I'd told Gareth the map was fake from the moment it came up, what do you think my chances would have been for surviving that day? Or if so, getting out of it with the bride price I needed? I played a card. I'd hoped I could convince him to take it himself, and leave us out. From then it's been a matter of reining in the damage."

"Damage?" said Raden. "Four men are *dead*."

"Three," said Tibs. He spat to make his point.

"I won't deny Dex had it coming," Raden said, giving Tibs a knowing look. "But we're down here for *nothing*?"

"We're down here," Brenish said, "because your boss is a greedy iron-fisted rascal who went Fell long before any of us were born. I could've come here myself, knowing the danger. I gave it up. He didn't. He chose to take us here. He chose this for us."

"Because you lied to him!"

"Aye!" snapped Brenish. "I lied to save my hide. It didn't work out the way I hoped. So be it. Blame me for everything. Blame me for Harry's death, at least, and Turk's; their blood is at least partly on my hands. It's no less on Gareth's, and Jase's death is on him entire. Do you think I'm proud that three children are fatherless?"

"Four," said Tibs. "You forgot Jase's bastard."

"I was counting him. Eddie at least has Finch."

Tibs shrugged.

"This," said Raden, "is why I say Gareth is still our leader. I'll honor my oath. When he learns the truth, it won't be from me. But he *will* learn it."

"Unless his secret papers have the answer," said Brenish. "Maybe he's done worse with solving those than the map itself. If I got but a peek, I might find what's missing. Tibs, do you see that?" Brenish pointed.

"The column?"

"Nay, the mark. Visak's mark. Like the one in Jarrett's Folly."

"I see nothing."

"I told you not to go swimming in that stuff," said Raden.

Brenish turned to him. "But the deed is done, and 'twould seem I've gained voidsight for it. If Visak marked the treasure room like that, all we need is the password for his spell. It may be on those papers. The clue could be there, somewhere. If I find it, I can claim to have solved the map. And then Gareth will never know. It's that, or we give up on the treasure and find a pit. He'll cut us out, but I can live with coming up empty; I've lived with worse."

Raden shook his head emphatically. "I'll not conspire for you."

"What choice have we? If we find the treasure and Gareth is never the wiser, all is well. If we don't, he may accept a fallback. But like as not, there will be more violence, and more death. Either way, the only route to finding treasure lies with me."

"Gareth has two potions that would let him see these marks. Two. He needs you not."

"A limited resource he'll be loath to waste. To convince him of the need you'd have to tell him the map was false. Even if you broke troth, which I'm sure you wouldn't do, there's naught but bloodshed that way."

Raden grumbled under his breath. There was no arguing with Brenish when his mind was made up. In that way, Brenish supposed he was a lot like Gareth.

Tibs threw his hand up in frustration. "I've followed you this far," he said. "Get us out of this with our lives and no debt, and I'll personally plead your case to Hamish when you try to seek his forgiveness, and his blessing. Get us out with money in our pockets, and I'll name my son for you."

"Snaketongue?" said Raden. "That's a mouthful of a name."

"What say you, Raden?" said Brenish.

Raden held his breath as he thought, but in moments he slumped his free shoulder and sighed in resignation. "Oh, aye. My oath is already given. You've upheld your end. God help us all, but I'll do what I can."

Brenish nodded firmly. He put out his hand. Raden and Tibs both took it, in compact.

"It will be well," Brenish said. "We should away. We've wasted time enough here."

The Streets of Shatterhelm

The three men sang on their way. They had no fear of monsters, for Raden's spell would yet protect them for hours—so said Brenish, who knew enough about the dread spell and its uses to guess as much. It wasn't exactly an orthodox spell the way it was performed, but it was the sort of unschooled magic that would have made Raden's grandfather proud. Not even a rat disturbed their road as they half marched, half hobbled their way to the city. Brenish walked with a slight limp; the weal from Tibs' whip ran deeper than he had expected, and he hadn't yet opted to stop for more of the balm.

The sounds of open song hadn't been heard in these deep places in hundreds, perhaps thousands of years. The goblins didn't roam near Shatterhelm, nor gremlins, and it was unusual indeed for the lizardmen to have come this far east from the neighborhood of Hanfore's Gate. Kalnosh the Great had held court in this region for many, many years, and though the wyrm was several generations dead, his influence was still seemingly feared.

Or, perhaps, the vigilance of Visak had kept the deep creatures at bay for so many years. Indeed the only thing Brenish feared now, besides Gareth and to a lesser extent Finch, was the possibility of running into traps set by the late wizard. It would be unsporting, but Visak was never predictable.

The road north was similar in construction to the Wide Road, but seemingly older. At regular intervals arched recesses were built into the wall, where candles or statues or plants might have stood. The deep river ran along a parallel course somewhere east of them. Fresher air blew at them from the north, most of it probably coming through the inaccessible cavern opening in the mountains.

The air from the outside world felt invigorating, and lifted their spirits further. In spite of Raden and Tibs having to come to grips with the truth, they were at least excited about the prospect of rejoining the others and being a step closer to getting home. Raden seemed happiest about that, for his leg appeared to hurt much more, and he sometimes stopped between lyrics to groan at his shoulder which was sore from the crutch.

Tibs was more openly joyful. Perhaps the news didn't impact him as badly, since Brenish had already cushioned him somewhat by voicing his concerns the day before. As far as Tibs was concerned, two men he had taken for dead were alive and well, and instead of spending eternity encased in magic glass—or worse, having it dissipate some unknown time later and leaving him alone in the dark—he had a new chance to live.

They covered two miles in an hour, which wasn't bad considering their condition. At the end of that journey, more doorways and side passages were built into the road as they had seen outside of other settlements. The men sang louder, fearing nothing, until at last the road ended. The tunnel opened into a great roofed cavern that stretched on northward beyond the reach of their lights.

Many tall buildings lay just at the edge of their light. A pale diffuse light came from above, much dimmer but enough to see more buildings in the distance. Some stretched to the roof and held it up. The men were slightly above the level of the city streets, which they could reach by following a wide, shallow ramp down. From their vantage, what they saw of Shatterhelm was arranged in an orderly fashion with many straight streets, like cities where the Vikings had had an influence. Some of the structures had crumbled, the work of both time and the dragon. The river was nowhere to be seen, apparently running beneath the streets.

Two tall pillars with pointed tops, very similar to the monument at Jarrett's Folly, marked the bottom of the ramp. One of them bore Visak's symbol. Almost directly behind it, Brenish sensed the teleportation orb.

The others would be in a building there, like the one they had stayed in at Lowcastle. They were close enough now that Brenish could make out lesser signatures near the orb: Finch's axe and censer, the goblin's staff, the wands and potions and scrolls on Gareth's person and in his pack.

He led the others down the ramp and into the outskirts of the city, feeling as though he were at the head of a parade of proud soldiers returned from war. There was no finery, no wagons or shining armor, no crowd to wave at, but the feeling of triumph was unshakeable. He rather liked it. If the discord organ were a real instrument, and using it wouldn't have such unthinkable consequences, he would have gladly made music upon it.

Their songs grew louder, grander, utterly carefree, and the cavern rang with the sound. Finally they drew within a furlong of the orb, but there was still no response, no challenge, no greeting. Brenish almost felt worry, wondering if the party had been overwhelmed and slaughtered in the night. Yet in their place, they might mistake the singing—surely they could hear it—for the voices of manthings or other unwelcome visitors. Gareth, he thought, was likely being careful.

In a few minutes more, the orb slid by to Brenish's left. He turned onto a small side street there, Raden and Tibs following behind. Naman stood in the street with a spell lamp, probably Jase's, staring in wonder. He said nothing as they approached, but beamed his gladness to see them alive as they finished their song. They barely got out the last chorus, as Cirawyn and Bob bolted out of a doorway.

Cirawyn ran to Brenish and threw her arms around him. He flung his torch to the ground and held her close.

"I knew you were alive," she said.

Gareth and Finch were the last out of the door. It was hard to read their expressions; they seemed as happy to see their companions as they were annoyed at them for raising the ruins with such a racket.

"Brenish," Gareth said, "you sly devil. I never expected to lay eyes on you again."

"We've come back from the land of the dead," Brenish said. "Somewhat worse for wear."

Gareth took note of Raden's splint and wrappings, and took off his pack.

"How'd you find us?" said Finch. "You didn't know which street we'd be on."

"Lucky for us," Brenish said, "we found a perfectly good tracker."

"I thought you were dead, too," Bob said. He said it to Tibs, but he couldn't stop smiling at the sight of his little brother still among the living.

"'Twas Raden's doing," said Brenish.

"And the noise?" said Gareth. He passed the green potion bottle to Brenish. He made a clucking noise as Brenish uncapped it and raised it to his lips for a sip, as though he had only intended it for Raden, but Brenish paid no heed. Just enough to wet his tongue was all he needed; he passed it back to Raden. The pain remaining in the burns on his hand, partially treated already, vanished immediately. So too did the ache and sting on his leg, and a hundred little bruises and cuts he didn't remember ever acquiring. He didn't even realize his back still hurt so badly from the fall off the cliff, until it suddenly felt well.

"Also Raden's doing," Brenish said. He heard a sharp click behind him, and Raden groaned. His shin had apparently needed resetting again. "He found a hidden talent, and cast a spell of dread just in time to scare off an angry troll."

"The fire did most of it," Raden said.

"You can channel magic?" said Bob. "How?"

Raden shrugged, with both shoulders now that he no longer needed the crutch. "Tim and the Dragon," he said. "We needed it to be a spell."

"Good old Tim."

"You both look like you crawled through Hell to get here," said Finch.

"Aye," Brenish said. "We've barely slept. We spent all night working our way upriver."

"Where'd you get that lamp?" said Gareth, pointing to the spell lamp hanging from the thong around Raden's neck.

"Same place we got that amulet. There's a lake of *esen* downstream, where a lot of unks collected. I still have a full bottle of the stuff. We found some kind of nasty alchemist's brew there, and a wand, but we used them both on the troll."

Telling partial truths again was like slipping on an old robe. It felt comfortable. Brenish felt like himself—but better than himself. He felt renewed confidence. Even their looming dilemma with the map seemed of little consequence.

"Is this true?" said Gareth, to Raden.

"Aye," Raden said. He didn't hesitate, even though he knew the bit about finding the wand was false. "Brenish was resourceful beyond measure. I owe him my life."

"Let's not get too thick," said Finch. "A simple 'aye' would have sufficed."

"This is wonderful," Gareth said. "Let's pack up our goods and finish this venture."

Brenish held up his hand. "A rest first, if you please. We're all very weary. A bite, and just a wink of sleep, would go a long way for us."

Gareth muttered. "I begrudge the delay," he said.

"As do I, but we're no good to you half dead."

"'Tis an improvement from *all* dead," Naman said.

"Aye. Give us an hour or two, Gareth. The spell will last a long while yet. Besides, 'tis all the longer to finish the next riddle. Tibs said you were stuck."

"I am," said Gareth, though he didn't seem pleased with it being said. "One step towards the winter, two steps towards the spring, three steps towards the water, four steps on the wing."

Brenish blew his lips disdainfully. "Visak," he said. "Give me a chance to unscramble my mind, and I'll help as I can."

Gareth slumped in defeat. "Very well," he said. "We may yet need all our strength. Do as you need."

Brenish made a slight bow of respect, or deference, that he suspected didn't entirely come across as sincere. He didn't care. He passed into the building where the others had made camp, removed his pack, and dropped to the floor in great relief.

There was food. Tales were lobbed at him. Cirawyn put her arms around him and kept them there. He fell into a deep, overdue sleep.

Brenish was roused awake by a hand on his shoulder. Cirawyn shook him gently. "Wake up, love," she said. "Time to go."

"How long was I asleep?" he said.

"Three hours," said Gareth's voice. "It's past noon. Time to get what we came for."

Brenish sat up. He still felt tired, but the rest had done him a world of good. His head felt clearer. His bravado was still there, waiting for his need when he would call upon it. Raden stood up, then Tibs. It was good to see Raden on his own two legs again. Raden carried Turk's sword now, leaving Cirawyn with just a pair of crossbows and a knife she had pillaged from the first gremlins.

Cirawyn had acquired a good pair of boots and a light helm sometime after the cliff. Brenish tried to sort through the scattered bits of what the others had told him about that time. More gremlins, more spiders, and the first of the lizardmen. Then the battle, which played out much as Brenish had deduced.

He tried to remember the other things he had learned: Gareth's accursed polymorphosis wand was spent, and discarded. (Good riddance.) The fire wand was drained, but still on hand in case Gareth had a mind to restore it with his replenishment scroll. The censer for the concealment mist was almost depleted. Bob had a shield now, a sturdy piece of polished iron.

"If you have any guesses to that riddle," Gareth said, "speak up. We'll try my idea to start."

"Which is what?" said Brenish.

"There are places mentioned on the map. Depictions of some buildings. They're vague, but it might be enough to set us back on track."

Willy had clearly intended for the owner of the map to spend days lost in Shatterhelm. No one would give up after coming so far. They'd run out of food first. He must have had a few buyers in mind, to produce something so devious: someone who'd deserve such a fate. Gareth probably wasn't on his list, being the sort of man who could survive a long trip back and exact revenge.

Gareth got the group moving and pushed them deeper into the silent city. Brenish and Tibs were at the fore. Finch, Naman, and Bob took the rear. Together they had four torches and four spell lamps: sun and flame in equal measure.

Shatterhelm was to Lowcastle or Wootenghast what those cities were to Paddystock. It was a massive ruin, unthinkable in scale. Cities of similar size were known: far north or northeast, in goblin territory, far east of Asaph's Gate where the blood drinkers lurked, and deep in the south near the old mines. And there were still others to the west, past Hanfore's Gate and beyond.

This city was largely intact, but significant pieces had been torn apart by the carelessness of the dragon. Bricks, whole sections of walls, and sometimes ancient statues lay strewn along the sides of the wider streets. The dragon seemed to have amused itself by trudging up and down every byway big enough to fit its girth, bringing ruin wherever it went. A number of the buildings were more than big enough to house the creature, which meant, logically, that one of them must hold its hoard.

But without Visak's password, or a spellbreak so powerful it could split the world in half, they could search forever and never find the gold. They could see the building and walk right past it, thinking they had checked it. They could see the gold in front of their faces and never register its presence. Visak had had decades to craft the spell, and could have enhanced it every year, every season, until the day he died. He had magical power and knew how to wield it; he had craftiness and knew that even better.

Why, then, all the invisible marks?

Gareth spent some time examining the lay of the city, paying close attention to the roofs, the forms of arches, to corners and lines. He seemed interested especially in towers, pillars, and buildings that looked like houses of government or of worship. He kept the map in his hand the entire time, opening it occasionally and speaking to himself in half-whispers.

After about an hour of this half-directed wandering, Brenish had had enough. "Gareth," he said, "this part of the city has barely been touched by the dragon. I don't think the treasure is right here."

"Of course it isn't," said Gareth. "I'm looking for the next clue. Look here." He brought the map over to Brenish. "This is a drawing of a tower and an arch. Very crude, but it must be connected to the riddle. One step towards the winter, that's north. One step towards the spring: south. Three steps towards the water would be east, and four steps on the wing."

"Which way is that?" said Brenish.

"West, of course. 'Tis all that's left."

"Three steps towards the water could also mean straight down, or west, depending on what part of the city we're in. On the wing could mean straight up, or straight in any direction. Birds fly south in the winter. It could mean south. Or it could be north, to the dragon's exit."

"You can't take steps straight down."

"You can on a ladder. Think like Visak. He wouldn't just give all possible directions. He'd do something tricky. You first met him when he was younger than I knew him. You must have better insights into his mind. Or perhaps you've seen more of his writings."

Gareth's eyes narrowed suspiciously, as if he thought this was another deception on Brenish's part. "I'm open to suggestions," he said. "You have a better idea?"

"I haven't had a chance to study the map in a week," Brenish said. "A good long look might set my mind."

Gareth handed it over. "Take it. If you see something, tell me."

"Aye."

Brenish took the map in one hand, but soon realized what a chore it would be to study it properly that way. If he couldn't get a proper look, he couldn't fake his way through if he stumbled onto anything useful.

"Oi, Raden," he said. "Trade." He held out his torch.

Raden looked insulted, because he knew now how pointless it was. But he took the spell lamp from around his neck and switched it for Brenish's torch.

With both hands free, Brenish was able to stretch the map out fully. It was easy to find the places they had already been, rough sketches copied from other rough sketches copied from real maps. But the last few pieces, mostly in the upper right corner, were vague to the point of absurdity.

Willy had drawn some buildings in a very hasty, hazy version of Visak's style. There was a corner wall with rather ordinary-looking windows, sketched in a way that suggested they should have been easy to recognize. A simple round tower was depicted there, next to a wall, but there were many such towers in Shatterhelm; the fact of them was rather well known to people who had studied ruins lore as extensively as Gareth and himself. An arch on the paper had more ornate detail than anything else near it, but there was nothing remotely noteworthy about its shape. And none of these sketches were close to each other, robbing the reader of any sense of perspective or how they might be related. The images were more decorations than clues.

"I forgot how bad these drawings were," he said. "Visak must have finished the map about the same time he finished a bottle."

"Aye," said Gareth.

"Think you he's jesting? These pictures are useless."

"The riddle's no better."

"I'm thinking on it. Perhaps the rest of the map has more clues. Why else would he draw a whole route to this city? There must be secrets buried in the other riddles."

"I thought you'd solved this," said Finch.

Brenish looked up, but Finch's ire wasn't directed at him; he was looking at Gareth.

"I thought the same," Gareth said. "Not all of the riddles, but the drawings were clear enough."

"Harry is dead, Gareth. Turk is dead. Jase is dead. Dex is dead."

Gareth looked at his lieutenant in surprise, and responded just short of exasperation. "I accept my responsibility, Ed."

"At least that wand is gone," Bob said brightly.

Gareth gave Bob the strangest look for that. He was angry, surprised, and confused all at once. At first Brenish wondered if Raden had said anything to him about the polymorphosis wand being such a bad idea, but no. Evidently Bob had figured that much out on his own. And with his usual skill, put his foot in it.

"Pray, continue," said Naman.

Gareth and Finch disengaged. Bob seemed grateful for the interruption.

"The map was meant for us," Gareth said. "Visak did nothing by accident. Have faith in that."

Finch turned away without acknowledging him. Raden shot Brenish a look of disgust, not entirely undeserved.

"Pity we didn't bring any goldsense," said Brenish. "My plan would have worked."

Gareth waggled his finger like a crone giving remonstrance to an errant boy. "Keep that tongue in your head, if that's all it has to say. Else I'll cut it the fork it wants."

Brenish heeded the warning and shut up. Gareth's patience was crumbling, but with it so was the respect of his men. At last, he saw a way out of the mess, a plan that would let him and the others leave not only with their lives, but with their fortunes. All it required was a little more time. He doubted now whether Gareth's other papers had given him any insights, which meant they were probably just as useless to him. Gareth didn't have it in him to pretend to be so flustered, he thought.

"We're covering too little ground," Gareth said. "As long as a spell wards us, let's use it. We'll split into four teams."

Brenish looked up from the map and gave Raden a secretive glance, as good as any smirk Jase ever wore. The logical way to split was one of Gareth's men with one of his "employees", Cirawyn counting among the latter. But if Brenish's suspicions of a double-cross were founded—though now he second-guessed them—it would be disastrous to leave any of them alone with Gareth, including himself.

"I'll stay with you," said Raden. The look wasn't lost on him. "I've a good eye."

"As you will," said Gareth.

"Naman," said Brenish, "you may as well come with me."

"Cirawyn," said Bob, as though they were choosing for a game. "Best for brawn to pair with a brain, they say."

Tibs snorted and nudged Finch. "I don't know which of us should feel insulted."

Brenish motioned the others around the map. "I'd as soon keep this for now," he said.

"Aye," Gareth agreed. He pointed to the drawings. "These are what you should seek, unless you should solve the riddle first. Don't stray too far. We'll meet in the city square, just north a way."

"I'm all turned around here," said Bob. "Hopefully milady has better direction."

"I have," said Cirawyn.

"Be on the lookout for anything tricky," Brenish added. He made eye contact with Raden. "Anything. Be suspicious." He turned to address the others, Gareth included, now that his point was made. "Traps are a possible danger. But most likely 'tis a puzzle you'll find.

Keep an eye for places damaged by the dragon, but look to structures nearby that might be untouched. We're dealing with an overlook spell. It could be something that seems right where it belongs, or looks too simple. Suspect what you least suspect. Visak loved nothing more than hiding things in plain sight."

"Like the map," Bob said.

"Aye, Bob, just like."

Gareth withdrew from the huddle. "As he says, men. We'll meet again in two hours."

Unseen

"That was a brazen performance," Naman said, once they were safely away from the others. They were headed northeast, within the very heart of the city.

"Thank you," Brenish said. "I hit the mark, then."

"Glad as I am to see you alive, our fate is unchanged. What do you intend to do now? You realize we'll not find a thing."

"Not necessarily. But if we find it, it won't be with the map's help."

"Even if you look in exactly the right place, you can't break that spell. Overlook spells have passwords or keys. You have neither."

"One problem at a time, Naman. Besides, we may not need to find anything."

"In Heaven's name why not? How do you expect us to live through this if Gareth is forced to leave empty-handed?"

Brenish grinned at him. Naman had been his conscience for so long. It was good to have him back, even though conscience seemed like such a burden now. Brenish had crossed over into some darker part of the mind, where words of caution were but a howling wind. He wasn't the sort of man who would let his friends come to harm for any price, but whatever other morals he ever had were, for the time being, suspended. As was his fear.

"The next few hours will solve that problem for us. Gareth is unraveling with frustration. Unless he has the key to the whole thing in his secret papers, he has nothing. For a time I was worried he might abandon the rest of us here, and leave with all the gold himself. But he doesn't act as a man with a loaded die."

"You think he'd turn on his own men? Even Gareth wouldn't stoop so low."

"He might. But Raden will keep watch. He knows of my suspicions."

Naman raised an eyebrow. "What else does he know?"

"Everything. Tibs too."

Without a word of warning, Naman slapped him across the back of the head. "Damn your mouth."

"I took an oath and kept it. There was no other way for us to work together. Anyway it had to be said."

Naman spat on the ground as his only reply.

"The others," Brenish continued, "they're seeing Gareth fall to pieces. The longer it takes, the more his frustration will consume him. They need never know the map is false. They'll turn on Gareth, we'll declare failure, and I'll offer to lead us to a treasure pit as I'd always planned. We'll walk away with a *full* cut, each."

"Fat chance of that, without goldsense."

Brenish smiled. Nothing scared him now. "Oh my friend, what tales I have for you."

Naman didn't ask him to clarify. He seemed tired of this conversation, wearied by Brenish's self-assurance. He did hold his head at an angle, jut out his nose the slightest as if to tell by sniffing whether this man was still the same one he'd botched highway robberies with outside of Ilyenis. The thief with big dreams and bigger worries was gone now. Clearly none of it sat well with Naman.

"The wyrm seemed to like that street," Brenish pointed. "Let's have a look."

Brenish walked off without waiting. He kept his eyes especially on the buildings and on the ground, looking for markers other than the ones on the map. He'd had long to ponder what an overlook spell might do to his mind, in this place. He knew aught of how the old man thought, which was still an advantage to him—though Gareth had at least the same advantage. His instructions to the others had been true: They should look for that which looked too ordinary.

Finding the spot where the treasure must be was one thing, but Naman was right: breaking or bypassing the spell was quite another. Even the goblin priest could have shouted itself hoarse trying to break Visak's spell; the wizard was too powerful and had years upon years to make the spell impenetrable as any fortress. Brenish regretted having so little experience in burglary, for it might have granted him insight in how to find chinks in the spell.

But then, perhaps he was looking at it all wrong. An overlook spell was nothing more than a lie sustained by magic. Who else in the party was as qualified to understand such a thing? Maybe Visak had never needed a password at all; he could have simply required a mind sharp enough to penetrate a powerful illusion.

They turned onto an avenue. They were deep in the city now, where the architecture was great and inspiring, most of the buildings large but with a number of multiple-story structures squeezed between that must have been boarding houses or tenements. The street had raised sidewalks, and occasional grates for water to drain away. Tall iron posts marched down the lane, though many had been bent or broken. At regular intervals there were squares of brick along the road, with circular openings in the middle and soil or dust in the center.

"There were trees here," Brenish said. "They grew by spell light. This city must have been beautiful."

"Fie," said Naman. He turned away in disgust. He was in no mood for sentimentality.

There was a great deal of damage to the fronts of many buildings, big and small. None of them looked much like a dragon would have spent a lot of time going in and out of them. It looked more like the beast had simply rampaged up and down the street, or else perhaps it had simply bumped into things in the dark.

"I'm not sure whether to look for buildings with more damage, or less," said Brenish. "Visak could have disguised the site any way he liked. A big place that looks empty might be too obvious."

"Why even pretend there's a point?" said Naman. "If you find it, the knowledge is useless to you."

"Not so. Gareth would be most pleased. Perhaps we could just *guess* the spellbreak."

"I'll not play this game."

Brenish shrugged. "As you will. We're the only team with that luxury. But if it's all the same to you, I'll keep looking."

"'Tisn't the same to me. You could be thinking a way out of this instead of flitting about."

"I think perfectly well on my feet. Besides, I told you, I already have a plan. Delay works in our favor."

Brenish walked down the street for a way by himself, until Naman tired of standing alone and began to follow. One of the buildings looked like a guild house or a meeting place, easily big enough to serve as a dragon's lair. A short set of broken steps led up to a portico with a rail, though only pieces of the rail were intact. He made his way carefully up and explored inside for a few minutes. The roof was intact and the doorway was too narrow, but Brenish was undeterred by common sense. He ran across the wide-open interior a few times just to convince himself there was no gold to trip on there.

He tried the same in another building, this one unscathed. Every accessible space was empty, not just visually. There were no hidden obstacles. He saw no hidden markings. This went on in the next likely building, and the next, and even a few unlikely ones. As Brenish became more and more dispirited, Naman's amusement grew to fill the gap.

Eventually Brenish realized his mistake: An overlook spell on any of these places wouldn't have let him enter, precisely because Visak wouldn't want anyone simply bumping into unseen gold. He would have walked into a different doorway instead, or walked right by the entrance without really understanding it was there. He was exploring the interiors for nothing.

After that, he moved on to a different street, and kept his eyes on the exteriors of all the buildings, looking for any signs that might leap out, any discrepancies. But it was just as useless. Even the simplest, most inept casts of overlook spells were a great challenge to see through. Brenish had encountered many in the city: mages loved to hide their purses that way. It was even common practice for overlooks to be used as spellbindings, though they were less effective. He knew his way around these difficulties, but they were child's play next to a master illusion.

The longer this went on, Brenish felt a need to rely only on his instincts instead. He tried a different street but barely spent five minutes there. Another, and he felt certain they were looking in the wrong place.

"Time's running short," said Naman. "I suggest you use the rest to plan."

Brenish's thoughts were already drifting that way, but as he took one last look around, a new idea came to him.

"One more," Brenish said.

He entered into a small doorway on a tall building, and found stairs. Instead of staying on the ground floor, he climbed up story after story. Naman trudged behind, barely willing to tolerate his capriciousness but perhaps interested in a change of scenery. After the fourth flight, they emerged onto the roof: a flat space with a low rail all around.

Brenish walked to the edge of the roof and surveyed the city. The paths of the dragon's destruction were easier to see from up there, except for places where taller buildings blocked his view. The greatest concentration of damage was plain: it was to their west, northwest of where he guessed the city square lay.

"There," Brenish said, pointing. "That mound of fallen stone."

"It could be naught more than that," said Naman. "'Tisn't the only one."

"Nay, but 'tis the only one big enough. Kalnosh didn't roost inside a building with a broken roof. That's the spot."

"You're fighting a spell that means for you not to see through it."

"Aye, but lies have limits. There has to be a grain of truth in them. There has to be a way they can be believed. I could talk you into a lot of things if I really tried, but I couldn't convince you you were a rabbit."

"Some days I'm not sure," Naman said. "But it's been about two hours. We should head back."

"Aye. We'll go to the square."

Brenish led the way. Although he had seen the square, he knew where it must be before he had ever reached the roof. Even without a proper map of Shatterhelm, he felt he understood its layout. He couldn't explain why. Cues from the way the halls and towers and street lines were oriented, perhaps, may have given him that sense. The bearing stone could have been another factor. The feeling that he knew his way around was so overwhelming he was certain the others must feel it too, to some extent or another.

The city square was a large open space, surrounded all around by shops and great edifices of forgotten importance. A fountain had stood there, some great statue spewing water from many points, but the fountain had been broken and all that remained were stony stumps and exposed bits of pipe. Its pool was dry, empty.

Finch and Tibs were already waiting for them when they arrived. "Any luck, men?" said Brenish.

"Nay," said Finch. "We sought clusters of features like those on the map, but found none."

"I looked mostly for places the dragon might have been."

Bob and Cirawyn were the next to arrive. "Oi," said Bob, "find anything?"

"Nay," said Tibs.

"We might have."

Brenish arched an eyebrow. "Go on."

"There's a place with a tower like the one on the map," Bob said, "and it's near an arch and a street corner."

"Ah. I'm sure Gareth will be delighted."

"It doesn't solve the riddle, though. We tried."

"We'll let Gareth try."

Brenish looked at Cirawyn, who seemed oddly hopeful in spite of knowing she and Bob couldn't have discovered anything of use. But another sight caught his eye, and he let his gaze skip past her. A glowing symbol was visible in the middle distance behind her, hanging above her head like a broken halo, on a wall just south of the square.

"Half a moment," Brenish said. He took off in the direction of the symbol.

"Oi," Gareth said, coming up the wide street from the east, alongside Raden. "Where are you going, Brenish?"

"Not far."

Brenish went past them as he approached the marker. It was Visak's mark again, like the others he had seen. It stood on the corner of a building, but one much too small to hold the treasure. Just to make certain he wasn't wrong, he stepped inside and walked around a little.

Gareth came in behind him. "What is it, Brenish?"

"I know not," Brenish said thoughtfully. "But I feel drawn here."

"An overlook spell wouldn't draw you."

"Call it a hunch. I like this spot. We should come back here, if the other doesn't amount to much."

"Other?"

Brenish didn't answer, but Gareth seemed cheered by his words nonetheless. He waited for Brenish to finish looking at the building, so they could join the others in the square.

"I hear some of you have made a find," Gareth said.

"Bob spotted the place," said Cirawyn.

"Excellent. Take us there."

The way wasn't long. Cirawyn led them one block to the south, one block west, to a place where the dragon had done considerable damage to a small cluster of buildings but left most of the others intact. The little street was mostly tenements, none of them any good for housing a dragon hoard, yet Brenish immediately spotted the markers Bob was talking about: a tower, and an arch. Gareth saw them too, and smiled wide.

"I was right the first time," Gareth said. He smirked at Brenish. "Starting at the square, it's one step north, two steps south, three steps east, four steps west. The steps are blocks!"

It seemed awfully prescient of Willy to know that just the right landmarks would be visible from this spot. There was even a wall on the corner with windows, just like the little sketch Willy had drawn. Had Willy copied those drawings faithfully from some other writings of Visak's? It made a great deal of sense that he would have done so.

And then Brenish saw, on a doorway behind Gareth and Cirawyn, yet another of Visak's invisible devices glowing its soft blue. What could the marks possibly mean? None of them were near the mound he had seen, which was north of where the party stood now. The room behind that doorway looked just as inadequate to hold Visak's treasure as the one on the corner. But what was the wizard's purpose in leaving them?

"Next riddle," said Gareth. "Brenish, if you'll do the honors."

Brenish turned, confused. He had riddles enough of his own. "Huh?"

"The next riddle. We're very close now."

Brenish opened the map again and found his place, near all the bad drawings. Assuming Gareth had already found what he believed were adequate solutions to the other puzzles, only one false clue remained after the riddle of the steps. "'Tis the last," he said.

"The key to the spell. This is the spot."

But Brenish's eyes froze on the page. He had forgotten what that riddle said until now, and now that he saw it afresh, he didn't dare read it aloud. Willy had, perhaps without meaning to, written him into a trap. It was Visak's kind of puzzle, probably something Willy had taken from a book of the wizard's jokes. It was doubtful this was the key to breaking the overlook spell, but there was no doubt at all what Gareth would do to try.

"Read it," said Gareth. "I think I already know the answer."

Brenish folded the map and let his weapon hand hang loose. He might need to draw a blade in a second. Gareth seemed confused as to why he would put the map aside.

"It can't be what you think," Brenish said. "Visak was a kind man, as you'll remember."

"The words, Brenish. Now."

He swallowed hard. "Seven men stomped 'pon the castle floor. The blood of the youngest opened the door."

Gareth laughed softly, though he was the only one. The others seemed to regard the idea of bloodshed as a means to breaking a spell as macabre, or sacrilegious. Even Finch looked vaguely horrified.

"I think we needn't spill *all* your blood," Gareth said.

Brenish tried to hide his surprise. Gareth's interpretation was better than his own. He didn't hesitate to draw his knife.

"Potion, please," Brenish said.

"First things first." Gareth motioned the men to form a circle, and stood nearly opposite Brenish.

Brenish tucked the map behind his armor and sliced along his left thumb. A slice was less apt to get infected. The blade hurt going in, but he ignored the pain, knowing that worse could come if he didn't make the attempt himself. A few drops of blood fell to the ground.

"Stomp, men," said Gareth. "Just the men."

All seven of them stomped on the ground, one foot after the other. It took them a moment to gain some rhythm, but soon they had the cavern booming the noise of it all around them. After a minute or so, Gareth called for them to cease.

"The pool hasn't moved. I expected it to trickle towards the hoard, or through a hidden crack. Perhaps we need more blood."

"I'll slash my wrist for you," Brenish said, "if you'll give me the potion bottle so I can sip it to stay alive."

Gareth waved him off. "Nay. Let me think a moment."

"Give me the potion anyway, if you're going to wait. I'm bleeding like a stuck pig."

"Oh simmer down. You're not a child."

Gareth began to pace around, thinking half aloud to himself, muttering, repeating the words of the riddle. Raden pulled out a strip of cloth and offered it to Brenish so he could wrap his thumb. Brenish accepted it gladly, and discovered it had been discreetly slathered with the healing balm. He turned his attention for the moment toward securing the wrapping.

Suddenly he heard a yelp and a scream, and looked up too late. Gareth held Cirawyn's black hair and his torch in the same hand, tightly; in the other hand he held a knife that Brenish had not previously seen, and it was at her throat. Several of the others reacted in alarm, some of them Gareth's own men.

"No, Gareth!" said Raden.

"The blood of the youngest," said Gareth. "Not the youngest man. Just the youngest. That's you, dear."

Brenish narrowed his eyes. "You'll not harm her, Gareth," he said coldly.

"Nay," Gareth said, but though it sounded like agreement he obviously meant something else. "She'll survive. She'll get the potion after. If it doesn't work, we'll try the wrist as you said."

"We'll try neither," said Brenish.

"This has gone far enough," said Naman, but he said it to Brenish.

"Agreed. Gareth, put down that knife and let's be reasonable men. You know Visak wouldn't have stood for something like this."

"'Twas he who wrote it. Why would he write something he felt would be misinterpreted so drastically?"

"To put off thieves, Gareth. What better way to divert them than making them harm each other?"

"Besides," Bob said, "Visak wouldn't have known there'd be seven men and a woman here."

Gareth nearly sneered. "Visak was a seer, Bob. Of course he knew."

"He wouldn't have approved of this, Gareth," Naman said. "You know that."

"I know there's a riddle with a plain answer. If he didn't expect this he should've chosen his words better. And it wasn't like him to choose wrong."

"Gareth," Brenish said, "you don't—"

"Nay," said Gareth. "We'll do it my way."

Gareth was quick as a snake; his training was too great. He moved the blade away from Cirawyn's throat, but in the very same motion slashed it across the exposed back of her right hand, just below the protection of Dex's vambrace. The cut was deep, and very long. She screamed as the blade sliced through, but just as quickly it was back at her neck. She dropped her torch from the other hand, in brief shock and panic.

Raw hatred exploded out through Brenish's head. Somehow he held his physical reaction in check; only his eyes gave him away. Others were less reticent.

"*Damn* you, Gareth," Tibs shouted.

Gareth's reply was perfectly calm. "Stomp," he said.

"You don't know what you're doing," said Naman. "You're just guessing what needs to be done. You don't even know what you don't know."

Gareth wiggled the knife. "Stomp. Now."

None of the other men moved a foot, until Brenish did. He stared death at Gareth, moving one foot down, then the other. The rest finally joined in, and then Gareth himself. Cirawyn wept and whimpered in pain. Every time she tried to jerk her hand back to her chest so she could apply pressure to it, Gareth yanked her braid and made her cry out again, keeping the blood dripping. Brenish increased the force on his feet, channeling his anger there.

"Stop!" Gareth said.

He looked down on the ground. Cirawyn had spilled quite a bit of blood, but her wound wasn't fatal. Another minute of stomping had produced no results.

"I would have thought that was enough," Gareth said.

"Gareth," Brenish said, as calmly as he could, "this isn't the way. This can't be the answer. Visak wouldn't want an innocent girl's blood spilled, nor mine, nor even yours. This is not the key to his spell."

"Then you'd best give me a different answer. I feel you've been lying to me this whole time. You've held something back."

"I'm always lying to you, Gareth. That's what I do."

"You know the true answer, don't you? You solved this riddle before summer was out. You had months."

"I swear to you I did not," Brenish said. "As I swore to Raden to tell the truth, I'll swear on my mother's soul I do not know the answer to this riddle. But this has gone too far. Let's fall back to my first plan. With goldsense, we can find a treasure pit. You'll still walk out of this a rich man."

"We have no goldsense."

"*I* have goldsense. Raden will confirm it."

Gareth glared at Raden, but Raden only said, "I swore an oath too."

For a moment Gareth considered the idea. The certainty of walking out with some gold against the possibility of leaving with none was a tempting one. Brenish however had little temper left to lose. He saw Cirawyn crying and trying to do something about her mangled hand, and made up his mind. One way or another, he didn't intend to let Gareth leave the ruins on his own terms. If there was treasure to be had at all, he would have at least as great a share as Gareth. If not, he would find another way to make Gareth pay.

Gareth made up his mind too. "Nay," he said. "It's Visak's gold or nothing. And you'd best tell me what else you've kept from me."

"Me?" said Brenish. "'Tis you who've held back."

"Watch your tongue," Gareth said, and pressed the knife a little further.

Brenish backed off and held up a hand for peace. He tried to withhold the will to murder from his voice. He squeaked out as deferential a tone as he could manage.

"Gareth, I never meant to be enemies here. But I know you have more knowledge than you've told me. Perhaps it didn't help you, but it might help us now if I can see it. Please. Put down the knife. Let her go, and for God's sake give her a sip of the potion. Show me the papers you have in your pack. We'll work this out together."

Gareth stared at him with absolute incomprehension. His whole demeanor said he thought Brenish had gone mad. "I've no papers in my pack but the scrolls I brought," he said. "The ones I have left."

"Nay," said Brenish.

"You truly think I'd have another source of lore, and not share it?" said Gareth. He didn't let up his grip on Cirawyn's braid nor move the knife any further from her, but his eyebrows dipped as a new idea took residence in his mind. "Oh, so that's your game. Yesterday you asked if I had a map of Shatterhelm. You've acted as though I knew something from Visak I don't. Today you asked if I'd seen *other writings*."

"I'd hoped you'd reveal them to me eventually, once you were out of ideas. That time has come, don't you think? Let's *both* have a look, before you do something that can't be undone."

"I have no other writings of Visak's," Gareth said. "Not for lack of trying."

"I saw them, Gareth."

Gareth tugged Cirawyn's hair again, eliciting another broken cry of pain, and held the knife still closer. "You think you can turn my men against me with a lie like that? I'm happy to prove you wrong. They'll see there's naught there."

"'Tis why you didn't want me in your pack at the garden. But I saw them."

"I didn't want you in it because the contents are valuable and you're a *thief*."

Finch was the one who stepped in now, trying to calm both men. "Brenish, maybe you thought you saw something there, but you were wrong. I've seen inside Gareth's pack, and there are no papers there."

"I know what I saw, Finch. I told Tibs what I saw. And Naman, and Raden."

"Aye," said Raden. "He did say that."

"Enough of this," Gareth said. "You couldn't have—"

"It was at the aqueducts, Gareth," Brenish said. "When the spell broke, and it was pitch dark. You opened your pack, so you could see by the light... of..."

Brenish fell silent. His head spun. He stumbled back as if kicked. Spellglow, radiating from the orb and a few of the potions, was a very different kind of light than the sunshine from the lamps or the flames of the torches.

Visak had a *way*.

He turned his head toward the sign of Visak nearby. It was a message for him, a simple call to action. And Brenish understood, now, what needed to be done. He turned back to Gareth and tried to choke out a few words.

"You were saying?" said Gareth. His tone was ice.

Brenish found his voice, though it was hoarse. "I need to see the orb," he said.

"My patience has ended."

But Brenish's confidence grew back anew. "The orb, please, Gareth. I can get you this treasure."

"You know the answer, then? Tell me now."

"I solved a riddle," said Brenish. "But not that one." He looked into his adversary's eyes. "Gareth, hear me. Do you truly fear I would use the orb to save myself, and leave her to die here? Think you I would abandon my friends? I accept your distrust. But trust your own reason now. I think I have an answer."

Gareth locked his eyes on Brenish. "When you begged me for 800p, I said you were a changed man. I didn't like it then. I like this less. Why think you I would lend you my trust now?"

"What I said then, I said for the same reason I say this now. You want to know what you can trust? Very well. You can trust, Gareth, that I will do anything for Cirawyn's sake. And right now, that means handing you the answer you want. To do that I require the orb. I swear I won't use it to teleport. Little good would it do me, anyway."

"Boss," Bob said, "I think he's genuine."

"I *know* he is," said Raden.

Gareth didn't let his eyes leave Brenish. "Ed?" he said.

"The other options are all worse," said Finch. "Let him borrow the orb."

"He doesn't have to use it, to cause mischief," said Gareth. "You don't need to hold it," he said to Brenish.

"Nay," said Brenish. "You could hold it, if it would put you at ease."

Gareth thought it through, and seemed to decide he was amenable to this plan. He gave a slow nod. He loosened his grip on Cirawyn, and pushed her towards Finch. Finch took hold of her only loosely, and pulled out a cloth for her bleeding hand.

With the same caution and still keeping eye contact with Brenish, Gareth removed one strap of his pack and then the other, placing it on the ground. He looked down only long enough to snatch out the teleportation orb, then pushed the pack behind him with his foot.

The pearly pale gold of the orb's spellglow was paltry next to the other lights. Gareth kept it cupped in his hand; it was too big to close his fingers around it entirely, but his grip on it would have made Lila envious of his strength. He crossed the circle in a few steps.

"The orb," he said. "Uphold your part of the bargain."

"I made no bargain," said Brenish. "Only a promise."

"Then keep your promise."

"Aye, Gareth."

Brenish took out the map, but didn't unfold it. Willy's writing looked the same as it ever had. He turned it around to find a blank space on the back. On that side the spell paper was, as one would expect, still blank.

"'Twas dark at the time," Brenish said. "I think the lights are interfering." He removed the spell lamp from around his neck and passed it to Naman. "Gareth, your torch too. Everyone else, please take a few steps back."

"I'm feeling dizzy," Cirawyn said, her voice thick with tears and pain.

Gareth waved a hand, indicating Finch should deal with it. Brenish watched Finch lead her to Gareth's pack so she could sit and lay her head against it.

"Your torch, Gareth," Brenish reminded him.

Gareth looked for any further signs of deception, though with Brenish that was a losing fight at best. After a few moments he relented and passed his torch to Raden.

Tiny lines, the faintest scratch marks of the thinnest ink, took shape along the back of the map. Their pattern and purpose was too difficult to tell.

"I see it!" said Gareth. His hostility broke apart like tattered rain clouds over the afternoon sun. "Visak, you clever old goat!"

"Still too much light," said Brenish. "Everyone, get the lights as far away as you can, please."

The others all moved away. Finch kicked away Cirawyn's fallen torch and stepped back further.

In only the spellglow from the orb, with nothing but the dim light of the cavern ceiling to compete, the writing revealed itself. Geometric designs, circles inscribing shapes inscribing other circles. Brenish unfolded the paper for a better view, and prayed his guess was right. Just as the Expert had said, the spell paper came from Visak's study. It was just the right size for Willy to work with. Just right.

The drawings that met Brenish's eye were nothing like a proper map. Most of the page was composed of diagrams, charts, and cryptic notations. It looked not unlike an astronomer's work, yet Visak had never had any interest in astronomy. It was likewise similar to alchemy, but the wizard had no more use for that art than the stars. Brenish let his eye drift, hoping to see something useful. Gareth, unsatisfied with the way Brenish held the map so loosely—to keep the blood from his thumb off it—took hold of it with his left hand and stretched it out taut, the easier to read.

Brenish used his free hand to point out some of the diagrams, drawing Gareth's eye about in the hopes of distracting him. He was no longer interested in letting Gareth find the treasure himself, on his own terms.

"Another riddle," said Gareth. He tried to point with his thumb. Brenish winced; he hadn't seen it himself at first, but there was a clear snippet of verse on the page. The words were facing Gareth; Brenish couldn't easily read them upside-down. "Hill under hill under lock without key. The usurper alone has eyes to see.' The wizard loved his rhymes, didn't he?"

Brenish mused on what the words could mean. He was certain the hill under hill meant the mound of debris he had seen from the rooftop, but if the overlook spell was the lock, the fact of it having no key was troubling.

Cirawyn made another high squeak of pain, and it focused his mind: He would be the usurper. And once he realized that, as his eyes wandered across the meaningless diagrams, he saw there what Gareth had never been meant to see.

Some of the writing that looked like arcane nonsense jumped out at his attention. A message was scrawled amongst the text and figures, or so it looked from a distance. Unfocused, the letters and numerals and strange runes looked like a rough approximation of guild code, his own guild's secret writing system by which they left messages for one another on the city walls. The message they formed was no illusion; it was coherent, and it faced him.

COUNT VL MARK THAT LAD

"Just as murky as the rest," said Gareth. "There are no hills here, and I imagine Visak himself was the usurper. But how does it pertain to the stomping and the blood?"

Six.

"Maybe the blood riddle has no answer," said Bob.

"What do you mean?" said Gareth.

Twelve.

"I was thinking. Maybe the other side's just a ruse."

"It could be," Gareth said, "but why would Visak have drawn a fake map on the back of his real one? 'Twould only draw attention."

"Aye, I thought that too. But then I thought, what if he didn't? Perchance he left it blank, and someone took it. Duggle and Ivers made off with his stuff when he died."

Twenty-eight.

"Only what they could find," said Gareth.

"Aye," said Bob, "but Duggle's good friends with Willy Alder. And Cirawyn didn't get the deepsick till Turk made mention of him. What if Brenish got it from Willy's wife?"

Thirty-nine.

Naman groaned deeply. "Damn it all, Bob," he said. Gareth looked his way.

Forty-five.

Just as Gareth began to turn his head back to level an accusation, Brenish launched a surprise uppercut. He caught Gareth squarely on the chin, knocking the man's head back. Gareth let go of the map; Brenish flung it aside.

Gareth and his men had no time to react. Brenish grabbed at the orb with both hands and pried it loose of Gareth's grasp. To keep Gareth from obstructing him, he stomped his foot.

Everyone else seemed to react too slowly. Time had become like winter sap to Brenish; he alone moved quickly. Bob acted panicked, unsure how to respond. Finch stepped forward, but Tibs' whip was already in motion to drive him back. Brenish pulled the orb further away from Gareth's reach, and flung it in a quick arc across to his target. Cirawyn caught it in her uninjured hand.

The moment ended suddenly, with the crack of a whip nearby and a fist in his face. Brenish stumbled back. Even though it wasn't Gareth's best blow, it was a solid enough hit to break his nose.

He didn't have the luxury of reeling and holding his nose, so he did neither. He corrected his balance almost instantly. Gareth was already turning away. Finch, previously distracted by Tibs, made a move towards the orb.

"Go!" Brenish screamed.

Cirawyn clutched Gareth's pack, closed her eyes, and vanished.

Mastery

Gareth's scream of wrath was sharper than his blades, almost inhuman. Fury gave him strength and speed he had never shown before. He raised his left arm and bashed the shield into Brenish's face. Another blow struck him as quick as the first. Brenish managed to raise his own arm to ward off a third blow, and a fourth, taking a nasty bruising hit with each one.

"You need me," Brenish said, coughing out blood. A tooth was gone.

"The devil needs you," said Gareth. He kicked Brenish in the stomach, then drew out his mace.

Brenish groaned but spoke quickly through the pain. "I'm your only chance to walk away with treasure. I have eyes you know not, and I know where to find the hill under hill."

Raden grabbed Gareth's arm. "Gareth, we do need him. He has other sight. That's the truth."

"Traitor!" Gareth growled. "How long have you been scheming with him? Before your fall, or after?"

"I remain loyal. Even now, Gareth. But hear him out."

"Nay," said Finch. "I've had enough." He stepped forward and brought his staff to bear, intending to drive it down onto Brenish's chest with a crushing blow.

"Kill me and Harry died for nothing," Brenish said.

Finch's lips curled in anger. Tremors ran down his arms into the priest's staff. "Fie," he said, and backed away.

"I'm sorry, men." Brenish stood and wiped his mouth, then spat out more blood onto the street. "Truly. He forced my hand."

Gareth sputtered, so beside himself was he with rage. "You gutter-crawling *swine*," he said. "I forced *you*?"

"I kept my promise, Gareth. I told you you could trust me to protect her."

"Then you've failed worse than you know," Gareth said. "Bind him up. We'll use his wits to get out of here."

"And leave *all* the treasure behind? I saw the hill. Naman was there."

"Aye," said Naman.

"More lies," Gareth growled.

"You were right about Visak, Gareth. He was a seer. He left a message for me on the map. And there's this: *The usurper alone has eyes to see.* I have voidsight. With it I've seen his markings nearby. And I have other ways of seeing still."

"Voidsight," said Finch, completely without inflection.

Gareth looked to Raden to confirm it. Raden nodded, still holding Gareth's arm. "He told us he saw Visak's mark at the crossing. I believe him. He was still under oath to tell me the truth."

"Oaths," Gareth sneered. "From Brenish."

"He upheld it at every turn. I've no cause to doubt him on that."

"He'd swear no such oath without one in return. What oath did he ask of you, Raden?"

"The one you'd expect."

Gareth ground his teeth. "What did he tell you about the map?"

"The truth," Brenish said. "Once we found Tibs I told them both. He was bound by his word not to tell you. But now you know. Pernilla gave me the map to sell for Willy, so he could get out of lockup early. When he made it, he picked a piece of spell paper big enough to serve as the map. Maybe Visak had scrawled on the back already, so it would be useless for most anything else. Willy didn't know it was there, else he'd have sold it years ago. *I* didn't know it was there, else I'd have told you sooner."

"You let us come here with a false map," Gareth said. His voice was a half-tamed screech. He was so flustered that he sounded more indignant than enraged, as if yelling at a servant for putting the wrong kind of plate out again at a dinner party. "You knew it was a forgery, and you said nothing."

"Aye. Once you made it clear you wanted it, you wouldn't have taken well to the truth. We both know that. You were already Fell. I lied, aye, but you left me no choice. Indeed if I'd told you the truth, you'd have believed what you wanted, taken out your anger on me, and all this would have happened just the same. Deny that if you can."

Gareth tried to lunge at him, but Raden still held his arm.

"Even if you can get us to the treasure," Finch said, "you've ruined our escape. We'll have to take only what we can carry, and hope to fight our way out."

"Aye," said Brenish. "Given the choice I wouldn't have done. It means we can't use a treasure pit, either."

"We'll manage without you, Brenish," Gareth said. "The truth is on the back of the map—nay, I should say the front."

"Which you'll read how? You've no spellglow to read it by." Brenish gestured toward where Gareth's pack had been. All that was left were some drops of blood.

Gareth turned back in anger, but Brenish, though battered, was serene. He spat out more blood.

"Oh dear," he said. "You've lost any potions you could've used for voidsight, too."

"How would you have gained voidsight?" said Naman.

"He swam in *esen*," said Raden. "Told him it was a bad idea."

Gareth let his arm droop, enough that Raden was finally willing to release him. He put the mace away. His anger seemed veiled by a cloud, leaving Brenish temporarily in the shade. With a few breaths he mastered himself, and found calm again. Gareth the Reasonable Man was out once more. This was the side of Gareth that Brenish usually feared most, the one who could win the hearts of his men.

Yet now Brenish didn't fear even that; he feared nothing. For perhaps the first time in his life, he felt complete certainty in his course.

"Well, men," Gareth said, "this is the Brenish we always knew. The liar. The thief. Who'd sell his friends for a stack of coin." The confidence was missing from his voice. He saw Brenish's mood plainly, and could read his own men at least as well.

"Perchance that speech would be more effective," said Brenish, "had your folly not killed Jase. Naman knew when we came that we were unlikely to leave alive. Coming here wasn't my idea, you'll recall. I tried to talk you out of it. 'Twas your greed that brought us here, Gareth, not mine. And you'd still have your precious orb if you hadn't threatened Cirawyn, nor rashly harmed her."

He turned to Finch, while Gareth was still frothing up a reply. "I know bringing her was your idea, Ed, but I don't blame you for this. You tried to stop him."

"Don't speak to me as a friend, Brenish," said Finch. "*My* friend is dead."

"Aye, and I hold my share of the blame. But no less than Gareth. You've a choice now. Follow me and we may leave with treasure, or follow him and we surely leave with none."

"We can return," said Gareth. "We need only walk out. We can teleport back here and try again. Without him. I'll give you two a full cut. And Harry a death benefit."

"Gareth," said Tibs, "I've never once trusted you over Brenish. Don't play that game with me now. Besides, he'd offer the same. And who made the decision to leave me for dead?"

"I wouldn't turn for you either," said Naman. "Not before, and not after what you did to Cirawyn."

Gareth tried to let their reproach go with a shrug, though it was disingenuous. "As you will. You can die here if you prefer. But mind you, men, Brenish lies when he says we need him. Usurper, is he? Then we only need his eyes. Making him talk will be easy."

"Try if you like," said Brenish. "I expected no more from you."

Gareth boomed back at him. "I still command! You'll show us the treasure because you'll have no other choice. If you don't, I'll find Cirawyn. She can't hide from me."

"And would you threaten your men's wives if they refuse to help you? Or Tibs' wife? Naman's mum? You don't understand the line you crossed, Gareth."

"This is pointless," said Bob. "Brenish, you want us to trust you? Then prove your worth and take us to this 'hill under hill.' We can decide later."

"Nay, Bob, we'll decide now. Gareth would kill Cirawyn out of spite, now. Or worse. You need me to get to the treasure, but he's naught left to offer but his prowess in battle and his back to carry gold."

"Wrong, Brenish," Gareth said. "I can lead us out of here without the need for the gold, or you. I can lead us all back to safety, and buy two orbs on credit. I'll still give Naman and Tibs a cut, to be fair, and erase their debts. Or they can walk away from it free. We can come back for the treasure another time. As for Cirawyn, if you're worried about her, you needn't be. I've decided to let her be. I'll even pay the bride price for you, and give her a cut. She can live out her days as a nursemaid *for what's left of you.*"

Brenish was unimpressed. Though Bob and Finch seemed to consider Gareth's offer worthwhile, if it let Cirawyn live, he didn't think they would fall in so easily now. "Or I can lead us to the treasure now," he said. "We'll take what we can carry, and take money off the top for two more orbs. Those who wish to cut out may do so then, out of whatever we've taken, and give up all claim on the rest. Those who return will get a cut of the full amount."

"That's hardly—"

"I'm not done talking." The interruption was worth it just to see Gareth's impotent rage. "All of us left alive right now will get a full cut, as will Cirawyn. Willy will get the same; he can share whatever he wants with Duggle. Harry gets the death benefit like the others. Those are my conditions. No lies. No tricks."

Gareth turned red where he stood. His face seemed ready to explode.

"How is that a better deal?" said Bob.

"You get the option to walk away with something. Also—"

Brenish ducked to the ground and rolled, snatching up the map with one hand and Gareth's dropped torch with the other. Before anyone else could move in, he held the two close together.

"I won't destroy the map," he said.

"I was right before," Finch said. "You are a deceitful little knob."

"A *desperate* knob, if you please, and I'll thank you to show some consideration for what that means. This is Cirawyn's worth to me. Is Maddie worth any less to you?"

Finch thought it through, and stood down. His anger seemed no less, but he held it back. This only infuriated Gareth all the more.

"Brenish, you filthy coward!" Gareth shouted. "Not man enough to face me on even terms? Let's settle this with honor, if you have any."

"My deeds are better than my words," Brenish said. "What say yours? Three good men and a piss-pot dead, an innocent woman's hand near severed? I fought for them, and for you. I risked my life for Raden's, and he lives. I wrecked my own escape plan—aye, *my* plan—to get Cirawyn to safety. That is my honor, Gareth. Coward am I? I brought no shield here; you brought twelve."

Froth spewed from Gareth's lips as he flung his invective. "Foul serpent! Your lies brought us to this pass. But for you we'd be safe and well. You miserable worm, you—"

"Just shut your gob, Gareth. I can take us to the treasure now, or you can try and take the map and I'll burn it before you can. That's all you need to understand. If you doubted my resolve you'd have acted already. Call me anything you like after you've accepted my terms. But I'll have your oath on it. Now."

Gareth had one last card to play, and did it before Brenish realized his mistake. Neither man's eyes moved from the other's, so he didn't see Gareth reach for the wand. He didn't see the draw until it was already pointed at his chest.

Pink lightning blotted out all else. The spell knocked Brenish onto his back. He hit his head against the stone. The torch arm got hit by the blast, throwing the flame clear of the map. He tried to get up but could not. He could move his eyes, focus them, blink. He could breathe. But his limbs and tongue wouldn't respond at all.

The others sounded calls of alarm, but though Naman and Tibs obviously wanted to intervene, Gareth's men sounded unsure of what to do. Brenish couldn't see any of them well, and what he could see looked overly dark and green from the afterimage. Little sparks flashed in his eyes, like glowing ash floating up from a fire.

A heavy weight settled onto his chest. Presently his vision cleared and he saw a knife, its point hovering very close to his left eye, and Gareth's hand holding it. He looked and could barely see Gareth over him, eyes wild and bloodshot.

"An oath you want?" said Gareth. "An oath you'll have. We don't need your voidsight. You'll return to the surface under my will, or not at all. Look well on my face, Brenish. Remember it well. Remember for the rest of your life what this moment has cost you."

"Gareth, stop!" Naman said. "You've made your point."

"Nay. He'll only try again, if he thinks he can. 'Tis better this way. And it fits the riddle."

"*Gareth!*"

The high-pitched shout caught Gareth's attention. He turned around, jerking the knife away as he looked. Brenish heard a *swoosh* and the sound of something impacting flesh. Gareth made choking sounds and reached at his throat. His head swung into view, turned back to face Brenish as muscles went slack. A crossbow bolt was stuck through his neck, just below the rim of his helmet. His blood gushed steadily.

Gareth blacked out. He pitched forward onto Brenish's shoulder, his helmet dinging Brenish in the side of head and clanging against the ground when he hit. He was gone.

No one seemed to know what was going on. Bob stammered inanely. Tibs shouted into the darkness. Someone shoved Gareth's body off of Brenish. He felt immediate relief from the weight, but still he couldn't move.

"Hold your fire," Naman said, though Brenish didn't know who he was talking to. Finch, maybe.

Someone settled beside him. He turned his eyes to look and saw that it was Cirawyn. She held the bottle of healing potion and tipped a splash of it into his open mouth.

His nose unfolded painfully from its broken scrunch. Pressure grew rapidly in his gums, and a new tooth erupted through them. In the midst of that brief agony his thumb and the back of his head felt better. The rest of the pain went away quickly. Life flowed back into his arms and legs, mouth and fingers.

"Thank you, love," he gurgled.

"You can see me?" she said.

Brenish replied with a nod at first. She must have drunk the rest of the invisibility potion. "Voidsight. 'Tis a long tale."

"Cirawyn?" said Raden. "Where are you?"

"I'm here," she said. "I never went far."

Brenish sat up and took her hand to stand. He spat out some more blood and looked down at Gareth. The anger he'd felt just a few minutes earlier was nearly gone. He should have been angry for what Gareth had planned to do to him; he should have been furious. But the well was empty. Seeing the man's corpse, he felt pity. The hatred for what he'd done to Cirawyn was still there, still fresh, although she had avenged that injury for herself. And there was the way he had brought her here in the first place, the way he had dangled her before Dex like a morsel to a dog. For those things he could still find anger.

Yet for his own part, for what had passed between the two men alone, Brenish could not condemn him. They had always understood one another far too well. This place, the darkness and the stone and the endless tales, had always bound them.

"I guess that ends that argument," said Tibs.

"Murder," said Finch. "It's come to murder." He glared in Cirawyn's direction, though he clearly couldn't see her.

"That was no murder, Ed," Cirawyn said. "I was defending Brenish. Besides, if anyone had a right to kill him 'twas me. He had it coming. But I'm in no mood to argue. Let's stop blaming each other for the fruits of Gareth's bad decisions. 'Tis a long way out of here."

"Nay, m'love," Brenish said. "The way is short. But first we'd best find that treasure. Are we agreed on my terms?"

"Gareth should get a death benefit," Raden said. "Split among his servants."

"Nay," said Brenish. "A full cut, as I promised. They've earned it as surely as we have."

"You forgot one small problem," Naman said. "The orb has been used up. Cirawyn may be able to see the map with spellglow if she has Gareth's potions, but we still have to take it out of here the hard way."

Bob slapped his own head. "Nay, Brenish is right. The way is short. Gareth never used that scroll."

"Which sc—" said Finch, and stopped. Sharp though he was, he lacked the instinct Brenish and Gareth had to keep track of every single resource. The goblin scout's replenishment scroll, which Gareth had been loath to use too soon or on the wrong thing, had been all but forgotten. "Oh."

"Men," said Brenish. "We have an orb. The question is, have we an agreement?"

Raden didn't hesitate. "Aye," he said.

"Aye, I'm with you," said Bob.

Finch fiddled with his thumbs and looked deeply annoyed, but met Brenish's eye. "Aye," he sighed.

"Then it's decided," Naman said. "You can take us to the treasure?"

"I believe I can," said Brenish.

Deception

Brenish led them to the northwest of Shatterhelm, a section searched by Finch and Tibs. Three blocks north of the square and two west, they came upon an area that had been all but destroyed by the dragon, just as he had seen from the roof. Several buildings had been knocked down almost completely, leaving little but huge, imposing piles of beautifully worked rubble. One of them was his goal, a lot where nothing remained standing at all.

There was no doorway left to enter the lost building, nor wall in which to set a door, nor space beyond the wall in which to hold a dragon's hoard. It was all brick and stone, tumbled on more brick and stone. A hill under the hills.

Brenish lay his hand against one of the broken sections of wall. "'Tis here," he said. "Here for sure."

"There's an overlook spell," said Naman. "You can't see through those."

"Visak said I could. I usurped Gareth's control, and I have eyes to see. But more than that, I understand what this spell is. Do you not see? 'Tis a deception. I understand how to craft such a thing without magic. Visak had years to make his, but in deception he was not my equal."

"That's cocky," said Tibs, "even for you."

"Aye. But that's how I read the riddle. Visak left signs all along our journey for me to see. Five I saw."

"Aye, I saw one," said Cirawyn. "Near where Gareth was slain."

"Near where you *slayed* him," Finch said testily. Again he tried in vain to give her the stink eye.

"You dispute my right to do it?"

Finch flared his nostrils like a bull and bowed his head sadly. "Nay."

"Enough chatter," said Naman. "If the treasure is here, let's go to it. I say we climb."

He didn't wait for Brenish, but reached for the first handhold himself: a broken piece of a column. Though his thick arms and legs seemed unsuited to the task, he took to the climb easily enough, and did it with one hand still holding a torch. Brenish took a lamp from Cirawyn to make the climb easier on her, and made his own way up right behind Naman.

The way was slow-going and interrupted by many halts where he had to search for a better place to set his hands, lest he slide backward. The surfaces of the stone and brick were rough on his palms and fingertips, and scraped the back of his left hand so much it stung worse than the burn he got from fighting Lila. Nevertheless he kept up a decent pace, so he thought. He fell a little behind Naman, who seemed to have a knack for it, and to his left he saw Finch work his way up. Tibs passed even faster on the right. All around and behind him, the others grunted or cursed as they went—but no more or less than he.

A slab of stone at the top of the mound, tilted at a slight angle, was good enough for a few people to stand on when they reached the top. Naman made it up first, then Tibs and Finch. When Brenish reached the summit himself there was no more room, so he stood aside and tried to find his balance in a loose collection of sharp-cornered brick pieces. He helped Cirawyn up in her turn, right behind him, and then Raden and Bob.

"Well," Tibs said, "what now?"

Brenish sighed and pulled the map out again. "The map will show us," he said. "First we'll need the orb."

Cirawyn took off Gareth's pack and set it at her feet. In a few moments she produced the orb, glowing yellow-white no longer. Now it was just a glassy sphere, dull in the center, for its magic had been expended. Remembering she needed a scroll as well, she returned to the pack again for that.

She held the orb carefully as she unfurled the scroll, and began to recite the words there. Brenish remembered his own experience reading one, how the runes had jumped into his mind. Her voice had the same notes of certainty, the same easy roll. He looked to the others, who turned their eyes in her direction without seeing. Though he could feel the pull of magic, it wasn't as pervasive as other spells he had known. The magic seemed to concentrate around Cirawyn, and was meant for the orb alone.

She completed the spell. The scroll turned to a puff of pulp fibers, and new life flamed up in the heart of the glass ball. At first the glow was unsteady, but gradually it grew back to its old strength.

Brenish handed his lamp and Cirawyn's to Naman, so he could join her near the edge of the group as far away from the lights as he could get. He found a good place to stand and opened the map.

"'Tis still blank," said Naman.

"Nay," said Tibs, "we just can't see the light. Did you see my lamplight when I was invisible? While she holds the orb we can't see it."

"Ah."

"The lights are too close, though," Brenish said. "I can barely see it. Move them back, please."

The others tried to move their torches and lamps out of view. Bob held his so that the map would be in its shadow; the rest of the men gradually copied him.

"Aye, there it is. Look for guildscrawl. Visak left me a message with it before. I'm sure he left another."

"I can't read guildscrawl," Cirawyn said.

"Aye, I meant—" He looked up at Tibs and Naman and saw them shrug. "Oh. Aye. My mistake. I forgot you two can't see it."

"What were we just talking about?" said Tibs.

"Right. Sorry. I was distracted. This is a big moment."

Finch shook his head, but he wasn't looking towards Brenish or the map; his gaze was elsewhere. "Nay."

He stepped off the slab and made his way to the far side of the pile's summit, where something had caught his attention. When he squatted to reach something there, he nearly lost his balance twice, but finally he reached out and picked something up. He stood again, and in his hand was a molded gold bar. A piece of parchment was tied to it with a leather thong. The parchment was Visak's stationery, with his symbol.

"Oh, he left a note here," Brenish said. "How thoughtful. Let's read it, then."

Finch scowled at Brenish's alacrity, but slid off the thong so he could unfold the paper. It was but a scrap, enough for a short message.

"'Dear friend,' says he. 'I offer you my deepest congratulations for finding the resting place of my fortune. Sadly I must inform you that for all your troubles, you have come to the very end of my gold, for I overstated the size of the dragon's hoard.'"

"That cheeky whoreson!" Naman exclaimed. "Probably he did this as a joke! I'll spit on his grave!"

Finch read on. "'For such deeds as you must have done to come this far, no man should leave empty-handed. Please accept this gold brick, the last of my estate, to use in good health.' He signed his name. There is no more."

Bob kicked a little chunk of brick with all his force, sending it off into the gloom beyond with the speed of a diving falcon. It clacked against another surface in the dark. "Fie," he said, "what a disappointment. All this way, five men dead, and for what? A single gold brick split seven ways?"

"Eleven," said Tibs. "You forgot Gareth and Willy, and the death benefits. Might as well give Dex half a cut; it won't be enough to pay Darius back."

"Ach. What rotten luck."

Brenish signaled for Finch to come back with the note and the brick. Naman handed back the spell lamp on the necklace, which he put back on to see them. Brenish looked over both items carefully, making sure to examine the note every way he could think to: upside-down, backwards, and even by shielding his lamp and using the orb to try and reveal something more like the map had. There was nothing.

"Well," Raden said, "that's that. Let's take this and go."

Brenish tried to hold up a hand for silence, but it was the one holding the gold brick and didn't much want to move. Once he realized that, he held up the other one instead.

Naman tried to speak. "There's naught—"

"Sshh!" said Brenish. Naman fell silent.

They waited Brenish out for a minute. Raden coughed once, quietly. Tibs turned to and fro, nervous and upset, his little eyeglasses reflecting the lights at odd angles and times so they kept flashing Brenish in the face. Brenish could only stare, expecting to find a clue. The gold bar was blank, and the paper appeared to be nothing more than a scrap of parchment after all. There was no hidden message, but he felt if anyone should see one, it should be him.

"Hill under hill," he finally said. "Lock without key. I assumed this was the hill, and the overlook spell the lock. Which of course has no true key."

"Aye," said Finch. "But nothing else is here."

"The usurper alone has eyes to see. It must have something to do with those marks. There must be something more."

"There isn't any more. All the treasure is gone. We got here. We must be within the perimeter of the spell, or I wouldn't have seen that. This is all the gold we'll find."

Brenish stopped and snapped two fingers in the hand holding the note. "Aye!" he said. "If we found this, and the spell hid it, we're surely inside the spell."

"I don't think overlook spells have a boundary," Cirawyn said.

"We'll find out."

Brenish handed the gold bar to Cirawyn and took out the bottle of goldsense. He took another tug on it, a bigger drink than any he had yet had.

Again the ruins around him took on new dimension, his sense showing him treasures and discarded items and lost (but valuable) trinkets for miles around. But there was no sense at hand of any more gold.

"Well?" said Finch.

Brenish looked around, feeling bewildered. He had been so sure the brick wasn't the end of it. "Nothing else," he said. "I don't understand."

"What's to understand?" Bob said. "There isn't any more. That's all the gold there is."

Brenish started to nod back at that, but he stopped. Suddenly a smile broke across his face. "Genius, you are, Bob. Genius. Truly. If we're inside the spell already, I should see anything that's here, by virtue of the goldsense."

"Aye."

"But I don't. I see us. I see what we have with us. Naught else. The goldsense says this brick isn't here."

"An illusion?" said Tibs.

"Nay. At least, what I mean to say is the gold is real. But 'tis protected by the spell. And if one piece is protected, so are all the others."

"Aw," Raden groaned, obviously irritated with Brenish's feeling that he knew it all. "Use your wits, Brenish. We can *see* this brick. We'd see others too."

But Brenish shook his head. "We see the brick because we were meant to see it. It's as I said. The overlook spell is a lie."

"Looks true enough to me," said Bob.

"I meant the spell is here to deceive us, Bob. Think you I only ever tell one lie? I tell many, each within the other. A man stops peeling when he thinks he's hit the center of the onion. Visak only did with this message what I would have done in his place. My God, 'tis so simple!"

"If 'tis so simple, Brenish," said Finch, "then break the spell and let's have done with it."

"Aye." Brenish stared at the brick as if by screwing up his eyes tight enough, he could force it to reveal everything. When that didn't do anything, he scanned around the top of the mound for any debris that might look like a gold bar in other form. A brick after all wasn't much different in shape and size. If he could see the outline of the shape, he felt he would understand.

Finally he gave up and shouted. "Visak!" he said. "We're here. I see your spell. I am the usurper of the verse. Open my eyes!"

His own voice echoed back from the far reaches of the cavern. The pile of broken waste was no different than before.

"I don't understand," he said.

"You see evidence of the spell," said Raden, "but you don't see the spell itself."

A light finally dawned in Brenish's brain. "Huzzah! Aye, Raden, I need the unk." He reached into the hidden pocket and removed Dex's owl. "This will show me the spell's nature."

"Ah, so you figured out what it does?" said Tibs. "What is that? Did Dex make it, as you thought?"

"'Tis a spellsight charm, Tibs. And aye, I think Dex made it and sold it to Enzo."

"You said you never found it," said Finch.

"I said a lot of things, Ed."

Bob scratched his head, not sharing Brenish's enthusiasm. "I understand that might show you the spell," he said, "but why ignore the signs you said you saw?"

"They were just guides, Bob. Meaningless now."

"There are none here?"

"None that I can see," said Cirawyn.

"Nor I," Brenish said. "But their purpose has been served. Like the one I saw, that Cirawyn saw also. I took it as a sign from Visak, and it led me to look closer at his writing to see the message he left for me."

"What did the others accomplish, then?" said Bob. "You saw one at Jarrett's Folly. Did that have a purpose?"

"Nay, except to keep me looking for others."

"If the usurper alone has eyes to see, then use them. If those signs were meant for you as you say, describe where you saw them."

"We're wasting time, Bob," said Naman.

"Nay, hear me out. Describe them, Brenish."

Brenish rolled his eyes. "Very well. I saw the first at Jarrett's Folly, as you said. Where Cirawyn made a rubbing of her dad's name on the stone. The second I saw at the crossing where Turk was killed, on a column. It had no meaning at all."

"None at all? I barely met the wizard, but that doesn't sound like him. What else saw you there?"

"Just a dead lizardman hanging by his hand."

"You mean the one Cirawyn shot, then finished with Turk's sword when the battle was won?"

"I guessed as much. Aye, that's the one. And the third was as we entered the city, on one of the stones by the road."

"What else was there?"

"Nothing." But Brenish paused and thought a moment. Suddenly he realized that wasn't strictly true. His eyes widened. "The orb was right behind it. I was tracking it with goldsense, to find all of you." He slapped his forehead. "How could I be so blind? The fourth and the fifth weren't special for their location. They were special for how I found them."

He turned and took the orb from Cirawyn, and pressed the unk into her hand, then the brick and the note as well. "Hold this to your head when you're ready, love."

"Why?" she said.

"Because I'm not the usurper. 'Twasn't me who killed Gareth. And though I know how to craft a lie, like the overlook spell, that's my only gift. But you always know the truth. You've always been the one to see."

Cirawyn nodded. She placed the owl upon her forehead and looked at the gold bar thoughtfully. She said nothing for a short while, studying the bar as a bee might study a flower. At last she smiled.

"Aye," she said, "perhaps I see it. Hand me the map, if you please."

Brenish handed it over and took back the rest. "Need you the orb?" he said.

"Not this minute. I don't need to read the map again." She folded it up gently and held it to her body.

"What do you need it for?" said Bob.

"Safe passage."

A minute passed in which no one spoke. Cirawyn looked at Brenish; her eyes were bright with wonder. Finch seemed impatient for the whole thing to be over with one way or another, as was Naman. The silence grew almost tangible, waiting for something to happen, until Raden broke it with a sneeze.

"God bless," Brenish said, turning his head back.

"Thanks. There's too much dust in this place."

"Aye," said Finch. "I've had enough of the dark. Cirawyn, is there a point to this? The map has faded, if that's what you wanted."

Brenish turned back to see her reply, but she was gone. His innards twitched in fear.

"She's disappeared," he said.

"Well spotted," said Naman.

"Nay, I mean I can't see her either. I think she's inside the spell."

"What if she doesn't come out again?" said Bob.

"Don't talk that way. You'll make me sick. I feel queasy enough already." But then he stopped to think. It wasn't actually queasiness he felt. There was tension present, something he felt less with his body than his heart. "Nay, it's—"

"I feel it too," said Finch.

The earth trembled. The rubble beneath them shook and tried to settle. Tibs and Finch were the first to crouch down to steady themselves. Brenish and the others did likewise. The air grew stuffier, thicker, and Brenish noted even his limbs felt heavier. A faint sliding, scraping sound rose up all around them, a high-pitched metallic hiss. It grew quickly to a muffled roar.

Brenish lost his footing and came down hard on the expanse of bricks, which no longer felt so sharp and bumpy. In falling, he barely managed to keep hold of the orb, but he dropped everything else. He turned around and saw Raden struggling, but Bob held his own. He shouted. "Everybody brace your—"

The spell completed. Space unknotted. The sense of impending change in his stomach went away, and the shaking vanished, but the rushing sound beneath them became briefly much louder before settling to a murmur. The cavern was instantly brighter, tinged with yellow in the reflections from their lights. Brenish reached down and felt no more brick, just a bed of coins.

He sat up and turned back to where Cirawyn had stood before she disappeared. She was there again, smiling at him.

"The map is gone," she said. "It got used up like a scroll."

"What a shame," said Brenish, getting slowly to his feet. "I was gonna give it back to Willy so he could put it in a frame."

The seven stood upon a shifting, still settling pile of gold and silver coins, gemstones, jewelry, staves, weapons, armor, goblets, utensils, chests, figurines, and baubles of every kind they could imagine. Artifacts made of strange metals were strewn about the pile, as were some of copper and bronze. Not all of the pile was treasure; though the mound was easily fifteen feet high, as much as half of it was real rubble. Yet the amount of sheer wealth beneath their feet was impossible to guess.

Naman tried to move but nearly fell over, and had to catch himself. Finch managed to fall over too, but he began laughing. His laughter was infectious; it spread to Tibs and Raden, Bob and

Naman, and finally to Brenish and Cirawyn. Brenish embraced her and slipped to one knee, slapping it against the unyielding gold.

"We did it, love," he said. Tears of joy came to his eyes. "We found it."

"Aye," she replied, beaming back at him. "But I'll not spend another minute here."

Brenish nodded and handed her the orb. She raised it up high. This time, she didn't close her eyes.

Sky

The ceiling was gone. There was only a painfully bright lavender hue, streaked with eye-searing pink. Everyone winced and shielded their faces. Brenish felt pressure in his head and involuntarily opened his mouth, popping his ears.

The temperature dropped abruptly. Where Shatterhelm had been warm, now they were deeply chilled, feeling the briskness of an autumn evening. A chill wind blew upon them from the east. Brenish turned to the west, and saw that though the sky was a viciously piercing yellow-orange there, the sun had already gone down.

Bob threw his arms wide open and slid down the pile onto the grass, like a child. Naman shrugged and followed him down. Finch took a more dignified walk. The others followed at their own pace and each in their own way. Brenish kept an arm around Cirawyn, partly to steady her. The pile was shallower than he thought, only nine feet high at most and not as wide as it had first seemed.

They were in a little meadow southwest of the village and situated higher up, near a patch of dense forest. Brenish didn't recognize the place, but he had seen the houses of central Ilyenis from the top of the mound, and a few lights. Cirawyn extinguished her torch and began to dismantle the pole; she was not the first to do so. Spell lamps were covered and put away.

Raden, carrying Turk's sword, headed into the woods. "Oi," said Finch. "Where are you going?"

"To cut firewood. What's it look like?"

"Cut lots. We'll need enough for the night." He turned to Brenish. "You understand we'll have to defend this till we can secure it. This has to go to the city right off."

"Aye," said Brenish. "Then we'll divvy it up."

"We'll need wagons," said Tibs.

"Gareth has some," Finch said. "They'll do. I'll go with Bob, and Naman maybe, and we'll bring some back for the first load. We might need to hire another few in the village, but I'll send some of

Gareth's stable boys to do that. They're stakeholders too. This is a lot of gold for wagons to carry, let alone horses to pull."

"Aye," said Brenish.

"Shame that Gareth's house and the village are both at least half a mile from here." If he meant that as a dig at Cirawyn for picking a bad spot, he didn't show it. Then again, it wasn't as though he could look her in the eye. She was still completely invisible to all but Brenish, and could be for most of the night, depending on how much potion she drank.

"The better not to be disturbed," she said. She looked about and smelled the air, and wrapped her arms around her torso. "'Tis a nice evening, if a bit bitter."

"The fire will take away some of that chill," Brenish said. He looked to Finch. "Go on and get the wagons. We'll stay here and defend the rest. Tomorrow when this is all locked up safe, we'll turn Willy loose and we'll all pick out our favorite bits."

"That's a full cut for each of us," Finch said. "And one for Gareth's household. One for the forger. Half each for Jase, Turk, and Harry. And we'll pay Dex's debts off the top."

"Aye. Though it's never been much to you, you have my word. I think my days as a thief and a liar are over."

Finch smirked. "Pity. 'Twas the one thing you were good for." But he meant it good-naturedly; he slapped Brenish on the arm and walked away to gather Naman and Bob.

Presently the wagon team walked off toward Gareth's estate, more or less in the right direction. Raden and Tibs came back to the grass and began building a fire; Tibs lit a torch again briefly so he could burn a circle into the grass and stomp the flames out as he went, so that the fire wouldn't spread beyond its bounds. Brenish and Cirawyn helped as they could, but Cirawyn soon found that Tibs and Raden kept bumping into her; she had to keep her distance.

The fire took little time to start, and soon blazed merrily. Though they were supposed to watch the gold, Raden yawned and sat on the grass. Brenish, too, still felt ill-rested from their ordeal the night before. Before long they all sat on the grass, ready to deal with any troublemakers.

But then, Brenish thought, most of the thieves and ruffians in the village were accounted for. There was Gavin, but he was likely already drunk at the inn.

"Was it all you'd hoped to see, love?" said Cirawyn.

Brenish nodded, thoughtfully. He stared into the distance, toward the horizon. The sky in the east was turning a deep, dark blue. "Aye. And nay. So many stories down there. Ours was but a little piece of them."

Raden laughed nervously. "You don't seriously mean to go back," he said.

"Nay, I've no such intention. That's as Fell as I'll ever get. But I think I'll never tire of the tales, nor the lore. A piece of that place feels like it came back with me. I needn't look far for it anymore."

Cirawyn put her arms around him. "I'm glad. My father will be glad to hear it too. He worried for you." She stiffened. "He must be back by now. I'm sure he worries for me too."

"We'll seek him out tonight, or early tomorrow. Nay, tonight. Better 'twere done sooner. I doubt he'll sleep well with you missing, anyway. I wouldn't."

"You won't have to."

Tibs clicked his tongue. "My missus should hear the good news too. And Sara, eh Raden?"

"Aye," Raden said. "Though the news is less good for some. Someone has to tell Elspeth about Turk."

"I'll do it," said Brenish. "This was mostly my fault anyway."

"Nay," said Tibs, "I saw the man die. Better me than you."

"As you will. You're right, like as not. And she likes you better."

The darkness deepened. Though in the west the sky was still luminous, many beautiful shades of purple, to the east night fell in earnest. The moon hung there, big and white, waxing to the full. Brenish yawned again, and sighed, and lay his head back in Cirawyn's lap. He didn't close his eyes.

"You saved me," he said softly, drowsiness slipping into his voice.

"Aye, m'love. And you me."

"Even before. You saved me from going Fell. I would've walked away from the dream of it, for you. But there was no one to save Gareth."

She smiled and stroked his hair. Her eyes seemed to glisten. They were happy tears.

The wind picked up, carrying shreds of cloud along. A few dim points of light sprang up in the sky, peeking from behind the last veil of day. Brenish sighed once more, struck by the beauty above him. He didn't need to close his eyes to find rest.

"What are you thinking, love?" she said.

He blinked long. Other images were driven out. His mind put away the sight of a burning troll, a girl lost in the dark, a smug yet heroic statue defying a monster long gone. There was only the firmament of royal blue, and the jewels embedded there.

"The stars are coming out," he said.

"Aye. So they are."

"I haven't looked up in a long time."

Afterword and Acknowledgments

In 1990 my family got our first PC, a step forward from the simple Atari 800XL I had grown up with. While this was a family machine, my father bought it largely because he knew I had learned about all I could from the old one, and the future was with the PC. It was a marvel of a machine for its time: It had an 80286 processor, one megabyte of RAM, a 40 megabyte hard drive, 256-color graphics, and one of the very first CD-ROM drives. Although it came with a raft of software, nothing captured my imagination or attention quite so much as when, on Christmas Eve, one of our family friends brought up some software himself. The software he brought included a C compiler and a game I had never heard of before: Rogue.

Growing up in the '80s, the idea of a game you play until you lose wasn't so foreign. Oh sure, you can *win* Rogue, but it takes an incredible combination of luck, skill, and persistence. When I was fourteen I had that persistence in spades. So for many hours, I explored the depths of the Dungeons of Doom in all their sixteen-color character graphics glory. I learned that bad potions can be thrown at enemies; monster zoos are a huge challenge but offer huge rewards; searching for secret doors isn't always worth it. But I never did win.

Over the years I came to know other Roguelike games. By no means have I sampled even a good fraction of them all, but I did enjoy Nethack and Dungeon Crawl, and these days I'm quite impressed by Brogue. Years ago I got to see an early prototype of a game called Darke Dungeon with more of a graphical edge. Even though my character was still nothing but a smiley face, the visuals of simple brick and dithered lighting in a dark place cut deep into my heart.

Reading Roguelike fiction seemed like a good way to slake that wanderlust, but it turns out to be hard to come by. Such a rich seed, but so little literature. If I couldn't read a story about a good old-fashioned dungeon crawl, the next best thing was to write one. *Below* began more than ten years ago as a novella, longer than any short-form work I'd ever turned out so far. I was immensely proud of the story, but as time went on the fabric wore thin. Gareth's early behavior, steeped in cliché, clashed so badly with the more rounded, intelligent villain he turned out to be. A lot of opportunities to develop character or setting were lost. As I later came to realize (and was told outright) how much my voice as a writer changed, the novella felt hollow; it demanded to be rewritten in long form.

Writing about the deep ruins doesn't really bring closure. Nobody ever played Dwarf Fortress and thought, "Well, that's the most epic story I could have hoped to see in this game. Guess I'll hang it up now." People who win Nethack don't declare their love for the game dead; they try to win again, and some will try to win under unthinkable conditions. Some succeed. Win or lose, they all bring back stories.

Those stories live on. I've spent hours reading Nethack FAQs, in which people discussed all the ways—past and present—they'd ever robbed shops without getting into trouble, abused polymorph on a huge pile of items, learned which creatures you could eat to gain valuable intrinsic abilities, kicked sinks for fun and profit, thrown gems at unicorns, and ascended to godhood on a strict diet of mango juice.

All of us who fall in love with Roguelike games go a little Fell. I'll always remember what it was like, evening after evening, going through those simple brown-walled rooms of Rogue and hoping to find a powerful wand, or a ring, and the means to identify it—or maybe a nice monster zoo with some epic loot handy, if I thought I could survive it.

There are worse ways to spend an evening than getting killed by centaurs.

For this book and the novella that came before, I offer my thanks to everyone who read them and offered input. That goes especially for Strange David Fuller, my wife April whose feedback about style led me to expand the story, and Katrina Kimpland for her hugely constructive notes. And of course, thanks to Dan Button, who first introduced me to the Dungeons of Doom a good quarter century ago.

If you enjoyed this book, I would be grateful if you post a review online—especially if it's a glowing review—to tell others what you thought about it. You get bonus style points for working in sly references to dungeon crawlers. My hope all along in writing this story was that others who enjoy these kinds of games would enjoy a book about the very same.

Maybe more writers will pass the Gate, and come back with more stories. When they return, they can find me by the hearth.

— Lee Gaiteri
May 2017

About the Author

Lee Gaiteri (guy-tare-ee) is a computer programmer from Syracuse, New York, where he lives with his wife and a fluctuating number of cats. His passions include bacon, Lego, caffeine, rooting for a perennially disappointing football team, and ranting with abandon. His chief aspiration is to become a beloved supervillain who would drive the mosquito to extinction and legalize the unrestricted sport hunting of Internet spammers. *Below* is his third novel.

CPSIA information can be obtained
at www.ICGtesting.com
Printed in the USA
LVHW031015050519
616703LV00001B/390

9 781541 093942